*Has she lost her heart
to London's most infamous rogue?*

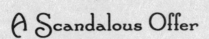

A Scandalous Offer

"Kate," he choked.

She spun around, the lace hem of her nightgown teasing across her bare toes, then leaned back against the ancient door. Her face was flushed beautifully, and her gray eyes could not possibly have been described as somber.

"Don't say a word," she ordered. "Oh, please don't! Edward, please don't ruin it."

He closed the distance, pulling her from the door and into his arms in an embrace he hoped was less carnal. "Kate," he said again. "Oh, Kate, love, be serious."

She set her cheek against his chest. He settled his hand on the back of her head, savoring the silky warmth of her hair. He shut his eyes and prayed for the strength to do the right thing.

But Kate was of no help whatsoever.

"Edward," she whispered, "what if I am being serious?"

And she was. Edward could hear it in her voice. She was entirely willing. Willing to give herself to him. Willing to make his dark dreams come true.

By Liz Carlyle

In Love With a Wicked Man
A Bride by Moonlight
The Bride Wore Pearls
The Bride Wore Scarlet
One Touch of Scandal

Coming Soon

The Earl's Mistress

Liz CARLYLE

In Love With a Wicked Man

AVON

An Imprint of HarperCollinsPublishers

This is a work of fiction. Names, characters, places, and incidents are products of the author's imagination or are used fictitiously and are not to be construed as real. Any resemblance to actual events, locales, organizations, or persons, living or dead, is entirely coincidental.

AVON BOOKS
An Imprint of HarperCollins*Publishers*
10 East 53rd Street
New York, New York 10022-5299

Copyright © 2013 by Susan Woodhouse
ISBN 978-0-06-210029-0
www.avonromance.com

First Avon Books mass market printing: November 2013

Avon Trademark Reg. U.S. Pat. Off. and in Other Countries, Marca Registrada, Hecho en U.S.A.
HarperCollins® is a registered trademark of HarperCollins Publishers.

Printed in the U.S.A.

10 9 8 7 6 5 4 3 2 1

In Love With a
Wicked Man

PROLOGUE
Becoming Ned

1829
Cambridgeshire

Winter had come to Bexham in a swirl of snow that likely wouldn't stick, and a clatter of skeletal branches whose frozen tips pecked and scraped at the headmaster's window like the fleshless fingertips of a wraith. From the quadrangle below came the sound of boys bursting from their classes for dinner, a clamor just loud enough to drown out Edward's growling belly.

Hunching forward on the stool, the boy jerked viciously at his coat, attempting to pull it tight against the chill, but he'd long since outgrown the thing. In truth, he'd outgrown a great many things at Bexham, for when the birch rod cracked down upon the headmaster's desk an inch from his nose, Edward did not so much as flinch.

"Well, boy," barked Mr. Pettibone, "your father's finally come. *Now* what have you to say for yourself?"

Boldly lifting his gaze, Edward had only a shrug.

It brought a small sort of satisfaction, the hard-honed ability to hold one's fear at bay; to sneer in the face of enmity and to give as good as one got. But then, his was a small sort of life. A life of utter inconsequence—and, for all that it mattered, not remotely like the life he'd been expected to live.

The headmaster had begun to tap the birch impatiently on his desktop. "Well, Mr. Hedge, do you see what Bexham's been up against?" he complained, staring over Edward's head. "That cold, calculating look in his eye! That unbridled insolence!"

"Aye, like his bitch of a mother," muttered Hedge, so low only Edward could hear it. Suddenly, Hedge turned from the bank of windows he'd been pacing, the buttons of his ostentatious frock coat catching the light as he came to loom over Edward.

"So you'll answer Mr. Pettibone, me boyo," he went on, seizing his ear in a ruthless twist. "Answer him, or the stropping you took here won't hold a candle to the one you'll take at my hand."

The lad lifted his chin another notch but the twisting did not relent, and this time Edward knew better than to strike back. No, he would not strike back—not until he knew he could strike Hedge *down*.

And that day was surely coming.

So Edward shrugged again, and spoke with the dulcet, upper-class clarity more common to Eton than Bexham. "Yes, I hit him," he said defiantly. "I hit him because he called me a bastard."

"Aye, and so you are," said Hedge on a chuckle.

"And when he called me a bastard, I called him a jumped-up costermonger's get," Edward clarified. "And then *he* struck *me*. So I had to strike him back. That's how it goes with this lot, Hedge. You daren't back down."

Hedge gave another grunt—this one a tad dismissive—then released Edward's ear and turned his attention to Pettibone. "So. Just the usual row, then. Lad's got a chip on his shoulder. No harm done, eh?"

The headmaster tossed down the birch with an impatient *thwack!* "The boy with the broken arm, Mr. Hedge, is the son of a City alderman," he said grimly. "I think I need not explain the inconvenience *that* might cause a man in your sort of business."

"Aye? And just what sort o' business would that be, Mr. Pettibone?"

The headmaster's nose lifted an inch, but Bexham was not the sort of academic institution that could afford too many scruples. "I believe you mentioned you were in London *finance*."

"Just so," said Hedge, extracting his purse. "Well, what's the damage?"

"The *damage*?" said the headmaster sharply.

"Aye." Hedge let a twenty-pound banknote drift onto the burnished desktop. "How much is it to be this time?"

The headmaster pushed the banknote back across the desk. "I don't think you grasped the purpose of this meeting, Mr. Hedge," he said. "Edward is no longer welcome here."

"What, at no price?" Hedge was accustomed to purchasing convenience. "What the devil am *I* to do with a twelve-year-old boy?"

"Take him back to London, I suppose," said the headmaster. "I fear we can no longer concern ourselves with Edward. The brawling, the broken windows, the sullen anger—yes, all this we've tolerated. But a fractured arm? Of a City alderman's son? No, my dear Mr. Hedge. Not even your ill-got gains can buy your way out of *that*."

Hedge drew a hand down a face that had once been handsome but had now begun to sag with dissipation. He lifted both eyebrows enquiringly. "A recommendation to another school, then, perhaps?"

"You're fresh out of schools," snapped the headmaster. "Bexham was his sixth."

Hedge grinned. "Aye, well, we've both been thrown out of better places than this."

"The better places won't have him," Pettibone retorted. "Eton, Rugby, Harrow—well, once, perhaps, they might have done. But not now. Not when it's become public knowledge his sire is the owner of a—a . . ."

"A *what*, Mr. Pettibone?" asked Hedge jovially. "Go on. Let it trip right off that learned tongue of yours."

"—a low gaming hell," snapped Pettibone.

"A low and extremely *profitable* gaming hell," Hedge amended. "Ah, well! What's to be done now, Pettibone? I know nothing of brats."

Pettibone's expression suggested that perhaps Hedge oughtn't have bred any. "Well, if it were me," he said tartly, "I'd apprentice him to a counting house. And a harsh one, too, for it will take a strong hand to keep that one in line."

"Don't I know it!" said Hedge wearily. "But a counting house? Surely that requires a sort of aptitude that is beyond—"

"My God, Mr. Hedge!" interjected Pettibone. "The boy is violent, not stupid! Have you read nothing we've sent home to you? Do you know nothing of your own son?"

Unabashed, Hedge shook his head. "Dropped on me, the boy was, like a stray cat."

"Well, your stray cat is a prodigy," said Pettibone impatiently, "with near total recall of figures, geometry, algebraic concepts—not to mention his grasp of probabilities."

At last, Hedge brightened. "No! A sharp one, eh?"

"Indeed." Pettibone had gone to the door, and flung it wide. "Sharp's the word."

"Ah, well, then!" Hedge hauled the boy out of the chair and frog-marched him toward the door. "Per'aps I can think of a use for the lad after all."

"What happy news," said Pettibone dryly.

"Aye," said Hedge, vanishing around the corner, "especially happy for *me*, I begin to think."

CHAPTER 1

In Which Lady d'Allenay
Plans a House Party

1850
Somerset

Family lore had long held that when the ancient Barons d'Allenay were no more, the Kingdom of Great Britain would crumble. For better than five hundred years, an unbroken if often tangled line of these noble gentlemen had held control of the vast Somerset estates collectively known as Bellecombe, which had been the seat of the Barons d'Allenay since the time of Henry V.

But at long last, after the fortunes of the barony had waxed and waned a dozen times, there finally came the day when there was no Lord d'Allenay.

No one was less pleased by this unfortunate turn than Kate, Lady d'Allenay. But the kingdom did not, after all, crumble.

And the fortune? Regrettably, *that* was definitely on the

wane—and all of Bellecombe with it. But Lady d'Allenay had never been without pragmatism. Indeed, from the earliest years of her girlhood, her grandfather, the thirteenth Baron d'Allenay, had been wont to pat her on the head and declare her *the sensible one*.

Indeed, she could hardly have been *the beautiful one*. That honorific had fallen to her late brother, Stephen. Certainly she was not *the charming one*, for her little sister, Nancy, had half the county's male population eating from the palm of her hand. So all that was left to Lady d'Allenay, it seemed, was pragmatism. And from the age of eight, when she had realized that her frivolous parents were not to be relied upon, she'd striven to cultivate that dull virtue.

"*—and do it pillowslip by bloody damned pillowslip!*" she added through clenched teeth.

"Beg pardon, m'lady?" enquired a voice behind her.

"Never mind, Peppie," Lady d'Allenay called back to her housekeeper. Then, with a clever twist, the baroness extracted herself from the depths of a massive linen press and presented Mrs. Peppin with a stack of fresh pillowslips. "New!" she declared triumphantly.

"Why, so they are!" Mrs. Peppin's eyes widened.

"I had a dozen put back," Lady d'Allenay confessed, "in anticipation of just such an emergency. The old ones we'll mend. Remind the maids to set them darning side down when they make up all the guest rooms."

"You always were such a sensible girl, miss," said Mrs. Peppin, gazing lovingly upon the crisp fabric.

"And full of pragmatism," added Lady d'Allenay rather too cheerfully.

But not beauty. Or wit. Or red-gold ringlets. Her housekeeper, however, had not seen new linen in a decade, and was awed into silence by its magnificence.

"Well, that's sorted." With a businesslike flip of her chatelaine, Lady d'Allenay checked the time on her watch. "I'm off to the new rectory shortly to inspect the construction."

But Mrs. Peppin pointed through a nearby window. "There be a gurt black sky out, my lady."

"Well, drat." Kate glanced at the gathering storm. "Nancy's taking tea at the rectory. Which means we can expect Mr. Burnham and his mother for dinner. He'll doubtless drive Nancy home."

"Oh, aye," Mrs. Peppin said dryly. "An act of pure Christian charity, that."

"Just warn Cook." Kate turned to lock the press. "I'll get busy mending for Mother's visit. Oh, and do remind Fendershot to inventory the cellars. Aurélie's friends do drink quite a *shocking* amount of wine."

"A body can scarce count the bottles flying," muttered the housekeeper.

"I do hope we don't have to order more champagne," Kate fretted, setting off down the passageway. "It's so frightfully expensive—but Aurélie declares she cannot abide Italian vintages."

"Oh, la, la, her delicate French blood!" Mrs. Peppin was not a devotee of Lady d'Allenay's mother—or her friends. "Per'aps you ought to tell Mrs. Wentworth we can ill afford to have them?"

"I did do last year, you'll recall," said Kate as they started down the sweeping staircase, "but this year . . . well, the thing is, Peppie, she's found out about the glebe land."

"My word! How?"

"Nancy probably wrote." Kate shrugged. "And I'm sure Aurélie has concluded that if we're building a new rectory and giving the Church acreage, Bellecombe must be a *little* flush."

"I wish, miss, you didn't have to call your own mother by her Christian name."

Kate sighed. "But *Mamma* makes her feel old, Peppie. You know Aurélie requires pampering. It seems a small indulgence."

Mrs. Peppin sighed. "How many is Mrs. Wentworth bringing for shooting season?"

"Just her usual." Kate mentally counted. "There will be the Comte de Macey again, I daresay—"

"—if the French pox hasn't carried him off," muttered the housekeeper.

"Really, Peppie, you're uncharitable," said Kate smoothly. "Besides, the two of them are just old friends now. Aurélie's current lover is a merchant banker, I believe."

"And a rich one, too, I don't doubt."

Kate paused on the landing. "Yes, but if one must love, is it not better to love someone rich? That's what I keep telling Nancy."

"Little good *that's* done," said Mrs. Peppin. "Who else, then?"

"Her bosom beau Lady Julia. And—oh, yes!—a young gentleman. Sir Francis something-or-other. I collect she thought he might flirt and sigh over Nancy, and thereby distract her."

"Your mother's wicked gentlemen friends generally expect a bit more of a lady than flirting and sighing."

"Mrs. Peppin, you quite shock my virginal sensibilities." Kate turned the next landing, and set off in a different direction from the housekeeper. "Well, I'm off to the parlor with this pile of tatty linen."

"Hmm," said the housekeeper. "Perhaps *you* ought to be off to tea with a handsome young man like your sister?"

But Kate marched on down the passageway, and pretended she didn't hear.

NED QUARTERMAINE WAS in a dark and pensive mood. With his coat and cravat long ago cast aside, he sprawled by a dying fire in his finely appointed suite, his knees splayed wide and his shoulders thrown back against the buttery leather of his armchair. Only the faint *chink!* of his brandy glass striking the marble tabletop broke the quiet as Quartermaine stared out into his garden; a garden that would have been awash in moonlight had this not been London, and the night sky not choked with damp and coal smoke.

But Quartermaine was a creature of the darkness—and, truth be told, more comfortable in it. And on this night, he was embracing that darkness with a bottle of eighteen-year-old Armagnac and a strand of small but perfect pearls adorned with one teardrop sapphire.

They lay heavy in the palm of his hand—and heavy in his heart, too. But that organ so rarely troubled him, the ache in it tonight might have been mistaken for dyspepsia. Best to wash it back down again, he'd decided. Still, from time to time, between sips of the burnt, ashy spirit, he gave the pearls a pensive little toss, just to feel them settle back into his hand, clicking against one another before stilling again; cooler, yet ever heavier, it seemed.

Just then, as if to punctuate the regret, the gilt clock on his mantelpiece struck the hour.

Three chimes. Three o'clock.

An hour at which there was good money to be made from the vanity and desperation of others. Above Quartermaine's head, the night's work continued on as little more than a soothing rumble of voices; one that was occasionally broken by the faint scrape of a chair leg across his marble floors.

He gave the brandy another sip.

The pearls another toss.

His heart another hard wrench. As if he might, just this once, manage to wring from it the will to do the right thing. But before he could steel himself to the duty, there came a faint knock at the door.

Peters. No one else had permission to disturb Quartermaine once he had stepped from his office into his private domain.

"Come!" he ordered.

His club manager entered with a perfunctory bow. "You might wish to come upstairs, sir."

Quartermaine tipped the Armagnac bottle over his glass. "Why?"

"It's Lord Reginald Hoke," said Peters. "I turned him off as you'd ordered but it didn't sit well. Apparently the damned fool feels lucky tonight."

After refilling his glass, Quartermaine lifted his lazy gaze back to Peters's, his eyebrows rising faintly. "Lucky enough to settle his accounts?" he murmured. "For if he does not, Lord Reggie shan't put so much as one manicured toe across the threshold of this establishment, lest I chop the thing off and use it for a bloody paperweight."

"A paperweight, sir?"

"To hold down that stack of worthless notes he's given us," said Quartermaine without humor.

Suddenly, from behind Quartermaine, the sound of hinges creaking intruded, followed by the rustle of fabric. He twisted in his chair.

"Ned—?" Her voice edged with irritation and her wild curls tumbling down, Maggie Sloan stood bracketed against the lamplight of his bedroom, Quartermaine's silk robe gathered around her in voluminous folds.

"I've business to attend," he said coolly. "Go back to bed, Maggie."

He sensed rather than saw the disdain flick over her face. "No, I think I'm off." Lip sneering, she slammed the door.

Emotionlessly, he turned back to Peters. "Where's Hoke now?"

"Pinkie stopped him in the entrance hall, sir."

"Alas, poor Reggie," said Quartermaine, setting his bottle down. "Shall I set loose the hounds, old chap? Or is there a bit of blood yet to be wrung from the Hoke turnip?"

Peters laughed. "Oh, there's blood," he said. "That's why you should come upstairs."

That elevated Quartermaine's brows another notch. "Indeed?" he said. "You shock me, Peters. I thought old Reggie entirely done in."

"He implies he's to meet some of his cronies here in half an hour for something deep," Peters suggested. "But he needs cash to stake at the card table, and he's in a mood to bargain."

Quartermaine sipped musingly at his brandy. "Well, I've never been known to sneer at a bargain," he said, rising. "But bring him down here. I'd rather not put my coat back on."

Peters bowed. "Certainly, sir."

Quartermaine followed Peters back through the suite and into the adjacent study where the heart of the club was centered. No bacchanalia or whoring went on within these walls; the Quartermaine Club was simply a circumspect, high-stakes gaming salon where many a noble scion had sent ten generations of wealth shooting down a rat hole beneath Ned Quartermaine's watchful eye.

But it was wealth, not blood, that determined whether a man—or a woman—could gain entrée to Quartermaine's world. Blue blood alone was next to worthless in his estimation—and he had enough of it in him to know.

Suddenly Quartermaine realized he still held the pearls in his hand. On a pinprick of irritation, he jerked open the drawer of his desk and let them slither into it, a cascade of creamy perfection. Then he took a cigar and went to the French windows that opened onto his garden.

The ash soon glowed orange in the dark. He could hear the rattle of a carriage coming up fast from the direction of St. James's Palace. The cry of a newspaper hawker in the street. And then the silence fell again. What the devil was keeping Lord Reginald?

Perhaps the craven bastard had turned tail and run back up St. James's Place to cower in one of his posh clubs. It little concerned him. Quartermaine always got his money—one way or another. He puffed again at the cigar and pondered at his leisure how best that might be done, for patience, he'd learnt, was truly a virtue.

Suddenly his front office door burst open in a great

clamor, with his doorman Pinkie Ringgold shouting down
a red-faced Lord Reggie as he shoved him into the room.

Reggie spat back, insulting Pinkie's parentage. Pinkie re-
ciprocated by twisting Reggie's arm halfway up his back.
The resulting howl could have raised the dead.

"Quiet!" commanded Quartermaine.

Silence fell like a shroud.

"Release him," Quartermaine ordered, "*now.*"

"But the blighter tried ter slip past me!" The portly doorman swelled with indignation. "Reckon 'ee finks I'm dumb
as I look."

"Which would be his mistake," said Quartermaine in a
voice quiet as the grave. "This, however, was yours. Ah,
Peters. There you are. Pinkie, you're within an inch of in-
curring my wrath. Kindly get out."

Pinkie snarled again at Reggie as he passed by Peters,
then thumped the door behind him as he exited.

"I want that upstart dismissed, Peters," snapped Reggie.

"Thank you," said Peters smoothly, "for your opinion."

Without asking either to sit, Quartermaine circled around
his desk to hitch one hip on its corner. Absent his coat and
cravat, his shirtsleeves still rolled to the elbow, it was a pose
of utter relaxation. A pose a man might assume late at night
in the comfort of his own home—which this was.

"Good evening, Lord Reginald," he said evenly. "Peters
tells me you've come to settle your debts with the house."

Reggie's uneasy gaze flicked toward Peters. Then, with
a sound of disdain, he gave his lapels a neatening tug. "I
can't think what sort of establishment you mean to run here,
Quartermaine," he muttered, "what with those Whitechapel
thugs shadowing the doors."

With a faint smile, Quartermaine made an expansive gesture. "My apologies, Lord Reginald," he said, "but it may
shock you to know there are occasionally gentlemen who do
not mean to settle their house accounts. Ah, but my termi-

nology is amiss, is it not? Such a fellow would not actually *be* a gentleman, would he?"

Reggie shrugged as if his coat were still uncomfortable. "Indeed not."

"But there, enough about our paltry establishment," said Quartermaine silkily. "Let's talk about you. Specifically, you propose some sort of bargain?"

Resignation was dawning in Reggie's eyes, but he was far too clever to admit it. Instead, he reached inside his coat and extracted a fold of letter paper.

No, not letter paper, Quartermaine realized when Reggie handed it to him. It was a legal document. After reaching across the desk for his gold-rimmed spectacles Quartermaine separated and scanned the papers, quietly refolded them, then lifted his gaze to Reggie's.

"And what, pray, am I to do with this?" he said, drawing the sheaf through his fingers.

"Why, not a thing," said Reggie lightly. "As I told your man Peters here, I produce it merely to prove I'm solvent. Or perhaps, even, to borrow against it?"

"But I'm not a bank," said Quartermaine, "and this, Lord Reginald, is a deed—along with an unsigned conveyance of said deed."

Reggie's gaze shifted uneasily. "Well, I'd meant to sell it," he admitted. "I never use the old place; it's just a little Somerset country house—a sort of shooting box, really, near the moors. But the deal fell through. Still, Quartermaine, the place is mine. I can sell it if I must."

"Lord Reginald," said Quartermaine quietly, "you owe me several thousand pounds. So I very much feel you *do* have to sell it."

Reggie looked at him as if he were stupid. "As I just said, the arrangement fell through."

"But your notes of hand were due—well, last month, two of them, if memory serves." Quartermaine snapped out the paper and pointed. "Tell me, Lord Reginald, is this the amount your buyer offered?"

"Well, yes," he said uneasily. "My solicitor drew it up."

"And was it a fair price?"

Reggie was caught between a rock and an ungentlemanly admission. He chose the rock. "Quite fair," he said, lifting his nose, "otherwise, I should never have agreed to it. As I said, Quartermaine, I've no use for the moldering old place."

Quartermaine refolded the papers, and thought of the strand of pearls in his desk, and of his own failings. Perhaps he ought not laugh at poor Reggie. Perhaps he was no better.

But he *was* laughing—and Reggie knew it. Still, it would take a bigger set of bollocks than Reggie possessed to play the haughty blueblood in the face of a man to whom one owed such a frightful amount of money.

Quartermaine laid his spectacles aside. "So let me understand, Lord Reginald," he continued. "You were doing the honorable thing: attempting to sell your small, superfluous, and unentailed estate so that you could settle your debts to me and pocket the balance. Do I have that right?"

It wasn't anything close to right, and all three of them knew it. Reggie's intent had been to sell the house in a fevered pitch for perhaps two-thirds its value in order to obtain quick cash in hand, and then stake himself at the tables with the naive but eternal hope of every bad gambler: that all would come aright in the end, and he would pay Quartermaine with his winnings in due course.

In due course meaning *when he damned well pleased.*

Quartermaine, however, was better pleased to be paid *now.*

He thwacked the side of his knee with the fold of paper. "I think you had a solid plan, Lord Reginald," he said pensively. "It's hardly your fault your buyer reneged."

"Indeed not," said Reggie haughtily. "We had a gentlemen's agreement."

"As do you and I," said Quartermaine, "though admittedly I cannot *quite* account myself a gentleman, can I, Lord Reginald?"

Reggie must have felt a stab of magnanimity. "Well, you're better bred than some fellows I know," he acknowledged, "and it's hardly your fault that your mother was a—well, never mind that." He gave a stiff, awkward bow at the neck. "May I get on about my evening, Quartermaine?"

"But first, back to the real estate," said Quartermaine. "What is the place called? What is its condition?"

The wariness in Reggie's eyes deepened. "Heatherfields," he said, "and I told you, it's just a little manor on the edge of Exmoor. The condition, so far as I know, is passable. Some old family retainers tend it."

"Tenant farms?"

"Three. All let, I think, along with the home acreage." Reggie smiled thinly. "I don't account myself much of a farmer."

"I see." Quartermaine smiled faintly. "Well, I'll tell you what I shall do, Lord Reginald. I shall take the moldering old place off your hands for the price your buyer offered— less, of course, what you owe me. And I'll do it now. In cash. Peters, unlock the cashbox and call down . . . what's that solicitor's name? Bradley?"

"Bradson, sir," said Peters, already fumbling for the key that hung from his watch chain. He shot a smile at their guest. "He's just upstairs, Lord Reginald, at the basset table. He owes us a favor or two. I'm sure he'll see to the deed of conveyance."

"We'll need three witnesses," said Quartermaine. "Bring Pinkie back, and fetch a footman who can read and write." Here, he turned to settle his watchful gaze on Reggie. "Doesn't that sound expedient, my lord? Soon you may go on about your evening—and with a tidy bit of cash in hand, unless either my memory or my arithmetic fails me."

Neither did.

Half an hour later, with Reggie looking pale and beaten, the deal was inked. Quartermaine offered Armagnac all around. Bradson took him up on it.

Reggie took his money and left.

"Well, that's that," said Peters cheerfully, shutting the great chest's doors when they were finished. "I thought it all went rather smoothly."

"Well done, old chap." Quartermaine chuckled, tossing the deed into his desk with Annie's pearls. "I cannot believe Reggie was fool enough to flash that paper at you."

"Desperate men, desperate means," said Peters. "He thought it might get him through the door."

"And so it did." Quartermaine shoved the drawer shut, and the laughter fell away. "Peters," he went on, "I need to go away for a time. A few weeks, perhaps."

Peters turned quizzically, but Quartermaine did not answer the unasked question. Peters had grown accustomed, over the years, to his disappearing with little explanation.

"Will you be all right here on your own awhile?" he said instead.

"Oh, indeed, sir," he said. "Off to gloat over your shooting box, perhaps?"

"Something like that," said Quartermaine, staring at the closed drawer.

Peters hesitated a heartbeat. "What do you mean to do with the house, sir," he said, "if you don't mind my asking? I've never known you to hunt or shoot."

At last Quartermaine lifted his gaze from the drawer. "It is a gift," he said quietly, "for Annie."

CHAPTER 2

In Which the Lovelorn
Are Cruelly Parted

It was a glorious afternoon three days after the rain had passed when Kate finally found herself riding alone across one corner of Bellecombe to examine the rectory's construction. Her path took her past several of the estate's tenancies, and along the back of the village, which edged the estate's largest farm.

Everywhere she looked, Kate beheld improvements. New roofs, better fencing, and even a new granary. Every ha'penny she and Anstruther, Bellecombe's steward, had managed to wring from the estate had been plowed back in again. Her grandfather would have envied Kate the chance to rebuild those things her father and brother had indirectly torn asunder. And he would have been proud, she hoped.

As the bridle path veered nearer the village, Kate passed by one of her tenant farmers bringing in the last of his hay. Touching her crop to her hat brim by way of greeting, she drew up her mare, Athena.

"Good day, Shearn," she said.

"M'lady!" Mr. Shearn tossed his rake to one of his sons. "Ike, pitch a spell, and Tom'll rake arter," he ordered, mopping his face with a handkerchief. "Whip it, now, in 'vore the rain come back!"

Sidling her mount nearer, Kate glanced skyward. "More rain?"

The old man winked. "Oh, I doubt it, m'lady, but I must keep the lads at it," he said, grinning. "Well, now. 'Tis good to see you out o' that gloomy estate office."

"I ran away when Anstruther wasn't looking." Kate leaned forward to run a hand down Athena's withers. "Tell me, how does Mrs. Shearn go on?"

The Shearns' cottage had been the one Anstruther had declared most in need of repair, and the cost had been a little daunting. Not just a new roof, but also a new chimney and a better shed for Mrs. Shearn's famed milch cow.

After passing a moment chatting with Shearn, Kate set off again, thinking of the esteem in which his tenants had held her grandfather. Indeed, the late Lord d'Allenay had always tried to put Bellecombe first, but in his heart, his children had ruled. Particularly Kate's father, James. And after him, her brother, Stephen. Yes, Kate had come to understand that James and Stephen Wentworth had been spendthrifts and gamblers of the worst sort.

The *losing* sort.

So what else could Grandpapa do save bail them out? The payment of a gentleman's debts was a matter of honor, plain and simple. But then Papa had died, and Stephen after him, and at last the awful bloodletting that had drained Bellecombe had been stanched in the most tragic of ways.

The ancient barony of d'Allenay held the unusual distinction of descending through heirs general, which meant that, if there were no sons, a daughter might do. So it had been decreed that Kate could hold the title. But she could not be permitted to sit in the House of Lords or hold any of the family's hereditary honors. That would have fallen to her husband.

Assuming she'd ever found one.

On a sigh, Kate cut Athena around a grove of trees, watching as the parish's new rectory—or at least the large, muddy spot allotted it—came into view. Already the foundation was in the process of being laid up by the masons Anstruther had brought down from Bristol. This being the workers' half day, however, all was silent.

Her uncle Upshaw, on whom Kate could always depend for sound business advice, had thought her quite mad to undertake such expenses until she'd explained her logic. The glebe holdings had not been expanded in a hundred years. The old rectory was small and beset by woodworm. Those were reasons enough, certainly, to do the right thing by the Church.

But Kate had had a better, more pressing reason.

Her fears. Fears that were abruptly renewed when she turned Athena through the gate and saw the other side of the new lumber pile. The earth being soft from rain, the Reverend Mr. Burnham didn't hear her approach and was instead assiduously—and enthusiastically—availing himself of the sins of the flesh.

Kate turned her face a little away. "*Richard Burnham!*" she said in a loud, carrying voice. "Kindly unhand my sister!"

The guilty couple sprang apart, Nancy's lips swollen, her fingers tangled in his hair.

"Oh, Lord," prayed the rector.

Oh, you had better pray, thought Kate. *You had better pray the minx won't have you.*

There came a sharp, feminine sigh of irritation. Kate turned fully around to see that Mr. Burnham had set Nancy away. Angrily spurring her horse forward, she could see her sister's cheeks were flushed bright pink beneath her riot of red-gold curls, her eyes swimming with angry tears as she glowered up at her swain.

Burnham's face had gone tight. "Yes, you *will* go back," he ordered Nancy, hands braced hard on her shoulders. "And you will go *now*."

"No! I shan't!" cried Nancy. "Let's have it out here and now—*all* of us."

"This is for me to deal with." Burnham let his hands drop. "We must have patience, my dear."

Nancy cut a nasty glance up at her sister. "Oh, yes, by all means, let us have more patience!" she said hotly. "Soon I shall be a dried-up old spinster, too!"

"My dear," said Burnham quietly, "that remark was ugly, and it was unworthy of you."

"I don't care!" cried Nancy. "Why should I grow old alone just because Kate shall?" Then, shooting her sister one last, killing glance, the girl turned on one heel and marched in the direction of the village.

"Nancy, wait," Kate ordered. "I wish to speak with you."

"No!" Her sister spun around and kept walking backward, hands fisted at her sides. "I have nothing to say to you, Kate! Not when you're determined to ruin my life!"

Burnham dragged a hand through his unruly locks, looking as if he'd been plowed down by a mail coach. Really, it seemed unfair for a man of the cloth to be so young—and so handsome. But the living was Kate's to bestow. And bestow it she had—taken in, no doubt, by those soft curls and innocent eyes.

"Mr. Burnham," Kate began in her most imperious tone, "my sister is inexperienced in the ways of the world."

Burnham looked as if he wished to wring his hat. Alas, he did not have one. Perhaps Nancy had knocked it off in her exertions. "B-but I love her!" he declared. "I wish to marry her. You *know* that I do."

"Indeed, I do," returned Kate grimly, "and it is only that which keeps me from shooting you where you stand."

Blanching, he lifted both hands.

"Oh, come, Richard!" Kate draped one hand over the

pommel of her saddle. "I like you too well to shoot you. But my sister's leading you a merry dance—and she'll do it the rest of your days if you're fool enough to let her."

"I am!" he cried, looking up at her. "I *love* her. Yes, Nancy's young. But she's a good Christian, Lady d'Allenay, and admired by all. She's kind and loving—and most importantly, she knows her own mind."

"Yes, and soon she'll know yours, too," Kate warned, "and she'll be telling you what to think every morning over breakfast. Her opinions will be yours, or you will have—and do pardon the irony here—hell to pay. Trust me. I know."

"Nothing could make me happier," vowed the rector, his eyes drifting about his new home's foundation. "But indeed, my lady, you must think me most ungrateful. Your generosity—it seemingly knows no bounds." Suddenly, he paled, and turned back to her, his mind working furiously.

Ah. At last it had occurred to him. "Yes, go on," said Kate wearily. "Say it."

"Surely . . . surely, my lady, you didn't think to dissuade my affections with this new rectory?" he croaked, "or . . . or the glebe land?"

"As in *a bribe*? Certainly not."

I meant to ensure you could afford to keep up my sister after she marries you.

As she inevitably would. Oh, Kate could buy the girl time, and build her a decent house. Aunt Louisa could insist she have a Season in Town. Uncle Upshaw could scowl. And Mamma could trawl her matrimonial nets through Belle-combe baited by a dozen of her handsome puppies. But in the end, it would all come down to this: a marriage of hardship and simplicity.

The awkward life of a parson's wife.

Kate cleared her throat sharply. "The glebe land is for the Church," she said. "For you, yes, and all who come after you, Richard. Besides, were I to bribe you, I should do the thing properly. With cold, hard cash—of which I have little."

The rector exhaled with relief. "Well, then," he managed. "Well. Then I—I renew my proposal for your sister's hand. I ask your permission to pay her my addresses."

"It looked to me as if you were already paying them," said Kate dryly.

His color drained again. "I—I can't think what got into me."

"A man of the cloth is still a man like any other," said Kate evenly.

"But I know your feelings in this regard."

"Richard, none of this is within my control." Kate softened her tone. "And if you persist in this folly—or I should say, if *Nancy* persists in it—Uncle Upshaw will simply order her to Town now instead of waiting for the Season to start. He is her guardian. I've no influence with my sister, and never have had."

The rector's eyes softened. "I . . . I'm sorry I brought her out here. Truly."

"I think it a vast deal more likely Nancy brought *you* out here," said Kate. "I know you're a man of honor. But I'm sure tidying the vestry became tedious. The dust, perhaps, made her sneeze. She began to sigh, then suggested the two of you take a little stroll. It no doubt seemed perfectly innocent at the time."

Mr. Burnham cut his guilty gaze away.

Deeply irritated with her sister, Kate spurred Athena half around. She had lost all interest in the new construction. "Just try to understand Uncle Upshaw's view, Richard, and keep the girl in check," she advised. "You must earn not just her affection, but her respect, if you mean to marry her. And if she chafes at that—why, that tells you something, does it not?"

"I . . . I hardly know," he said. "Does it?"

Kate shrugged. "As Nancy is so quick to point out, I am myself unwed and apt to remain so," she replied. "But here's the long and the short of it. Nancy is almost nineteen, and has never had a Season. Never seen London. Never been courted beyond this county. Before she does something so drastic as to—"

"—marry beneath her," the rector supplied, his mouth twisting.

"Oh, Richard! I do not think that. I *do not*."

"Lord Upshaw thinks it."

"No, he merely fears she has lived a rustic life," she said, "and wants Nancy to see a bit of society. He would never make her marry a man she didn't love. I counsel only patience, Richard. You must both be *sure*."

Burnham lifted his hand to take hers, his soft curls ruffling lightly in the breeze. "I *am* sure," he said, gazing up at her. "But I understand, Kate. I will be more firm with her."

On a nod, Kate let his hand slip away and wheeled Athena a quarter turn. "I trust you will," she said over her shoulder. "Oh, and Richard—steel yourself on another front. My mother means to come for the shooting season."

"*Mrs. Wentworth?*" Dread sketched over the rector's face. "How . . . delightful. And her lively friends, too, I daresay?"

"I fear so, yes."

During last year's visit, in the middle of a languid stroll through the village, Kate's mother's paramour, the Comte de Macey, had espied Burnham's tiny, provincial church through his jeweled lorgnette and declared—on something that sounded suspiciously like a chortle—that he found himself in dire need of confession.

The entire household had known, even then, of Nancy's infatuation with the new rector. Doubtless the comte's ruse had arisen from pure devilment, and a prying wish to lay eyes upon this manly paragon. Left with little option save to graciously oblige the Frenchman in his hour of Catholic need, the Reverend Mr. Burnham had made do with a dark Anglican corner and a vestry curtain.

Whatever de Macey had teasingly confessed to the poor man had evidently singed Richard's ear hair. He had come back out of the church pink-faced, and never spoke of it again. Kate's mother had barely contained her laughter, and merely smacked *le comte* with her parasol in mock disapprobation.

"Well," said Richard, dragging his hand through his hair again. "When do you expect her?"

"Richard, it is Mamma," she said evenly. "One does not so much *expect* her, but rather simply battens down the hatches and watches the horizon darken."

With that, Kate touched her crop to her hat brim, and wheeled Athena about to urge her into a canter. Through sheer force of will, she had not let Richard see the anger that still roiled inside her. Setting aside the cruelty of Nancy's insult, Kate knew there was no one she'd sooner welcome into the family than Richard. But the couple might well have to wait until Nancy's majority.

Instead, Nancy was attempting to force the issue. But if she could not give a fig for her family's wishes, thought Kate angrily, could she not, at the very least, think of Richard's good name? *He was the village rector*—and Nancy had tempted him into a situation where any passing villager might have seen.

Driven by temper and, yes, by the hot sting of her sister's insult, Kate gave Athena her head. They flew across the field, tossing up divots of turf almost silently. The Shearns had turned their wagon and were raking up the last of the hay. Intent on her errand—and a little blinded, perhaps, by temper—Kate passed by with merely a nod.

Reaching the main road, she leaned over Athena's haunches and sent her sailing over the fence and through the wide gap in the hedge. And in the next moment, all hell erupted.

In a roadway that should have been empty, a massive dark shadow loomed on her right. Athena reared in surprise. The great, black beast barreling down the hill reared, too, pawing so close Kate felt the hoof breeze past her forehead.

The rider cursed, and fought for control. Too late. The

hard, wheeling jerk he forced upon his rearing mount sent him flying from the saddle. His head struck the moss-covered millstone that sat like a massive, immovable toad at the intersection.

Kate screamed, kicked loose her stirrup and leapt, leaving Athena's reins to dangle. Falling to her knees in the grass, she needed but a glance to see blood was streaming from the man's temple, his eyes open yet sightless.

Terrified, Kate turned and rushed for the fence, hurling herself half over. "*Shearn!*" she screamed at the top of her lungs. "*Shearn! Bring the wagon!*"

"OH, DEAR!" NANCY gingerly set down her basin of steaming water by the massive mahogany bed. "Oh, Kate! I'm so sorry. Poor man! I ought not have goaded you."

"No, you ought not," Kate admitted. "But the fault is mine; I was careless."

"Yours?" Nancy gave a little sniffle. "*You* are never careless."

"I wish you were right." Willing her hand not to shake, Kate stroked the heavy, gold-brown hair off the man's forehead. "Here, give me the sponge."

Nancy blithered on between damp sniffles about her guilt and regret and something about Richard being angry enough to throttle her as Kate dunked the sponge and wrung it out, assessing the best way to attack the drying blood that had streamed down his face and ruined his shirt.

The injured man lay now in Stephen's bedchamber at Bellecombe, directly across the passageway from Kate's. From the time Ike and Tom Shearn had gingerly lifted him from the verge until the moment they'd settled him onto the bed, the man had made no sound. More worrisome still, when Kate had clambered into the hay wagon to close his eyes, they had not so much as twitched beneath his lids. Nor did they now.

"Kate . . . is he going to die?" murmured Nancy, her eyes searching the man's face.

Kate paused, twisting about on the bed to lean over the man. "He's not going to die," she said firmly. But looking at the man's pale, strikingly handsome face, Kate was reminded of her brother, who had lingered months after his fall.

But that was different. Stephen had fallen from a great height. His spine had been badly twisted, if not broken. It had been terrible. The panic began to rise again, and Kate forced it down.

Maintain calm, she told herself. *Press on.* She was of no use to this poor man in a state of agitation. "He's just taken a blow to the head, Nan," she said more gently. "He's merely concussed. His heart sounds strong as an ox."

Tucking a clean towel around his face, Kate began to sponge away the blood matting the blond hair at his temple. No, not blond, and not quite brown, either, but a dark, shimmering gold—at least six different shades of it, too, as if he'd spent a great deal of time in the sun.

And yet his thin, long-fingered hands were impeccably manicured. His shirt was of the finest cambric, the blood-stained collar starched to an inch, though a hint of surprisingly black bristle now shadowed his long, lean cheeks. A gold watch chain swung from his waistcoat, and on his right hand a faceted sapphire winked upon his little finger. There was no mistaking it. The man was a gentleman through and through—and a wealthy one.

Soon the water in the basin was tinged pink and Kate's care was rewarded by the sight of an ugly, two-inch gash that now merely oozed blood at his hairline. "There," she said, settling back onto the edge of the bed. "It will want stitching, I daresay, but the blood's clotted. Who went to fetch the doctor?"

"Tom Shearn." Nancy was still twisting her hands on the opposite side of the bed.

Just then Mrs. Peppin came bustling into the room with a dark coat slung over one arm, and a brown valise in hand. "Lawk, poor man!" she declared, setting the case atop the chest at the foot of the bed. "Here be his postmantle and gurtcoat, miss. 'Twere strapped to his saddle."

The bag, like the rest of him, looked expensive, the leather worn soft as butter. A brass escutcheon glittered below the handle. Kate bent, and tilted it a little toward the light. The tiny strip was engraved with four initials, the first of which were legible as *N.E.D.* but the last one Kate could not make out; either a *Q* or an *O* with a scratch in it.

After hanging the coat, Mrs. Peppin took his hand, chafed it briskly for a time, then laid it down with a sigh. "If he don't rouse in a bit, Miss Kate, you'd best roke about in that postmantle and try to make out who he be. Someone, somewhere is apt to be missing the poor gentleman."

Kate set her head to one side and studied his face. "For the life of me, I cannot recognize him."

"No, miss, he's not from hereabouts," said the housekeeper. "Handsome enough, though, idn' he?"

"And he had not been to the house, you say?" Kate asked again. "He was, after all, coming back *down* our hill."

"No, not a sight of him. Perhaps he took a wrong turn, saw the castle, and knew his mistake? Mayhap he'd meant to turn down the hill instead of up?"

"There's nothing down the hill, either," said Kate. "Nothing save Heatherfields, which is shut up."

"And about to cave in," added Mrs. Peppin sourly.

"Ike Shearn is going to ask about the man round the village," said Nancy.

"Good. Well. Tom and the doctor might be a while." Kate tossed the bloody sponge into the basin and shoved away a tendril of hair with the back of her hand. "I think, Peppie, we had better get him undressed and make sure he's not otherwise injured."

The housekeeper tilted her head at Nancy, and lifted one eyebrow.

"Nancy, go downstairs and watch for Dr. Fitch," Kate instructed. "Oh, and ask Cook to steep some beef tea."

For once Nancy went without argument. There was no question, of course, of Kate being sent from the room. Despite being both unwed and under thirty, she had headed the household for several years. And during those years—perhaps even before them—she had come to be viewed by those around her as an entrenched spinster, comfortable with her state and station in life, and more devoted to the land than she could ever be to a husband.

Even Aunt Louisa had given up hoping Kate might marry. Kate's London Season—and the brief betrothal that had followed—had been a debacle of epic proportions. Kate had fled back to the isolation of Bellecombe with her tail between her legs, and lost herself in learning to manage the estate. No, despite her occasional jest to Mrs. Peppin, the luxury of possessing virginal sensibilities was not Kate's lot in life.

After tugging off his tall riding boots, they set about drawing off the man's coat. His elegant cravat having been whipped off by the roadside to wrap his head wound, Mrs. Peppin's capable fingers began instead with the buttons of his brocade waistcoat.

"Lawk, miss, did ever ye see such fine stitching!" the housekeeper declared, fingering the silk lining.

Kate lifted her gaze from the sleeve she was wrestling. The waistcoat looked more expensive than anything even her dandified brother had worn, while at the same time utterly understated. "Savile Row," she murmured, "or something near it. Here, help me lift him."

The man was solidly built, but little by little his outer garments were tugged, pushed, and peeled off, then laid aside for brushing. Mrs. Peppin folded his waistcoat and set his pocket watch on the night table by the basin.

Then, as if reconsidering it, she picked the watch back up, and flipped open the cover. Her worn blue eyes flicked over it, then sharpened.

"Engraved?" asked Kate.

"Aye." The housekeeper turned it around. "*To Edward with love*," she said, "*from Aunt Isabel.*"

"To Edward." She leaned across to examine it. "The initials on his bag are not quite decipherable, but the first three are clearly *N.E.D*. Well done, Peppie. It seems at least one of our patient's names is Edward."

"Well, let us pray he'll live to see his poor auntie again." Mrs. Peppin seemed touched by the notion that such a tall, strapping man might have someone to mourn him.

Kate turned her attention to the man's shirt. "This is ruined with blood," she said ruefully. "I'd better just cut it off."

After fetching scissors from her sewing basket, Kate tugged the man's shirttails from his trousers, the fabric still warm. That was good, she reassured herself. Warm was good. But that rising warmth merely served to carry the man's tantalizing scent, a faintly woody aroma that reminded her of chestnut and fresh citrus. And *man*. Yes, for all his infirmity, their patient still smelled very much—and very temptingly—like a man.

A little irritated with such fancies, Kate seized his shirt and slit it stem to stern with her scissors. The fine lawn fell away to reveal a smooth, broad chest literally layered with muscles.

"Lawk, look at that!" Mrs. Peppin whispered. "I'd have wagered the fellow never did a day's work in his life."

Perhaps not, Kate ruefully considered. But he'd certainly been doing *something*. "I daresay he boxes," she murmured. "Many wealthy men seem to have a proclivity for that brutal sport."

But on her next breath she saw the ugly white pucker of flesh alongside his rib cage. Mrs. Peppin lightly touched it. "Poor love," she said. "Looks to be a knife wound. Could he be a military fellow?"

But at that very moment, a faint sound escaped his lips, no

more than an exhalation, really. Kate set away the scissors with a hasty clatter. "Edward?" she said urgently, leaning over him. "Edward, can you hear us?"

His eyes flicked back and forth beneath his lids, and he seemed to give an odd sort of shudder. On impulse, Kate seized his hand. "Edward, you're at Bellecombe Castle," she said a little loudly, "in Somerset. Can you hear me?"

But the man's eyes had stilled, and his hand went limp in hers. She held it thus for some minutes, but he did not stir again. A cold fear settling over her, Kate laid it down, his ring winking blue fire in the afternoon sunlight.

He is not Stephen, she told herself again. *He will not die. I shan't permit it.*

After a time, they set about drawing off the man's trousers, leaving him in nothing save drawers and stockings. Kate could not help but eye the dusting of dark hair between the mounds of his chest muscles. It thickened as it trailed down his belly, then vanished suggestively beneath the linen of his drawers.

Drawers that now hung almost tantalizingly low, having been dragged down by the removal of his trousers, leaving the thin, snowy fabric pulled taut—and leaving little to Kate's imagination. She was debating the decency of attempting to pull them back up again when a knock sounded and Hetty, their kitchen maid, stuck her head in the door.

"Beg pardon, Mrs. Peppin, but the stillroom's locked." The girl's gaze swept down the man, catching on his thick, strong hipbones. "Lawks, hang my stars and garters! Dangerous 'andsome, in't he?"

"Mind your London tongue, Hetty; good country girls don't make so bold." Mrs. Peppin was already sorting through the keys at her waist. "Now do ye watch his eyes, Miss Kate," she added as she rose. "I've a notion he's stirring."

When they had left the room, Kate took the man's hand again. It was warm and heavy, yet utterly lifeless. Where the devil was Dr. Fitch? She glanced at the mantel clock.

But little more than half an hour had passed since his fall. It seemed an eternity—and a dangerously long time to remain unconscious. Despite her guilt, Kate let her gaze trail over his nearly bare body again—merely to observe the rise and fall of his chest, she assured herself.

Kate wasn't entirely innocent, but never had she seen a man so thoroughly undressed. What woman would not feel a certain fascination at the sight of the honed, hard muscles that layered the man's arms and chest? And those hipbones. Yes, she could understand Hetty's absorption, for there was something distinctly virile about them. But what? They were just bones. And yet they seemed to suggest *something* . . .

But Kate was too stupid to know what. Flicking another glance at his closed eyes, she yielded to the temptation to stroke a hand down the hard swell of his biceps; all the way down to the warm, velvet-soft skin at the crook of his elbow.

His eyes did not move. Tentatively, she eased her palm down his belly, her hand rising and falling with the firm abdominal muscles that rolled from the bottom of his breastbone, and went . . . well, Kate was not perfectly sure where they went. Underneath the tie of those drawers, certainly . . .

For an instant, her curious fingers hovered.

Then good sense returned on a rush of embarrassment. Kate snatched back her hands. Good Lord. She was not a fool. She knew how men were made. How they . . . *reacted.* She'd had a brother. A London Season. Been held, on occasion, inappropriately close. And once—*just* once . . .

Kate drew a deep breath, and forced it from her mind. Then, desperate for something to do besides stare at the beautiful man, she leapt from her chair and seized his valise. Snapping it open, she methodically laid out the contents atop the chest.

Immediately she began to reconsider the possibility of an army career, for this was a man who moved fast and light. Three sets of fresh linen were rolled tight together with a pair of breeches and waistcoat. A razor, but no strop. Soap in a pierced silver case—the source, she realized, of his tantalizing scent. A comb. Tooth powder and a brush. But nary a scrap, she noted abashedly, in the way of nightclothes.

Only three things remained in the bottom of the bag. A pair of gold spectacles in a leather case, a copy of Niccolò Machiavelli's *The Prince*, and lastly, in a blue velvet bag, a strand of pearls.

Kate flipped open the book in faint hope of finding a name on the flyleaf. Nothing. She repacked the case, giving the soap one last sniff, then returned to her vigil. It belatedly occurred to her that what she had *not* found was money. Surely such a wealthy man would not travel without funds?

It scarcely mattered; he was her obligation, now that his quick, near suicidal action had saved her from being brained by a flying hoof. She could only pray the man didn't pay the ultimate price for such selflessness. On an unexpected wave of tenderness, she set her hand to his warm, slightly bristled cheek.

His eyes flew open—eyes the most startling shade of green.

Kate gasped, jerking her hand away. But the man caught her wrist—*hard*. She was trapped, her nose but a few inches from his, their gazes locked.

"E-Edward?" she whispered.

His eyes searched her face for what felt like an eternity, then he swallowed hard. "Who are you?" he choked, his voice like a rasp.

"Kate," she blurted. "Lady d'Allenay. You've been injured. Do you remember?"

His grip tightened. "Where the devil am I?" he whispered, his gaze darting about the room.

"At my home," she said, "in Somerset. You took a fall, sir. Please, can you kindly release me?"

His head swiveled on the pillow, his gaze going to his fingers, still locked around her wrist. He stared as if wondering to whom they belonged, and for an instant, Kate feared he was blind.

"Edward," she said more commandingly. "Let go."

Slowly, he did. His eyes were moving across her face now, taking her in. Relief rushed through her. "I'm so sorry," she blurted. "I didn't expect anyone on our road. I took that fence too fast."

He blinked once. "*Who* are you?"

"Baroness d'Allenay of Bellecombe," she said. "And you . . . well, you are Edward, yes? I'm sorry; I don't know your surname. Is there someone—your wife, perhaps—for whom I might send?"

"I'm not married," he blurted.

"And your name?"

He blinked again, and shook his head, his lips thinning. "Edward—?" he said.

But it was not a statement. A cold chill washed over Kate. Impulsively, she returned her hand to his face. "And . . . and your surname? Your home?"

She watched in horror as something like fear spread across his face. "I . . . I do not know." For a moment, his throat worked furiously. "Good God!" he rasped. "I do not know!"

CHAPTER 3

In Which Dr. Fitch Attends the Patient

Dr. Fitch shut the flap of his satchel with an efficient snap as he trudged into Kate's private parlor. Waving off the chair Kate offered, he set his bag and a brown bottle down on the tea table.

"Well, all in all, Mr. Edward is a healthy man in his prime," proclaimed the elderly doctor. "I have left him resting comfortably, Lady d'Allenay."

Nancy, her contrition fading, had begun firing questions, comments, and opinions upon Kate and Mrs. Peppin as soon as the doctor vanished into the invalid's room. She now turned her interrogation upon Fitch.

"Is that laudanum, Doctor?" she asked, pointing at the bottle. "Is that perfectly wise, do you think? And when will his memory return? Has he remembered *anything*? The accident, perhaps?"

"Miss Wentworth, if you please!" Dr. Fitch threw up a hand. "One question at a time."

"Perhaps the laudanum is for me," said Kate grimly, "so that I can sedate myself."

Nancy cut her a dark, yet faintly rueful look. "Well, I only meant that, given the poor man has sustained a head injury—"

"Do ye be still, Miss Nan," Mrs. Peppin chided. "I hope I know how to dose a man with laudanum! He's apt to be sore come morning."

"Precisely," said Fitch. "In addition to a severe concussion, he's badly bruised and has set an ankle wrong. Further, he's cracked his left collarbone, and there's little to be done for it. So yes, though it's not ideal, Mr. Edward may have laudanum should he develop an unbearable headache or severe pain."

"We'll see to it, and never you worry," Mrs. Peppin reassured him. "Now, what may the poor gentleman eat?"

"Anything, but begin with the beef tea and porridge," the doctor advised. "He must rest, and make no more movement than nature requires. No reading or close work for a fortnight."

"No *reading*?" said Kate, horrified.

"His brain is concussed," said Dr. Fitch tightly. "Indeed, he mightn't even be able to read—alexia, it's called. Moreover, patients sometimes exhibit odd behaviors, or suffer a degree of disinhibition. My colleague had a patient who imagined himself Prince Albert and got himself arrested climbing over the palace gates. Yes, rest is essential."

But Kate had already seen enough to know the man would not be so quiet. "Surely he'll go mad?"

"Then you must see he does not," said the doctor. "Read to him. Converse with him."

"Cards?" Nancy suggested. "I could play piquet with him."

"Not until two weeks have passed," said Dr. Fitch, "at the very least. Besides, Miss Wentworth, if you will pardon my saying, you are too restive a person for sick-bedding." He paused, and snatched up his satchel. "Now, my good ladies,

I shall return in two days' time. But send for me if there's any change."

Kate slicked her hands down the front of her skirt. "And . . . and his memory, Doctor? We should very much like to contact his family."

Dr. Fitch shrugged. "Ordinarily the loss is fleeting," he said, "but I will not lie to you, Lady d'Allenay. Mr. Edward may be your guest for some weeks."

"And if his memory doesn't return?"

The doctor shook his head. "Never seen it happen," he said confidently. "Oh, one reads of such things. But to see it? No. Even our Prince Albert eventually came round."

With that, the doctor bowed, and started to the door, Mrs. Peppin following.

Kate picked up the small pile of nightclothes she'd assembled. "Well," she said, looking pensively across the hall, "we had better go in and check on our guest."

"Not I!" Nancy's eyes twinkled with mirth. "I am too *restive*. Besides, you're the one who nearly killed him."

"Ah, back in form, I see," said Kate dryly. "What will you be doing, I wonder, whilst I tend my patient?"

"Writing to Uncle Upshaw," she said, flouncing from the room, "to tell him I wish to get married at once."

"Ah!" Kate followed her out. "*At once*, is it?"

"It seems the prudent course," said Nancy, making a dramatic pirouette in the middle of the passageway. "This frightful accident has reminded me that life is precious, Kate, and I don't want to waste it."

On a sigh, Kate knocked softly on the door. Inside, she was a little dismayed to see that her guest now lay beneath the bedcovers, the sheets pulled to his chin. She felt, strangely, more awkward than ever. He moved as if he wished to stand, as any gentleman would have done. Then, realizing the awkwardness of the situation, he froze.

"No, you mustn't move," she declared, holding up a staying hand. "Here. I've brought you some things. A nightshirt and a robe. Oh, and slippers—which may or may not fit."

"Thank you," he said simply. "And please thank whomever—your husband, perhaps?—who so kindly loaned—"

"They are Fendershot's," said Kate, shaking out the night-shirt. "Our butler. I'm not married."

"Oh." He looked at her solemnly. "I'm very sorry. Lady . . . d'Allenay, was it?"

"Yes—oh, but no—" Realizing his conclusion, she shook her head again. "I am not widowed. I have never been married."

He looked a little askance at her. "I inherited the title," she explained, "from my grandfather some years ago."

"Ah," he said, looking almost as awkward as she. "That is . . . unusual, is it not?"

"Not common," she acknowledged. "Here, may I help you into this nightshirt? The castle is drafty, I fear."

His eyes widened. "I may have taken a blow to the head, my lady, but even I realize the impropriety of being dressed by an unwed lady."

"I *un*-dressed you," she replied.

"And now I can *re*-dress myself," he said a little fractiously.

"No doubt," she said evenly, "but you may not move about in doing so. Now, stop standing on such ceremony. I'm going to drag this over your head, Edward, and you will—"

"How do you know my name is Edward?" he interposed.

"It was engraved on your watch."

"What watch?"

"A magnificent gold pocket watch." On a shaft of sympathy, Kate went to the chest and retrieved it.

He took it, and snapped the cover open. "From Aunt Isabel," he said quietly, his gaze meeting hers. "*Aunt Isabel*," he said again, and if repeating the words might summon forth a recollection. "Good God. Who is she?"

Kate laughed. "A rich and doting aunt, from the look of it," she said, snapping out the nightshirt. "That watch is eighteen-karat gold, from London's best maker."

He scowled a little, his brow furrowing. "That's not what I meant," he said, laying the watch aside.

"I know it isn't," said Kate more tenderly. "You must feel so frightfully frustrated—and so frightfully *cold*—or will do, at any rate. So I'm going to pull this over your head, and over your shoulders. Then, when I turn my back, you will wiggle it down—without moving, if you please."

"And how the devil am I to do that?"

She popped it over his head, careful of the fresh stitches, then regarded him with a little smile. "I knew it would not take long before you asserted yourself," she said evenly. "Now, there. Wiggle into it—*gently*!"

She turned and listened to his efforts, noting with some concern a little grunt of pain.

"Shall I call a footman to help?" she ventured.

"No," he barked. "I mean—thank you, no. And what is that supposed to mean, anyway? *Assert* myself? Go on, turn round if you wish."

"I do wish," she said, turning to survey his work. "And it's just that I know the type of man you are."

"Ah!" He looked askance at her again. "And what type is that, exactly?"

"The *take charge* type," she returned. "The *I'll get out of bed when I bloody well please* type."

"I must say, my lady, you're mighty free with your language." But he was grinning a little. "And you seem remarkably well-informed, considering I don't even know my own name."

"Yes, you do. It is Edward."

"Did it ever occur to you that I might have stolen that watch?" he suggested. "Or bought it from some pawnbroker?"

Again, she laughed, and this time she sat down by the bed to regard him more seriously. "No, you're a gentleman—

from London, I'm fairly certain—who has ventured into the West Country for a reason," she said, and this time she took his hand and gave it a hard squeeze. "We must merely wait for that reason to surface. While waiting, however, the doctor advises you not strain your mind. Just rest, Edward. You are welcome here."

His eyes glinted with humor. "A crackbrained watch thief, welcomed with open arms by a woman who ought to be married but isn't," he said. "This is a curious predicament in which we find ourselves, Lady d'Allenay."

She let his hand go, and propped her elbow on one of the night tables, attempting to strike a casual pose. "Kate," she said quietly. "Until we know your full name, you must call me Kate, for I can call you nothing but Edward."

"Kate," he said, his expression suddenly serious. "For Katherine?"

"Yes," she said. "Now, I'm going to ring for some beef tea. Tell me, does your head hurt?"

He smiled vaguely. "A bit," he said. "How did you know?"

"I see it in your eyes," she said. "Dr. Fitch left laudanum. Will you take a little?"

"God, no! The wretched stuff makes me ill," he said. "Wait—how do I know that?"

His gaze met hers again, and this time she saw the alarm rise.

"You knew you weren't married," she said.

His gaze turned inward, and she could see him fighting down the fear. "I do know that," he said, swallowing hard. "I do know laudanum turns my stomach. And I do know that I should like—above all things, it seems—some beef tea! Lord, my manhood may never recover!"

"Oh, I'm fairly confident your manhood never forsook you," she said on a laugh. Then, feeling faintly awkward, she leapt up to ring the bell. "Perhaps you oughtn't try to think so much."

"Try *not* to think?" he said irritably. "How can I not

think? I'm trying like the devil to remember something—anything—about myself."

She returned to the chair, and regarded him gravely. "I rather doubt memory is something one can force," she murmured, pensively setting her chin on her fist. "Not even someone as formidable as you."

"Formidable?" He snorted. "I'm terrified."

"And yet you maintain your—I don't know—your gravitas, perhaps? Or composure?" she said evenly. "You seem very much in command of yourself."

"Frozen with fear," he muttered.

She laughed, and leapt up at Hetty's knock. After ordering his tray, she returned to her chair. "I will make a deal with you," she said. "If you will try not to think, I will remain here and we will just chat until you're drowsy."

"Chat?"

"In the way of people just getting to know one another," she said. "As if we just met . . . on a train, say. On a long journey. Perhaps some memory will inadvertently stir."

He gazed about the room, which was admittedly large, and dramatically furnished in an almost medieval style. "You are Baroness d'Allenay of Bellecombe," he said, "and can doubtless afford a private, first-class carriage."

"Oh, you would be surprised at what I cannot afford," she said.

"In any case, you would not be traveling with the likes of me," he replied.

She looked at him, puzzled. "What does that mean? The *likes* of you?"

His brow furrowed again. "I do not know," he finally said. "But for all you know, Lady d'Allenay, I am a very bad man. And here you are, alone with me."

"Nonsense," she said tartly. "I am in my home, surrounded by people who, I do assure you, have my best interests at heart—and yours, too. Moreover, you are a gentleman. I see it in your attire. Your voice. Your demeanor. Never take me for a fool, Edward."

But it seemed suddenly odd to call him by his Christian name. And he was still regarding her with grave intensity. "There are a great many *gentlemen*, my lady," he finally said, "who are very wicked indeed. In fact, I would venture to say the odds run a little higher of that being the case than they would within the general population."

"You sound quite certain of that," she said. "Are you a student of human nature?"

"I believe I must be," he answered in a cool, certain voice. "I may be half naked and two-thirds terrified, but my talents, such as they are, seem not to have left me. And by the way, Lady d'Allenay, *most* people are fools."

"I find I cannot disagree with you, but you do sound a little like a radical," she said. "Do you mean now to read me a lecture on universal male suffrage? If so, you quite waste your breath. I support it entirely—or would do, if they'd let me take my seat."

"Ah, a secret Chartist!" he said on a chuckle. "Will women want the vote next?"

"I hardly think we could fare worse in wielding it, do you?"

"*Touché*, Lady d'Allenay," he murmured. "A rabble-rouser. I begin to like you better and better."

Against her will, she burst out laughing, then set her fingers to her mouth. "Dear heavens, you're *thinking*," she said. "Dr. Fitch will have my head on the platter."

"And a lovely head it would be," he said smoothly. "Dare I suggest a surround of parsley and winter cabbage? It would set off your creamy complexion to quite good effect."

Kate felt her heart hitch, then jerked herself back to reality. "I'm afraid, sir, that you're flirting," she said, "which is more of a mental strain, I daresay, than thinking. I must insist you stop it at once."

His eyes glittering, he opened his mouth as if to parry

words, then abruptly shut it again, twitching at his bedcovers as if uncomfortable. "I beg your pardon," he said. "You're right. It seemed to . . . just slip out. I must strike you as ungrateful."

"No, I—I'm sorry." Good heavens, the man seemed to keep her eternally off balance. "If it amuses you to pretend to flirt—"

"*Pretend?*" His eyes lit with mirth.

"Yes," she said tartly, "and if you find it diverting, I daresay I must bear it with grace. Were it not for me, you wouldn't be here in this awkward situation."

"Yes, you suggested as much earlier," he said. "And I'm sure it's not the case. Still—and tell me precisely—what the devil *did* happen?"

"It is very much the case." Kate wrung her hands, and explained how their horses had nearly collided, and how he had forced his horse to wheel around, thereby taking the worst of it upon himself.

But the man brushed aside the story and simply said, "And why, Lady d'Allenay, were you in such a temper? I confess, you do not look the type."

"Because you do not know me," she said. "I've a frightful temper, and it often serves me ill. As to why, well, I had quarreled with Nancy. My sister."

"Ah, the beauteous Miss Wentworth," he said blandly. "I met her when the doctor came in. Do you mean to tell me what the quarrel was about?"

"Certainly not," said Kate. "It would be of no interest to you whatever."

"I am bedridden," he reminded her. "By this time tomorrow, I'll likely find Bristol's tidal charts engrossing."

Just then, a knock sounded and his tray was brought in. Kate had ordered a light repast; not just the broth, but a little sliced chicken and a bit of bread and cheese.

"Oh, bless you," he said, falling on it as if famished. "I was afraid of being reduced to porridge."

"It was suggested," she said lightly, "but you do not seem all that incapacitated. And it is, after all, your brain which has been concussed, not your stomach."

That did indeed appear the case. After a little help in situating the tray, and with the most discerning of table manners, Edward made short work of it while Kate nattered on about the weather, and tried not to hover.

When she returned from helping Hetty out the door, she paused at the foot of the massive bed, her hands lightly crossed. "Well, I should leave you now, I daresay," she said. "There is a footman in the great hall at all times. Should you need anything, you have only to ring that bell."

He crooked his head to look at the wire that was now wrapped about his bedpost. "Yes, your housekeeper threaded that round the room slick as a ribbon."

Kate unfolded her hands. "The hooks were already in place," she replied. "This was once my brother's room. He lived here as an invalid for a time, and the regular pull was too far for him to reach."

"Ah, I see." He fell quiet for a moment. "But now he's gone, I collect? Otherwise, the title would have fallen to him?"

"Yes," she said simply. "So the wire goes directly to the footman's station. Even in the middle of the night, he'll promptly attend you. And on no account must you get up. Not this evening, and certainly not in the night. Well, not unless—"

She cut an uneasy glance toward the dressing room door.

He waved away the embarrassment. "I understand, Lady d'Allenay," he said, "and to be honest, I feel as if a cartload of bricks fell on me, and haven't the least wish to stir from this bed."

"Good." She gave him a little nod. "Then I shall wish you a good evening."

"But I thought we were going to have our train conversation," he said, his gaze very direct.

"In the morning, perhaps." Kate pulled open the door.

"I have offended you," he said quietly.

"Not in the least." Kate forced her gaze to soften. "But you look tired. And I wish to go into the office and study my maps."

"Your maps?"

"Yes." She nodded. "Tomorrow, if it is agreeable to you, I mean to send one of my grooms off on your black horse," she said, "to poke about."

"To poke about?"

"You're not from here," she said again. "Of that I'm certain. And it makes no sense to think you rode here from London, or even from Bristol. You certainly haven't a carriage. So you must have come by train."

He seemed to consider it. "Perhaps I was visiting somewhere," he proposed, "and simply went out for a ride?"

She set her head to one side. "I think not," she said. "You were carrying a greatcoat and a valise full of fresh linen."

He grinned. "Poked through my smallclothes, eh?"

"I did," she said. "I was looking for something, you see, that might identify you, for I was afraid—"

His face softened. "Afraid I mightn't wake up again," he said. "I'm sorry to have frightened you."

"You certainly didn't mean to," she said a little stridently.

"No." Fleetingly, he looked hopeful. "But you found nothing?"

She shook her head. "I fear not," she replied. "But you do wear spectacles, and have a rather refined taste in reading. Tomorrow, when you're looking more the thing, we'll see if anything in it jogs your memory."

"Yes." He looked disheartened. "Yes, a good plan."

"In the meantime," she added, "my groom will visit the livery stables and country houses hereabouts, in greater and greater circles, until someone recognizes either the horse, or our description of a large, recalcitrant man who does not care to sleep when he's told to do so."

Thus chided, he drew the covers up to his chin again. "Killjoy," he grumbled.

She lit the lamp, and turned it very low. "I will check on you again after dinner," she said, "at which time I expect to find you insensate with sleep."

He responded with a loud *snorkk!* with his eyes already closed.

Kate laughed, then returned to the door, pausing halfway out. "Good night, Edward."

But he said no more; not until the door was shut.

Then, "Good night, Kate," he said very quietly.

CHAPTER 4

Becoming Edward

Edward woke to the sounds of a house coming to life. For an instant, he wallowed deeper into the softness of his bed and attempted to push away reality. It didn't work; he sat up on a shaft of uncertainty to find that in the faint light of morning, nothing looked familiar. Confused, he threw back the bedcovers and looked down at a nightshirt he didn't recognize.

Indeed, he didn't even *own* a nightshirt.

There it was again. Another obscure fact.

He did not own a nightshirt.

Reality began to trickle back—the preceding few hours of it, at least. On a sigh, Edward fell back into the bed again, drawing with him the lofty eiderdown and wool counterpane, both of which smelled of clean country air.

There was an odd sort of pleasure in coming awake in such a homey place, he realized. Though he felt a degree of uncertainty weighing him down, he also felt an odd sense of comfort and rightness about him, and the buoyant realization of having nowhere to be, and no obligations.

He likely oughtn't get used to it. He surely must have obligations.

In fact, he knew he did. And one of them was rather pressing.

But what was it? Something flickered just on the edge of his conscious mind, like a pennant snapping in the wind. He could not reach it. Left with no alternative, he heeded the doctor's advice and let the memory go, then stretched himself luxuriantly, like a cat stirring.

He could feel a good deal of soreness in his shoulder and ankle—bruises, perhaps—but nothing intolerable. And though his vision seemed not quite right, his head no longer hurt.

For a time, he lay simply listening to the house; to the soft, swift sounds of servants' feet on thick carpet, and to the occasional clack or clatter of a bucket or broom. Such great houses were all very alike at such an hour, he supposed. Except that this, his hostess had said, was a castle.

Bellecombe Castle. In Somersetshire.

And apparently, he had ridden here. From *somewhere*. Edward closed his eyes and tried to conjure up a memory—or at least a notion—of what the castle might look like. Was it massive, ancient, and generously crenellated? Or was it one of those faux castles so favored by the nouveau riche, with outlandish turrets and barbicans built for show?

No, this was a real castle. He was sure of it.

And his intriguing hostess, Lady d'Allenay, was a real aristocrat.

Oh, you would be surprised at what I cannot afford, she had said to him last night.

It was the mark of a true blueblood, that quiet admission—and an honest one. These monstrous old houses drained them, oftentimes. Or their sons did.

How did he know this?

Edward shrugged. He knew it as he knew the sun would inevitably rise. Indeed, it *had* risen, and was beginning to

warm the room now. He looked up at the great black beams
of a ceiling that had not, thank God, been covered over with
decorative plaster, and at the massive tester bed, almost eb-
onized with age, which appeared to have been sitting in the
same spot since Elizabeth's reign.

He liked that. He liked this place. It felt like a home,
though he could not have said why.

Then he tried to think again of what might have brought
him here.

Again there was the flicker of *something*—something important, or so it felt. He was not witless, he reassured himself. He was fairly certain he *was* Edward. That he'd come
here for a reason—a good reason, he thought. Moreover,
his conversations since waking in this room yesterday were
quite clear to him.

Gingerly he sat fully upright, somewhat reassured that the
pain was not worse. But he did still feel a little unsteady, as
if he were suffering a bad morning after. Good Lord, he had
not suffered one of those since . . .

Since when?

Since . . . the army?

Wait. Had he been in the army? He had some notion—
some fragment of memory about sitting around a fire . . .

He gave a bark of laughter. For all he knew he was a cattle
drover. Or a shepherd.

But there it was, that little sliver of memory; a flickering
campfire, and a bottle sent around, catching the light as it
passed. Then the memory was gone, and Edward was left
with the sudden, sinking sensation that he didn't want it back
again.

That he did not want *any* of it back again.

But what a mad notion! What sort of man would not want
his life back?

He was simply unnerved by all the uncertainty. He wished
she would knock on his door again. Lady d'Allenay. Kate.
The Goddess.

Except that she was not a goddess, really. She was too tall, with the plainest gray eyes and brown hair imaginable. Colorless, he would have called her.

Except that her eyes were keen with intelligence and wry humor; one got the feeling Lady d'Allenay laughed often— and frequently at herself. Yes, there was a vast deal of color inside her. And her hair—though it appeared not to have so much as a wave in it, and despite the fact that she had dressed it as severely and plainly as was possible—it had suited her; it had looked efficient and practical.

But if a woman have long hair, it is a glory to her, for her hair is given her for a covering.

The words sprang to his mind unbidden. Why?

Because it was *that* sort of hair. The hair of a modest woman, he thought; hair that would fall about her naked form like a silken curtain. Hair that shimmered with deep, mysterious hints of chestnut red, but only when the light caught it.

Perhaps she was a goddess after all. Not Venus, but Vesta; blazing with the flames of hearth and home instead of a simmering seduction or a facile charm. And yet he found her enticing all the same.

Good Lord, what fanciful notions. He wondered if he'd always been such a sapskull or if the blow to his head had disordered him. He had the deep-seated certainty that he was not behaving like himself, at least not the self he had been. And what other sort of self was there?

Irritated, Edward threw back the covers and, despite the discomfort of his bruises, did precisely what he was not supposed to do. He got out of bed. After the room stopped spinning—well, slowed—he went a little unsteadily to the tall mahogany wardrobe, already knowing what he would see. He threw the latch and pulled both doors wide.

His riding coat, two waistcoats, and three freshly pressed shirts hung within. Folded neatly on the shelf below lay two pairs of breeches; one of them the pair he'd worn yesterday, now freshly brushed, along with a folded stack of cravats and drawers. Even his boots had been freshly polished.

Yes, somehow he recalled what he'd worn yesterday. Why could he not recall where he'd been when he put it on? Or where he'd purchased it?

In any case, it was time to get up and about. The deep bruising and pain would abate all the sooner, he reassured himself. And there must surely be water? He staggered his way into the antechamber that served as a sort of dressing and bathing room, clutching at pieces of furniture as he went. There he attended to nature's call, then poured out an entire pitcher of water into the basin atop the washstand.

It was his last clear thought.

He didn't hear the crash of the basin as it fell, nor the sound of his door bursting open a moment after that. And his next memory—by no means a clear one—was of hands, many of them, cool and competent, bearing him back into the soft, fresh bed.

When he woke again, daylight blazed through the crack in his draperies. Woozily, he sat up to find a small cot had been placed beside his bed, and that a liveried servant—a young man of perhaps twenty—now sat just inside his door, his chin buried in his neck cloth as he drowsed.

Well. His goddess had set spies upon him, it seemed.

And wisely so, perhaps. A little irritated, he yanked the wire wrapped around his bedpost. To his surprise, Miss Wentworth came in, her wild, red-gold curls somewhat contained beneath a cap, and a feather duster in hand.

"Jasper?" she said, looking around the door at the servant.

"Let the poor boy rest," Edward rasped.

She turned to him brightly. "Good morning," she said. "Are you feeling a bit steadier now?"

"Thank you, yes."

Edward did not much care for being viewed in a nightshirt by so pretty a young lady. Which was not to say that many a female had not often seen him in far less, he sensed. But in this case, he felt awkward—and at a distinct disadvantage.

That was what irritated him. He was not a man often caught at any sort of disadvantage. Of that he was quite certain.

The footman had leapt from his chair to neaten his waistcoat in an attempt to pretend he had not been asleep.

"Thank you, Jasper," said Miss Wentworth. "Kindly go downstairs and ask Cook to send up a light breakfast for Mr. Edward."

He was hungry, dash it. But food, interestingly, was not foremost on his mind. "Where is Lady d'Allenay?" he asked.

"She rode out early with Anstruther, her steward," said Miss Wentworth. "She often does. But as you see, she altered your arrangements a bit before going."

Miss Wentworth had gestured toward the cot. "Blast," he uttered under his breath. "Was she here when I fainted?" he said more audibly. "I did faint, did I not?"

"Oh, you did, and she was," said Miss Wentworth, eyes wide. "She ran across the passageway in her nightgown and helped Jasper and Fendershot lift you back into bed."

Edward felt a rush of mortification. "*Lifted* me?"

"She had only your feet, I believe, but Kate is surprisingly strong," Miss Wentworth went on. "Jasper and the butler had a shoulder each. I came in just in time to mop up the water."

"I do beg your pardon," he said gruffly. "I have put everyone to a vast amount of trouble."

"Not in the least," said the girl. "After all, this *is* Kate's fault—and, well, mine."

"Yes, you were quarreling, I hear," he said, grinning. "What, I wonder, could two such agreeable ladies find to quarrel over?"

"A man," said Miss Wentworth, lifting one shoulder. "Really, do women ever quarrel over much else, when you strip it bare?"

Edward didn't know what to say at that. *A man.* How odd. He had somehow imagined that . . .

"What time will Lady d'Allenay return?" he asked, trying to hide his impatience.

Miss Wentworth's eyes glittered with humor. "Oh, it will be hours," she replied. "They're riding the lower pastures, getting ready for the autumn damp."

He lifted one eyebrow. "Damp?"

She smiled brilliantly. "Yes, the sheep must be counted, and checked to be sure they are sound for the winter, then driven off the coeing ground. Coe being a disease of sheep, you see."

"It sounds dreadful," he said vaguely.

"Yes, tapeworms or liver flukes or some such thing." She shrugged. "Kate can explain it better than I."

"Your sister must have a remarkable knowledge base," he said dryly.

"Oh, if you live here long enough, you'll learn all about sheep, whether you wish to or not," she replied. "Besides, Kate has to know. Our lower pastures are too wet for wintering."

"I believe I must not be country bred," said Edward, none of this sounding familiar to him. "But I should apologize. I have detained you, and it looks as though you were busy."

"Oh, yes!" Wrinkling her nose, Miss Wentworth stirred from the door, and made a dramatic gesture with her duster. "Desperate duty calls!"

"Desperate? How so?"

A look of exasperation dashed over Miss Wentworth's face. "My mother, Aurélie, is coming to visit," she said, "so we're scrubbing the place crown to baseboard, and turning out all the guest rooms. Everyone pitches in."

He laughed. "How many guest rooms does she need?"

"Heavens, who knows?" She threw her arms wide, nearly catching a vase with her duster. "That's half the problem. She'll say four, and a baker's dozen will turn up. Once she came with eight carriages and twenty servants in tow—she dislikes trains excessively—but her gentlemen friends inevitably *must* shoot, and Aurélie never stirs without an entourage."

"Impressive," he said. "But your mother does not reside here?"

"No, she finds it too bleak by the moors. She spends the Season in London, and the winter in France."

"And you do not go with her?"

Miss Wentworth lifted one shoulder. "No," she said, "and our aunt Louisa says that Aurélie hasn't the patience—or, frankly, the reputation—to bring out a debutante, which I very nearly am."

"Hmm," he said. "And what is this dashing lady's full name?"

"Mrs. James Wentworth," said the girl, "but she has been a widow some years now."

Edward didn't recognize the name, but then, he hardly recognized his own. "So you're to have a country house party descend upon you shortly. I must get myself well and out of your way."

"Oh, by no means! We've twenty-three guest chambers, and even Mamma cannot fill up so many as that." Her nose wrinkled again. "Still, those in the south tower are a little tatty."

Edward remembered Lady d'Allenay's remark about what she could not afford. But he had no opportunity to explore the topic further—not that it was his place to do so.

The footman returned with a tray and Miss Wentworth stepped out. "Oh, by the way, Edward," she called back, as Jasper lifted off the cover of a plate of a warm omelet, "your things have been pressed and hung in the wardrobe, and your luggage stowed in the coffer."

"The coffer?"

With her duster, she pointed at the medieval chest that sat at the foot of his bed. "Mind the lid," she warned. "It was made frightfully heavy—to keep Viking marauders from carrying off our silver, I collect."

"Thank you," he said again.

Then Miss Wentworth vanished along with her duster. Edward ate with gusto, then surprised himself by promptly falling back asleep.

As AUTUMN SETTLED more certainly over Bellecombe Castle, one day turned to three and Edward's bruises turned from red to ugly shades of purplish-yellow. Dr. Fitch came again, pronouncing his patient as well as could be expected, and Richard Burnham came to offer his prayers.

Kate came to regret ever having seen the man all but naked, for the vision of that solid chest and its dark, tempting trail of hair had begun to torment her nights.

"How is our invalid?" asked Nancy at dinner that evening.

"Resting comfortably." Kate looked at her across a forkful of parsnips. "Which you would know, perhaps, had you not chosen to spend the whole of the afternoon at St. Michael's."

"Heavens," said Nancy lightly. "Was ever a person more chided for spending too much time at church?"

"Well, it must be the tidiest church in Christendom, what with you and Mrs. Burnham at it six days a week."

At that, Nancy took insult. "I'll have you know Peppie and I turned out four bedchambers in the south tower this morning," she retorted, "whilst you were reading the *Eclectic Review* to Edward."

"I thought reading from a London magazine might jog a memory," said Kate evenly. "How bad was it?"

"How bad was what?"

"The south tower."

Nancy lifted one shoulder. "Not as bad as I'd feared," she admitted. "Now that we can afford fresh mattresses and new glazing, the musty smell is gone. Well, that and the fact that Peppie had all the draperies washed."

"Washed?" said Kate incredulously.

Nancy went to the sideboard and returned with a decanter of wine. "They were beyond being beaten and aired," she said, refilling their glasses. "It was wash them, or burn them."

Kate flicked up an anxious glance. "Did they survive?"

"Passably." Nancy sighed. "Kate, it's a castle. Those rooms were built in the sixteenth century. No one expects luxury; the bedchambers will do now if needed. The Mongol horde descends shortly."

Kate felt her mouth twist. "Then let us pray we do not have to put any of our horde in the south tower."

"I'd sooner put the whole lot of them in it," said Nancy. "It's about time for a good, sharp frost, and a frozen rime on that new glazing might send them all packing again."

"Heavens, poor Richard!" Kate shook her head. "To wish for a wife so lacking in Christian charity!"

Nancy just shot her a dark scowl. "No one needs a practical wife more than a softhearted parish priest," she replied. "Besides, you don't want Aurélie's horde here any better than I do. But that does beg the question, Kate—what are we to do with Edward?"

It was a topic that had weighed on Kate. Her houseguest had grown increasingly impatient during his recovery, and would not remain abed much longer. It was one thing to house a man too ill to go elsewhere. But once he was up and around—once his injuries were more unseen than apparent—it might not be thought entirely proper for him to remain at Bellecombe.

But where to send him?

It scarcely mattered, for Kate could not bear the thought of his leaving Bellecombe until he was entirely well again, and able to pick up the threads of the life she had so recklessly arrested. Yes, the guilt weighed on her. And if there was a little part of her that was faintly fascinated by the man . . . well, that didn't bear thinking of just now.

She had spoken sharply to him, of course, about getting out of bed. And ever since, he had been . . . well, if not a model patient, at least an obedient one. Indeed, he had declared himself determined to please her, claiming that he had much sooner look at her than at Jasper.

It had been said with a wink, too; one that made her stomach do that odd little flip-flop again. This was followed by his shockingly rakish grin; a grin that seemed, on further consideration, entirely out of place on a countenance that was otherwise so stern.

"Kate," said her sister impatiently, "what are we to do with Edward?"

"There's nothing we can do until he's himself again," Kate answered. "Besides, Aurélie will think it a great lark."

"She will," Nancy agreed, "and all her gossiping friends will, too. And Aurélie hasn't enough sense to think how unfortunate rumors might reflect on us."

Kate sighed, and crushed her napkin in her lap. "No, she'll simply flirt with the poor man outrageously, and convince herself it's all in a good cause—bucking up his spirits, and all that rot."

But Nancy had set her chin in her palm almost morosely. "Sometimes I marvel," she said, "that Richard is willing to take me on at all, given my bloodlines."

Kate had no reply to that. Instead, she motioned for their plates to be removed, and tried not to think of the coming storm.

CHAPTER 5
Jasper's Perfidy

Three or four days after his accident, Edward woke to see the afternoon sun dappling the wall opposite his bed, the pattern shifting with the trees outside. The footman had fallen into another deep drowse, his chair cocked back against the wall in a remarkable feat of physics.

Edward shook off the last vestiges of a strange dream, and fumbled on the table for his pocket watch. But his vision still seemed off, and even with a squint, he could not make sense of the dial. Impatiently, he glanced over his shoulder at the angle of the light streaming in through the tiny, diamond-shaped panes. Yes, very low indeed.

He had slept away another day. And he was just about done with doing so. It was one thing to lie here and listen to the goddess's perfectly modulated, almost sensuous contralto as she read to him from the *Times*, or regaled him with one of her glib stories about life on the home farm, while his gaze trailed lazily down her porcelain skin, her swanlike throat, and all the way down to what looked like a pair of small, perfect breasts.

But to sit here and stare at Jasper's overbite as he snored?

At least Edward's headache had entirely left him. But his right ankle still hurt like the devil and besides the stitches in his head, he had a nasty bruise from the small of his back halfway down the thigh. Worse, the tedium was making him crotchety.

He needed distraction. Damn it, he needed *action*. He was not a man who could simply lie about like this; even absent his memory, Edward knew that much. And with his body beginning to stir almost frustratingly to Kate's presence, he knew, too, that he was far from death.

He scrubbed a hand around his stubbled face, then cleared his throat a little sharply. The footman came awake at once, the front legs of his chair clacking hard upon the planked floor.

"Yes, s-sir?" he stuttered, quite literally jerked awake.

For an instant, Edward considered the situation. He got out of bed on legs that were reasonably steady, and pulled on the butler's robe. "Jasper," he finally said, "are you by chance a married man?"

Jasper shook his head a little too emphatically. "Indeed not, sir."

"Have you a mother, then?"

"Yes, sir. In Nether Stowey, sir."

Edward figured Nether Stowey to be a small crook in the road. "Well, doubtless she tries to smother you with kindness and wool sweaters," he said, "and you probably came to work here in part to be your own man. To get off the farm and out from under the cat's paw—not that it isn't a kindly meant paw, mind."

Jasper smiled, revealing his overbite again. "'Twas a little like that, sir."

"Women are all like that." It was another of his mysteriously known facts. "In fact, Lady d'Allenay is, I daresay, a little like that?"

Jasper's eyes widened. "I'm sure I'd not know, sir."

Edward hardened his jaw. "It's like this, Jasper," he said. "She's got me wrapped in cotton wool, but I must have a bath. And a proper shave. Could you arrange such a thing, do you imagine?"

Jasper's eyes widened further as he declared he did not know.

"Isn't drawing a bath something you would ordinarily do at the request of any houseguest?" Edward suggested. "Moreover, have you been forbidden to draw me a bath?"

Jasper shook his head. "Not . . . exactly."

"Then kindly do so at once," said Edward. "I know you fear Lady d'Allenay will scold you, and if she does, I'll make it plain I gave you no choice. I'm done with being washed in a saucer of warm water."

Jasper's eyes just shot to the door, as if looking for assistance.

"Damn it, man, I've lain in that bed hours unending, and I'm fit company for neither man nor beast," he said. "Now take yourself downstairs and come back with some hot water whilst I pull out that old slipper tub."

At that, Jasper leapt into action. "No, sir," he said firmly. "You just sit yourself back on that bed, sir. I'll pull out the tub."

KATE WAS ENJOYING tea with Nancy, Mrs. Burnham, and the wife of a local squire when Mrs. Peppin began to hover outside the wide double doors. The entire conversation had centered around the identity of Bellecombe's mysterious guest.

Mrs. Cockram, the squire's wife, opined as how he *might* be a French spy come creeping up from the Channel. The facts that Bellecombe was too far inland to be worth reconnoitering, and that the entire nation of France was still occupied with the aftermath of their most recent revolution could not dissuade the good lady from this theory.

Mrs. Burnham, herself a vicar's widow, suggested that

this was an uncharitable view of a gentleman too ill to defend himself. Kate didn't imagine her houseguest to be remotely incapable of defending himself, but she held her tongue and began to worry more about the urgent look on the housekeeper's face.

She was somehow sure that look had to do with her obstinate patient, and rose with a rueful smile.

"I believe our guest must require my attention," she said, not entirely disappointed to be called away. "I beg you will excuse me. Nancy, do pour again."

But the ladies both rose with her, declaring that it looked like rain, and that they had overstayed their welcome—which was not *quite* true.

"Still, it is *such* a distressing thing," said Mrs. Cockram, drifting toward the drawing room door, "that two unwed ladies must harbor a man of unknown character. I vow, I wonder if you oughtn't send him to Mr. Cockram and me at the Hall?"

"Well, if anyone is to have the poor gentleman," interjected the rector's mother, "he must come to the rectory. Would that not be the very thing?"

"It would not." Kate folded her hands firmly before her. "Thank you, ladies, but I assure you we are managing perfectly well. And he cannot be moved from his bed. He's extremely frail."

"Then Richard must come again to minister to his spiritual nee—"

Mrs. Burnham let her words fall away, for a massive shadow had just fallen across the threshold. As Mrs. Cockram's eyes widened almost comically, Kate slowly turned, praying she was not about to see what she very much feared.

But it was precisely what she feared. Her wayward houseguest stood bracketed in the doorway attired in his elegant black coat and a burgundy brocade waistcoat that practically sculpted the lean turn of his waist. And he was *much* taller—and altogether too male—seen standing, as opposed to lying in a heap, or reclining on a pile of pillows.

"Edward!" she managed. "What on earth—?"

Freshly shaved—and smelling very unlike a man at death's door—he was dressed for riding in his tall boots and snug breeches. Then again, Kate remembered, he had nothing else *to* wear.

But this fact being unknown to Mrs. Cockram and Mrs. Burnham, the good Christian ladies were glancing from Edward to Kate in a way that made it clear they doubted her veracity.

"Good afternoon," he said a little tentatively.

"Edward, you are not to be up!" Nancy had jerked into action, and yanked out a chair. "Do sit down, sir, before you fall down."

But Edward didn't look at the chair. Instead, he looked faintly mortified. "I do beg your pardon," he said stiffly. "I had no idea you were entertaining, my lady, and thought merely to take a little exercise."

He was, at least, bearing a bit of his weight onto a brass-knobbed walking stick she recognized as Stephen's, to save Kate from looking a complete liar. And his wet, golden hair was slicked back off his forehead, starkly revealing the mottled, stitched-up wound.

"A little exercise?" she echoed. "Without Dr. Fitch's permission?"

"He didn't tell me I mightn't move," Edward countered. "He said I must rest, avoid bright light, and not think."

"Indeed, sir, you do look much better this afternoon," said Nancy with a little curtsy. "It is something like a miracle, to be sure! But if you will excuse me, I was just escorting Mrs. Burnham and Mrs. Cockram to the door."

Here, the good ladies seemed suddenly to regret their notion of leaving. But nothing by way of encouragement being offered by their hostess, the good ladies lingered only a little. After simpering over introductions, they duly presented their hands to the handsome invalid, fluttering and blushing as if he were the prince himself, then wished him a speedy recovery.

But Kate could not miss the speculative looks they cast at her as they parted.

Edward watched them go, then turned to her. "I have the most appalling fear I should apologize," he said. "Did I behave wrongly?"

Her temper yielding in the face of his earnestness, Kate threw up her hands on a laugh. "I was just being gently chided for harboring *a man of unknown character* beneath my roof," she said. "I reassured them you were so deathly ill as to be perfectly harmless, and—oh! *Now* you begin to look unsteady!"

And he was. Abruptly, Kate slipped a hand under his elbow, and urged him into a chair near the table.

"I beg your pardon," he said again when he'd settled himself, and set the walking stick away. "This blasted leg, you see, is half my trouble."

Kate resisted the urge to kneel down and examine it. "Is it worse?"

"I think I didn't grasp how thoroughly I'd wrenched the ankle."

"Nor did I." Kate had begun to pace the room. "Did Fitch examine it properly, do you recall?" she added fretfully. "Could it be broken?"

"Yes, he did, and no, it could not," said Edward. "Kindly sit, Lady d'Allenay. You will give me mal de mer with all that striding about. I'm in a weakened state, you know."

Regarding him warily, she did sit, carefully sweeping her full skirts aside. "There," she said, "now kindly tell me which of my servants conspired against me and toted up your bathwater?"

"It was Jasper," Edward confessed, "but I had to chase him down and flog him unmercifully first."

Kate lifted one eyebrow. "On that leg?"

"Yes. Remarkably slow, poor lad."

"Hmm. Well, I will say no more. As I may have mentioned, I know your type."

At that, he grinned hugely. "You did say, didn't you?" he agreed. "Let that be a lesson to you."

"A lesson?"

"Yes, the next time you mean to run down some poor, unsuspecting fellow, pick a more biddable sort of chap." He paused long enough to peer at the tray. "Is that tea, by any chance?"

Kate gave up all hope of sending the man scurrying back to bed. "Yes, Nancy didn't take any," she said, taking up the pot again. "You may have her cup. Do you take milk? Sugar?"

Edward paused for a moment. "I do not know," he said. "I think I shall have both. I find myself in a mood to indulge in all that life has to offer."

She laughed and tipped the pot. "How odd," she said. "Nancy said something a little like that recently."

They settled back and sipped tea in companionable silence, Edward relaxing into his armchair and Kate perched on the long sofa she and Nancy had shared mere moments earlier. After a time, he set his cup onto his saucer with a soft *click*, and looked at her a little mischievously.

"So, Lady d'Allenay, I gather I have competition for your favors?"

Kate almost spewed her tea back out. "*What—?*" she said, after forcing it down. "Are you utterly mad?"

"I'm not perfectly sure," he said earnestly. "For all we know, I may have just escaped Bedlam and fled for the moors."

"Edward, what *are* you talking about?"

"Isn't that what the villain usually does in gothic novels?" He lifted both his harshly angled eyebrows. "Hies off to hide amidst the heather and the bracken until the hounds run him to ground in some miserable, marshy hole?"

"Oh, heavens! That isn't what I meant, and you know it."

"Ah, you meant the part about the competition?" he said. "I merely ask because, having thus far enjoyed your nearly undivided devotion—well, except for the sheep and the late harvest—I find myself loath to give it up."

"How flattering, Edward, when your stay here has been so brief," said Kate a little tartly. "But by all means, do carry on."

He shrugged a little wanly, though Kate had begun to suspect there was nothing wan about the man. "It's just that Miss Wentworth suggests that you have your eye, perhaps, on another," he said, his green eyes warming. "I am not perfectly sure, Lady d'Allenay, that you shall have time for anyone else. I begin to fear my recovery may be protracted, and that I may require the whole of your attention."

"Well, you certainly have it now," she said darkly. "Why do you not tell me *exactly* what it is my sister said to you?"

"That the two of you were squabbling over a man."

"Ah, and so we were." Kate relaxed back onto the sofa. "But it has nothing to do with me."

"It must do," he pointed out, "or you wouldn't have been angry."

Kate surveyed him warily across the tea table. "My sister has formed something of a mésalliance," she said. "And it was that which we were quarreling over."

"Ah! So you have no interest in the gentleman?"

"In Richard Burnham?" Kate rolled her eyes. "Goodness, I should hope not."

"Ah, Richard!" he echoed. "Such a strong, stalwart name."

"Had you been awake Wednesday," she pointed out, "you'd know Richard is our rector."

"Oh, well. He might still be strong and stalwart, mightn't he?"

"He had better be, if he means to marry Nancy."

"But you said it was a mésalliance," he pointed out.

Kate shrugged. "A poor choice of words," she said. "I've the highest regard for Mr. Burnham. But Nancy is, as you may have noticed, the beauty of the family. It was hoped she might make a brilliant match."

"Hoped by whom?"

Kate hesitated, blinking for a moment. "Oh, my aunt Louisa, who is Lady Upshaw," she finally said. "She and Uncle Upshaw live in London and are very grand. He's Nancy's trustee until she comes of age. They wish to bring her out in a high style and marry her off to a duke, I collect."

"Ah," he said quietly. "And what do *you* want?"

"I want my sister to be happy," said Kate.

He paused a heartbeat. "And that happiness requires the wealth and status such a marriage would bring?"

Kate gave a sharp sigh. "Actually, I begin to believe that her happiness requires Richard. But I don't know what's to be done about it."

"Interesting," he said quietly. "But that was not, actually, what I meant by my original question."

"What original question?"

"What do you want *for yourself*?" he asked, his voice pitched almost suggestively low.

"For myself?" She looked at him blankly. "What more could I want? I have Bellecombe."

"Yes, what indeed?" After a long pause, he continued, "Well, may I gather you have discouraged your sister's pursuit of your rector?"

She nodded. "I have."

"Why?"

Kate began to neaten the folds of her skirt. "Nancy is just eighteen. She knows nothing of the world."

"And you do?" He was looking at her quizzically.

Kate flashed a muted smile. "I know all I wish of it," she said. "I did go to London for a season or two. I . . . met people—some of whom were quite nice, but many of whom were simply self-absorbed. I prefer Somerset."

"And mightn't your sister do the same? Prefer Somerset, I mean?"

"Young girls do not know what they want," Kate chided. "They make poor choices. It falls to their elders to vet those choices."

"Hmm," said Edward pensively. "Why does that sound like the voice of bitter experience, I wonder? Tell me, Lady d'Allenay—"

"Kate," she lightly interjected. His discussion was growing too personal—and perhaps too near the truth—for her comfort. "We must stand on equal footing, sir. So if you cannot call me Kate, we must make up a temporary surname for you. I propose . . . *Clutterbuck*. Yes, Mr. Edward Clutterbuck."

"*Clutterbuck?*" he said, genuinely amused.

"No," she amended. "Bracegirtle. Edward Bracegirtle. We've a whole clan of them over Lynmouth way. Smugglers, they used to be."

"Well, Kate," he said teasingly, "I might well be a smuggler for all we know. But a Bracegirtle? No, I fancy not. And if we discover that I am, why, I shall feel obliged to throw myself over a parapet. You must have a parapet hereabouts, have you not?"

"We have," she said, "and a body or two has indeed been flung from it over the centuries. But I should prefer yours not be next, as I feel personally responsible for you."

"Ah," he said quietly. "Then it seems I have you just where I want you."

"Do you indeed?" She looked at him quizzically. "And where is that?"

"Obligated," he said, dropping his voice an octave, "*to me*."

These last two words seemed to ooze like warm honey around Kate, and she didn't like the strange, fluttery feeling they engendered in the pit of her stomach. Edward, she had realized early on, was a bit of a tease.

On the other hand, Dr. Fitch had said their patient might suffer a temporary lack of inhibition, so she had thus far brushed off that teasing. Now, however, it seemed wiser to reel him in, before he embarrassed himself.

"Edward, I fear you're flirting again," she said darkly. "It cannot be good for your concussed brain."

"Oh," he said evenly. "Well, it certainly felt pleasant enough. But there, my lady, if we cannot talk of us, I should love to talk of you."

"Of me? In what way?"

"How does a lady so charming and intelligent come to be unwed at such a mat—" Here he paused to clear his throat. "—er, *marriageable* age?"

"Yes, I'm approaching my dotage," she said dryly, "at not quite twenty-eight. And it comes about, I daresay, as much of life does. Gradually, but inexorably, and with very little planning."

"So you've no specific dislike of the male species?" he said lightly. "There are some women, I'm given to understand, who do."

She shrugged. "Well, I've met more than a few men whom I thought arrogant and presumptuous."

"Does that include me?"

"Not yet," she said warningly.

A teasing smile split his face, deepening into a pair of glorious dimples that softened his bladelike cheekbones. "And so your Nancy has her worthy suitor," he said musingly, "but what of yourself? Were you never tempted to step into the parson's mousetrap?"

"For a man who cannot remember his own name, you're remarkably forward," she remarked, but with little rancor.

Indeed, it was surprisingly easy to talk with Edward—perhaps because he *didn't* know who he was. Thus, he wasn't anyone. He was also entirely without prejudgment—and, so far, entirely without advice.

"I was betrothed for a time," she confessed, "to an old family friend, as it happened. I had adored him from afar since childhood. But in the end, we decided we would not suit."

"In other words, *you* decided?" said Edward.

"Yes. Yes, I suppose I did."

"Poor devil." Edward smiled thinly. "Left brokenhearted by Vesta, goddess of hearth and home, likely never to recover."

"Oh, nothing so maudlin as that, I assure you."

"So your swain just dusted himself off and moved on?" His lighthearted tone returned. "The fellow made a brilliant marriage elsewhere and happily bred himself half a dozen brats, I suppose?"

At that, Kate looked away.

"Well?" he said expectantly.

She glanced up to see Edward studying her with more gravity than the conversation warranted.

"Actually, he never married," she answered. "I think, really, that he never met anyone whom he loved nearly so well as he loved himself."

"Not even you?"

"Certainly not me."

"Ah, then you made a wise decision, fair Vesta."

Something in his tone unnerved her, and Kate leapt up again. "We had better see if Motte has returned," she said, starting toward the window.

Edward turned in his chair as she passed. "Who, pray, is Motte?"

"Our head groom. I sent him off again this morning on your horse. We need to find out where you've come from."

And then send you back there on the very next train . . .

But this she didn't say aloud. Indeed, she scarcely meant it—which was half the problem. She feared he suspected it, too. Kate could feel his intense gaze following her across the room, could almost feel the weight of his words upon her.

Had she made a wise decision?

Pondering it, Kate drew back the drapery with one finger

and stared blindly down at the castle's lower bailey. At the time, she had been quite sure of her choice; sure of what she'd seen, and sure of what it meant.

That Reggie did not love her.

And Kate had *needed* him to love her. Desperately so. Indeed, she had convinced herself that she loved him. But had she? In her way, yes. But to be *in* love? The notion seemed ludicrous to her now.

Moreover, in light of the rumors Aunt Louisa so often passed along from London, Kate had made a lucky escape; Reggie's notoriety had become the stuff of legend. Kate certainly didn't approve of how he'd managed his estate. And eventually, he would have dragged Bellecombe down with it. She knew that.

So why, then, had she begun to question her choice these past few years?

Because she was now nearer to thirty than twenty, and no one else had come along?

No, more likely it was because she now understood that, even if someone *had* come along, the awkward explanations honesty would have required of her would likely have undone Kate—and ruined any hope she might have had for her happiness.

So would it have been better, in the end, to have simply married Reggie? To have merged their estates, had his children, fought the good fight to preserve their capital, and simply looked the other way when his eye—and some of his other organs—went wandering?

No. No, it would not have.

And Kate would be damned before she'd let loneliness drive her into the arms of regret. She was a stronger person than that. She let the curtain drop.

"The bailey is empty," she said, fixing a smile on her face as she turned. "Motte must still be—"

But to her shock, she practically hitched up against a wall

of manly chest. One hand braced on a nearby chair, Edward stood directly in her path.

"What are you doing up?" she scolded.

A mere flicker of uncertainty sketched across his face. "I think I'm about to be arrogant," he murmured, "and *very* presumptuous."

Kate froze like a rabbit in the path of a large, and very dominant predator. She was staring up into eyes that were a remarkable shade of green, and only faintly teasing now. To her shame, she made no move to resist, knowing, even in her naiveté, what was about to happen. And when his hand reached for her, she let her lashes drop half shut.

Edward threaded his fingers through the hair at the nape of her neck, then slowly lowered his mouth to hers. It was a kiss as languorous as it was possessive, his lips first settling warmly to hers, shaping and molding, then opening to a plunging taste of sheer intimacy.

For a moment Kate simply closed her eyes and did nothing but savor the warm, swirling sensations as his mouth moved gently but commandingly over hers. Slowly, his other arm circled around her, the palm of his hand settling at the base of her spine to make slow, melting circles as he urged her against him.

Somehow, her hands were sliding around his waist, skimming along his flanks beneath his black coat, the silk of his waistcoat smooth and warm as his ribs rippled against her palms. On a low groan, Edward deepened the kiss, his tongue stroking slowly, then twining sinuously around hers as he thrust.

Kate let her hands slip around to skate up his back under the warmth of his coat, releasing his heat and his scent in an erotic cloud of soap and male essence. She sighed, a warm, sweet lethargy washing through her on a shudder, tugging her will away with it; leaving only the wish to have this— whatever *this* was.

Something more than a kiss, she feared. Something warm and safe and cozy; a thing that made her want to melt into his strength even as the warmth began to snap and crackle into a reckless flame that blocked the world around her, and drew her deeper into his maelstrom.

But Kate was saved from her folly when, somewhere nearby, a door slammed. Startled, she jerked, then set her palms to his chest, pushing herself away.

Edward slowly surrendered, lifting his mouth from hers. His eyes were heavy and hooded, his expression that of a sybarite, languid but a little thwarted.

"Ah," he said quietly, removing his warm, heavy hand from her spine. "The world intrudes, my goddess."

Kate stepped back, eyes locked to his, her fingertips flying uncertainly to her lips. Good Lord. She was not a goddess. She was not his *anything*. What she was, more likely, was mad.

Or desperate.

Pathetically desperate.

Edward, however, was regarding her gravely, yet with a hint of wry humor in his eyes. "You flay yourself, Kate," he said, in his deep, seductive voice, "so needlessly."

"But we . . . we shouldn't have."

"Probably not," he said blandly.

Edward was again bearing his weight onto the back of the chair, and the hand that had embraced the back of her head was now set on his hip, pushing back his coat to reveal the sleek turn of his waist.

"No, probably not," he said again, more pensively, "but alas, I could not help myself."

Kate slowly shook her head. "I don't believe that," she said. "You are a man of utter self-discipline. I doubt you've ever done even the smallest thing against your will."

The rueful look returned. "You might be right," he admitted. "But we neither of us know, do we? Indeed, we know nothing about me." He sighed. "You're right, Kate. We *shouldn't have*. Not because you're spoken for; you are not. And not because I am, for I am not. I might, however, be the most egregious scoundrel on earth. That, you see, is the problem."

"How do you know?" she whispered.

Puzzlement appeared. "How do I know what?"

"That . . . that you are not spoken for." She felt heat rush to her cheeks. "How can you really know?"

He shrugged. His hand left his waist, hesitated almost uncertainly for a moment, then dragged pensively through his thick, almost leonine mane.

"I know it in the way a man knows if he's left-handed or right-handed," he finally said. "I know it in a way that cannot be put into words, Kate. There is no other half of me; I'm only what you see before you. And I have the sense . . . I have the sense that I've never been anything else."

"You are not a young man," she said quietly.

His eyes crinkled. "No, I am not," he agreed. "A man of lesser years would not be aching and limping after a mere tumble."

Kate sighed again, and stepped around him. "Oh, it was no mere tumble, trust me."

He laughed, and set an arm about her waist, but in a companionable fashion. "So do I gather that, even should I prove *not* to be an egregious scoundrel, I would simply be too decrepit for you?" he asked, strolling back to the sofa with her.

She swatted at him, and pushed him back into his chair. "Do not be ridiculous," she retorted. "I have never seen a man so . . . so very . . ."

"So very what?" he prodded, winking.

"*Arrogant*," she snapped. "There, you have achieved it."

The wide grin flashed again. "Oh, I don't think that's what you meant to say, Kate."

"Very well, then, *vigorous*," she snapped. "Vigorous and virile. There, are you pleased? If sin, danger, and temptation were an unholy trinity, their embodiment would look something like you."

For a moment, he was stunned into silence. She continued to glower at him.

Then softly, he chuckled. "Good Lord, Kate," he finally said. "Perhaps I had better go fetch my spectacles. Nothing undercuts a man's virility quite so quickly. Well, that or a creaking corset."

"Or a posset," she said on a snort. "Or a pillow for your gout. Or, if you wish, I can wrap that ankle in mustard and flannel."

Then, to her chagrin, they both burst into laughter.

"My dear," he said, settling back into his chair, "you have managed to entirely unman me."

Oh, not nearly, thought Kate.

And more was the pity. Indeed, situated as he was in the small chair, he looked entirely too large and too dangerous now. Yes, too *virile*.

Just then, Nancy came back into the room, a piece of note-paper in hand.

"Miss Wentworth," said Edward smoothly, bracing his hands to rise.

"Don't you dare rise." Nancy threw up a hand. "I just wanted to tell you that Motte returned, having learnt nothing. He's brought his route for the last two days." She handed it to Edward. "Here, see if anything looks familiar."

Edward's piercing green gaze focused upon the paper. "Taunton, fourteen miles," he murmured, scanning it. "Bridgwater, twelve miles. On to Nether Stowey, eight miles. Up to Minehead, eighteen miles."

"Good heavens! That's quite a trek." Kate rose, intent upon looking over Edward's shoulder.

"And he has visited every inn, livery, train station, and tavern in between." Nancy was behaving oddly, and had backed away as if uncertain of her welcome. "Motte and that black horse looked utterly fagged."

Kate set a hand on the back of Edward's chair. "All the way round to Minehead," she marveled. "Poor Motte! How many miles is that, totted up?"

But Edward was still staring at the groom's notes.

Nancy started nearer. "Edward?" she said sharply. "Do you see something?"

But Edward didn't look at her. Instead, he looked up at Kate, his gaze almost stricken. "Here," he said, handing it to her. "Take it. I cannot—"

Kate felt a cold shaft of fear. "Edward, what is it?"

He shook his head, his eyes bleak. "I can see it," he said, "but I can't *add* it."

Kate snatched the paper. "It's just Motte's hand," she said. "It's near illegible."

Edward seized her wrist in a near death grip. "*No*," he said harshly. "I can read them, Kate. But I cannot . . . I cannot *add them up.*"

Kate could hear the alarm in his voice. She dropped to one knee by his chair, Nancy standing at the other side, and held out the paper. The words and numbers were indeed perfectly legible.

"Oh, dear heaven!" said Nancy in a panicked voice. "Kate. Oh, Kate. We weren't supposed to let him read anything!"

"It's all right, Nancy; it isn't that. A little reading hasn't ruined anything." Kate turned to look at Edward. "When you look at the numbers, Edward, what do you see?"

He opened and closed his mouth soundlessly, then swallowed hard. "Markings that . . . that aren't letters," he said, moving a finger down the page. "It was the same with my watch. I thought it was—I don't know—my vision, perhaps."

"So you can tell which ones *are* numbers?"

He shook his head, his harsh brows drawing together. "Yes, I see them," he rasped, pointing. "Things that I know, logically, are numbers. But . . . they don't mean anything. And they must do, mustn't they? They *have* to. I *have to* understand numbers, Kate. I *must*. Everything depends upon it."

"Everything?" His vehemence shocked her, but she took on a soothing tone. "Yes, yes, of course. It does to all of us. It is part of our everyday lives. But it will come back, Edward. It will."

"Will it?" Edward unclenched his hand from her wrist. "Yes, yes, of course it will. It must, mustn't it?"

"Look, as Nancy says, we have gone and done the very thing Dr. Fitch told us not to do," said Kate, rising. "We have let you strain your mind." She reached down with her hand. "Nancy, kindly tell Peppie I want Fitch back in the morning. Now, come, Edward. Let me escort you back to your room so that you can rest."

"Damn it, Kate, I'm not a child," he said irritably.

"Oh, I'm quite certain of that," she murmured, refusing to drop her hand. "But you have tired yourself out. Your brain will not recover without rest. That is what Fitch said, and we see now how right he was. We must be thankful, I daresay, that you don't imagine yourself Prince Albert."

"What?" He looked at her incredulously.

Kate gave her hand an inviting wiggle. "Come, I will tell you Fitch's funny story as we walk back to your room."

"Oh, and Kate?" said Nancy as they started from the room. "Motte said something else, too. It might be important."

"Yes?" Kate turned to look over her shoulder.

"He says that Edward's horse is not young," Nancy added, "perhaps fifteen or sixteen years old. But far too fine, all the same, to have come from any livery. And the tack is that of a wealthy gentleman's; the saddle, Motte says, is by Sowter's in the Haymarket—custom made, and one of their very finest."

Edward cut her a sidelong glance as they made their way upstairs to his bedchamber. "Kate, what are you thinking?"

"That you have a sentimental attachment to your horse," she replied. "George Motte is an expert groom, trained in Uncle Upshaw's household in London. If he says your mount is old and your tack exquisite, then it is."

"Hmm," he said.

But Kate got the strangest feeling that she had not replied to the question he really wanted answered.

It was no easy feat to return Edward to the care of Jasper, and to convince him that an hour's nap before dinner would be the very thing. It was not, in his opinion, any sort of thing at all. It was a nuisance. A trespass upon his manhood. And in the end, only the promise that she would read to him again the following day would placate him.

But they were already fast approaching the time, Kate sensed, when Edward would not be gainsaid, and no sort of symptom, however dire, would keep him within the purview of a mere female and a cowering footman.

She sighed, and stayed long enough to watch Jasper help him out of his coat. Thus reassured, if only marginally, that he meant to stay put, Kate returned to the drawing room to see that Nancy had ordered a fire built up against the evening's chill.

She was standing by the hearth, her hands outstretched to the feeble heat. Her face was a mask of worry as she glanced toward the door as Kate's footsteps approached.

"Will he be all right?" she said quietly.

Kate clasped her hands before her, then slowly nodded. "I believe so," she said. "Dr. Fitch said, you will recall, that sometimes one lost the ability to read. I think this must be something similar. I think with rest, his faculties will return."

"Good," said Nancy, her voice gone a little cold. "Then he'll be out of here, perhaps, before you ruin yourself irredeemably."

Something sank into the pit of Kate's stomach. "I beg your pardon?"

At last Nancy turned from the fire, her mouth twisted a little bitterly. "Who do you think slammed that door so loudly?" she said. "It was a warning, Kate. And you're dashed lucky it was me and not one of the servants who walked in on you."

"Good heavens." Kate put a hand to her temple. "But my dear, it was . . . it was just a kiss."

It was a pathetic defense, and Nancy bluntly said so. "And it was a good deal more than a kiss," she harshly added. "My God, Kate, had Reggie ever kissed you in such a way, Grandpapa and Uncle Upshaw would *never* have let you beg off that betrothal."

"If Reggie had ever kissed me in such a way," said Kate coldly, "perhaps I would not have wished to beg off."

Nancy rolled her eyes. "Oh, Kate! Are you mad?"

"Certainly not," Kate countered, "and furthermore, *you* are hardly in a position to level any criticism over a kiss."

"Well, Edward has taken a stultifying blow to the head," Nancy retorted. "He cannot be counted upon to show any sense."

"And you suggest I cannot?" But Kate feared her sister might be right.

Nancy flounced toward the door in a huff. "Well, at least I know I'm committed to Richard," she said snidely, "and that he has the most honorable of intentions. I know his name. I know he's not married. Or a scoundrel. Or a gambler. Or an outright felon."

"Edward is a good man," Kate countered feebly. "He meant no harm."

"Well, Richard is a rector, and he wishes to *marry me*!" Nancy shouted back. "But *you* won't let him! We know him nearly as well as we know ourselves. Consider, Kate, the hypocrisy in that!"

For good measure, Nancy slammed the door on the way out, causing half the candles to gutter in the draft.

Kate stood for a good half hour in the gloom, considering what a fool she was.

She knew that the criticism Nancy had leveled at her was hardly unfair. But she was not Nancy. Her situation was very different, more different than Nancy could ever know. And

Edward desired her; Kate was not such a fool as to be unable to recognize that simmering emotion in a man's eyes.

No, she should not have let him kiss her. And if he tried to do it again . . . well, she was going to let him. The realization caused a little frisson of sensual awareness to shudder through her.

Yes, she was going to let him.

It seemed madness.

It seemed the most logical thing on earth.

He was a strikingly handsome and virile man who looked at her with such heat it took her breath. Such things didn't happen to Kate in her ordinary—*tediously* ordinary—life. And if he wanted her in that way, why should she not have him?

There were risks, yes. Risks to her heart—and other risks, too. But would it not be better to live with a heart that was broken than a heart that was frozen and empty? As to the other, there were ways to mitigate that, too.

Kate looked down at the flickering shadows cast up by the fire and realized she was twisting Grandpapa's signet ring around and around on her finger again.

Oh, this *was* madness! It would not do. Edward was a charming flirt, no more. And she—well, she was just what she'd always been. Ordinary, tart-tongued, and plain, with little to recommend her.

On that thought, Kate blew out the rest of the candles. She had enough real problems without dreaming up more. Letters to write. Accounts to balance. And a few cases of expensive wine to somehow wedge into her household budget, for Aurélie's most recent letter had arrived. The horde was indeed descending—and bringing, her mother threatened—a *shocking surprise*.

Aurélie was often both shocking and surprising. And those two things together in one sentence—however redundant— could not possibly bode well.

CHAPTER 6

A Fragile Friendship

Determined to cast off his role as invalid, Edward went searching for Kate the following afternoon in Bellecombe's estate office where, he was reliably informed by the good-natured Jasper, the lady spent most afternoons.

Having bathed, shaved, and dressed himself, he set off on his quest feeling a little more sure of the world. And very sure he owed his hostess an apology.

He could not for the life of him think why he had kissed her, and so lasciviously. Or why he had dreamt such torrid, sensual dreams of her last night. In his fantasies, Kate had trembled beneath him, her fingers tangled in his hair, her small, perfect breasts his for the tasting. He had woken in a tangle of bedsheets, burning to kiss her again, sweat beading his forehead.

It was . . . disconcerting.

Perhaps it really was the blow to his head? The good doctor had ordered him not to think, and apparently, he had succeeded.

Oh, he didn't fancy himself an upright paragon of virtue—

quite the opposite, he feared. But nor did he have the sense that he was the sort of fellow who went around seducing virginal young ladies—and if he was, then he was in need of a good horsewhipping.

Except that Lady d'Allenay was not exactly young. And she didn't kiss like a virgin. Nor quite like a lady of experience, either.

She was something in between, perhaps?

She had once been betrothed, she had said. To a man who had not loved her. How could such a thing be? The lady was not a beauty, but she had a purity of character one could not mistake, and a wicked, scathing wit. A man could not for one instant find himself bored, he imagined, in her company.

There seemed to be no huge fortune involved—the usual thing that drew suitors. An entailed estate like Bellecombe could not be sold, but only carried forth into the next generation. Until it was flourishing, there would be no money to fritter.

So it seemed that, where Kate was concerned, at least one gentleman had been wise enough to see the jewel shining within—and then let it slip from his grasp. It intrigued him, Edward told himself, and that was all. He was just a man who liked a puzzle.

And perhaps a challenge.

Certainly his goddess was more interesting to muse upon than was the great, black void that constituted his past, and his brain's pathetic inability to add two plus two. For if he dwelled upon that, he soon began to sink into the sands of despair.

And so he went in search of her. To apologize. And yes, perhaps to pick up their light flirtation where he'd left it. But more than that? It was a line he would not cross. No, he would not be living out his sensual fantasies with the enticing Lady d'Allenay.

Bellecombe's estate offices encompassed the whole ground floor of the south tower, Jasper explained, and were most easily accessed via the inner bailey. But despite his room being situated in the main house, Edward decided to first hobble up six flights of stairs and onto the open parapet that connected the east and north towers.

From this soaring vantage point, one could see that the original medieval construction consisted of four towers linked by wide, crenellated walls like the one on which he stood. However, a pair of more modern wings extended beyond the walls, making Bellecombe Castle what must surely be one of England's most splendid homes.

Far below him lay the cobbled inner bailey, and beyond that, the outer bailey, surrounded by the secondary walls that appeared to house the stables and other utilitarian functions. There was an outer gate and an inner gate, both likely portcullised, with a long, high bridge between; a solid defense for times of turbulence. And while the castle had no moat, the undulations of earth when seen from above indicated there once had been one.

Rising up around all this rugged beauty were green and rolling Somerset hills, the castle nestled like a diamond amongst it all.

Bellecombe. *Beautiful valley.*

He looked down at the south tower, and saw that the thick, wooden doors were opened wide onto the cobbled courtyard, to catch the morning's warmth, he supposed. He could see Kate sitting just inside, bent industriously over a massive desk, her glossy hair shining in the sun. Suddenly raw lust twisted through him again, seizing his breath.

He forced it away, swallowing hard. He willed himself to look at her objectively. How slight and fine-boned she appeared from this distance. It was a grave responsibility she bore upon those slender shoulders. What a remarkable thing that this great and ancient estate had come to her, and at a relatively young age.

After reading to him this morning from the newspapers, Miss Wentworth had reiterated the story of how her sister had been made heir after their brother Stephen's death. The young man had apparently injured his spine in a fall, then lingered, bedridden, until pneumonia took him one winter.

Stephen Wentworth had been brought up for this; Kate had not. She had been entirely unprepared. And yet she seemed confident and capable now.

There were a few ancient English titles, Edward knew, that could convey through the female line, but only if there were no males. A string of six or eight entirely competent elder sisters could be displaced by one brother, be he only aged two. Or a spendthrift drunkard. Or an outright fool.

Edward knew many such men—or at least he knew that he knew them. Who they were and under what circumstances he knew them escaped him, perhaps mercifully. But it struck him as reprehensible that a competent female had less standing than a fool with a pair of bollocks between his legs.

Alas, such was English law.

Having taken it all in, Edward descended through the east tower, ending up in a small, vaulted chapel with soaring clerestory windows, their exquisite stained glass shimmering with reds and golds and blues in the morning sun. It made him feel that if God were in a place, it would surely be a place such as this. Beautiful, and yet, with its stiff-backed oak pews and uneven stone floor, just a little humble.

Moreover, it made it ever more plain to him that, whatever their circumstances now, there had once been a vast deal of wealth in the d'Allenay dynasty. Like the right to crenellate for defense, the right to possess one's own chapel was a privilege bestowed only upon those deemed both wealthy and trustworthy.

Closing the thick, oaken door behind him, Edward secured it by dropping an iron door latch as wide as his wrist, then crossed the bailey. Kate's office doors still stood open. He hobbled inside, giving a light rap upon the blackened oak slab.

"Edward!" Kate looked up from the letter she was writing,

her face breaking into a wide smile as she rose, both hands outstretched in welcome. And he realized in that moment that nothing about her was remotely plain. How had he ever thought otherwise?

"Hullo, Kate."

"I'm glad, of course, to see you," she said, the tone both welcoming and chiding at once. "But what are you doing out of bed?"

He took his weight off the elegant, brass-knobbed stick he'd purloined, and smiled. "Getting better," he said, letting it dangle, aloft, between two fingers. "My balance is improved and Fitch says I should exercise the ankle an hour each day. Moreover, he orders you to free poor Jasper from his nursing duties. I've already ordered the cot removed."

"Have you indeed?" She shot him a chary glance, then motioned to a chair beside her desk. "Well. Sit down. Where have you been since Fitch left?"

"Exploring your castle," he said. "It is a medieval marvel, my dear, and delightfully untouched by time."

She shot him a rueful glance. "Yes, I fear the Wentworth line has always had a shocking propensity to fritter money that might have been better spent on modernization."

"It looks to me as if you're slowly setting that to rights."

"Five hundred years of dissolution?" Her mouth twisted. "Well. One does what one can."

"Surely not all your ancestors were wastrels?"

She laughed, that throaty, unselfconscious laugh he liked so well. "No, you're right," she admitted. "A great many were excellent managers, and my grandfather did what he could. But the place has been lost once or twice—Cromwell, the War of the Roses—the Barons d'Allenay always managed to get on the wrong side of every little spat. That, along with a few entrenched gamblers, a couple of womanizers—the sixth baron, we're told, was an outright bigamist—*et voilà!* as Aurélie would say—the roofs rot and the coffers sit empty."

He cast his eyes around. "Oh, it doesn't look that bad," he

said. "Someone's been working hard at trimming the wicks and polishing up the brass."

She smiled in acknowledgment. "My grandfather trained me well," she said, "and Anstruther, our steward, is like a member of the family. But enough of that. What did Dr. Fitch say? And the whole of it, if you please."

"Madam, a man would cower at the thought of keeping a secret from you."

"Ha!" she said on a laugh. "You've never cowered in your life, I daresay."

But she had relaxed into her chair, and pushed it away from the desk. She wore riding clothes, he realized; a plain brown habit that could only be described as serviceable, with an almost mannish cut. Her shirt collar was high and starched, and only her velvet lapels softened the coat. He suspected she'd already ridden out to one of the farms this morning, for there was mud caked around one boot heel.

Oddly, he liked that. Kate looked capable and brimming with vitality. She had not lingered in her bedchamber until noon, fretting over nothing more significant than which jewelry to wear to tea.

Did a great many ladies do that? Yes, he somehow thought they did.

"Well?" she demanded. "Your prognosis, sir?"

"Fitch says time heals all wounds, even those one can't see," said Edward. "He thinks my stitches can come out soon. He wasn't surprised by the problem with arithmetic. And whilst I may walk a little, he still wishes me to rest and avoid eye strain."

"So no reading?"

He shook his head, and felt another pinprick of frustration.

"Have you felt anything stir? Even a fragment?"

He smiled thinly, hesitating before he spoke. "Well, I had some strange dreams all night," he confessed, "most of which don't bear repeating. But in one of them, I found myself walking through a park. And in the dream, I *knew* that it was Green Park. In London, yes?" He glanced at her for confirmation.

"Yes, in London."

He nodded. "I could tell that I'd been there before, and often. And I felt as if . . ." He paused, trying to put it into words.

"As if what?" Kate leaned across the corner of the desk, and he wanted, suddenly, to kiss her again. He let his gaze drift over her face, hoping she could not see the hunger there.

"I felt as if I were going somewhere familiar," he said quietly. "There was an urgency about it—I *needed* to get there. And then I was striding through this narrow passageway—like an alley—with gaslight at the end. Then I woke up, feeling strangely relieved."

Kate was tapping a finger on the desktop. "There are a couple of places where one can enter St. James directly from the park," she said after a moment had passed. "Perhaps you live near there?"

He lifted his eyebrows. "I didn't realize you knew London well."

"Not especially," she admitted. "But before Belgravia became all the rage, Uncle Upshaw and Aunt Louisa lived in St. James's Square."

"Ah, yes! On the fashionable side, I daresay?"

Her eyes widened. "See? You know that. You know there is an unfashionable side."

"I did know it, didn't I?" he mused.

"One might also go that way to reach, say, the Carlton Club, which is very near Spencer House," Kate suggested, absently scrubbing the toe of her boot across a crack in the flagstone. "Or perhaps you might belong to White's? Or one of the other fashionable gentlemen's clubs? And there are one or two less savory places, I believe, in St. James—if some of my brother's stories were true."

"Hmm," he said. "Those do not sound like tales suitable for a lady's ear."

She shrugged. "Well, in any case, if all else fails, you might go to London when you're entirely well, and walk about the neighborhood."

"Ah, is my goddess eager to cast me from Mount Olympus?" he murmured.

Her breath hitched a little oddly. "No, certainly not," she said. "Please, Edward, do not tease me. Not . . . not in that way."

"I beg your pardon." He reached across the desk again, and took her hand. "It is an excellent idea, and I will go."

"When you feel up to it," she said.

Edward sighed. "I feel, Kate, such an imposition to you here."

Her eyes flared with something like dismay. "You *must not*," she said firmly. "Were it not for me, you wouldn't even be in this predicament. Besides, we will eventually discover where you've come from, Edward. We *will*. And when we do, you can return to—to your family, or to whatever it is you've left behind. And that will almost certainly reawaken your memories."

But there was an increasing tension inside his chest. The last of her words came at him as if from a distance. And then the strangest thing happened. Suddenly the tension became a rush of emotion—no, *dread*—so strong he had never known the like. As if the whole of his body had gone numb. For an instant, his breath stopped.

He did not want to go back.

He was sure of it.

He exhaled sharply. Good God, what kind of life had he led? What was it that lay there like a chunk of hard, black tar in the bottom of his heart? Had he been unhappy? Or, God forbid, unhappily married? He had been so sure he was not. He was still sure. But there was a darkness in his past he truly did not wish to revisit.

Could he be quashing those memories in some hidden recess of his soul? Allowing himself to stay here, where he felt so . . . so strangely at ease? So very much at home? Bellecombe seemed to him a place of warmth and security.

But what a mad notion that was! Good Lord, he was a man grown.

"Edward?" Kate's voice was gentle, but probing. "What is it?"

He lifted his gaze to hers, and knew that it was bleak. "What if I don't want to remember?" he said, forcing his mind to be calm. "I . . . Kate, God help me, but I sometimes think I *don't*. And how can that be?"

"It cannot be," she said firmly. "You're still a little unwell, that is all. I beg you will not fixate upon it. And I confess, I'm glad to have you here."

"Glad?" he said, lifting his gaze to hers. "Are you, Kate?"

It was her turn to look away. "More, perhaps, than I ought to be," she murmured, hesitating a long moment. Then she picked up the thread of her thoughts, speaking, perhaps, a little too swiftly. "But I'm glad to know you're not uncomfortable here. Why do you not just rest, and think of this as . . . a sort of holiday? What is the harm in that? What can be accomplished by worry? No one, Edward, wishes to lose their past."

Edward stared past her, at a glass-fronted bookcase stuffed with agricultural tomes. "I sometimes have the feeling the past isn't far from my grasp," he admitted. "At times, I can almost glimpse it—it's a little like following someone you think you know down the street. Then, at the last instant, just as you get near enough to see their face, they vanish round a corner."

He didn't realize he had laid his hand upon her desk, his fingers fisted so tight his knuckles had gone white, until Kate covered it with her own.

She gave it a hard squeeze. "Edward, just stop following. Stop looking. Virtually everything we seek in life comes to us only when we stop seeking it."

He gave a harsh laugh. "You're right, Kate," he said. "I

know you are—though I don't know how I know it. Hell, I don't know how I know anything. Oh, but you must pardon my language! I'm not at all sure, Kate, that in my past life I was the gentleman you think me."

"You are a gentleman bred if not born," she said with both asperity and certainty, "and likely both."

Edward shrugged, and glanced at the letter she'd been writing. It was crossed and recrossed in a few places, with scribbles written up and down the margins.

"Ah, well, enough of my pathetic mewling," he said, extracting his hand. "What are you doing?"

Her cheeks seemed to turn a little pink. "I'm writing to Aunt Louisa and Uncle Upshaw," she said. "I'm inviting them for a visit."

Edward was surprised. "Are you?"

"Yes." She dropped her gaze to her lap, and began to twist at the unusual gold ring she wore upon her second finger, a habit he'd noticed before. It was a man's ring, and he wondered, not for the first time, if her fiancé had given it to her. "Yes, I wish them to come down for the house party. For two reasons."

"Ah," he said quietly. "And may I know what they are?"

She made a feeble, airy gesture. "I just want them to meet Richard Burnham," she confessed. "I quarreled with Nancy again last night. And I've come to realize that it is not my place to oppose this marriage, or to give her any advice whatsoever."

"If it's any consolation to you," he said quietly, "I don't think your sister is anything near a fool."

At first Kate made no reply to this, and instead just twisted the ring around again. "No," she finally answered. "No, she's not. Nancy is so charming and pretty, one sometimes expects her to be flighty. Or to have her head turned by all the flattery. But she is not, and she has not. She says she wants to marry Richard, and that only he will do."

"And you've come to believe it?"

Kate nodded. "I think so," she said. "For whatever my opinion counts—which technically is very little, for I'm not her trustee. Though I may own Bellecombe and administer what is, by most definitions, a vast fortune in real estate, I cannot legally be my sister's keeper. Is that not silly?"

"It is," he said.

"I granted Richard the living of St. Michael's, so I think my opinion of his character is plain," she went on. "I would not entrust this parish to any man whom I did admire and respect. And perhaps if Uncle spent some time with Richard—and Richard's mother, too—he might come to see that Richard could make Nancy happy."

Edward regarded her for a long moment, wondering what it was he saw lurking in her eyes; a furtive sort of doubt, he thought.

Her hand now lay flat on the desk beside the letter. He picked it up in his own, marveling at the thin elegance of her fingers and the short tidy nails. Kate made no effort to draw away, but he watched the unease fade from her gaze.

After a long moment had passed, Edward gave her fingers a reassuring squeeze. "My dear," he said quietly, "have you considered simply insisting Lord Upshaw permit the marriage? You could tell him you're confident they are suited."

For a moment, he thought Kate didn't mean to answer him.

When at last she spoke, it was hesitantly, as if the words were being dragged from her. "But what if my judgment is no better than hers?" Kate finally said. "What do I know, really, about life? About marriage? I chose wrongly, and made . . . well, a mess of my life, really."

"It strikes me that you made no sort of mess at all," said Edward calmly. "You betrothed yourself, decided after a time that you didn't suit, and extricated yourself from a potentially lifelong mistake."

But Kate was biting her lip almost brutally, and Edward realized there was something she was not telling him. It was not, however, his place to press.

Indeed, he had already pressed his attentions upon the lady. He would not press his opinions. Lightly, he lifted her hand and brushed his lips across her knuckles, then released her.

It was not a sensual gesture, but instead—he hoped—one of reassurance. Of solace, perhaps. This house—and Kate—comforted him in a way he could not explain. Whatever sort of man he turned out to be, in this time and place, could he not do the same for her?

"And what was your second reason?" he said quietly.

"I beg your pardon?" Kate looked confused.

He smiled. "You said there were two reasons for inviting your aunt and uncle."

"Oh, that." Kate blushed prettily. "Well, it is just that Aurélie—Mamma—is coming, you know, and Aunt Louisa sometimes provides a . . . well, let us call it a calming influence on her."

"Interesting," he remarked. "And Lady Upshaw is your mother's sister?"

"Half sister, though you'd hardly know it." Kate smiled. "Louisa's mother died when Louisa was small. A year later, her father shocked the entire family by marrying their pretty French governess, and promptly having Aurélie."

Edward could not suppress a grin. "Oh, my."

"Oh, my, indeed," said Kate. "But to Louisa's credit, she has never held it against Aurélie. Her elder siblings, however, harbored some resentment, I think. After their father's death, Aurélie spent much of her time in France whilst the others did not. They look to Louisa to . . . well, to hold the whip hand over Aurélie occasionally. But whether Louisa will come for the house party, I don't know."

"Why wouldn't she?"

"She has quite a large family," said Kate. "The eldest three are settled, but Louisa still has daughters in the schoolroom. It is not fair to bother her with my troubles."

"I notice both you and your sister are more apt to call your mother by her Christian name."

The blush deepened. "Aurélie says it makes her feel old to be called Mamma," said Kate. "She did marry almost scandalously young. And indeed, it is no great trouble to indulge her."

It seemed rather more than an indulgence to Edward, but he held his tongue.

"Kate," he said instead, "I didn't come all the way down here just to quiz you about things that are really none of my business."

"I haven't found your questions the least intrusive," she returned. "But why, pray, did you come?"

"I think you know why," he said.

"No," she replied. "I do not."

He lifted his gaze to hers again, one eyebrow crooked. "I came to apologize," he said, "for my bad behavior last night."

"What, for being irritable when I tried to get you to rest?" She cut him a sidelong, almost coy look. "Or for saying to Jasper—within my hearing, no less—that he might go to the devil when he insisted on helping you out of your coat?"

"Kate," he said chidingly.

Her eyes lit up with specious recognition. "Ah, you meant for that kiss!" she said. "Do you regret it?"

"Of course. How could I not?"

"Heavens, how mortifying for me!" she murmured. "I daresay you don't mean to do it again, then. I own to some disappointment."

For a moment, it was as if his heart stilled. "Ah, Kate," he said softly. "I think we can both be sure I'm not the sort of man who ought to be kissing you."

Her eyes flashed. "Oh? What sort should I chose instead? A fortune hunter, perhaps? I have no fortune save Bellecombe, and now I'm tasked with preserving it. My options, Edward, are limited."

Edward tried to understand. "You expected to marry," he said. "To leave Bellecombe to your brother's care, and have a family and home of your own. To have children."

She glanced away.

"Kate, you can still do those things," he pressed. "Perhaps you should go back to London instead of sending your sister? Couldn't Lady Upshaw introduce you to some eligible gentlemen?"

Her lips thinned, and she shook her head. "I haven't time," she said. "Things are too precarious here. It's taken us five years just to push the estate books back into the black."

"Kate, can't your steward—"

"*I* cannot," she interjected. "What's more, I don't wish to. Look at me. I'm not beautiful, and I know it."

"That is not true," he countered. "And it strikes me you have many virtues that—"

"You don't understand." She shook her head again. "I'm no longer Miss Katherine Wentworth with a modest but serviceable dowry. Do I *wish* to marry? Yes, of course. But even if I had the time to meet eligible gentlemen, how could I be certain that a man wanted me, and not the revenue this estate might someday—*someday*, if I work my fingers to the bone—begin to throw off?"

She had been somehow spooked, he guessed, by her former fiancé. "Kate, not everyone is like that."

"Men who are seeking wives, Edward, must be practical," she said. "They must consider what that wife will bring them. No one will look at me and see a plain woman with a good heart. They will see only the heiress of Bellecombe. But my father and my brother nearly bled this place dry, and I'll be damned before I'll let another man do it."

He had upset her, he realized. How tragic Kate could not see her own worth. And yet she was right; her value was now inseparably entwined with that of the barony's, and if he understood the law, whoever married her would likely control both.

"And yet you can be very persuasive, my dear," he said, attempting to lighten the mood. "I have no doubt you could keep that sort of man in his place."

"I cannot be bothered with *that sort of man*," she snapped. "I have real problems here. I haven't the time to take on a battle that needn't be fought. I can't run that risk—not to Bellecombe, and not to my family."

"And so you will trade . . . what?" he asked. "Your future children for the future of this estate?"

Something like pain flashed in her expressive gray eyes. "Yes, if one wishes to look at it that way," she said quietly. "I think it a worthy sacrifice."

"And what will become of all this when you're gone?" he pressed. "Who do you build it for—*sacrifice* for—if not your children?"

"Nancy is heir to Bellecombe, as it now stands," Kate answered. "The estate would be well served if it descended through the Burnham line."

Edward threw up both hands. "Then it seems your decisions are made, my dear," he said. "I'm sorry I kissed you. This . . . thing we have, Kate—this fragile friendship—I oughtn't have risked it for the sake of something so trifling."

Her smile was muted, but the warmth had left her eyes. "You're just bored here, and thwarted—as any man of ambition and energy would be." She pushed her chair a little away from the desk, and flicked a glance at an ancient bracket clock that stood on the mantelpiece. "As for me, I'm sorry to say I must leave you now. I'm promised to Anstruther."

"Ah. More sheep?"

Kate smiled, but it no longer reached her eyes. "No, we've some mining operations on the other side of Dulverton," she said, snatching a worn leather saddlebag from the floor. "We're heading that way now."

"Coal?" he asked.

"No, we have coal interests nearer to Bath," she said, "but this is just a small silver mine."

"You don't look happy about going," he said. "Or is it me? Please, Kate. Tell me I haven't made you unhappy. I should rather anything, I think, than that."

"How silly you are, Edward." She stood and began stuffing files and ledgers into the bag. "It's just that . . . well, I understand farming. Sheep. Corn. The turn of the seasons. But mining? I loathe it."

"Do you? Then sell it."

"Tempting, but unwise." Kate latched the buckle of her bag. "Fully half Bellecombe's revenue is derived from non-agrarian assets. Now the superintendent wishes to discuss a new business proposal, and I'll understand about half of what he says. No, it is not you, Edward, trust me."

Edward hoped she spoke the truth. "It's no easy business, being Baroness d'Allenay, is it?" he said with a smile. "Well. I mustn't keep you from it any longer."

After securing her brown top hat and drawing the light veil over her face, Kate snared her crop in her empty hand, and stepped briskly toward the courtyard. "Oh, there was one other thing," she said, turning back. "I might be late tonight. But since Fitch has given you permission to be out of bed, I hope you'll dine with us tomorrow evening?"

"Thank you." Edward exhaled slowly, and with a good deal of relief. "Nothing would give me more pleasure."

"Excellent," she said with a formal tilt of her head. "I shall ask Anstruther to join us. You will like him."

Edward watched her make her way across the courtyard, her heels clicking briskly on the cobbles and the long skirts of her habit neatly caught up along with the saddlebag, as if she did it often. Kate's figure was trim and straight as a duchess's as she strode beneath the first portcullis, then turn into the outer bailey, vanishing from sight.

And suddenly, he wanted to go after her. Go after her and say . . . what? Good Lord, he wasn't even sure what she'd offered him. Just another kiss?

Whatever it had been, his rebuff, however lightly made, had almost certainly driven a stake through its heart. Just as it had been meant to do. And yet Edward had actually followed her halfway to the portcullis before he stopped himself.

What madness it would be to follow her! He didn't even know his own name, for pity's sake. Nothing had changed. Suddenly he heard the clatter of horseshoes on the cobbles. Kate's bay mare came trotting out at a brisk clip then turned smoothly onto the long bridge that led from the castle.

She was followed out by a tall, unfamiliar man on a great beast of a horse, a gray that soon edged alongside the mare.

Kate sat her mount elegantly, her posture as perfect as her command of the creature beneath her. Neither she nor the man on the gray so much as turned to look at him standing in the shadows of the gatehouse, frozen like some lovelorn schoolboy gazing after her.

But he was not a schoolboy. He certainly was not lovelorn.

And yet as he stood there watching Kate and her horse vanish from his sight, Edward was struck with the certainty that he'd just made a terrible mistake; perhaps the greatest of his life.

But then, how could he know?

He was nothing. His life—and his mistakes—were invisible. He could not know his future when he hardly knew his past. He did not know his own name, for God's sake. Could not even add simple numbers—perhaps not even think straight. And for the first time since his accident, Edward wanted to rail at the heavens in anger.

CHAPTER 7

Beautiful Music

Kate prepared for dinner the following evening with more care than she wished to admit, even to herself. Mrs. Peppin sat in her usual spot by the hearth in Kate's private parlor, her feet up on a small stool, knitting as she watched Kate pull out her dinner gowns in turn, then shove them back into the wardrobe again.

"The claret-colored satin," the housekeeper finally said, her needles busily clicking. "'Tis simple, miss, but it does become you."

"All my gowns are simple," Kate muttered, yanking out the claret to study it.

Peppie set her basket aside. "Aye, and by whose choice?"

Kate shot her a chagrinned look, and hung the gown on the door hook. "Mine," she acknowledged, fluffing out the skirt. "I was never meant to be a peacock, Peppie."

"Nor a wallflower, miss," Peppie advised, rising and going to the bellpull. "And Hetty needs to press out that skirt. Even a peacock looks poor when wrinkled, and you've a hand-some man to dinner tonight."

Kate felt her eyes widen. "Peppie, for pity's sake," she chided. "It is just Edward."

"Aye, just Edward," Peppie agreed. "Still, 'tis one thing to observe a man when he's laid up an invalid, and another thing altogether when he's up and around, striding about like some Roman statue come to life."

Kate shot her a chiding glance, and came fully into the parlor. "He's limping, not striding," she corrected. "Besides, Peppie, we don't know anything about him."

She could have been talking to herself, Kate realized. Indeed, she *should* have been. Good heavens, she had tried to *flirt* with him yesterday! And if Edward's response to her veiled suggestion had not brought her crashing back to earth like Icarus on wings of wax, perhaps Peppie's blunt tongue could get the job done.

The truth was, like John Anstruther, Mrs. Peppin had been more of a parent to Kate and Nancy than their own had been. Peppie had a right to speak—and no one could dash cold water on foolishness with more aplomb than she.

And yet she didn't quite do that. Instead her wrinkled face fell a little. "Aye, you're right," she said. "Still, it has been a pleasure to have a gentleman stirring about again—and a handsome one, at that."

"Yes," said Kate a little darkly. "I just keep wishing he'd wear his spectacles round the house. Maybe it would be a little off-putting?"

Peppie chortled. "Oh, miss, 'twill take more than a pair of spectacles to tarnish the brass on that man," she said. "I thought Miss Nan might have her head turned, but not a bit of it."

"I fear it isn't Nancy we need to worry about," said Kate grimly. "I find him entirely too diverting. At least he's start-ing to remember bits and pieces."

"Aye, and one day—or so Fitch claims—his memory

will come flooding back, and we'll be shut of him," said the housekeeper on a sigh. "But for my part, I'll be a little sorry."

Kate would not, she told herself. She would be glad. Glad to return to her ordinary life, and to be rid of the fantasies that had begun to torment her. She kept telling herself that, too, even as Hetty pressed her gown, and Peppie persuaded her to braid her hair up into a high coronet on the back of her head.

"There!" said Peppie, securing it with a comb of intricate gilt filigree that had been her grandmother's. "The spit and image of the late Lady d'Allenay, you are. 'Tis no wonder, miss, you were His Lordship's favorite."

The arrangement did become her, Kate admitted, turning to look at it sidelong in her mirror. The fan-shaped comb was set with a spray of garnets that caught the light, and somehow gave the arrangement not just elegance, but a sort of queenly grace.

"*Was* I Grandpapa's favorite, Peppie?" she asked a little wistfully.

"Lawks, yes, miss!" Peppie bent to fluff her skirt around her crinoline. "Oh, he loved Mr. Stephen dear. But Lord d'Allenay knew all along that you'd be best for Bellecombe. He died a good death knowing it would be yours."

"I'd like to prove him right," Kate muttered, "but it is hard. I declare I did not understand half of what was said about that mine yesterday."

"What mine?" said a dry voice from the door. "Heavens, Kate! Aren't you togged out to the nines!"

Kate turned to see Nancy standing on the threshold that separated her bedchamber from the parlor.

"I'm wearing a five-year-old gown you've seen a hundred times," said Kate evenly. "If that's the nines, then I've a Parisian revue shoved in my wardrobe."

Nancy had crossed her arms over her chest in a gesture Kate knew well. "But you're wearing Grandmamma's garnet comb," she said accusingly, "and now you're putting on her matching earbobs that dangle halfway to your collarbones."

"Yes, and *you're* wearing her emerald and diamond choker," Kate pointed out, speaking over her shoulder as she fastened the last earbob. "Would you care to trade? I can have these off in a trice, I do assure you."

"Emeralds for garnets?" said Nancy dismissively. "I think not. But you *are* getting dressed up for Edward. We both know it."

"I certainly am not," Kate lied.

"You *are*," Nancy challenged, "and why it is acceptable for you to flirt with a man who, for all we know, is a highwayman, whilst I cannot marry one whom we know to be a saint, I'm sure I don't know."

"Miss Nan!" Peppie put her hands on her hips. "Let's have none of that, now."

"None of what?" said Nancy innocently.

"If your sister finally feels like dressing up a bit and entertaining a guest, we should all be happy for her," said Peppie. "Mr. Edward is a gentleman. And your sister has little enough pleasure as is."

But Kate had turned from the mirror, seizing her red and gold shawl as she went. "Edward may well be an outright rogue, I'll grant you," she said airily, "but I'm not remotely interested in him. Moreover, I'm ten years your senior, Nancy, and have seen a little of the world."

"A precious little," her sister grumbled. "I should write to Uncle Upshaw to tell him you're harboring a mysterious man beneath our roof and that something must be done about it."

Kate turned and smiled brightly. "Do you know, Nan, you're too late," she said. "I've already done precisely that. Now come along, do. We are keeping Anstruther and Edward waiting."

EDWARD FOUND JOHN Anstruther drifting about the drawing room with a glass of whisky in hand, and recognized

him at once as the man on the gray horse. The burly, bewhis-
kered Scotsman stood on no ceremony, introducing himself
at once, and pulling the stopper on the decanter to pour
Edward a drink as if he were very much at home.

"Devil of a shame, sir, aboot your tumble," the steward
remarked, passing the glass. "You must be champing at the
bit to get on wi' your business."

"That's the thing," Edward mused. "I don't know. I don't
feel a great sense of urgency. But I do feel an inconvenience
here."

"Not a bit of it! The ladies don't think it a moment," said
Anstruther giving him a hearty thump on the shoulder. He
then began to regale Edward with a tale of a schoolmate
who'd suffered a similar fate at university.

"Fell drunk oot an east windae at Old College," said Anstruther, "ontae a gaggle o' first years. Lucky thing, for the
lads broke the fall. But his head hit the pavement anyway.
Poor devil didn't ken his own name for a bloody fortnight."

"And then what happened?"

Anstruther's wide brow furrowed. "I dinna recall how,"
he said, cutting a glance at the open door, "but it came back
all of a rush. But there—we must na' speak of it before the
ladies. 'Twas too much like poor Mr. Stephen."

For an instant, Edward didn't follow. "Ah, yes," he said.
"Miss Wentworth mentioned her brother died after a fall,
but not how it happened."

"Och, he went off on one of those continental larks with
his boon companion, Lord Reginald," said Anstruther, "the
drunken lout."

"Lord Reginald?"

"Aye, the lout." Anstruther jerked his head in the general
direction of northwest. "Ah, but I'm talking out o' turn. The
ladies have a soft spot for him still, I daresay."

"But you don't, I collect." Edward grinned.

A look of misgiving sketched across the steward's face.

"He was youngest son o' the Marquess of Yelton, and fair full of himself," he complained. "Lady Yelton's mither was raised just t'other side of the hill, and the lad was his granny's wee princeling. And no guid did that auld woman do us when she died."

"Oh? In what way?"

Anstruther's ample muttonchops trembled as he shook his head. "Left that dunderheid the hoose and three tenant farms to piss away," he muttered, one eye on the door. "Not my place to say, mind, but I niver thought him a good influence on Mr. Stephen."

"Young men, it seems to me, are eternally in search of a bad influence," said Edward dryly.

"Aye, weel, Mr. Stephen was'na wicked, just spoilt. So he went off to Tuscany on a lark wi' Lord Reginald, climbed up some bell tower aff his head wi' drink, and somehow fell oot it. Lost worse than his memory, too."

Edward looked at his borrowed stick. "I gather Mr. Wentworth couldn't get around very well after his accident."

Anstruther shook his head again. "Niver walked again, really," he said, "though he was helped to hobble about a wee bit. But a man lies quiet like that too long, and he's done for. Pneumonia will seize hold of his lungs every time. You may have come a cropper, sir, but you're up and about, praise God."

Just then, Edward caught the sound of ladies' footsteps coming swiftly down the stairs. Anstruther shot him a warning look, tipped his whisky, then drained it.

"Anstruther!" said Miss Wentworth, sweeping gracefully into the room to kiss his cheek, "how handsome you look out of your boots and surtout."

The Scotsman colored a little, and worked a finger under his cravat. "I'm trussed up like a Christmas goose, Miss Nan," he said. "Och, ye've got your granny's necklace on! How I do miss that crabbit auld lady."

They fell then into a discussion of the previous Lady d'Allenay's virtues, which—her crabbiness notwithstanding—were apparently myriad.

"It means crotchety," Kate murmured, eyeing him over the sherry she was pouring. "And she wasn't, really. Just pragmatic."

With a muted smile, Edward lifted his whisky. "Well, then," he said, tipping his glass to hers, "here's to pragmatic women. I find them charming."

To Edward's delight, Anstruther allowed himself to be engaged in conversation by Miss Wentworth on the opposite side of the room for some minutes, the two of them chattering like a pair of jays, and leaving Edward alone with Kate.

She looked remarkably beautiful tonight, he realized, in a full-skirted gown of deep red velvet, split and cut away to reveal an underskirt of ecru-colored satin. The snug bodice was pleated to either side, and cut so low across her shoulders it just skimmed her breasts before plunging. But the neckline was more suggestive than titillating, for a chemisette of ecru lace lent it discretion.

She wore no necklace to break the creamy expanse of bare shoulders and had removed the ring she usually wore, he noticed. Her only jewelry was a pair of elaborate gold earrings shaped like long, thin leaves set with graduated red gems and a filigree comb, set like a little crown atop an arrangement of braids. Edward had no strong grasp of female fashions, but he recognized elegance and simplicity when he saw it.

She returned from pressing a glass of sherry into her sister's hand. "I see Anstruther's let you at his whisky," she remarked.

"Ah, *his* whisky, is it?"

Kate wrinkled her nose. "I can rarely drink it," she said. "But I keep it for him, so that we can occasionally entice him into the house."

"You make him sound like a stray dog." Edward shot her a grin.

"Hardly," said Kate. "He has the whole of South Farm to himself. That has a large manor house, so he's quite snug."

"Has he been with you long?"

"Oh, nearly since I was born," said Kate. "He was Grandmamma's godson, you know, and they were very close. Grandpapa hired him."

"And you trust him?" asked Edward lightly. "He is a good business manager?"

"Anstruther is like family," said Kate. "Heavens, when Papa was alive, Anstruther was the only person who could talk sense to him. Grandpapa, for all his wisdom, doted on his only child too well. Yes, I trust him—as do all our tenants. Even Mamma adores him, though she teases him unmercifully for his dour ways."

"His duties must be vast."

"Frightfully," said Kate. "He stewards the estate, helps with our mining interests, and goes to London at least once a month to deal with all our business and banking there. He knows how much I dislike Town."

Her words agreed precisely with what Edward's instincts told him about the man's character.

"Speaking of mining," he said, "how did the two of you find your meeting yesterday? Was it as dreadful as you feared?"

She managed a thin smile. "No, but I left our superintendent disappointed," she confessed. "He wishes to sink a new shaft in the spring."

"What did you tell him?"

"That we could afford it, *perhaps*," she said pensively. "But what we cannot afford is to expand into Cornwall, where he has his eye on a potential tin mine."

"Tin is a steady business," Edward remarked.

"Tin is subject to undercutting by competition in the Far

East, or used to be." She shook her head. "No. I think it too risky a venture. Perhaps, if I understood it better . . . but I do not. And I haven't the time to learn, sadly."

Edward thought it was probably worth a good deal of study. Steam-pumping technology, now improving by leaps and bounds, was predicted to revolutionize tin mining. He opened his mouth to say so, then abruptly closed it again.

What did he know, really, about mining? And if he knew anything, *how* did he know it? *Where* had he learnt it? But he did know quite a lot, he was sure of it. Still, how presumptuous it would be of him, of all people, to give Kate advice on capital investments.

"Were you going to say something?" she politely enquired.

He shook his head. "No, I was just—"

Edward was saved from his potential folly when Fendershot came in, bowed stiffly, and announced that dinner was served.

He was surprised to find that the Wentworth sisters didn't seem prone to gossip or talk about the latest fashions over dinner as he might have expected, but instead stuck to more practical topics that were of interest to Anstruther.

Over the course of the meal, Edward learnt more about late harvests, wool markets, and apple orchards than he felt strictly necessary, but he found it interesting to study Kate in her element. Save for those few glimpses of her life he'd seen in the estate office, all he really knew of Kate was her kindness.

Over a fish course of fresh whiting in a brown butter sauce, Anstruther spoke contemplatively about the potential tin mine. He was, however, unable to counter Kate's logic that a loan would be necessary, and that improvements to the home farm would have to be put off.

It could not, in short, be done.

"Aye, niver a borrower or a lender be," he remarked wistfully. "Still, 'tis a rare opportunity."

After this, however, no more was said, and they eventually retired to the drawing room, where Miss Wentworth was prevailed upon to play the pianoforte. Anstruther, to Edward's surprise, had brought in a violin in a battered case, and tucked it behind the sofa. He brought it out now, and settled himself onto a chair almost facing her.

"How marvelous," Edward whispered. "Are they any good?"

Kate gave a muted smile. "Suffice it to say that, for this skill alone, I would keep the man in whisky. And where Nancy got such a talent, I shall never know. I'm tone-deaf."

Edward was soon to realize what she meant. The pair began with a complicated sonata for keyboard and violin, and played it flawlessly. Clearly they had played together for many years, each easily anticipating the other's timing, and he felt himself being lulled into an almost dreamlike state of relaxation by the perfection of the music.

And yet he felt fully aware and grounded; perhaps more so than he had felt in some days. He could feel Kate next to him now, radiating warmth—a sort of simmering sensuality that went beyond mere beauty. Indeed, it had nothing to do with beauty. But it had a great deal to do with the sudden shaft of desire that twisted into a knot in the pit of his belly.

Good Lord. Edward drew a long, steadying breath. He was no callow lad. Many a woman had warmed his bed, he felt sure. Why should this one possess his every waking moment, and draw his heated glances? Ever since their long conversation in her office, he'd felt something shifting—changing inside his head, really—though whether it was a change he would welcome, he was not entirely certain.

She looked at him as the last notes faded, her smile soft. "Impressed?"

"It was beautiful," he admitted.

"Mozart," she said, fluffing the pillowslip she'd taken out to darn.

"Yes, I know." Edward frowned. "But how do I know it, I wonder?"

"Don't think of it," said Kate, for they were already beginning a second piece. "Just enjoy the music. I doubt you've heard their like in London—or Paris, for that matter."

"I wonder if I've ever been to Paris?" he mused.

She cut another appraising glance at him. "Many times," she said, lifting one eyebrow. "I can tell just by looking at you."

He laughed, and some of the sensual tension fell away, replaced by something sweeter. Edward felt suddenly as if he were enjoying a restful evening with a dear friend.

Except it was not quite like that at all.

No, it was something more.

But in what way *more*? Edward felt suddenly confused— well, more confused, that was to say, than he had been since falling off his damned horse. What was this strange sense of longing that assailed him when he looked at Kate?

Or was she simply all he had? All he knew? When he recovered his memory, would Kate still matter?

He felt very certainly, and a little fearfully, that she would.

He cut a sidelong glance at her now, noticing the skill with which her needle darted in and out of her fabric. She was not beautiful, it was true. Her gray eyes were serious, almost somber, her skin a smooth, pale ivory that was utterly absent of any artifice. But her face was a small, perfect oval, and there was no mistaking the keen intelligence in her eyes.

She didn't mean to marry, she had implied.

It was a shame, really. Kate could have made some worthy fellow a fine wife. There was an unmistakable passion and intelligence simmering in that steady, unflinching gaze.

He tried to force his attention back to Miss Wentworth and Anstruther, but failed. Their music, a faster selection this time, was already rising to a crescendo.

Kate looked at him and smiled. "Sometimes," she said

quietly, "I find myself missing my mother. This is her favorite piece."

"She loves music?"

"Very much," said Kate.

"But she does not care for life by the moors, your sister said."

"Oh, she flits in and out, but Aurélie seems to thrive on the excitement of London," Kate conceded, letting the pillowslip crumple into her lap on a sigh. "Papa did, too. And Stephen. But Nancy and I, we have always been content at Bellecombe."

"You've always lived here?"

"More or less," she said. "Papa thought London an unhealthy place for children to be raised. Especially Nancy; she had weak lungs as a babe. Once she came along, we were sent here to stay."

"Quite a sacrifice for your mother to make," Edward murmured.

"Well, no, it was not like that." She looked at him with what might have been chagrin. "Aurélie stayed with us when she could, but Papa would grow irritable. Mostly we lived here with our grandparents and Anstruther. Eventually it was just Nancy and me. Well, until Stephen was injured. By then Papa had died. And Aurélie thought the country air might be best for Stephen, so she sent him here to recover."

Edward was beginning to have some notion of Mrs. Wentworth's maternal instincts, and it wasn't particularly endearing. But if Kate didn't perceive her mother's inattention as neglect, who was he to argue?

And there it was again.

The turn of a face. A flash of ice-blue satin. A high twist of glorious golden hair, caught by the sun. And then it was gone, leaving nothing but the scent of lilies behind, and an awful, aching sense of longing, and of loss . . .

But the scent was not real. None of it was real. It was just a glimpse, like a scene flickering past the window of a moving train, only to vanish on the next breath.

"Edward?" Kate's voice came from far away. "Edward, are you all right?"

"What?"

He looked up and realized he was staring at Kate again. She was watching him intently.

"I think my mother was very beautiful," he said on a rush, as if the thought might leave him again, "with a . . . a mole just to the left side of her mouth. And dark blonde hair that reached her waist. But she always wore it up very high when she went out."

"Did she?" said Kate calmly. "In a chignon? Or braided? How?"

"A sort of twisted style, with a diamond tiara," he said. "I don't know what one calls it."

"And what was she called?" asked Kate very softly.

He shifted his gaze, wracking his brain. "*Mamma?*" he finally said.

A long moment passed. Edward tried again to recreate the fleeting vision. But there was nothing. Kate, too, realized it.

"Well," she said with a faint smile, "at least she allowed you to call her that."

Edward said no more, and Kate, bless her, didn't press, as if sensing that more questions might drive the fragments away. "Yes," he finally agreed, "we must take our little victories where we find them."

"That has always been," said Kate quietly, "my policy."

And he had the oddest feeling that hers had been few and far between. Yes, victories both small and rare; all were to be savored. At least he could see—could *almost* see—his mother's face.

And the inexplicable rush of mixed emotions her vision engendered? Those explanations would doubtless come another day. But he was not at all sure he would welcome them. Beneath it all lay a sense of dread, and a certain knowledge that theirs had been a troubled—perhaps even an unhappy—parting.

Could that have something to do with his almost visceral reaction when it came to Kate's mother? But how fanciful that was.

"Ah, well," he said as Anstruther began restoring his bow and violin to its case. "Tonight seems like too pleasant an evening to conjure up visions of my dead mother."

Kate leaned nearer, her expression intent. "*Is* she dead?"

He was sure of it; she had been dead for a while, he thought, and told Kate so.

"I'm sorry," she said with a sympathetic smile.

But Miss Wentworth had risen from the pianoforte, and was crossing the room toward them. "Not another tatty pillowslip, Kate?" she said, looking down at her sister's lap. "How many does that make?"

"An even dozen," said Kate ruefully.

Just then, Anstruther came to thank Kate for dinner and say his good-byes. After laying aside her mending, Kate rose to see the steward out, their heads bent together as they began wrestling with the topic of the tin mine again. They walked from the room arm in arm, looking more like dear friends than employee and employer.

Edward watched them go, and fleetingly wondered if Anstruther was up to anything, but he cast aside the notion on his next breath. No, John Anstruther was solid as a rock, of that he was oddly certain.

Miss Wentworth perched herself on one end of the sofa and chattered happily at Edward until her sister's return. When Kate returned some ten minutes later, she immediately flicked an assessing glance down his length.

"I've been thinking, Nan, that it's time we did a little shopping."

"For once, sister dear, we are in total accord," said Miss Wentworth. "Where do we go?"

"To Taunton, I think," she said, still looking more at him

than at her sister. "Anstruther says he can spare me tomorrow. There are still a few things that want ordering up for Aurélie's visit. And Edward, there are several fine haberdashers there—not what you're used to, of course—but you cannot live in riding clothes."

"I could simply ride back to London in them," he suggested.

Her eyes flashed prettily. "And go where?" she demanded. "To one of those vile London hotels? Then wander about the streets asking random strangers if they know you?"

"It could be done," he said softly.

And the truth was, he felt well enough to go. More than well enough. And yet he held his breath, feeling a little like Hephaestus about to be cast from paradise for his imperfections.

But it was Miss Wentworth who spoke first. "Oh, Edward," she chided, "that is quite out of the question."

"It certainly is," Kate agreed with asperity. "And if it comes to that—which it certainly hasn't—then you will take the train, and take Jasper with you."

"And thus inconvenience you even further, Kate?"

She gentled her tone. "Again, you're the one inconvenienced, I think."

"Yes," said Miss Wentworth, her gaze softening. "You've likely left your family—or at least your aunt Isabel—terrified. Give it a few more days, Edward, at least. Stay here, and meet Uncle Upshaw."

Edward cast the girl a dark look. "I cannot imagine Lord Upshaw will wish to meet me," he answered. "Indeed, my presence here is apt to meet with his sharp disapproval."

"Your presence here *is* apt to bring him rather more quickly," Kate agreed. "A circumstance I have used to my benefit. Our uncle knows everyone, and has a slew of solicitors at his beck and call."

Edward bowed. "I see you ladies will not be dissuaded,"

he murmured. "You must do as you see fit, then. But I believe my presence here can only cast a pall over your mother's house party."

On a trill of laughter, Miss Wentworth rose. "Oh, Edward, there you could not be more wrong!" she said. "No, *your* presence—oh, the mystery! The drama! Lord, if Aurélie knew we were harboring a handsome and mysterious man, she'd be coming all the faster!"

Kate smiled. "I fear she's right," she said, sliding her sewing basket back under her chair. "Off to bed, then, Nan?"

"Heavens, no! Off to make my shopping list," said the girl, her blue eyes still sparkling with humor.

When she was gone, Kate sighed. "It must be half past ten, and I shall have letters to write before we head out tomorrow."

Edward cut a glance at the longcase clock by the door. "Nearly eleven, I'm afraid," he said, sketching her a little bow. "Well. Thank you, Kate, for a lovely dinner."

ONCE UPSTAIRS, EDWARD didn't ring for Jasper to help him undress. Instead, he whipped off his cravat and his coats, then managed to yank off his boots before going to the decanter of brandy the efficient Mrs. Peppin had left a day or two earlier. He had some hope that, given enough of it, he might wash away his burning lust for Kate.

After pouring a glass, he went to the window and looked out across the moonlit landscape. It was a cloudless evening, and in the bailey below, he could see Anstruther locking the inner gate behind him, securing the castle for the night. Edward hitched a hip high on the thick stone windowsill and sipped pensively at his glass.

In a matter of two or three days, he gathered, Mrs. Wentworth and her friends would arrive. He really did not want to be here. But nor did he wish to leave, either.

He was just fooling himself, he feared. This strange interlude—this languorous respite from his ordinary life—

could not go on. He had responsibilities. Duties. He had
begun to feel their weight even if he could not remember
their particulars.

His reverie was fractured by a light knock at the door.
He crossed the room in his shirtsleeves and stocking feet,
expecting the dutiful Jasper, perhaps, though he had firmly
dismissed him hours ago.

But it was not Jasper who stood on his threshold.

It was Kate. Kate in her nightgown and wrapper, her hair
down and her face alight.

"Edward!" she said, seizing both his hands in hers.
"Think! Think what just happened! The most marvelous
thing!"

"Marvelous?" He laughed, and squeezed her hands.
"Vesta just descended from the heavens to knock upon my
door?"

But she brushed past him almost impatiently, drawing
her hands from his. "No, no, just a few minutes ago, when
we were downstairs," she said breathlessly. "Just before we
came up?"

Edward turned back his mind. And then it struck him.

"My God, the clock!" he said, going at once to his night
table to snatch up his gold pocket watch. "Look. It's a quarter past eleven now."

"Yes!"

He lifted his gaze to hers, and swallowed hard. "Kate. The
numbers—they make perfect sense!"

"Can you do arithmetic?" she asked, sketching in the air.
"Imagine . . . oh, six plus twelve?"

"Eighteen," he said. "Eighteen. A one followed by an
eight. I see them even without pen and paper."

"And everything else must surely follow!" Kate had
caught him by the shoulders, and was dancing him around
the room. "You have remembered your mother. Your *arithmetic*. Oh, Edward, I am *so happy*!" Then she slowed and
looked up, a little breathless, her face alight with joy.

And then Edward did the most foolish thing; a thing which, much later, he could not possibly blame on a blow to the head.

He caught Kate hard against him—dragged her literally off her feet—and kissed her. Kissed her like he meant it, with one hand going up to cradle her perfect face, stilling her as he covered her mouth with his own.

For a mere instant, Kate held the heels of her hands against his shoulders. And then she, too, surrendered to the moment. He let her slide slowly back down his length, never taking his lips from hers. He slid a hand through the silken hair at her temple, then stroked over her shoulder and down her back, and then lower still, pulling her fully—sensuously—against him.

On a soft sound of pleasure, Kate's hands slid down his flanks, raking him lightly with her nails.

Blood began to pound in his head as he thrust his tongue along hers and felt her breathy sound of pleasure. Need shuddered through him, then pooled red-hot in his loins. Against the softness of Kate's belly, his shaft hardened almost abruptly, like some callow schoolboy's.

Her delicate nostrils flared wide as she kissed him back with an innocent recklessness. Fleetingly, he wanted to urge her down on the bed, ruck up her nightgown, and take her. The madness came so swift and so urgent, he had to fight it down with all the will he possessed.

He knew he needed *to stop.* Knew he was losing control, body and soul. Instead, he let his palm skate around the sweet swell of her hip, drawing her even harder against him, until he felt Kate's hands pushing hard at his shoulders.

An awful mix of relief and almost crushing disappointment flooded him. He pulled his mouth from hers, his breath already rasping.

But it was not the deliverance he'd imagined.

"We forgot to shut the door," she said breathlessly. She flew across the room, pushed it shut, then snapped the lock.

"*Kate*," he choked.

She spun around, the lace hem of her nightgown teasing across her bare toes, then leaned back against the ancient door. Her face was flushed beautifully, and her gray eyes could not possibly have been described as somber.

"Don't say a word," she ordered. "Oh, please don't! Edward, please don't ruin it."

He closed the distance, pulling her from the door and into his arms in an embrace he hoped was less carnal. "Kate," he said again. "Oh, Kate, love, be serious."

She set her cheek against his chest. He settled his hand on the back of her head, savoring the silky warmth of her hair. He shut his eyes and prayed for the strength to do the right thing.

But Kate was of no help whatever.

"Edward," she whispered, "what if I am being serious?"

And she was; Edward could hear it in her voice. She was entirely willing. Willing to give herself to him. Willing to make his dark dreams come true.

It stunned him for a moment, but he quickly regained himself. He had, after all, been teasing her—and calling her his goddess. Obviously he'd taken that teasing much too far.

"My dear, we aren't entirely sure what manner of man I am," he whispered. "I'm certainly the sort who hasn't any business trifling with a young lady's affections."

At that, she planted her hands against his chest again, and pushed herself firmly away. "I am not young," she said, looking up into his eyes. "And I'm no longer fool enough to allow any man to *trifle* with me."

"Kate, Kate," he murmured. "How you honor me. But love, we cannot—"

"Have you any idea, Edward, the sort of life I live here?" she interjected.

He set his head to one side, and studied her a moment. "The sort of life you *wish* to live, I hope," he said. "Am I wrong?"

Her lips thinned pensively as she formulated her words. "Not entirely, no," she finally admitted. "But it is not remotely like the life I expected to lead. And it's often lonely. There are parts of it that are too full—too crammed with expectations and problems and hard work—and then, sometimes late at night, there are pockets of this . . . this terrible, swamping *emptiness*."

He cupped his hand around the turn of her face again. "Oh, Kate," he whispered, "as tempting a notion as it is, I should rather not be the means of a lady's self-destruction, if that, God forbid, is what you contemplate."

Her pale coloring deepened to pink, and he realized once again how lovely she was. "I don't know what I contemplate," she said huskily. "I beg your pardon, Edward. I didn't mean to put you in an awkward position."

She started to pull away, but he could see the hurt in her eyes.

"No, no, Kate," he said, drawing her back again. "Don't ascribe any hidden meaning to my words. Oh, I want you, my dear. I have wanted you, I think, almost since the moment we met."

She buried her face against his shirtfront. "When we met, I nearly killed you."

"And still, here we are," he said on a choked laugh. "It seems I've a penchant for dangerous females. But I'm far from a saint; of that I'm quite certain. Don't waste your virtue on me, Kate, for I cannot deserve it. And you would surely regret it."

She lifted her face to his then, her expression stricken but earnest. "I have some experience with regret," she said very quietly. "And strictly speaking, I have no virtue. I already wasted it, you see—to please a man who *truly* did not deserve it. No, Edward, we do not need to talk about regret. I have felt it often these last eight years."

It was a brave speech, but he could feel the pain behind it. He held her gaze very steadily for a time, trying to swallow down an anger that was bitter as bile in the back of his throat. Then he surrendered, and said what he wished. "Oh, Kate," he rasped. "I could kill the bastard with my bare hands."

"Why?" she said simply. "It was my doing. I was not . . . coerced."

She meant that she was not raped, he thought grimly. He very much doubted she'd known what she was doing.

The gentleman, however—or rather, the *scoundrel*—almost certainly had known.

But Kate was still watching him, her eyes unwavering. "It was, quite honestly, an awful experience," she confessed. "I thought I loved him. That it would be somehow magical."

Edward elevated both eyebrows. "Ah, the fiancé!" he murmured.

Her lashes swept down. "Yes."

"Who was he?"

She gave a little shake of her head. "Just an old family acquaintance," she said. "He was beautiful, and so charming. But too late I learnt that I loved an illusion; that I merely idolized him for being all those things that I was not."

Kate's eyes were shimmering dangerously, he realized. Edward reached up and ran a thumb beneath her eye, but the tears hadn't spilled.

He resolved that they would not.

"I'm sorry, Kate, that your lover was not what you'd hoped," he said. "You're the sort of woman who deserves to have her dreams come true."

"I think so, too," she said simply. "And lately . . . well, lately, I have dreamt of you."

He shook his head, but drew her fully against him all the same. "Kate, my dear," he murmured into her hair, "we must be mad. Both of us."

"I am not mad," she said, her cheek pressed to the wall of his chest. "I am perfectly aware of what this is, and what it is not. I know you will not stay here. That you're getting well and must go back to your life soon. That we will not meet again."

He suspected she was right, and knew that he should have been glad. But her words instead filled him with an inexorable sadness; a longing so deep he ached with it.

"Kate." Edward's hand sculpted the small of her back as her lips brushed his again.

There was no more need to talk. She was Kate, and she desired him. And he would do his best to be—at least for tonight—the lover she wanted. The man she deserved.

And yet he could not mistake something hot and burning behind his own eyes. The longing he felt for her seemed to be rushing toward a crescendo of its own. The ache seemed drawn from a well of sadness and longing he could not explain. And for better or worse, he was going to slake it.

Kate's lips softened beneath his as he kissed her, hot and openmouthed, with his eyes wide open. Her hands moved over him again, then began to tug eagerly at his shirt, drawing it from the waist of his breeches until it billowed nearly free. Like warm silk, her tongue slid willingly along his, allowing him to plunge deep.

Edward knew precisely what he was doing—and thought he knew precisely how his body would react. He could not have been more wrong. For when Kate's slender hands slid beneath his shirt, raw need surged again, and left him shivering beneath her artless touch.

She touched him tentatively at first, and then more urgently. Gingerly, he moved her nearer the bed. Pulled free the ribbon of her wrapper. Pushed it over her slender shoulders and listened to it whisper its way onto the floor.

Kate made a sound of pleasure, and began to push off his shirt. Impatiently, Edward yanked the last of it free, then stripped it off and over his head. Kate's eyes widened innocently. And then—like the siren she secretly was, he feared—she set her lips to his breastbone, her tongue stroking ever so lightly, drawing a ribbon of heat up his flesh.

"Edward," she whispered as she moved her lips over his skin, "I've wanted to do this from that first day; from the moment we took your shirt off. You're so exquisitely, perfectly *male*."

At those words, raw lust twisted deep in his belly, an agonizing knot of sweet, throbbing pain. His erection pulsed insistently between his legs. And any hesitance he might have felt vanished on the sound of her next sigh.

He kissed her again, and pushed her gently down on the bed, wedging one knee between hers. She fell back into the softness on a sigh, smelling of sunlight and of grass after a spring rain; all innocence and sweet seduction. He followed her down, his face buried against her neck. Kate's body arched beneath his weight, her dark brown hair scrubbing the pillowslip.

On the night table, the lamp flickered, casting dancing shadows across the white sheets. "Now, Edward," she said throatily, her hands pushing at the band of his breeches.

But she was not ready for *now*.

He kissed her again, exultantly, then slowly moved away, pressing butterfly kisses along her throat. Then he twisted around to sit on the bed, the floor cool against his feet as he propped his hands on his knees.

For an instant, he tried to talk himself out of what he was about to do. But it was far too late, and he was far too lost. Behind him, Kate made an impatient sound, and drew a fingertip down his back. Edward reached over and turned down the wick until it was nothing but a glow in the darkness. His need for her was like a palpable thing, the ache in him so deep he wondered already how he would ever extricate himself from this.

But that was a problem for the morrow. He and Kate, they were the here and now. Edward jerked to his feet and began to slip loose the buttons of his breeches.

He heard the mattress creak behind him. "Edward—?"

He cut a glance over his bare shoulder. Kate was on her

knees behind him, her fingers drawing up the hem of her nightgown. But her eyes were fixed upon his buttons.

"No," he rasped. "Leave it on."

Her hands fell. "Must I?"

He slipped the last button free. "Leave it on *if you wish*," he clarified.

Apparently, she did not wish.

Seizing the hems in both hands, Kate stripped the thin cotton up and over her head, tossing it into the darkness behind him. His hands froze in the act of pushing down what remained of his clothing, and his throat seemed to catch.

The glorious silk curtain of her hair had slid over one shoulder to spill about her feet. In the candlelight, its chestnut sheen warmed to russet red. Her breasts were high and round, almost surprisingly full, with small, dusky-pink nipples already erect. He let his gaze trail down the soft swell of her belly, all the way to the thatch of hair between her thighs, and felt something carnal stir deep in his loins.

It was the male need to have her. To take. To dominate. To thrust himself inside Kate and worship her pure femininity.

He closed his eyes, shucked off what was left of his clothing, and crawled back onto the bed, taking her down into the softness with him. He kissed her again, slowly thrusting as his hand tangled in her silky hair. Kate began to move urgently against him, her hands moving hungrily if inexpertly over him.

After a time, he forced his breath to calm. Twisted the burning lust down with a fierce chokehold so that he might pleasure her properly. He rolled to one side and stretched out along her length to face her. He tilted up her chin with his finger. Kissed the tip of her perfect nose.

"Kate, love, are you sure?"

She nodded, and reached for him. "Oh, Edward," she whispered, "I am *so* sure."

It was the sound of his name on her lips that nearly broke him.

"I am sure of you," she went on. "I am sure this is right."

God help him, but he was sure, too.

And even then, Edward knew that a part of him was holding the truth at bay. He felt in that moment as if he could have remained by her side forever, lost in the sweetness of her. Lost in the solitude of this place, and the steady warmth of Kate's gaze.

And he knew, just as surely, that it would never be. That he was taking what he did not deserve. Tainting, perhaps, a pure innocence. And for an instant, he felt the hot press of tears behind his eyes again.

"Make love to me," she murmured. "Pleasure me. *Please*."

He hadn't the strength to say the word that honor required. Perhaps he hadn't any honor at all. He did not know.

"I will, love," he assured her. "In time. But you're the sort of woman a man should love slowly."

She reached for him then, but he caught her wrist, gently restraining her. Then he pushed her over, dragging his leg over hers. "*Slowly*, Kate," he said again, his tongue flicking out to stroke her nipple.

"*Aah*," she said.

Capturing her breast fully in his mouth, Edward suckled her, drawing the plump flesh into his mouth, then stroking the tip with his tongue. Kate cried out in the darkness, her hips arching hard beneath the weight of his thigh.

"Be a good girl," he murmured, brushing his lips down her breastbone.

Instead, she tangled her fingers in his hair on a soft, needy cry.

He forced her to still with the weight of his arms and legs, kissing and suckling each breast in turn. She whispered his name. He was lost in the sound of her voice.

She was like no other woman he'd made love to before; he knew this even though he could remember no woman before her. He had the feeling that, even were his memory intact, he still could not have remembered them.

Kate sighed again, artless and eager. He wanted her; wanted, he feared, more than this mere moment in time. And when her hips began to arch restlessly, Edward set a hand alongside her inner knee and drew it slowly upward, skimming along flesh so warm and so soft he wanted to drown in it.

He drew the hand higher, until he reached the nest of curls that guarded her center. Kate's eyes were closed now, her mouth open on a soundless cry. He stroked deep, almost brushing her nub.

"Open your eyes, love," he whispered.

They flared wide, her pupils dilated in the darkness. "Edward," she murmured.

"I want to touch you, Kate," he said. "I want to make you mine."

"Touch me," she whispered, her eyelids heavy. "Touch me, Edward."

On that, he plunged one finger into her and felt her body spasm with the shock. She moaned, a sound that was not a sound but something that vibrated from her deep into him. He stroked again and again. Kate's breath sped up, one hand fisting in the sheets.

His thumb found the wet, trembling jewel and lightly stroked. Kate cried out, then murmured his name again. He felt caught in the madness. And foolishly, he let that deep urge to dominate get the better of him. He let himself say the thing that was not true; let himself make the promise—or the threat—he could not keep.

"Kate, this is mine," he rasped. "Do you understand?"

She shut her eyes and nodded almost imperceptibly, her hair scrubbing the pillow.

His breath was coming hard now, his body focused on just one thing. *Claiming her.* "Do you understand?" he demanded. "If we do this—no, *regardless*—this is mine. *You* are mine."

"Yes." The word was soft, thready with need. She swallowed hard, her throat working up and down. "I am yours, Edward. Make it so."

He pushed inside her again, two fingers now, his thumb lightly circling. Kate cried out, and began to pant, her head turning a little into the pillow. Again and again he moved, the silken muscles of her passage tugging at him. Urging him.

Desire throbbed inside him now; not just his cock but the whole of his being. He could not wait. He dragged himself fully over her, and pushed her knees apart with his own. Guiding himself between her legs, he pushed himself inside and felt her stiffen at the invasion.

"It's all right, love," he whispered, drawing out ever so slightly.

"I know," she whispered, reaching up for him.

Edward lowered his weight onto her and took her mouth in a kiss both fierce and unyielding. A kiss that truly claimed her. He thrust deep, parrying her tongue, intoxicated by her taste.

He drew back and thrust his cock again. Kate cried out, and drew up her knees to cradle him. He set his arms rigidly against the mattress, lifted, and rocked into her, praying for strength.

It was as if Kate knew just how to madden him. Tilting her hips, she let her warm hands slide down his back, then down his buttocks, drawing him to her with unerring womanly instinct. He felt his body shudder, thrust again, and squeezed his eyes shut.

This was making love.

The thought flashed through his mind, clear as a lightning bolt.

This was rare. Singular and perfect. This, he dimly realized, was what it meant to be as one with a lover. Beneath him Kate was moving more urgently. Ruthlessly, Edward bit back his impatience and set a steady rhythm, matching his movements to hers. Kate made a sound of pleasure, and hitched one leg around his waist.

"Yes, love," he crooned. "Show me what you need."

"*You.*" Her nails raked his flesh, setting his back aquiver.

Each thrust was better, sent him spiraling higher, pushed him nearer the edge. He could fall in love with her, he realized; perhaps already had. He pushed away the truth that kept threatening, and followed her pace, determined to pleasure her. Determined to bind her to him.

She cried out, and arched hard against him. He stroked deep, and stroked again, urging himself against her at that sweet, perfect angle. And then her head tipped back into the pillow, and Kate shook beneath him, her flesh drawing his. Her fingers curled into the muscle of his buttocks, and her knees clasped his hips until the shuddering rush of pleasure finally slowed. Edward pushed deep one last time, and felt reality splinter.

It was as if his very soul rushed out of him with his seed, flooding like a relentless surge into Kate. He thrust again, felt the tendons of his neck and back draw taut as a bowstring. Felt Kate's arms come around him, drawing him down and down and down.

Down into a cosmos that went beyond his understanding.

Down into her exquisite embrace.

CHAPTER 8

In Which Fendershot Sets to Work

Still a little heavy-eyed from lack of sleep, Edward dined the following morning with Miss Wentworth, a little troubled she might somehow see the truth in his eyes. What would she say, he wondered, if she knew what he and Kate had done last night—*all* of last night—save for those last three or four hours spent in sweet oblivion?

She would not approve.

Hell, *he* did not approve.

But he'd done it, and given the chance would likely do it again, despite the fact that he could feel himself sliding near a perilous precipice. Though he was sure he'd bedded many beautiful women—and likely without a great deal of forethought—Kate was dangerous.

Kate was worth forethought. And afterthought. Actually, Kate was becoming bloody near an obsession.

It should not be so, Edward reminded himself. She was not glamorous or even classically beautiful. She was quiet, almost demure at times. But he no longer believed her plain. No, not remotely.

Still, however lovely she was to him, a woman he'd just met simply could not constitute the whole of his life. It was not wise—especially for her. Sooner or later, reality would return to him whether he wished it to or not. And then, yes, he would have to leave her.

And what then? For either of them? What would be left save the ashes of a fire that had burned so fierce but so fleetingly?

But there was, of course, one thing far worse than ashes he might leave behind. He could leave Kate with child.

In the light of day, it chilled him to realize how cavalier he'd been about that. Kate might pay a terrible price for his recklessness; the price of bearing a child to a man she didn't know.

If Kate could not see the horror in that, then he must see it for her.

"Edward, more tea?"

He looked up to see Miss Wentworth at the sideboard, the pot held aloft.

"Oh." He smiled absently. "Thank you, no."

She returned to the table and set her own cup back down with a clatter. "What can have got into Kate this morning?" she murmured. "My sister is never late for anything."

"Strictly speaking, she's not yet late," he said, extracting his pocket watch. "She told me we would leave at eight."

He had already given Miss Wentworth the good news about his ability to grasp numerals again. Now she spared her attention only for his watch, which was, admittedly, exquisite.

"Yes," said Miss Wentworth absently, "but Kate never misses breakfast. Edward, may I see your watch?"

He lifted a curious gaze to hers. "But of course."

He unfastened the chain and passed it to her. Miss Wentworth stared at the inscription, turning it this way and that in her hand.

"What is this mark?" she asked after a moment had passed.

"What, that little design?"

"Yes." She turned the watch and tapped on the small engraving below the inscription.

He took out his eyeglasses and leaned nearer. "I believe it is properly called a lozenge," he said. "It is a heraldic mark used by ladies in lieu of a full coat of arms."

"I thought as much," said Miss Wentworth. She turned it back around and stared at it. "This is the style used by a widow or a spinster, isn't it?"

Edward considered it. "I have no idea," he said. "Why?"

Miss Wentworth caught his gaze meaningfully across the table. "It must belong to your aunt who gave you this watch," she said, turning around in her chair. "I suppose Kate and Peppie were so busy reading the inscription, they never studied the design. Jasper?"

The young man darted in from the corridor with a bow. "Yes, miss?"

"Fetch Fendershot for me, will you?"

A moment later, Bellecombe's butler, a tall, stately man of at least sixty years, came in. "Mr. Edward, Miss Nancy," he said, bowing. "How may I be of service?"

"You know a little something about heraldry, Fendershot, don't you?" she said.

"My father was a clerk with the College of Arms," he said. "I know a little. And his late Lordship kept a good collection of heraldic materials in the library."

Miss Wentworth passed him the watch. "What do you make of this?"

He gave it the briefest of glances. "Those are the arms of a noble widow," he replied. "The shape and the little ribbon tell us that."

"And the symbols?"

"A combination of the lady's father's arms and her late husband's arms," he said, "or it should be, if done properly."

Miss Wentworth's gaze caught Edward's again. "I think your Aunt Isabel is likely your mother's sister," she mused. "Were she your father's sister, she would have used the family's full coat of arms, wouldn't she? But perhaps she wanted your grandfather's arms on the watch?"

"I don't know," said Edward. "The etiquette of heraldry is beyond me."

"It is beyond most people," Fendershot murmured, still studying the lozenge.

Miss Wentworth returned her attention to the butler. "What are the chances, Fendershot, you could identify who this Isabel is?"

The old man shook his head. "Very difficult, I'm afraid," he said. "But I would enjoy nothing so much as a morning spent perusing your grandfather's old books. May I keep the watch today, Mr. Edward?"

Edward waved his hand dismissively "Oh, by all means," he said, "but please do not put yourself out on my account."

Indeed, a little part of him wished to snatch back the watch, and circumvent the inevitable. But the butler had already vanished from the room, his morning's work in hand. A moment later, Kate dashed in, already attired in a carriage dress of dark blue, a cloak over her arm.

"Heavens, I overslept!" Her gray eyes flared with heat as they lit upon him. "Quick, Nan, pour my tea whilst I grab a piece of toast. I've sent Jasper for the carriage."

Ten minutes later, Edward was helping Kate on with her cloak.

"I'll fetch my wrap and my reticule," said Miss Wentworth, rushing from the room.

Edward followed Kate to the open door. Then, at the last instant, his patience slipped. He caught her by the arm, and spun her around, setting her back to the wall. Kate's eyes widened with shock.

Heedless, he kissed her until she was breathless, kissed her deeply and possessively, with his lips and his tongue and his hands, until his breath came rough and her arms were entwined about his neck.

Kate. Kate. Kate. It was as if her name coursed through his blood, driven by the very beat of his heart.

She maddened him. He needed her. Desperately, he feared.

When at last sanity returned, he set his forehead to hers, searching for the words he needed. "Damn it, Kate," he finally said, "I don't know where this is going, but—"

"*Shh*," she murmured. "Don't talk, Edward. Don't ruin it."

"We have to talk about it," he said. "This is not . . . This is not *nothing*, Kate. I don't know what it is, but it is *something*. Something . . . vast and near incomprehensible to me."

"Not now," she said, brushing her lips over his cheek. "Jasper is coming."

Edward forced his mind back to the present, and heard rapid footsteps approaching from the castle's great hall.

He came reluctantly away from the wall, turned with a muted smile, and offered Kate his arm.

THE DRIVE TO Taunton was not overly long. Kate had ordered her landau, which was driven by a coachman who looked to have been born a century earlier. The day was frosty, but the ladies wanted the top folded down. Edward was glad to oblige them, praying that a brisk drive might clear his head—or at least cool his ardor.

After a long drive through the Somerset countryside and half a dozen picturesque villages, they reached the outskirts of Taunton.

Edward could not have said precisely when it dawned on him that the passing shops and houses looked familiar; it was more of a slow, uneasy realization. When he saw a squat, stone bell tower in the distance, he was certain.

"What is that place?" he asked abruptly.

"Staplegrove," said Miss Wentworth, pointing over the trees. "Richard's cousin is vicar there."

But Kate, more perceptive, had caught the unease in his voice. "Have you been here before, Edward?"

Slowly, he nodded. "Yes," he said. "I am very nearly certain of it."

"Could you be *from* here?" Miss Wentworth's pretty brow furrowed. "I really think not. Richard would have recognized you. Likely *we* would have recognized you."

Since Richard Burnham had come twice to offer his prayers for Edward's swift recovery, Edward expected she was right.

Burnham was an astute gentleman with a piercing gaze who had almost certainly come not to minster to Edward's spiritual needs, but rather to reassure himself of his beloved's well-being.

Edward had done his best to put the young man at ease, and to appear as unthreatening as a man of his height and bearing could do. The rector had gone away satisfied that at least his intended bride—if not Edward's soul—was entirely safe. But Burham certainly had not recognized him.

"What about that inn, Edward?" Miss Wentworth pointed in the opposite direction. "Does it look familiar?"

"Nancy, let be," Kate warned, settling back against the banquette. "Eventually Edward will remember, and until then, pressing him won't help. Now, have you your shopping list to hand?"

Edward did indeed try to put it from his mind but he could not escape the uncomfortable sense of familiarity. He told himself that it was a good thing. But it didn't feel like a happy thing. No, the familiarity carried a haunting sort of sadness, and brought with it that weighty sense of obligation that had been troubling him the last few days.

His mood notwithstanding, the visit was a commercial success for the shopkeepers of Taunton. It was a town of some size, and as Kate had predicted, there was no difficulty in finding haberdashers, hatters, and bootmakers sufficient for the average gentleman's needs.

After graciously loaning him a generous sum of money—
and teasing him that she meant to keep his pocket watch
as collateral—Kate left him to his own devices, agreeing
they would meet for luncheon at the hostelry where the carriage had been left. The ladies set off in the opposite direction along the high street, Kate casting him one last, heated
glance over her shoulder as she went.

After recovering from the memories *that* engendered,
Edward went from shop to shop ordering—and in some
cases outright purchasing—those basic bits of kit that a
country house visit might require, and giving Bellecombe
Castle as the delivery address for those things requiring
tailoring. But all the while he remained on edge, searching
every face he saw, waiting for that inevitable moment when
someone would recognize him and shout out his name.

It did not come.

He had been so very certain it would. That today would
be the day. Why? Because of some squat church tower that
looked vaguely familiar?

But there was no denying the familiarity of that scene, and
no denying the heavy weight it left in the pit of his stomach.

Nonetheless, no one spoke to him save to thank him for
his custom and to press receipts into his hand. Having deliberately left his stick in the carriage to keep both hands free,
Edward went about his business, trying to take comfort in
how little pain he felt in his leg. And that free hand came in
handy; by one o'clock, he was carrying enough packages to
put a simpering London dandy to the blush.

After they had dined on a luncheon of cold chicken and
late vegetables, Kate sent for her carriage and the three of
them returned in the direction from whence they'd come,
Miss Wentworth teasing him unmercifully about his outrageous collection of boxes.

Having taken the rearward seat, Edward was watching
Taunton vanish in their wake when the carriage went clat-

tering over the railroad track. Just then, he caught sight of a gray-haired woman in brown descending from an open carriage near the station.

It was as if he'd been struck in the head by a lightning bolt. He realized at once that she was known to him.

Well known to him.

Indeed, he was already groping desperately in his head for her name when she turned around to stare at him, her posture stiff as a statue, her hand held up to a girl of perhaps twelve years who remained in the carriage, waiting to clamber down after her.

Still seated, the girl, too, turned, as if to discover what had caught the woman's attention. Her gaze caught Edward's. Then, with an expression that was perplexed—almost injured—she lifted her hand in greeting, and gave a tenuous little wave.

It was as if he froze inside.

It was Annabelle.

Dear God.

Annie and her grandmother, Mrs. Granger. They were still staring after him as if he were a ghost. Which of course they might do, since he was supposed to be . . . be where? Where the hell was he supposed to be?

Where had he gone after leaving Mrs. Granger's cottage?

The house. The damned house he'd taken from Reggie. What was the bloody thing called?

Heatherfields.

Had he arrived there?

No. No, he had taken a wrong turn. Seen a magnificent castle down in a vale. Not Reggie's little manor. Irritated, he had turned around and given Aragon his head . . .

Bits and pieces of his memory began to go *click, click, click*, sliding back into their logical places like beads on an abacus, making for a horrific sum total.

He had taken Aragon from his happy retirement in Mrs.

Granger's stable. He had been on his way to Heatherfields, to see what might be made of the estate he'd taken from Reggie.

Lord Reginald Hoke.

Lord Reginald Hoke *of Heatherfields*.

He could hear Anstruther's disgust in his head.

Left that dunderheid the hoose and three tenant farms to piss away, he had said. *Not my place to say, mind, but I niver thought him a good influence . . .*

He could see the picture being laid out before his very eyes. Knew his face must look white as a sheet. He could feel the hope and the joy draining out of him, and he knew without a doubt what that hard black knot inside him was. It was his heart.

The ladies were arguing over a certain pair of shoes they should or should not have bought. They were not looking at him. Could not see him for the liar he was.

And suddenly a flood of thoughts came roaring like a swollen river through his head. Rising in waves, like white, frothy peaks in his brain. A crashing, rushing reality. And a history. He looked about, and recognized the milliner's shop on his left.

He could see the yellow bonnet that had hung in the window the summer before Colombo and Trincomalee. Maria had wanted it. He hadn't the money. But that was before the fire. Before the army. He could see the encampment again; they had been out shooting. Someone . . . someone had drowned. A terrible tragedy.

Maria?

No. Maria died in England.

The drowning—that was Ceylon. Edward shook his head, attempting to reorder his thoughts. To sort what mattered from what did not. Ceylon didn't matter; it was over. But Maria mattered. *Annie* mattered.

"Edward?"

Miss Wentworth was looking at him strangely across the carriage.

Recalled to the present, he swallowed hard. "Yes?"

"Are you all right?" she gently prodded. "You look as though you've seen a ghost."

Even then, he was not perfectly sure why he hesitated. Perhaps because the thoughts—the memories—were still so jumbled in his head.

"No," he rasped. "No, I'm fine."

Miss Wentworth smiled, and returned her attention to Kate and the shoes. She was quite sure they had been more green than blue. And the heels either too high or too low.

Faced with no alternative, Edward did what he made it a strict policy never to do. He took the coward's way out.

He was not proud of it. But he pretended to go to sleep anyway, tipping his tall hat down over his eyes and crossing his arms over his chest.

"Look," said Miss Wentworth after the business with the shoes was settled. "Edward has drifted off, Kate! Indeed, I'm a little worried. He didn't look at all well this morning."

"Did he not?" said Kate vaguely. "Perhaps he didn't sleep well."

"Obviously, he didn't," she said tartly. "Something must have kept him awake last night. Perhaps we should call Dr. Fitch?"

"There was a barn owl, I think," Kate lied. "Up on the parapet. I didn't sleep well myself."

"A barn owl?" Miss Wentworth said incredulously. "Why would a barn owl be on a parapet?"

"I have no idea," said Kate. "Perhaps it was some other sort of owl."

"Perhaps you have owls in your belfry," said her sister.

They squabbled good-naturedly all the way home.

Edward passed the time attempting to breathe beneath his hat brim, and trying to think of heroic ways in which a gentleman might kill himself—then, on his next feeble breath, reassuring himself that things could not possibly get worse.

The rest of the day was to prove him wrong.

Over and over and over again.

UPON THEIR RETURN, the trio was met in the great hall by Fendershot and Jasper. The latter was soon staggering under bandboxes and cloaks, while the former was motioning them into the library.

"The most amazing thing, Your Ladyship," he was saying to Kate. "Do just come this way."

All three of them followed the butler into the library to see a stack of books on one of the long oak tables, and Edward's watch laid open on a velvet pillow, a magnifying glass beside it.

Fendershot cast an expectant gaze over them, then drew a deep breath. "The more I studied the lozenge—it was, you see, that unusual griffin *segreant* that caught my eye—and my great-uncle, you see, was once in service to the Earl of Oakley, and I remember he had a—a sort of silver tray that the earl gave him in honor of his many years of—"

"It's all right, Fendershot." Kate laid a hand on his arm. "You needn't fully explain. It is clear you've seen something familiar?"

Fendershot drew a deep breath. "Just so, my lady," he said, pointing to the watch. "This part of the lozenge is taken from the Earl of Oakley's coat of arms."

"I do not know Lord Oakley," said Kate. "But then, I know scarcely anyone. Who is he?"

"I don't know who he is *now*," said Fendershot. "A cousin of the sixth earl, I believe, for the sixth earl had only daughters, two of them. And his title, unlike your own, could descend only patrilineally."

Kate was nodding. "Only from father to son."

"Just so," said the butler. "Moreover, if we refer to your

grandfather's old peerage, we will see that Oakley's eldest daughter was named Isabel and his youngest was named Caroline."

Edward felt a rush of emotion; something cold and a little sickening.

But Kate and her sister were studying the book that lay open beside his gold pocket watch.

"So, if we follow this—" Fendershot was drawing his finger along a line of type.

No, let's not, thought Edward.

"—then we see that Isabel married Baron Keltonbrooke," the butler droned on, "and became Isabel, Lady Keltonbrooke, now his relic. Further, my lady, it is important to note that Baron Keltonbrooke was an only child—"

"Yes, yes," said Miss Wentworth, leaning over the book, "but we don't want to learn all these names. What can they have to do with Edward?"

"I'm merely explaining that Lady Keltonbrooke has no nephews on her husband's side," said Fendershot patiently. "She hasn't *anyone* on her husband's side. And she hasn't any children, either. Moreover, she has only two nephews on her sister Caroline's side."

"Yes?" said Kate, her brows knotted. "And who was her sister again?"

"She was Lady Caroline Smithers," said Fendershot, pausing dramatically, "*but she married the Duke of Dunthorpe!*"

"Oh, my God!" squealed Miss Wentworth, clapping her hands. "*Is Edward a long-lost duke?* Edward! Kate! How romantic!"

"Er—well, no," said Fendershot, "but I'm fairly certain he's Lord Niall Edward Dagenham Quartermaine, the duke's second son."

Edward must have made a choking sound. Kate had turned to look at him.

"Edward," she whispered. "There were initials. On your valise. *Those* initials. Fendershot must be right. Mustn't he?"

He shook his head. "No," he said quietly. "Not . . . exactly."

KATE WATCHED A strange emotion pass over Edward's face. No, not emotion. It was more an absence of emotion, bizarre and a little chilling.

Indeed, he had been behaving more than a little oddly since leaving Taunton. She had not for one moment believed he had been asleep on the drive home. She had assumed—mistakenly, she now feared—that he'd merely wished to avoid Nancy's nattering over shoes.

But it was not that. No. He had seen something. *He knew something.*

"Lord Niall Quartermaine!" said Nancy effusively. "It does suit you."

"*Do not* call me that," he uttered. "I was never called Niall. Nor do I now use a title."

His voice was cold, and as absent of emotion as his expression. Nancy's face fell, and she looked at him a little woundedly.

Kate drew a deep breath, and clasped her hands before her. "Well, Fendershot," she said, "you are, as always, a marvel. Thank you. Now, would the two of you kindly excuse Edward and me? We will have particulars to discuss, I think, in light of this shocking development."

The butler bowed. "But of course."

Nancy opened her mouth to protest, then, with another glance at Edward, followed Fendershot from the room.

"This is not welcome news, Edward, is it?" Kate managed as soon as the door was shut.

Edward had begun to roam the room, which was not especially large. "No," he said flatly. "I fear it is not."

Alarmed at his tone, Kate followed him to the windows.

Hands clasped tightly—too tightly—behind his back, Edward stood looking blindly out at Bellecombe's formal rose garden, now bare save for those last, dry leaves that still clung hopelessly to the rose canes. His posture was utterly rigid, like that of a soldier, and the soft laugh lines about his mouth and eyes had hardened into something far more brittle.

"You remembered something on the drive, did you not?" Kate tried to sound matter-of-fact.

He did not answer. It was as if he had gone elsewhere, and could not even hear her.

"Edward?" Lightly, she touched his arm, and felt him flinch.

After a moment, he spoke. "You have been nothing but kind to me, Kate." His diction was as flawlessly upper class as ever, but his voice seemed to belong to a different man. "And I owe you, of all people, an explanation. But it is to be an unpleasant one, I fear."

She let her hand drop. "Edward," she whispered, "Edward, please, you're scaring me."

He said no more, as if turning something in his mind. As if determining how much to tell her, or how he might soften the blow. "Kate," he finally rasped. "Last night I lost my senses. I said things to you that I'd no right to say. I suggested things. I'm . . . so sorry."

Kate felt a sort of cold numbness flooding through her body and into her extremities, and for a moment she feared she might faint, because the most horrific thought had just struck her.

"Dear God," she murmured. "Edward. Please tell me you . . . you are not *married*?"

"No." Finally, he turned from the window, but his eyes were soulless. "No, I have never been married. I was once betrothed. Or believed myself betrothed. But she died whilst I was in the army."

"Oh." Kate's face fell. "Oh, Edward. I'm so sorry."

He shrugged as if it didn't matter. "Perhaps it would not have lasted," he said. "She was young. And her family disapproved."

"I . . . oh, I see."

"I very much doubt you do," Edward returned. "But that is neither here nor there."

It was very much here and there to Kate, but she had grown a little frightened of the look in his eyes. She said nothing, and let the shoe hang.

"Your butler suggests I'm the son of the Duke of Dunthorpe," he said. "It is true that I was born to the Duchess of Dunthorpe and called for some time Lord Edward Quartermaine. But when I was ten it was explained to me that I was not, after all, the duke's son."

"Oh." Kate dragged in a breath. "Oh, *Edward*. That is terrible."

"Oh, I think the duke rather relished telling me," said Edward, the corners of his mouth drawing taut. "He had never been fond of me, for I looked very little like him. Indeed, I looked much like my mother who, I gather, had not the strongest of moral fiber."

"Still, what a cruel thing to do!" Kate cried. "To . . . to tell such a thing to a child! And really, the law does not allow him to put you aside. If you were born to the Duchess of Dunthorpe, the law concludes you to be his son. One cannot simply declare a thing to be . . . to be *not so*."

Edward shrugged, his profile harsh and stark against the window's light. It was a dismissive, almost haughty gesture. "The law is one thing, and the practicalities another," he said. "In the heat of an argument, my mother made the mistake of throwing my parentage in the duke's face. And that, as they say, was that."

"And that was *what*?" Kate whispered. "What happened?"

Edward turned at last to look at her—to truly look at her. "He told her to get me out of his house, and to take me to my father where I belonged," he said calmly, "and that if she could not bring herself to do it, he would put the both of us out, and petition the House of Lords for divorce. And he would have got it, too."

The feeling of cold and lightheadedness had returned. "And she . . . *she did that?* She took you from your home? To your father? But who was he?"

"Not a nice man," said Edward, the words clipped. "Indeed, he was the sort of man, frankly, whose son should probably not be welcomed into your home. And beyond that, I would prefer to say no more."

"But you are still the duke's son in the eyes of the law," said Kate, "if he did not take legal action."

Something like rage fleetingly flared in Edward's eyes. "If that is the straw your kind heart clings to, my dear, then it is a tenuous reed, indeed, that you grasp." He thrust out a rock-steady arm, and pointed at the long library table. "I may well be listed in those fine, leather-bound tomes of your grandfather's, but no one imagines me to be anything but what I am—the bastard of a beautiful but flighty duchess, and a vile piece of trash who was not fit to wipe the dirt from her shoes, let alone seduce her into his . . . into his . . ."

He spun away, back to the windows, pinching hard at the bridge of his nose.

"Christ!" he said. "I cannot believe this has happened. That I have dragged you, of all people, into this quagmire of filth."

This time Kate did not touch him. "Edward, listen to me," she said warningly, "this has happened because we had an accident—an accident which I caused—and that is the end of it. Moreover, I do not concern myself with what others think or wish to believe—"

"Well, you had better concern yourself," he snapped. "If you cannot think of your own good name, Kate, you had damned well better think of your sister's. She wishes to marry the rector, you will recall. And then there is Lady

Upshaw. She has, what—? Two or three daughters in the schoolroom? And they are about to descend upon you within the next few days?"

"Edward, I'm sorry for all this, but your worry is premature," said Kate, drawing herself up to her full height. "As to Richard, he's a better man than to concern himself with such foolishness. As to my aunt, she's not bringing her daughters, and even if she were, it is my opinion that carries the weight in this house. Do not for one moment think it otherwise."

"Christ!" he said again.

"*Edward.*" This time she did touch him, but lightly. "Edward, do not fret so. *Please.* Listen to me. I'm glad your memory is returning. It will be all right. It *will.*"

But Kate was shaken. She could not escape the fear that her life had just changed inexorably; that it had just turned as brown and bare as the rose canes clattering in her garden, casting off the last shriveled leaves of autumn.

And there were still more shoes left to drop; Kate didn't deceive herself. She still felt like Marie Antoinette with the guillotine cranked but halfway up.

Moreover, it dawned on her, too, that the house was no longer silent; that the sound of servants' feet had begun to fly up and down the passageways and stairs. Surely Edward's news had not carried far and wide already?

Suddenly, there was a sharp knock upon the library door.

"Kate?" said Nancy, breathless. "Oh, Kate. You had better come out."

Kate spun around to glower at the door. "What?" she snapped.

For a heartbeat, Nancy hesitated. "Kate, I'm afraid Mamma has come," she finally said, "and I think . . . well, I think you won't be happy with her surprise."

Kate looked down to see her hands were shaking. The weakness made her angry with herself. "Well," she said with asperity, "you will excuse me, Edward. It seems my guests have arrived."

"Kate." Edward caught her arm, his face fleetingly softening. "Oh, Kate. We really need to talk further. There are things I must say."

"I know, but not now," Kate whispered. "I must go and deal with what will doubtless be but the first of Aurélie's cock-ups. As to you, Edward, you're our welcome guest until you wish to leave, so I insist you come, too."

Kate strode into the great hall to see poor Jasper staggering beneath another towering heap of boxes that Nancy was helping to steady, and Aurélie warbling in her pidgin French while simultaneously trying to kiss Fendershot and Peppie on both cheeks, a hatbox dangling from one elbow and Filou, her flatulent pug, draped over the other. A huge red hat was perched upon a towering pile of inky curls, and trimmed with a black feather that curled elegantly backward, almost brushing her shoulder.

On the threshold, Kate paused. "Mamma fancies herself French," she murmured over her shoulder, "but it's mostly just a show."

"Good Lord," said Edward quietly. "*She* is your mother?"

"Remarkable, isn't it?"

"How many carriages does she require?" He was craning to look out the door.

"Heaven only knows. Mamma hates the train." Then, with a parting smile, Kate stepped into the fray. "Aurélie!" she said, opening her arms. "It is very bad of you to come early."

"Oh, *ma chérie, ma chérie!*" her mother declared, flinging a hatbox wildly aside. "*Alors*, give poor *maman* a kiss. Oooh, how I have missed you."

The pug oblivious, Aurélie swept Kate up in a cloud of ermine, eau de cologne, and dog hair, then set her away again. "Well, Katherine, how do you go on? Oh, *ma fille!* Your hair! What have you done to it?"

"Why, not a thing," said Kate, wriggling from the embrace.

"That is my very point." Aurélie's lips made a pretty moue. "Oh, *ma chérie*, you look like a brown mouse."

"Yes, well." Kate forced a smile. "Where is *le comte?* Lady Julia?"

"La, somewhere!" Aurélie made an absent gesture over one shoulder. "Sir Francis wished to stop in the village whilst I brought on the baggage. But we are speaking of the hair, *ma petite chou!* In Paris, you know, the braids are all the thing, *oui?* Very high, very glamor— *Ça alors, who is this—?"* Suddenly, her eyes widened dramatically.

She had noticed Edward.

Kate stepped back a bit. "Aurélie, this is Mr. Quartermaine, who has been our guest a few days. Mr. Quartermaine, this is my mother, Mrs. Wentworth—and, er, Filou."

Kate's mother was a beautiful, almost fairylike creature with inky black hair and flashing blue eyes who appeared at least a decade shy of her years. Men always looked twice—often thrice—at Aurélie, but Edward's gaze was inscrutable, and utterly without affect.

Aurélie's eyes, however, widened even further. "Ah!" she said lightly. "Mr. *Quartermaine,* is it?"

"Indeed." Edward bowed coolly, and brought her hand to his lips. "A pleasure, *madame.*"

Aurélie gave a light laugh. Then, before he could straighten up, she cut Kate a dark—and very knowing—glance, sharply arching one brow.

"Mr. Quartermaine and I had a little dust-up near the village road." Kate explained. "I fear he took the worst of it, and was unconscious for a brief time."

"*Quel dommage!*" declared Aurélie, her gaze taking in his wound. "And such a pretty man, too. Ah, well! It is time for Filou's nap, *ma fille.* The road—oh, la!—you cannot fathom the filth! The fatigue! We have been mercilessly jostled. Oh, but wait! Where is Kate's surprise?"

With a sly smile, Aurélie turned to look through the open door and down the steps. Suddenly on edge, Kate leaned around to look past her. And there he stood.

Dear God.

Suddenly, Kate couldn't get her breath.

Of all the riffraff Aurélie might have dragged with her from London, she'd chosen Lord Reginald Hoke, Kate's former fiancé? Of course Aurélie and Reggie did run in the same fast London circles; Kate knew that. And it wasn't as if Kate didn't see him on rare occasions.

She was always civil, and Reggie was always speciously fawning. It was a polite, two-minute charade. But this was different. This felt as if he'd come to invade her peace. The very sanctity of her home.

Well, she'd be damned before she showed even a hint of weakness—or heaven forbid, regret—before that arrogant devil.

"So, you've brought Reggie with you," said Kate darkly. "Why, pray, would you do such a thing?"

"Ah, *ma chérie*, he misses you!" declared her mother with a huge, theatrical wink. "Alas, Reggie is much cast down at present. You will cheer him up, *oui*?"

"I will do no such thing," said Kate firmly. "I will not turn him out. But if Reggie is to be cheered, Aurélie, you will have to do it yourself."

"Oh, how wearying you are, Katherine! Reggie is an old friend." Lashes aflutter, Aurélie set the back of her hand to her forehead. "*Eh bien*. Mr. Quartermaine, perhaps you might give me that very strong-looking arm of yours, and help to my room? And my blue portmanteau? I must have it now, for Filou's blanket is in it."

But Edward was looking more forbidding than ever. "Certainly, ma'am," he said stiffly.

Just then, Reggie himself came through the door herding his put-upon valet, who was bent under the weight of a large, brass-bound dressing case. Reggie looked as sleek, slender, and satanically handsome as ever, and Kate wanted to backhand him in the teeth.

He espied her at once. "Kate, old thing! How famous!"

Left with no alternative, Kate crossed the hall to greet him.

Edward veered toward the mountain of baggage long enough to snatch the blue portmanteau.

"How do you do, Reggie?" she asked, catching his hands in hers.

"Katie, darling!" He kissed both her hands in turn. "You're like water in the desert to me."

Kate smiled. "Don't trouble yourself to flatter me, Reggie; it is unbecoming to us both," she said matter-of-factly. "I do hope your journey wasn't tedious. How is your mother in Devon?"

"Very well," said Reggie. "She sends her regards."

"Lovely," said Kate. "Now, may I introduce you to—"

"Good God, *Ned Quartermaine*?" Eyes rounding, Reggie faltered, his gaze going to the blue case Edward held. "Has Bellecombe taken you on as a footman? Or are you just here to gloat?"

"Reggie, don't be an ass," said Kate.

"How do you do, Lord Reginald?" said Edward coolly.

With a wicked grin, Reggie thrust out a hand. "Well, old chap, I see it's true what they say. You never sit on a mere profit when you can turn it into a windfall."

"No, I do not," Edward agreed.

It was a strange comment. And how very odd, thought Kate, that they should know each other. Still watching Edward from the corner of one eye, Reggie returned his attention to Kate and, before she could protest, looped an arm companionably through hers.

"Well, old thing, how goes life at the family pile?" he said, once again blithe. "Walk with me upstairs and help me choose a bedchamber far from the Comte de Macey's wretched snoring, won't you?"

Kate pulled her arm from his. "I must greet the others, Reggie," she said coolly. "Just tell Peppie where you wish to—"

Reggie shot her a darkling look. "My dear girl, de Macey, Julia, and Sir Francis are two miles behind," he said, dropping his voice intimately. "Doesn't our past entitle me to a mere five minutes of your time? Trust me, you will wish to speak with me before those three arrive—for *they* will be well acquainted with Mr. Quartermaine."

Her expression stiffening, Kate strode back in the direction of the library. But she did not go far; just around the corner. There, she stopped.

"Very well, Reggie." Kate crossed her arms over her chest. "Your five minutes have begun."

The fawning pretense vanished, and his expression darkened. "Kate," he rasped, "what in God's name can you be thinking, to permit that man inside this house?"

Kate arched one eyebrow quite deliberately. "Inside my home, do you mean?" she echoed. "I rather got the impression he was an acquaintance of yours."

"Certainly not!" sniffed Reggie. "Not socially. And just because Heatherfields is now in his hands does not give him the right—and certainly not the social standing—to enter a gentleman's seat at his leisure."

In her outrage, Kate didn't fully absorb his words. "But this is not *a gentleman's seat*, is it?" she said warningly. "It is *my* seat, Reggie. *My* home. Oh, you're welcome here— you were, after all, Stephen's best friend. But do not for one moment forget to whom Bellecombe belongs."

"Well," said Reggie, anger twisting his face. "That's what it always comes down to, doesn't it? *Your* house—and good old Reggie put thoroughly in his place!"

"Don't be ridiculous," said Kate, tapping her toe impatiently. "So, he has got hold of Heatherfields, has he?"

"Good God, he hasn't *told* you?"

Kate avoided the question, but her brain was furiously churning. "How, exactly? Did you sell it?"

"Well, yes." Reggie looked confused. "What's that black devil up to? Dropping round in some vain attempt to befriend the local gentry?"

"Actually, Reggie, Mr. Quartermaine has been staying

here," said Kate, "in Stephen's old room. I collect your shock was such that you failed to notice the sutures in his forehead?"

"Staying here?" Reggie looked stricken. "Kate, you . . . you do know who he is, don't you?"

"Yes, he has made it plain to me who he is," she said. "The gentleman met with an accident along the road—one that was, regrettably, my fault—and since he could not possibly stay at Heatherfields in its present condition—"

"The devil!" said Reggie. "Heatherfields is the prettiest house in Somerset."

"Indeed," said Kate, "and apparently the most decrepit. Anstruther says you've let the roof fall in on the south wing."

"Kate, never mind Heatherfields." Reggie still looked grim. "You have guests arriving. You will not wish them to know you have been harboring a—"

"Careful, Reggie," said Kate, leaning near him. "I will not hear you insult him."

Reggie's face had lost its color. "My dear, think what you say," he replied. "You have London's worst gossip, Lady Julia Burton, practically on your doorstep. Do you want this to get out? She'll gazette the whole wretched story!"

"Lady *Julia*—?" said Kate incredulously. "Even *I* know Julia has bedded half the men in Mayfair—and I live two hundred miles away! The Comte de Macey is just an elegant scoundrel. And what of Mamma's new puppy, Sir Francis Smythe-Whoever? A paragon of virtue, is he? Or Mamma's new gentleman friend, the banker? Oh, saints all, I'm sure!"

"Kate, she has thrown the banker off," said Reggie in a warning tone. "I collect she took offense to his admiring one of the singers at the Royal Opera House last week."

"Merely that?"

"Well, you know how she is," said Reggie. "In any case, I had to listen to her peevishness all the way here—so you can strike him from your guest list."

One less mouth to feed, thought Kate uncharitably.

"Yes, well, I'm sorry to hear of Aurélie's travails," she said, "but no one here is in any position to look down upon Mr. Quartermaine, and I tell you, Reggie, I will not have it."

"Kate," he said, catching her hands again. "Kate, my girl, you don't know what you're doing."

But Kate was quite sure she did.

And she was, once again, quite wrong.

"Reggie, I'm not your girl," she said.

Reggie's expression softened with what looked like true tenderness. "No, Kate. You are not," he said, "and I have rued that circumstance every day since you left me."

It was such arrant nonsense, Kate didn't bother to respond. "I must go, Reggie, and help Mrs. Peppin get everyone settled," she said stiffly. "Welcome back to Bellecombe. It is good to see you."

"Kate." He caught her arm and spun her around. "Kate, don't speak to me so coldly. You'll break my heart."

"Don't be ridiculous, Reggie. You haven't any heart."

"Kate, my God, how can you be so cruel? After all we've been to one another?"

"Oh, Reggie, such drama!" she said. "You likely haven't spared me two thoughts since last you laid eyes on me."

"Kate, that just isn't so." Reggie let his thick black lashes sweep down. "I've longed to see you. Longed for it so desperately I came all the way from London—and not in a train, like some civilized person, but in a lumbering coach, trapped for miles with your mother and that damned farting dog of hers."

His words ended on a faintly petulant note. Had he truly expected her to fall into his arms?

"I'm sorry about the dog," said Kate impatiently. "As to the other, Reggie, we're childhood friends who were briefly betrothed. Stop making more of it."

"But, Katherine, my dear," he replied, leaning inappropriately near, "there was *more*, wasn't there? I do hope you haven't forgotten?"

"I have not forgotten you made it plain you preferred another."

Reggie tried to snake a hand around her waist. "Kate, love, men will have their little trifles," he murmured. "Why didn't you tell me how you felt?"

"Oh, and *then* you would have cast your mistress off?"

"Bess?" Reggie shrugged. "Yes. Why not?"

Kate sighed, and tried to pull away. "Reggie, I would call you a liar if I cared enough to quarrel, but I do not, so kindly take your hand off my—"

Instead, Reggie kissed her. It was swift but hard, and when he lifted his head away, his eyes were glittering almost dangerously. Kate was still staring at him when she felt a cold chill down her back.

"Katie, love," Reggie was whispering, "you know we are meant for one another. You know I can make you feel—"

"I beg your pardon, Lady d'Allenay." Edward's deep voice pierced the gloom of the passageway. "Your mother requires you upstairs."

Humiliated, Kate pushed Reggie away and turned. Edward stood silhouetted against a shaft of low afternoon sunlight, large and impossibly male.

Behind her, Reggie laughed. "Pardon us, old fellow," he said, pushing past them both. "Just rekindling an old romance. Kate, my love, I'll see you at dinner."

Edward looked her up and down. "Are you all right?"

Kate wanted to spit the taste of Reggie from her lips. "I'm fine," she said, "but Reggie is a presumptuous ass."

"Would you like me to deal with him?" asked Edward evenly.

She gave a sharp laugh. "What? Pistols at dawn for *that*?"

"No," said Edward. "I'm not a gentleman. I don't have to go through the dainties of dropping a damned handkerchief to get my satisfaction."

Kate gave a dismissive wave of her hand. "I wouldn't do him the honor of caring enough to encourage you," she replied. "Besides, he amuses Aurélie. And he was like a brother to Stephen." She paused to sigh. "Have the other carriages come?"

"Yes, three, I'm afraid."

There was an edge in his voice Kate didn't like. She stopped and looked up at him. "Edward," she said quietly, "is there anyone else you know?"

His face was still without emotion. "Yes. In fact, they are all precisely the sort of people I do know."

"Does that include Lady Julia?"

"Yes."

"My mother?"

"I recognize her name now," he admitted, "and I know she is much admired in certain circles for her beauty and charm."

It was a diplomatic way of putting it. Kate eyed him warily for a moment, but she did not have the luxury of time. Reggie's words had spooked her a little. "Why didn't you explain to me, Edward, that you had bought Heatherfields?"

"In part because you would not slow down and listen to me just now in the library," he said. "And because it isn't an easy explanation to make. You see, I did not, strictly speaking, buy it. I took it."

"*Took* it?" Her brow furrowed. "But Reggie said . . ."

"I don't care what he said," Edward grimly replied. "I forced his hand, but ever so politely. I took Heatherfields in lieu of his gaming debts, and he was in deep. That's what you need to understand. Like so many of his kind, Lord Reginald owed me. And I always—*always*—get what I am owed, Kate. I operate a private gaming club. A high-stakes hell, for lack of a gentler phrase. That, you see, was my father's—my *real* father's—line of work, and I learnt it from the master."

She could only stare at him, horror blooming in her chest like blood from a stab wound.

"Do you understand what that means, Kate?" he pressed, as if to shove the knife deeper.

Mutely, she nodded. "Yes, certainly," she finally managed, "and in the most vile of ways; my father and brother practically lived in the hells. What did you imagine ran Bellecombe into the ground, Edward? A run of bad luck on the exchange?"

He stood silent before her, his shoulders filling the passageway, his expression still cool, utterly businesslike. He made no move to touch her; indeed, from the set of his jaw, it looked as if he had resolved never to touch her again. And yet, if one looked closely, there was something like pain stirring in the backs of his eyes.

Kate closed her own and remembered his touch.

Remembered that he was still Edward.

That whatever he was, she still . . . what? *Loved* him? What balderdash. She'd once believed she'd loved Reggie; look how that turned out.

"Good Lord," she murmured, feeling suddenly wan. "So your inability to read numbers—to make sense of them—that's why it horrified you so?"

"It horrified me, yes, but I wasn't sure why. Kate, I would never lie to you." She felt his hand slip under her elbow, warm and steady, but beyond that he didn't touch her. "Kate," he said again, more softly. "Oh, Kate. I'm so sorry. For all of this."

Something in her heart wrenched. "You overheard, then? What Reggie said?"

"Yes."

"Well, it's just Reggie, Edward," she managed. "We mustn't mind him."

"I do mind him," he said. "I mind him very much indeed. But . . . he is not wrong."

"So you still wish to leave—" She bit back the last word, *me*.

"Kate, I do not *wish* to leave," he said. "Will you make me say it? Very well. I don't wish to leave *you*."

She opened her eyes. "Then don't," she replied. "Don't give him the satisfaction."

His lips thinning, Edward slowly shook his head. "Tell your mother the truth; that we just discovered who I am. I can assure you that *she* knows me by reputation, if not sight. Fendershot will support your story. Tell her you were duped, if you wish. Then tell her you've sent me away. Mitigate the damage."

But whatever the damage, it was done, Kate realized. Reggie had seen him. Her mother had seen him, and apparently did indeed have some notion who he was—which, given her circle of friends, was quite likely. Edward had just admitted some sort of acquaintance with Julia, de Macey, and Sir Francis. And one could never stop the servants from talking.

No, far better to brazen it through. Besides, she would not give Reggie the pleasure of knowing he had been right.

She set her hand on Edward's arm, felt her fingers digging into the wool of his coat sleeve. "A gaming hell," she whispered. "Where?"

"Does it matter?" he replied, looking down at her. "In St. James. Between the Carlton Club and Spencer House."

At her gaping stare, he added, "As I said, it is a very exclusive sort of club."

And situated amongst some of the most expensive real estate in Christendom, she realized. Decadence and vice had been very good indeed to *Ned* Quartermaine.

Yes, Reggie had been right. She had not known that Edward was the sort of man who bankrupted young gentlemen for personal gain. But she had known his touch—known it intimately. And just now, it was clouding her judgment. Kate knew it, even as she spoke.

"Please, you mustn't go," she said. "You still have stitches. I'm still responsible. Edward, I'm still . . ."

"What?" he said, the word so soft she barely heard it.

She lowered her lashes. "I still want you here," she managed. "I will not pretend I approve of what you do; I do not. But that . . . that is not who you *are*. Not to me. I cannot reconcile all this in my mind. Not yet."

Nonetheless, something inside Edward had changed in the minutes since their return; shifted in a way she could not define. Even his face looked harder. And his wicked smile, those laugh lines about his eyes—had she simply imagined all that?

"Kate, my dear, don't be naive," he finally replied. "It's precisely who I am—and I learnt my trade in a hard, cold school."

Kate shook her head, mystified. "If you say so," she replied. "But you are a gentleman born, and a better man, I suspect, than those who are about to descend on me."

"From what I saw in your hall just now," he said dryly, "that is not far from true."

"Aurélie does prefer people who amuse her," Kate acknowledged. "How well do you know them?"

"De Macey, by reputation only," he said. "Sir Francis is a frequent client. Lady Julia Burton has come in once or twice on a gentleman's arm."

Kate sighed. "Well, I had better go and greet them," she said. "Tomorrow . . . tomorrow, Edward, we will all be less on edge. Let us decide not to decide anything just now."

Edward gave her an almost mocking bow. "As you wish."

She nodded, and started down the corridor. Then suddenly, she jerked to a halt and turned back around. "*Can* you stay?" she asked. "I am sorry; I didn't think. Have you a family? Is anyone worried about you? Expecting you? Surely—"

"No one," he interjected. "There is no one. The club's manager expected me away for a few weeks, perhaps. There might be a letter awaiting me at Heatherfields, but I doubt it."

"I see," she said.

But something uncertain had flickered in Edward's eyes,

and Kate knew there was more to be said. Something he didn't wish to say, perhaps. But she didn't press him; she had had all the surprises she could bear for one day.

"Well, then," she said. "I shall see you at dinner?"

He nodded, but held back rather than accompany her.

Dreadfully torn, Kate returned to the great hall. There she found herself thoroughly hugged and kissed by Lady Julia Burton—a plump, pretty widow who, like Aurélie, was of uncertain years and even less certain morals—and by the Comte de Macey, her mother's near-constant companion and occasional lover.

"Kate, my dear!" The dapper gentleman kissed her lightly on the cheek, his enormous mustache tickling her ear. "How good you are to have us."

Kate managed a smile. The man was an aging roué, yes, but one could not help liking him. Years ago, she'd half hoped Aurélie might marry the man and put him out of his misery—that her restless mother might finally settle down—but just now Aurélie and de Macey were in one of their *merely friends* stages.

"It is a pleasure, de Macey," she said. "My home is ever yours."

"So you've always said." The comte beamed. "Come, let me introduce our young friend, Sir Francis Smythe-Feldon."

Across the great hall, a dashing gentleman of fashion tore himself away from cooing over Nancy to join de Macey, bowing over Kate's hand and declaring himself enchanted.

The three of them made for a blessedly small crowd, given Aurélie's usual entourage.

About age thirty, Sir Francis possessed dark, pomaded curls and a pair of dangerous-looking eyes. Had Aurélie really intended him for Nancy? Just now Lady Julia had her arm hooked in his, and was looking a tad proprietary.

Perhaps, like Filou, the gentleman was just the ladies' pet, brought merely for amusement? If so, Kate could only pray he didn't break quite as much wind.

"De Macey says the shooting here is outstanding this time of year," said Sir Francis. "So kind of you and your mother to have us. We three shall endeavor to be entertaining house-guests."

Kate forced a dazzling smile. "Aurélie's friends are always entertaining," she said truthfully. "Speaking of which, she has ordered me upstairs. Lady Julia, Mrs. Peppin will situate you next to me, just across the corridor from Aurélie. I know you will wish to be close to her. De Macey, Sir Francis, I believe you're one floor above. Do let me know if you're not comfortable."

Kate left them well occupied—along with her mother's maid and two servants she didn't recognize—sorting the last of the baggage. But rather than go to her mother's room, she instead turned coward and pushed open the door to her parlor, tears pressing hotly against the backs of her eyes.

"There you are, *mon chou!*" Her mother's lazy voice carried from the hearth. "I knew you would eventually show yourself."

After Kate's eyes adjusted to the dim light, she could see that Aurélie lay upon Kate's favorite divan near the fireplace, her feet propped up on a pillow, and one arm cast over her eyes. Filou was snoring, nestled in the folds of her skirts.

"Mamma?" Kate sniffed the air, displeased.

"This is such a lovely suite of rooms," her mother murmured dreamily. "I have always preferred it."

"Then by all means, take it." Kate was jerking back the draperies. "But Mamma, you cannot shut everything up. What did you feed that dog for luncheon?"

"Ooh, this chaise is heavenly!" declared Aurélie on a languid, catlike stretch. "And Filou had . . . let me think . . . *oui*, rabbit confit."

"Are you sure it wasn't cabbage?" muttered Kate.

On a grunt, Filou leapt down and came waddling and snuffling in Kate's direction as she threw open one of the windows.

"*Vraiment*, Filou has missed you, Katherine!" Aurélie declared, lifting up perhaps two inches to peer over the arched back of the divan. "Go on, pick him up. *Oui, oui*, you may kiss him if you wish."

Mostly to dissuade the tears that still threatened, Kate picked the dog up and absently scratched his ears. "Really, Mamma, you drag this poor creature about almost cruelly."

"*Mais non*, Filou cannot be without me!" Aurélie declared. "Nor I without him! Now, *ma chérie*, you must pour me a glass of something—have you any of Peppie's black-currant cordial?"

"I expect so." She set the dog back in her mother's lap. "But I thought you were going to have your nap now."

"*Mais oui*, I was," she agreed. "And then I ask myself— Aurélie, you imbecile, how often do you get to share life's little intimacies with your eldest daughter?"

Kate blanched. "Intimacies?"

Aurélie threw a limp, white hand over the back of the divan. "The cordial, *ma petite*," she said plaintively. "I find it most restorative. Then *oui*, come sit. We must have—what does dear Peppie call it? A comfortable cose?"

"Something like that," said Kate, resigned to an unpleasant fate.

Despite Aurélie's wan demeanor, limp gestures, and constant declarations of being frail, faint, and just generally put-upon by the world at large, Kate didn't for one moment misjudge her mother's indefatigability. Her ears had pricked up like Anstruther's favorite pointer, for Aurélie was on the hunt for something.

And Kate feared she knew what it was.

Scrabbling about behind one of the small cupboard doors, she found Peppie's bottle, thumbed out the cork, and poured her mother a glass. After setting the bottle down on the silver tray atop the sideboard, Kate thought better of it, picked it up again, and poured herself a glass.

A generous one.

After thrusting the first at her mother, Kate sat down on the adjacent sofa. "Very well, have at it, Mamma," she said. "I daresay you mean to rip up at me over Mr. Quartermaine. Or my treatment of Reggie."

Aurélie sat up gracefully. "*Moi—?*" she said, pressing the limp, white hand to her bosom. "Oh, *chérie*, far be it from me to lecture anyone over a man!"

That, at least, was an astute observation.

But Aurélie was waving at the door that stood open to Kate's bedchamber. "Look, *ma petite*, at what *maman* has brought you from Madame Odette in Paris. It is hanging on the door."

Setting the glass aside, Kate went to the door and unfastened the linen sheath that hung there. Inside was an emerald-green dinner gown over a lacy underskirt shimmering with gold. The sleeves, bodice, and all the hems were delicately piped in gold, and the plunging neckline looked far, far too daring for Kate.

Still, it was utterly breathtaking.

"Mamma, it is lovely, of course," she began, "but—"

"*Non, non*, Kate! How you tire me with your protests!" whined Aurélie from the divan. "This, *ici*, it is too tight; and this place, too low. *Non, non*. Put the dress on for dinner, *mon chou*. And *oui*, it is cut precisely to your measurements so do not even think of giving it up to Nancy."

Kate's eyes widened. The dress certainly would not have done for Nancy. Sometimes it seemed as if Aurélie had feathers for brains.

And other times . . . well, that didn't bear thinking about. But *Filou*, as best Kate recalled, was loosely translated as *trickster*. She sometimes wondered who might better wear that title.

"The gown is magnificent, Mamma," she conceded, going back to the sofa. "Yes, perhaps I will put it on one evening. Not tonight, I think."

"*Oui*, as you please," said Aurélie, with a very French

shrug. "But wear that dress to dinner, *mon chou*, and Reggie is like to fall prostrate at your feet."

Kate sighed. "Oh, Mamma. What can you be thinking?"

A slow grin curled over Aurélie's lush mouth. "*Oui, oui, mon chou*, he pines for you!" she chortled. "Indeed, he begged me on bended knee to bring him to your side. It was most affecting."

"He pines for his bank account, more like," said Kate sullenly. "I don't dislike Reggie, Mamma, but it will be a cold day in hell before I reconsider marrying him."

Again, the Gallic shrug. "Eh, *tant pis*," she said evenly. "I promised him only that I would see what might be done."

"And now you see," said Kate. "Recall, if you will, that I broke my betrothal for a reason."

"*Oui*, and a silly one, perhaps," said her mother, cutting her a sly, sidelong glance. "You are not getting any younger, Katherine."

Silence fell across the room. Kate set her wine down with a sharp *clack!* Her hand went to her forehead. She didn't need her mother to remind her.

"Mamma, I caught him *in flagrante delicto* with his mistress. It was, to my mind, the very best of reasons."

"*Oui, oui*," her mother murmured. "It was badly done of Reggie, to be sure."

Badly done?

Was there a proper way to humiliate one's betrothed wife?

The awful memory still made Kate's cheeks burn. A mere week after the announcement of their betrothal, she'd gone to the Season's last, most extravagant masque dressed— quite ludicrously—as Venus. She had meant to surprise Reggie. And she had. Behind a curtain, with his hands and his tongue in a variety of places they ought not have been.

Worse, she had not been the only one who'd seen. Her bloodcurdling scream, perhaps, had not helped in that regard . . .

Afterward, her mask still in place, she had rushed into

the ladies' retiring room, hidden herself behind one of the screens, and burst into tears. Ten minutes later, a trio of well-dressed ladies had followed her in, tittering over it.

Really, had the country mouse expected to tame the wicked Lord Reginald? Did she not realize he meant to marry her for her money? She should account herself lucky such a handsome charmer had deigned to offer for her at all.

The worst part of it was, Kate had been left with the suspicion that perhaps Reggie had engineered the awful scene; that perhaps he had *wished* to be relieved of his betrothal.

Stephen had been dead just eight months, and during that time, she and Reggie had drawn ever closer. And yet, Kate's grandfather had emerged from negotiating the marriage settlements looking worn and unhappy.

She had never asked her grandfather about it, Kate realized. Perhaps she had been afraid of what she might hear. But she'd come to suspect that Reggie had not fully grasped the grim state of Bellecombe's finances before proposing marriage.

After the scandal in London, Lord d'Allenay had not uttered a word of protest when Kate had announced she was ending the betrothal. In fact, he had looked relieved.

He had been an astute old gentleman, her grandfather . . .

"Are you listening, *ma petite*?" Aurélie's thin, wheedling voice cut into Kate's reverie.

She jerked her head up. "Yes. No—I'm sorry, Mamma. What did you say?"

Aurélie heaved a put-upon sigh. "I was asking about dinner," she said. "I wish to have Cook's leek soup. And I wish Nancy and Anstruther to play afterward. Will you make him?"

Kate's eyes widened. "Mamma, I cannot *make* him," she said. "But I will invite him to dine with us, and hope that he agrees."

Her mother's mouth drew into a petulant line. "I doubt he will agree," she complained. "John Anstruther is the most obstinate man on earth. And you—this business with Reggie—*you* are the very same. It is that frightful Scotch blood, just like your grandmamma. And the two of you share her old-fashioned notions, too."

Kate wasn't sure just when she'd been lumped in with poor Anstruther for a scathing, but it was good company, at least. "I cannot think it is old-fashioned to wish one's husband to be faithful."

"*Non*, just unrealistic," said Aurélie under her breath. Then she relented, and cut Kate a knowing look. "Oh, come, *ma chérie*, I am no fool. I know Reggie for what he is."

"Then why in heaven's name did you bring him?"

Over her glass, Aurélie winked. "Because, *mon chou*, one never knows what might happen when the pot is stirred, *non*? Things at Bellecombe have been simmering too long. And now your sister—" Here, Aurélie wrinkled her pert, pretty nose. "Now she thinks to marry this . . . this rector? *Zut!* How dull he sounds!"

"Do you really disapprove because he's a *rector*?"

Aurélie's eyes widened innocently. "*Mais non, ma petite*," she said. "I disapprove because the man is faint of heart and drags his feet."

"He is waiting on Uncle Upshaw's permission," Kate reminded her.

Aurélie snorted disdainfully. "Bah, a man worth his salt does not wait! He sweeps the lady off her feet! One may always marry over the anvil. What is Lord Upshaw to him?"

"Oh, merely Nancy's guardian!" There was no point in explaining to Aurélie that Anglican rectors did not abscond to Scotland with stolen brides, so Kate took another tack. "Moreover, Upshaw holds her purse strings, too."

Aurélie's face fell. "Ah, that is so, *n'est-ce pas*?" she said. "Still, it is a . . . a mere technicality! Even Sir Francis, I assure you, would have enough sense to manage such a small, trifling detail."

Kate shook her head, mystified. Then it struck her.

"Mamma, just what are you suggesting? A contrast? A . . . a competition? Is that what you're trying to engineer?"

Aurélie smiled. "Well, if I am, may the best man win," she said. "If, after a week in the company of the handsome Sir Francis, your sister still prefers her dull rector, *eh bien*, what is to be done? I think I shall tell Reggie to flirt with her, too. If you do not want the poor man, I shall make some small use of him."

Kate just shook her head, for she'd come to believe Nancy would not be dissuaded. But Aurélie meant to put it to the test, clearly. Yes, *eh bien*, indeed.

"Richard Burnham is not dull, Mamma," Kate chided. "As to Reggie, he must have his pockets inside-out to have given up Heatherfields."

Her mother sighed, and sipped pensively at her cordial. "I confess, I was not aware of that little misfortune until we had left London," she said a little ruefully. "And now, to find wicked Ned Quartermaine—of all people!—here at Bellecombe? Ah, *chérie*, perhaps the pot has already been stirred, eh?"

"Ned." It was what Reggie had called him, too, but the name did not suit him. "It is a brutish-sounding name."

"He can be a brutish man," said her mother.

"Do you know him?"

Aurélie's eyes widened. "*Bien sûr*, who does not?" she said a little breathlessly. "The man is notorious."

"Notorious? That seems harsh."

Aurélie gave another dismissive wave. "Oh, he does not trouble me," she replied, "but to pretty young men like Sir Francis? *Oui*, he strikes fear into the very heart of such as them—and still they go! Like little lambs to the slaughter, carrying their purses of gold like precious offerings. And he takes it. *Oui*, every time, in the end, Ned Quartermaine wins."

"He is very rich, then?" said Kate.

"Very." Her mother grinned. "Watch Julia fanning herself at dinner tonight if you don't believe me."

"And you really know him?"

"*Mais non*, Katherine, I only know *of* him," declared Aurélie. "Whilst I have many vices, *mon chou*, it would not be possible to sustain two gamblers in one family. Your father was all we could afford."

"We had Stephen, too," said Kate darkly. "And we couldn't afford either of them."

"*Oui, oui*," said Aurélie a little forlornly. "At least it was a passion they shared, father and son. Some families, you know, have nothing."

Only Aurélie could cast a hopeful light on such a bad habit. "*Nothing* would have been better," Kate said.

Again, the languid shrug. "*Mon Dieu*, Katherine, one cannot scold the dead!" Absently, she drew the pug closer and began to rub its distended belly. "No, I do not game. All the gentlemen of my acquaintance, however, do—*oui*, my frightful crowd of friends you faintly disapprove of. So, yes, Mr. Quartermaine is not unknown to me. Be very careful, *ma petite*, of that one."

"He is leaving," said Kate, "in a day or two."

"*Vraiment?*" Aurélie looked suddenly attentive. "And you do not wish him to go?"

Kate shrugged. "I don't know what I wish," she confessed. "Reggie took such pleasure in telling me what a bad man he is, I'm very nearly tempted to beg him to stay."

"Oh, he is a very bad man," said Aurélie with a languid toss of her hand. "But as I say, *mon chou*, the other sorts are really too dull to be contemplated."

"He certainly is not that," Kate admitted. "He is . . . intriguing."

Still, her mother's point struck straight to the heart of Kate's crushed dreams; dreams she'd not allowed herself to acknowledge, even inwardly. What a fool she was. The first man to turn her head in years was far more wicked than Reggie. *He was the owner of a gaming hell.*

Kate had now fully grasped the full import of that fact—and still she would mourn his leaving Bellecombe, and her life. If that was a moral failing, it was one she'd have to live with. She desired him beyond all reason.

Kate was, it seemed, her mother's daughter after all.

"So, Ned Quartermaine, I take it, has been here some days?" said Aurélie coyly. "I begin to have hope for you, *ma chérie*. Perhaps you possess more spirit than I once feared. Tell me how this visit came to be?"

Kate rolled her eyes. "I gather he was looking for Heatherfields and took a wrong turn," she said. "We nearly collided, and he was thrown from his horse and struck his head."

"How frightful," said her mother blandly. "I hope you nursed him back to health—and spent a good deal of time leaning over his sickbed in the process."

"Mamma, only you would encourage such a thing," she said. "I wonder which of us is the greater fool."

"*Are* you a fool?" asked Aurélie lightly. "There is no shame in it, *ma petite*, for wiser women than you have fallen for Quartermaine's golden looks. I confess, frankly, to some reassurance. Your letter last month sounded wistful. I feared you were lonely. Indeed, perhaps I need not have come at all?"

"Mamma, is that what this is about?" Kate demanded. "I make the mistake of sending my mother a heartfelt letter, and this is my thanks? You drag my castoff fiancé back here because you think me desperate?"

Her mother gave her lazy shrug again. "Well, as I say, you are not getting any younger, Katherine. Further, Julia has quarreled with Lady Bushwell over having slept with her favorite footman. And I—well, amidst many tears, I have broken with my banker."

"Tears?" Kate lightly lifted one eyebrow. "His? Or yours?"

Her mother smiled tightly. "His, *ma chérie*. At my age, I am beyond crying over men. But in any case, it did seem a good time to quit London."

Kate managed a smile. "Well, as to Edward—to Mr. Quartermaine—his golden looks notwithstanding, he is leaving," she said. "Indeed, some would find it scandalous he's been here at all."

Her mother sighed. "Yes, no doubt," she acknowledged. "Well. Do you wish to come to London for amusement?—no, Paris, I think, is better this time of year—*oui*, I shall take you, *mon chou*. There, am I not a good *maman*? I will order the carriage for tomorrow. The gentlemen may shoot without us."

"Mamma, I cannot go to Paris at the drop of your hat, and no, I don't want to. Really, you mustn't refine too much upon my letters. I was just feeling sorry for myself."

Aurélie pulled a genuinely sorrowful face. "Is it because of Louisa's new grandchild?" she gently suggested. "That is what—little Lydia's second? Or third? *Vraiment*, I cannot keep count. And was it Lydia's? Or Cassandra's?"

"Is that really what brought you, Mamma? Your newest grand-nephew? My maudlin letter?"

Aurélie shrugged. "Perhaps," she said, "or perhaps not. Alas, I am an indifferent parent, Katherine, I know, but not, I hope an utterly unfeeling one? Now, tell me more about Mr. Quartermaine."

"There is nothing to tell," said Kate sharply. "At first he was knocked senseless and Fitch confined him to bed. He's getting about quite well now. The stitches can come out, I think, but Fitch is away a few days. Once he's back, I expect Mr. Quartermaine will be on his way."

"Must he go? Truly?" murmured Aurélie, her gaze growing distant. "Well, well. What is to be done about this?"

"*You* are not to do *anything*," said Kate sternly.

At that, her mother sat up, hugging the pug to her chest.

"To be sure, Kate, that is entirely up to you," she said, "and I would not think of interfering."

Filou chose that moment to audibly expel the odiferous effects of his parsnips.

It seemed a fitting punctuation point to such an arrant lie.

Kate sighed, and threw open another window.

CHAPTER 9

An Invitation to a House Party

Edward returned to his room by a circuitous route, desperate to avoid the crowd in the great hall—and desperate to avoid himself, perhaps, though that was not really an option. He felt utterly cold inside, as if he were slowly going numb, a sensation almost comforting in its familiarity.

How long had he lived this way?

Years, he supposed. And since numbness was an absence of feeling, one didn't know one suffered from it until the feeling began to return. Then, as with a case of frostbite, one suddenly realized what true pain was.

It was too late for him; he had thawed by Vesta's blazing hearth too long—but with a strange reprieve. Only when his memory returned had the pain truly set in.

Yes, he welcomed the numbness. Let it return, he prayed, in all its cold fury.

He thought again of the crowd downstairs, and cursed beneath his breath. Yes, he fit in perfectly. Even at a distance he had recognized the scandalous beauty, Lady Julia

Burton, arm in arm with one of his regular customers, Sir Francis Smythe-Feldon.

The Frenchman, de Macey, he knew vaguely. For all his elegance, the gentleman was not one Quartermaine particularly welcomed in his club, for he was that rarest of the rare: a disciplined gambler. And a man who, despite his bonhomie, could be dangerous when crossed.

Still, their skills notwithstanding, Edward wished to avoid them all.

He particularly wished to avoid Lord Reginald Hoke.

Upstairs, he closed the door and leaned back against it, taking the weight off his leg, which ached a little. Somewhere in the afternoon's chaos, he'd mislaid Stephen Wentworth's walking stick—a provident loss, perhaps, for if he'd had it to hand upon discovering Lord Reginald Hoke kissing Kate, he might have snapped, and beaten the damned fool to a bloody pulp.

Slowly he exhaled and let his head fall back against the door, his throat working up and down. Good Lord, the coincidence of it all! Lord Reginald's debt. Heatherfields. His meeting Kate. What were the chances of such happenstance?

Still, Edward was a man who had long survived—and thrived—by plying the slender blade of chance. Always, in the end, it had cleaved down on his side. But this time? When it felt, strangely, as if it might truly matter?

He was doomed. He'd seen the disdain in Kate's eyes when he'd told her who—no, *what*—he was.

And he had brought that disdain on himself. Even without his memory, Edward had suspected something of his own character, for surely a man's character was as much an immutable part of him as the color of his eyes. He had sensed very clearly that he'd no business in this beautiful Eden. That he'd no business *with her*.

Yet he'd let himself—what? Grow close to Kate? He would not call it more than that, for naming a thing gave it power over a man. He had learnt that lesson long ago.

But dear God, he had to get past this. This nameless long-ing; this emotion that could not—and would not—matter in the end. On a shaft of frustration, Edward pushed himself away from the door and went to the massive oak coffer at the foot of his bed and shoved up the lid with both hands.

There, just as Miss Wentworth had promised, he found his valise. He took it out, shut the chest, and sat down upon the ornately carved surface to unbuckle the bag. His memory clear now, Edward ran his hand around the bottom until he felt the familiar notch, then he hooked the tip of his finger in it and pulled up the false bottom.

The deed conveying Heatherfields lay beneath. And under it, some five hundred pounds in banknotes. A fortune to most people. Mere pocket change to him.

At least he would be able to repay Kate's loan—assuming she would even touch his filthy lucre. But her compassion? The kindness of everyone at Bellecombe? Those he could never repay. Unwittingly, they had given him respite from a life that once had meant survival, but had long ago become just plain, reflexive ruthlessness.

It was as if the twisted course through his harsh and ugly world ran like parallel paths with one more pure of purpose, more sweetly ordinary, and now the line between them had blurred. One misstep had led him to slip unwittingly across that narrow vale and let him glimpse what he could not have. What he had, perhaps, thrown away long ago.

Once upon a time, he had persuaded himself that he lived such a hard, wicked existence for Annie. That he wished her to have a life free of want; one that was imbued with as much grace as a man's ill-got gain could purchase a child.

But Annie's wants—if not her grandmother's—had long ago been satisfied. Mrs. Granger had been sent gowns and governesses aplenty for the girl, and along with them Edward had provided a dowry sufficient to make all but the most scrupulous of men overlook the obscure circumstances of Annie's birth. And now there was Heatherfields to go with it; an estate, he hoped, that could be made worthy of being called a gentleman's seat.

Thinking of Annie, however, made him realize what was *not* inside the valise. Annie's pearls. The pearl and sapphire necklace he'd taken in such haste when he'd flown from Ceylon; his wedding gift to Maria.

Except that there had been no wedding.

There had been only a funeral, and a child so small and so weak of limbs and lungs that it seemed surely destined to die. And Mr. Granger, so angry and disbelieving, refusing to accept the responsibility for the unutterable tragedy his pride had brought down upon his house.

And now Edward was left to wonder what had become of the pearls. Though he had dreaded his every trip to Somerset—and made few enough of them—he had carried the pearls like a talisman. But Mrs. Granger still refused to allow Annie to have them.

Not yet, she said.

But *never* was what she meant. She didn't want him in Annie's life. Indeed, she did all she could to keep him from the child—as much as she dared, at any rate.

Still, pride usually went before a fall, and most of Mrs. Granger's had gone shortly after her husband's death, when Annie was just six. With her daughter and husband in the grave, and their small manor sold to settle Granger's long-onerous debts, the lady had finally answered one of Edward's letters.

Yes, she had been glad enough, at long last, to take his filthy money. To call him, with grim reluctance, Annie's godfather. To live in the cottage he had bought and paid for, and to dine upon the food his stipend provided. But the pearls—and the story that went with them? No. Annie was too young to understand, she maintained.

It was a curious refusal when Edward was not even sure what story he'd even meant to tell the child. The truth? It was too ugly.

Probably he would have simply said that long, long ago he had seen her mother standing on the Chain Pier at Brighton with the wind whipping at her bonnet ribbons, and had fallen headlong in love. That he had worshipped her for her beauty and her blithe spirit, and had hoped with all his heart to marry her, but that it simply hadn't worked out.

Which was the truth, so far as it went.

And amongst the truths he would *not* tell was that, after Maria's death, he had set about making himself rich. Because rich men took what they wanted and to hell with arrogant refusals. Because with Maria dead, the good name and the military career he had so carefully crafted were no longer of any use to him. He had no need to become respectable.

And so he had become, once again, his father's son.

He had immersed himself in that foul family business that traded in the frailty and foolishness of humankind, and had made, yet again, a blazing success of himself. And he had done it with spite seething in his heart.

Because he had known Granger for the prideful fool he was. He had known that, before the man was done, he'd finish driving his estate and his family into the ground. That in the end, it would all come down to whoever was capable of supporting Annie.

And he had known that that person would be Alfred Hedge's hard-edged bastard, and that the Grangers would bloody well learn to like it. Because the child needed a supportive, responsible male presence in her life. No one knew that better than he did.

Edward had never doubted what he was capable of with the sweat of his brow and the toil of his brain. Never had he acknowledged defeat—not even in those darkest, bleakest hours of his childhood. He had always believed in himself. That he could—and *would*—fight his way through to prevail, and that he'd make those who had thwarted him rue the day.

But yes, pride did indeed go before a fall. And Kate, he very much feared, was his. If that gormless fool Granger was looking down from heaven—or up from hell—he was likely having his last laugh at Edward right about now.

He looked down and realized his hand had taken a death grip on the handles of his valise. Letting go on a stab of grief, he restored the false bottom atop the documents, and rose to go in search of Miss Wentworth. Since she'd stored the valise, she had probably taken Annie's pearls for safe-keeping. It was unlikely, he thought, that anyone in this bucolic Eden would have stolen them.

It was also unlikely that it would be Kate whom he practically ran into.

And yet, it was. She was coming out of her parlor behind Mrs. Wentworth, her mother's fat pug caught up in her arms, her face pale, and decidedly drawn.

"*Bonjour*, Mr. Quartermaine!" Mrs. Wentworth trilled, her gaze sweeping his length. "Do you deprive my three friends of your excellent company? You are indeed as cruel as they say."

"Ma'am." He made the lady a small, stiff bow, cutting a glance at Kate as he did so. "I was not aware my presence would be missed."

"But how could it not be?" The lady beamed a smile so beautiful that he was reminded of why, even at her age, she was the toast of half London's gentlemen. "What an exciting prospect it is, I am sure, for my companions to anticipate a few days in the great Ned Quartermaine's company—and for me, certainly. A social coup, even, I daresay."

"You're very kind," he said, still watching Kate from the corner of one eye, "but Lady d'Allenay and I have discussed it. I believe it is time I left Bellecombe."

"Ah, but you must have heard, Mr. Quartermaine, of my wicked propensity to surround myself with handsome rogues?" Mrs. Wentworth hooked her arm in his, and cut him a coquettish glance. "Besides, you have been ill.

What sort of holiday is that for a gentleman? We are here to dine and dance and hunt. You will stay as my guest. I command it."

Edward looked steadily at Kate. "Thank you, ma'am. But I believe that choice must be Lady d'Allenay's."

"Bah!" With a dismissive gesture, Mrs. Wentworth cast her daughter not so much as a backward glance. "Why should Katherine mind? I'm forever dragging my friends to Bellecombe. She is used to it—and what opinion can society have of it? This was my husband's home, was it not? How can anyone expect Katherine to turn me—or my choice of guests—away? Would she not be an unnatural daughter indeed, to be so cruel to her dear *maman*?"

The lady was offering him an out, he realized.

Or was it an in?

Whatever one called it, her message, however coquettishly delivered, was clear. He was to be *her* guest at Bellecombe—to join a party of houseguests who already clung to the fringe of polite society. A party that would be little more scandalous for accounting the Duchess of Dunthorpe's baseborn son amongst their number. He might stay with no damage done to Kate. Was *that* her purpose?

Still, he knew he should go. But what about that blackguard Reggie? Would he continue to press his attentions on Kate? She was no fool, of course. And yet, he found himself loath to leave her side.

"You're very kind," he said again.

"*Bien sûr*, always," said Mrs. Wentworth sweetly, "so long as I get my way."

"A couple of days, then," he said reluctantly, his gaze catching Kate's. "Unless your daughter wishes otherwise?"

"She does not," said Aurélie sharply. Then she turned, took the pug from her daughter's arms, and waltzed off, leaving Kate alone with him in the passageway.

Staring after her, Edward was suddenly uncomfortable. He had the odd sense of having just been played in some way, and by a woman so silly and so vain, it seemed impossible. He didn't like it.

"Behold a force of nature," Kate murmured, watching her go.

"I cannot believe she is your mother," he said honestly.

"Who could?" Kate replied. "All that beauty and charm skipped me altogether."

"Blast it, Kate, I wish you wouldn't—" He stopped and pressed his lips into a firm line.

She turned to face him. "Wouldn't what?"

He dared not hold her gaze. "Nothing," he said, his voice tight. "You know how I feel. It does not bear repeating."

She shook her head, her eyes round, fathomless pools in the dim passageway. "I know how Edward felt about a great many things," she said softly, "and I perhaps had some grasp of his regard for me. But I do not know Ned Quartermaine."

"And you do not want to," he said grimly.

"It's possible you're right," she acknowledged, folding her hands before her in that quiet, slightly prim fashion he loved. "But isn't that for me to decide?"

He made her no answer, but nor did he leave her and go back into his room as he should have done. Instead, his hand came up, only to freeze in place. He yearned to cup her cheek, to draw her to him and tell her she was twice the woman Aurélie Wentworth could ever hope to be. That she was flawless; prim and proper and perfect just as she was. That flirtation and flattery were ephemeral and easily found, but that good character was bone-deep and forever.

But she was watching him with a newfound guardedness. Besides, what would a man like him know of good character? He let the hand drop, having scarcely lifted it at all.

The tenderness in Kate's eyes was at once veiled. "Edward, Aurélie has given you some time," she advised. "There is no need for you to leave Bellecombe unless you have become unhappy here."

"It has nothing to do with *here* or *there*," he said tightly. "I am just . . . damn it, Kate, I don't know what I am. I barely know *who* I am. And what I know I do not much like."

"Then be something else," she said simply.

At that, Kate, too, turned away, and set off in the direction her mother had taken. "Oh, by the way," she said over her shoulder, "dinner is at seven."

"Kate, please—" he called after her.

She turned at once. "Yes?"

He hesitated a long moment, caught between the words on his lips, and his better judgment.

Better judgment, for once, won out.

"There were some pearls," he said, "in a blue velvet bag. In my valise, I mean."

"Oh, yes." The confusion cleared from her brow. "With the sapphire teardrop. Nancy put them in our vault for safe-keeping. In the estate office. Anstruther is there; he'll get them out for you. Just ask."

He could see the curiosity plain on her face, but she didn't ask. No, she doubted him—and his character—now. She would not press her luck with questions she mightn't wish to have answered.

Edward gave a tight nod. "Thank you."

They regarded each other for a time across the chasm of the passageway. He wanted to go to her and say . . . *something*. Something that might reassure her of how he felt— however that was. And he wanted to tell her about the pearls. But he wasn't sure what to tell her, and not at all sure she would believe him.

Almost no one else did. Not when it came to Annie. And he, God help him, had left it that way. Until now, ambiguity had seemed better for Annie than the truth.

"Thank you," he said again.

Disappointment sketched across her face. Then, with an-other faintly regal nod, Kate turned and vanished down the passageway.

An hour later, after penning a letter to Peters, his club

manager, Edward crossed the inner bailey to see the door to the estate office closed against the chill. He cracked it to see John Anstruther seated at the battered and ancient desk, the front of which abutted Kate's.

Apparently absorbed in thought, the man sat with his back to the massive fireplace, one of his magnificent muttonchops twitching as he dotted his pencil down a long, green ledger.

"Good afternoon," said Edward from the threshold.

Anstruther glanced up at once. "Ah, Mr. Edward! Come in, come in." His smile amiable enough, he laid the baize ledger aside. Still, Edward could see a hint of mistrust in the big Scot's eyes.

He lingered a moment on the threshold. "It's Quartermaine, actually," he said evenly. "Mr. Fendershot finally jogged my memory for me."

A sort of wince passed over Anstruther's face. "Aye, I heard aboot that," he acknowledged. "You're a man of business, I take it."

"That's a polite euphemism," said Edward. "May I sit down?"

"Surely, take Her Ladyship's chair," said the estate agent. "Would you have a wee dram?"

Anstruther already had his desk drawer open. At Edward's assenting nod, he extracted a bottle and two glasses, which he eyed judiciously against a low shaft of afternoon light.

"It's clean enough for me," said Edward.

Anstruther didn't spare the whisky, filling the glass two-thirds full and pushing it across his desk and onto Kate's.

"So it's just Mr. Quartermaine, is it?" said Anstruther casually just before lifting his glass.

"As opposed to Lord Edward?" he answered on something of a snort. "I haven't answered to that name in better than two decades."

"Aye, but you could," said Anstruther evenly. "Some men would."

"A courtesy title isn't worth a boot full of piss, Anstruther," said Edward, "and we both know it. Besides, I'm content enough as I am."

"Ah, and how fares Her Ladyship on that subject?" asked the estate agent.

Edward shook his head. "I don't think Kate—Lady d'Allenay—gives a damn about titles," he said. "But she's none too pleased with my line of business. I should get out of here, Anstruther. I've overstayed my welcome. You know it as well as I do."

"Aye?" said the estate agent, taking a good sip at his glass. "Then go."

"I shall—or I meant to—but then Mrs. Wentworth said . . ."

"Ah!" Anstruther said knowingly. "In the middle of it, is she? I would na' doot it."

"She seems almost cavalier in her disregard for Kate's wishes."

"Nooo, not a bit of it," said Anstruther. "She's a canny one, though, is Aurélie Wentworth."

"So she's manipulating me, then?" asked Edward, lifting his gaze to Anstruther's. "First simply ordering me to stay, then flattering me and batting her lashes in turn?"

Anstruther laughed a little grimly. "Better men than you, sir, have underestimated that lady's will," he said. "As to her purpose, none knows it save Aurélie Wentworth herself. Mayhap there is none."

"You've known her a long while," said Edward.

An inscrutable emotion flickered in his eyes, but when he spoke, his tone was as bland as ever. "Oh, aye," he replied. "Miss Kate was a wee babe when I came to Bellecombe, and I was an auld face hereabout even before that. The previous Lady d'Allenay was my kinsman."

"Yes, your godmother, Kate said."

"Aye, that's right. I've known Aurélie Wentworth long and well. Dinna be deceived, sir; the lady is far from a fool."

They drank in silence for a time, and Edward was struck again with Anstruther's sagacity. He was blunt and plain, both in speech and in appearance. He was exactly what you saw before you, and Edward did not doubt that his work habits were just as straightforward.

For a man who dealt with duplicity and dissemblance firsthand for a living, Anstruther was a heartening change.

"So, how many up at the house now?" asked Anstruther conversationally, cupping the whisky in his big hand.

"Well, your old friend Lord Reginald, for one," said Edward with a half smile. "Lady Julia Burton, along with the Frenchman de Macey, and a young blade with whom I have . . . well, let us call it a passing acquaintance."

The estate agent lifted his bushy eyebrows. "Aye, and I hear Lord Reginald is fairly weel known to you, also."

Pondering what to say, Edward dangled his glass between two fingers, then set it down with a *thunk!* onto the desktop. "My club is by necessity a very private sort of establishment, Anstruther," he said. "One cannot be both profitable and exclusive without a great measure of discretion."

"Oh, aye," said Anstruther evenly. "Gentlemen wishful of pissing away their money and time are ever in need of *that*. God forbid they be known for the fools they are."

Edward laughed. "But I in turn must thank God for those fools," he returned. "Without them I'd likely be nothing but a poor army captain living on half pay."

Anstruther crooked one eyebrow. "No' a gambling man yourself, then?"

"No, for I've observed that vice since boyhood," said Edward. "But some men are bound and determined to throw away money on chance, Anstruther, no matter whether I exist. If I do not take their gold, some other enterprising chap will—and he may not be honest in the doing of it."

"*Hmmph*," said the steward with no malice in his tone. "And you are? Honest, I mean?"

Edward was turning his whisky glass absently around in circles atop Kate's desk. "Well, whatever else people may say of me, I've never been called a cheat or a liar," he said. "A hard-hearted bastard, perhaps—but I could hardly dispute either, could I?"

"'Twouldn't be my place to say, sir," Anstruther answered.

"Well, I can tell you this," said Edward. "I know Lord Reginald intimately enough that I have found myself in possession of the estate which I believe adjoins this. I have relieved him of Heatherfields."

"Ah, have you now?" Anstruther grinned.

"It was part of my purpose in coming to Somerset. Thank God I've remembered it." He hesitated an instant, then forged ahead. "By the way, Anstruther—"

"Aye?" He lifted one eyebrow.

Edward carefully considered his next words. "Is there any need to worry about Lady d'Allenay being . . . well, *bothered* by Lord Reginald?"

"*Hmm*," said Anstruther. "Up to old tricks, is he?"

"I don't know his old ones," said Edward grimly, "but I dislike what I've seen today."

Anstruther scrubbed a hand around his jaw. "Oh, Kate can handle Reggie, I expect. But I dinna ken what her mither was thinking, to be honest."

"Well," said Edward, "perhaps I shall stay on a few days. I must, after all, see to Heatherfields."

"Aye, someone better," the steward grumbled.

"As to that, Anstruther, you strike me as a man of some knowledge," said Edward. "I would welcome any advice you might have with regard to bringing the estate back to all it should be."

"Aye, then roll your London money out here in a great wheelbarrow, Mr. Quartermaine," said the steward, "for you're to have need of it."

"That bad, is it?" said Edward. "I suspected as much when I took title. I suppose, however, I held out some hope . . ."

"Well, abandon it," Anstruther interjected. "The roof's

giving in o'er one wing o' the hoose, and the outbuildings and farms are worse. One's no longer even tenanted, for the rats won't e'en take up in it. Reckon Lord Reggie might no' have told you that."

"He's unaware, more likely, no more attention than he seems to have paid it." Edward sighed. "Well. Time is on my side, I suppose."

"Dinna ye mean to live in it, then?" The steward's wary expression had returned.

Edward pinned the man with a steady gaze. "The estate is merely an investment, Anstruther," he said certainly. "Once the place is habitable, I will not further trouble Lady d'Allenay."

Anstruther lifted his massive shoulders. "As to whether or not you've troobled the lady, it's no' my place to say," he answered. "Miss Kate can speak well enough for herself on that score. However, if it's an investment you're after, Belle-combe might look at it by way of expansion, and save you the cost of repair—assuming we could come to terms."

Edward hesitated. "I misspoke," he said. "*Investment* is not the right word. I've a purpose for the house, but it is not for me."

Anstruther's expression turned uneasy again, and Edward was searching for a way to clarify his words when a hard knock sounded upon the door and Nancy Wentworth flew in in a swirl of blue velvet and red-gold curls.

"Oh, I beg your pardon!" she said upon turning around and seeing Edward.

"I was just on my way out," he assured her.

"Oh, not on my account!" Miss Wentworth perched herself on one corner of Anstruther's desk, but she was looking at Edward appraisingly. "So, I hear you're to switch allegiances?"

"Allegiances?" Edward looked at her curiously.

Miss Wentworth's pretty face broke into a wide smile.

"You're to be Mamma's guest instead of Kate's and—oh, that reminds me!—Anstruther, we've a command performance after dinner. And Cook is making her famous leek soup. Perhaps that will ease the sting?"

On a great grimace, Anstruther cut an unhappy look up at the girl. "Dinner wi' that lot?" he complained. "Have I nae choice?"

"Certainly!" Miss Wentworth had begun to brush what looked like sawdust from one shoulder of his tweed coat. "You may go to Aurélie and beg off. But I think we both know how that will turn out."

Anstruther swatted the girl away. "Leave it, Nan," he said, pushing himself up from the chair on a sigh. "Quartermaine, I beg your pardon. I'd better go and dress."

The estate agent strode from the room, snatching his greatcoat from its hook as he went.

"Well," said Miss Wentworth when he had vanished. "Let me try this again." She extended her hand, along with her usual bright smile. "How do you do, Mr. Quartermaine? May I still call you Edward?"

There was something all too knowing in the girl's eyes, and he regretted having snapped at her earlier. He took her slender hand into his own. "You may not," he said, giving it an almost affectionate squeeze. "Not in company, miss. Do you understand me?"

Her smile turned teasing. "Oh, yes," she said, dropping his hand, "because you operate an iniquitous gaming hell."

"I think those terms are a trifle redundant," he replied. "And who told you that, by the way?"

Her eyes glittered. "Reggie did," she said conspiratorially. "And straightaway, too. He didn't scruple an instant to tell me how wicked you are."

"And if you've a brain in your head, Miss Wentworth, you'll heed it," said Edward, "as should your sister."

The girl gave an impudent shrug of one shoulder, and slid

off Anstruther's desk. "Alas, we are Aurélie Wentworth's daughters," she said as her heels clicked onto the flagstone, "and likely haven't a teacup of brains between the three of us."

Edward did laugh then. There were enough brains between those three to overthrow the British government, he suspected, and it was entirely ludicrous that he should sit here discussing wickedness with a country innocent. Indeed, he wondered that Anstruther had left them alone together.

But no one at Bellecombe seemed quite as scandalized as they ought to have been, hardened, perhaps, as they were by the scandals that had come before him.

"Well, I'm off." Miss Wentworth was already halfway out the door. "I shall see you, *Edward*, at dinner."

This last was cast cavalierly over her shoulder, and it was on the tip of his tongue to call her back and chide her. But Nancy Wentworth had bolted after Anstruther, shouting something about his remembering to rosin his bowstring.

Edward went out into the cool shadows of the bailey, and watched them standing beneath the inner portcullis, chattering like the most amiable of friends. He liked this place very much, he thought again; liked the camaraderie and the cooperation of it. He was growing fond of the plainspoken Anstruther, just as he was with everyone else at Bellecombe, and was a little sorry Mrs. Wentworth and her friends had come to taint it.

But then, he had been here before any of them.

Yes, it was time for him to go. He knew it. Hadn't he just said those very words to Kate's estate agent?

And yet, not half an hour past, he had written Peters to give him his new direction. More telling still, he had enclosed a letter to Maggie Sloan. She would likely be relieved it was at an end; theirs had been a sporadic romance, and beautiful actresses expected to be catered to.

Edward did not cater. And Maggie—well, Maggie didn't shed tears. Not unless she was paid to.

So, no, he was not leaving Bellecombe, was he? Not yet. He would stay as Aurélie Wentworth's guest, just another day or two—merely to keep an eye on Lord Reginald Hoke, and ensure the man intended Kate no insult.

Or so he told himself.

It had grown cold now inside the castle walls, and dusk was coming on fast. His mind deeply conflicted, Edward turned and went back into the main house.

Only then, halfway up the steps, did he remember Annie's pearls.

CHAPTER 10

Kate's Quandary

Kate went through the next few days like an automaton, socializing with her guests at breakfast and at dinner, then spending the rest of each day out and about, attending to her estate duties. She left all else to her mother—who would have done as she pleased regardless.

To her undying relief, the fine weather held and she was able to escape Reggie's cloying attentiveness when the gentlemen went off into the valleys and woodlands in pursuit of wildfowl during the daylight hours.

With his leg so greatly improved, and his cracked collarbone opposite his gun shoulder, Edward surprised her by joining the shooting party—along with Lady Julia, who, though she was not quite so bold as to actually shoot, nonetheless tugged on her boots and went off to admire the hunters. A few neighboring gentlemen having been invited, Richard Burnham also came—not so much from any love of sport, Kate guessed, but because Nancy accompanied Aurélie daily at noon with the lavish luncheon prepared and packed by Cook.

In accordance with Aurélie's wishes, the hampers of food—along with Bellecombe's second-best china, white wine for the guests, and ale for the beaters—were then hauled out into the hinterlands to be laid out like a moveable feast on purpose-built folding tables made by the estate carpenter.

The tables were covered in the best Irish linen. The wine was French. Filou sat in Aurélie's lap wearing a little scarlet coat and eating tidbits from her plate while Bellecombe's pointers howled in protest for having done all the work with no reward.

Kate was in charity with the pointers. It was all rather farcical, really, and made all the more so since Nancy and Aurélie were driven out not on the ordinary wagons with the servants, but in Anstruther's well-sprung curricle, since he, however irascible he pretended to be, indulged Aurélie's every whim even as he complained of her extravagance.

In defense of Aurélie, Kate was forced to acknowledge that her mother had not been wrong in predicting Lady Julia's behavior. By the afternoon of the second day, Julia returned to the castle with her arm linked companionably with Edward's, waxing awestruck over the gentleman's deadly skill, and declaring breathlessly that he had *actually allowed her to hold his gun!*

Uncharitably, Kate wanted to put a gun to Lady Julia's head.

Instead she kept her mouth shut and ate enough braised woodcock to last her until Lady Day.

Thus neglected by Lady Julia, Sir Francis turned the full of his charm upon Nancy. This brought a dark scowl to the Reverend Mr. Burnham's face and a look of deep disapproval to Anstruther's. *Le comte* came down with a sniffle, which he attributed to damp boots. And despite attempts both subtle and obvious, Lady Julia could not *quite* corner Edward—and his gun—alone.

In the end, no one save Aurélie was happy—and she was as giddy and gay as ever.

So far as Kate was concerned, Edward kept his distance, even at meals. Having surrendered the task of seating charts and menus over to Aurélie, Kate was irrationally irritated by her mother's habit of putting Kate and Edward at opposite ends of every table, and situating Reggie somewhere near Kate's elbow.

Aurélie, one could only conclude, did not grasp Kate's definition of a cold day in hell.

Even the servants began to notice. In the village and across both Bellecombe and Heatherfields, word of Kate and Reggie's broken betrothal had provided gossip fodder for a fortnight. Now the gossipmongers had begun to weigh the possibilities of a reconciliation; Kate could see it in their eyes, and it horrified her.

This was confirmed as she and Mrs. Peppin drove back from the village one afternoon, the housekeeper having needed a pound of beeswax and some linseed oil for waterproofing *le comte*'s boots.

"And never, miss, was there ever such a slipshod valet as de Macey's man," Mrs. Peppin was complaining as Kate cut her gig around Edward's fateful milestone and started up the hill. "He can black a boot well-a-fine, I'll grant ye, but it's as if the fellow never met a puddle!"

"I think when Fitch comes to remove Mr. Quartermaine's sutures this afternoon, Peppie, we should ask him to look in on the comte." Kate was staring over her horse's head. "I cannot like his cough."

"This afternoon, eh?" Mrs. Peppin sniffed. "Well. I daresay Mr. Edward will pack off straightaway then. And none will be better pleased than Lord Reginald to see the back of him."

Kate smiled as if she'd given no thought to Edward's leaving. "Do you suggest Reggie has designs on Lady Julia, Peppie?"

"Miss Kate!" Mrs. Peppin shot a disdainful look across the gig. "Mr. Edward pays that one no mind. She just sniffs arter him like that pug running behind your mother. As to Lord Reginald, I think we know how the wind blows."

Kate cut a dark look at the housekeeper. "Peppie, was Mrs. Shearn gossiping with you just now? When you were paying Mr. Hastings for the wax?"

Mrs. Peppin's face colored furiously. "She were talking," the housekeeper acknowledged, "and I were listening."

"Ah, thank you for that fine hair-splitting!" said Kate. "And what, pray, was the good woman talking *about*?"

The housekeeper hesitated. "There's talk in the village that Lord Reginald's come back," she acknowledged, "and much speculation as to whether the pair of you have reconciled."

Kate all but turned around on the seat. "I hope you quickly disabused her."

Mrs. Peppin shrugged. "There's no discouraging gossip," she said evenly, "when there are those as wish to believe it."

"Why would anyone care?" asked Kate incredulously.

"It's Heatherfields, miss," said the housekeeper, "all gone to rack and ruin. A village suffers when a great house sits empty. Fewer to be employed, fewer candles and flour and soap to be bought. All totted up, Miss Kate, it do hurt."

"And Reggie is charming," said Kate under her breath. "That's what it comes down to."

"I think it's not that," said Mrs. Peppin musingly. "Oh, he's the greatest charmer ever lived, but everyone knows he's let things go. No, I think it's you, miss. I think the village would like a proper family at Bellecombe again."

A proper family.

She and Nancy, Kate supposed, didn't constitute such a thing; not in the eyes of the village. No, they wanted a lord of the manor with his boots up by the fire, and half a dozen children to carry on the name. As if she did not want the same.

"I'm sorry I've been such a disappointment to the entire countryside," said Kate bitterly. "I wonder what everyone would have me do? Kidnap a husband?"

At that, Mrs. Peppin laid a hand on her sleeve. "Oh, miss, don't take hard," she said. "There's not a soul as doesn't want the best for you. Surely you know it?"

"Yes, I suppose." Kate topped the next hill, and reined her cob back a bit. "But *Reggie*? Really?"

Mrs. Peppin was silent for a long moment. "Mr. Edward's in a nasty line o' business, I hear," she said a little too casually.

"Indeed." Kate felt her lips thin. "He owns a gaming hell."

"And that is very wicked, I reckon?" said the housekeeper speculatively.

"Well, he's hardly Circe calling from the rocks to lure men to improvidence," said Kate. "They go of their own accord. But yes, it's wicked. I'm sure we ought not know him. But Mamma does not care a fig for that—and I'm not sure I do. I should, I know, but . . ."

She let her words trail away. There really was no explaining, even to dear Peppie, just how she felt. Wounded. Disappointed. Thwarted. *Deceived.*

And yet she'd been deceived by no one save herself. Edward had warned her, and often. He had not known *who* he was, but he had seemed to have a sense of *what* he was.

For all you know, Lady d'Allenay, he had said, *I am a very bad man.*

It had been but the first of his many cautions. About his character. His unknown past. And yet she had not listened. Indeed, she was not even *sorry* she hadn't listened!

Good Lord, what was she coming to?

In the passageway but a few days past, Kate had told him

that she did not know Ned Quartermaine. But that was a lie, wasn't it? She had known him all along. She had known him *intimately*. She had gone to his bed knowing his character was questionable, for he'd told her so. And given half a chance, it seemed she might do it again.

Mrs. Peppin sighed deeply. "Can you not find it in your heart to forgive Lord Reginald, then?" she said. "I know, miss, that you don't love him, and that he's riddled with fault, but—"

"*But I should settle?*" Kate interjected. "Oh, Peppie! Not you, too?"

"Not *settle*, lovey." Mrs. Peppin set a hand between Kate's shoulder blades and rubbed it in little circles as she'd done so often in Kate's childhood. "But Heatherfields has been in the hands of Lord Reginald's family for nearly as long as Bellecombe's been in yours. Besides, I know you want children. And how else to get 'em if you will not go to London, and you will not have Mr. Edward?"

"Have *Edward*?" Kate could feel the warm weight of tears threaten. "He . . . Heavens, Peppie! He has not asked me. And . . . my God, a gaming hell owner? After all Bellecombe has been through? Is that not the very antithesis of what we need?"

Mrs. Peppin merely grunted. "I'd say it's time some money flowed uphill to Bellecombe instead o' trickling down," she said dismissively. "Wentworth men, if you'll pardon my saying, are mostly good at the down. Besides, 'tis no one's business save your own."

But it was not just Kate's business, was it?

Even if Edward were interested in her, what of Nancy's prospects? Nancy, who wished so desperately to be a rector's wife. Mightn't a scandal ruin that prospect? And what about Aunt Louisa with three young daughters yet to bring out? And Uncle Upshaw's certain outrage?

Aurélie's antics were trouble enough to Lord and Lady

Upshaw, but should Kate—the titular head of the Wentworths, and the one they depended on to behave rationally—oh, should *she* make such a scandalous match . . .

Well, it was out of the question.

As she had just said, Edward had not asked her, nor would he. The very notion was mad. Besides, there could not possibly be any place in such a man's life for marriage, let alone children. But he was still every inch a man—and quite a lot of inches there were, too, if she was any judge. And while even a green fool could see Edward was not the marrying kind, mightn't he—with a little coaxing—return to her bed?

Must the rest of her days be not just barren, but something worse?

Kate thought again of the shimmering dress her mother had brought from Paris; of the low neckline and the way the too-snug bodice pushed up her breasts. Heavens, if that wasn't coaxing, she didn't know what was.

Then, realizing the perilous path her thoughts were taking, Kate shut her eyes. Good Lord, gambling and wickedness had impoverished her childhood and the entire estate. Did she now mean to literally climb in bed with it?

But last time, she had not climbed, had she? Edward had urged her down into the softness of the bed linen, crawling over her like some lithe, golden predator . . .

"In any case," said Mrs. Peppin, as if reading her thoughts, "that one's as fine a man as ever I've laid eyes on—and I've seen him naked, mind. No real charm, o'course. But charm won't keep a woman warm at night."

"Peppie," said Kate tightly, "you're not helping me."

"Well, the Lord helps them as help themselves," said Mrs. Peppin, "and if I were young as you, miss, I might be helping myself to that man."

"Peppie." Kate clasped a hand over her eyes. "This is scandalous."

"Yes, mayhap," said the housekeeper, "but don't tell me, miss, you weren't thinking it."

Kate did not tell her. Instead, she set a spanking pace for home.

So everyone expected her to do the sensible thing, did they? To marry Reggie, and be glad the scoundrel would have her? Well, they could all go to the devil. She was getting tired of being dependable and predictable and sensible.

She was going to go home and try on the dress—*without* the fichu.

She was going make a fool of herself.

Again.

BELLECOMBE'S ILLUSTRIOUS PARTY numbered a lively twelve for dinner that evening. It being customary for the great house to entertain the local gentry on such occasions, several neighbors had been invited. And Aurélie, of course, had again demanded the put-upon Anstruther's attendance.

They sat down to dinner in good spirits, with Edward finding himself situated between Lady Julia and Squire Cockram's wife, whom he'd met only briefly, the day he'd embarrassed Kate in her drawing room. As usual, the pug lay under the table at Mrs. Wentworth's feet, occasionally rising to snuffle about on the floor. Edward was beginning to grasp the means by which the lady preserved her svelte figure.

Throughout the meal, he listened attentively to Julia's chatter but found himself bored, and incapable of keeping his eyes from cutting down the table in Kate's direction. He had become accustomed, he realized, to her simple mode of dress—and if asked, he would have said he much preferred it.

But that was before he'd seen the gold and green confection that bared her lovely shoulders, wrapped her slender waist like a second skin, and . . . well, there was no peace to be had in observing what it did to the rest of her fine attributes.

He was not alone in admiring it. Even before the party had sat down to dinner, Lord Reginald had alternated between allowing his gaze to drift lazily—almost possessively—

down Kate's length, and shooting dark glances across the room at Edward.

Reggie's snit was the least of Edward's concerns; the fellow was nothing but a nuisance so far as he could see. But then the party reunited in the drawing room, and Lady Julia leaned into him in a cloud of too-sweet perfume.

"Will they make a match of it, do you imagine, Mr. Quartermaine?" she murmured, making a discreet gesture toward the pair who stood alone together in a private corner. "De Macey thinks not, but Sir Francis has wagered him twenty pounds."

Edward felt his spine go rigid. "I beg your pardon?"

Lady Julia's grin deepened. "Lady d'Allenay and Lord Reginald," she clarified. "I was warned off, you know, by her mamma, before we'd even left London. I assume the family hopes for a reconciliation. Indeed, I collect the poor girl has had no other suitor these last many years."

"If that is true," he said tightly, "then it is doubtless by the lady's choice."

"Do you think so?" asked Lady Julia, snaring a glass of madeira as Jasper passed with a tray. "It is said she wishes to marry. The barony needs an heir. Her mamma hoped, I think, that her position toward Reggie had softened."

Just then, amidst much cajoling from Nancy Wentworth, a neighbor sat down at the pianoforte and struck up an exuberant tune. In a trice, Mrs. Wentworth ordered the rugs rolled up, and soon one of the gentlemen was leading Miss Wentworth out in a lively country-dance. Mrs. Wentworth attempted to drag Anstruther onto the floor with them, but the big man shook his head.

The lady turned her attention to de Macey, who cheerfully obliged her.

"How quaint! A country entertainment." Julia edged her elbow in Edward's direction. "Shall we show them how it's done in Town, Mr. Quartermaine?"

"I think not," he said laconically. "Try Sir Francis."

The dark-eyed Sir Francis was indeed approaching. Lady Julia cast Edward one last, faintly pouting glance, then abandoned him for the better offer, pressing her untouched glass into his hand.

Edward gave an inward sigh of relief, then wondered why he did so.

Lady Julia was precisely his sort of woman; a beautiful widow with enough knowledge to entertain him in bed, and enough practicality to know he would never marry her.

It should have been ideal. And for a moment, Edward actually tried to persuade himself to go after her. Forcing his gaze to follow her as she dipped and swayed, her eye flashing prettily, Edward sipped Julia's wine and considered what he was giving up in not pursuing the lady's hints. But then his attention caught on a flash of emerald green, and the thought was lost.

Her lips a little tightly compressed, Kate was allowing Lord Reginald to lead her into the dancers. He felt his ire stir, then reined it back. He was jealous, and had no right to be so. Reggie was duplicitous and lazy, but not, he thought, precisely evil.

As gentlemen went, there were worse. *Much* worse.

The truth was, Edward disdained most of his clientele. Decent gamblers—men like de Macey, with whom one might actually sit down and enjoy a drink and some intelligent conversation—were rare. Worse, they were unprofitable. Until now, he had simply viewed Reggie with his usual contempt. But he was coming to actively loathe the man.

He didn't deceive himself as to why. But he knew on that same breath that it would not do; that he could not help Kate in any meaningful way save to keep his distance.

Kate danced as she did everything else, with grace and competence, and few flourishes. The confection she wore, with its bold colors and plunging bodice, was made for no debutante. It was a daring gown for a bold woman; one who knew what she wanted.

Did Kate know what she wanted?

Did she want Lord Reginald Hoke? Had she once loved him?

She wished to be married, Julia had suggested. Was it true? Kate had hinted otherwise to him; that marriage was a risk she had rather not take. He wasn't sure he'd believed her, even then. He was ever more confident he didn't now.

Edward watched her until the music tinkled to a halt, remembering how she had moved beneath him in bed with that same lovely grace and sense of purpose. And for an instant, he felt that same aching sense of loss; the feeling of having slid into something deep, from which he might never extract himself.

Since regaining his memory, he had struggled to become himself again. Cold. Aloof. Outwardly civil, but ruthless inside. Yet it sometimes felt as if his very nature was trying to shift like loose gravel beneath his feet.

He knew the sensation would not last; that he was what he was, and that even his affection for Maria had not changed him. Nor would his feelings for Kate—whatever they were. He would as soon not analyze them too thoroughly.

Reggie had caught Kate's hands and was spinning her about the room. Well. A husband. She needed one, he thought. Deserved one. A kind and good man.

But she didn't deserve him. No, it would not do.

And she certainly deserved better than Lord Reginald Hoke.

When the music ended, Kate stepped back from Reggie, her face flushed pink. He reached up and tucked a loose strand of hair behind her ear. Aurélie Wentworth circled an affectionate arm around her younger daughter, and whispered something. Nancy laughed, drew away, and snatched Reggie by the arm to drag him near.

The three of them looked very gay, as if they shared a happy secret that he could never be a part of. Here at Bellecombe, even Mrs. Wentworth evoked something of that sense of domestic contentment he had enjoyed during his recovery. Before he had known who and what he was.

Now he was just another outsider looking in; a hard man who had lived a brutal life. He didn't belong here in this paradise with its quiet and beauty. Grace was wasted on the likes of him, however he might yearn for it. Or yearn for her, the epitome of grace.

He paused in his pathetic musings to glance back. Kate had vanished—through one of the windows that gave onto the formal rose garden, he suspected, for the draperies covering it still stirred. Suddenly he felt an intense warmth at his side, and turned to see Mrs. Wentworth at his elbow, her seemingly irrepressible smile curling one corner of her mouth.

"*Ça alors*, Mr. Quartermaine, you do not dance?"

"Rarely," he said. "Are you inviting me?"

She laughed, a light, trilling sound. "*Vraiment*, sir, the word *invite* seems far too benign to be applied to a man with so grim a gaze. Does one *invite* a lion to dine?"

"You did," he pointed out.

She giggled as if he were the cleverest creature on earth. "This is true," she acknowledged. "Ah, I see Fitch has dealt with your stitches! Now you have only a scar to lend character to your handsome face."

"A man of my ilk," he said blandly, "should probably take his character where he can get it."

Mrs. Wentworth shrugged, then set her head coquettishly to one side. "*C'est bien*," she murmured, studying his forehead. "You were *too* handsome, I think, before."

Edward took a long, slow sip of the wine he held, and carefully considered his next words. "Mrs. Wentworth," he said quietly, "are you by any chance flirting with me?"

She laughed, but it was uneasy. "And if I were?"

"Then I would thank you for the compliment you pay

me," he said, setting Julia's glass down with a sharp *chink*, "and tell you that perhaps it's best I went on my way back to London."

Her beautiful eyes widened with alarm. *"Non,"* she said, seizing his arm. "You must not go! Not yet!"

"Must not?" He looked down at the thin, pale fingers curled around his coat sleeve like beautiful talons. "Those are strong words, *madame*."

She released his arm. "Perhaps, but I think you tease me," she said, her lashes lowered. "You will stay, *oui*? I see a reluctant willingness in your eyes. I am grateful. I have need of you, sir."

"I can't think why," he said. "You have a coterie of admirers, *madame*."

"It is not a coterie that I need," she said, cutting a sidelong glance at Reggie. "I fear, sir, that I have brought a serpent into my daughter's house. Perhaps you might help me—*zut*, what is the phrase? Guard the wicket?"

Edward crooked one eyebrow with a look that usually sent his customers and staff scurrying. Mrs. Wentworth was made of sterner stuff, and merely batted her lashes.

"Explain yourself," he said.

The lady swallowed hard, her swanlike throat working. "It is Lord Reginald," she whispered. "He persuaded me to bring him here with tears and pledges of adoration. But now I learn—*ma foi!*—he has lost everything, or near it! Worse, he has lost Heatherfields. To *you*."

Edward beheld her for a moment in stony silence. "I took it fairly, *madame*," he finally answered, "and in accordance with gentlemen's terms. Do not be so bold—or so foolish—as to ask for my sympathy. You will not get it."

"Mais non, I do not," she replied, the words rushing out. "I ask merely for your—"

At that moment, Reggie glided up beside him. Over his shoulder, Edward could see Nancy Wentworth looking at her mother with dismay.

"Careful of this one, Quartermaine," said Reggie silkily, hooking his arm through Mrs. Wentworth's. "In Madame Heartbreaker, even you may have met your match."

The lady smacked him almost playfully. "Reginald!"

He smiled, and leveled his gaze to Edward's. "Oh, she may pet over little cubs like Sir Francis," he said on a chuckle, "but she eats wicked men for breakfast."

"I think," said Edward, "I can manage."

Then he gave Mrs. Wentworth a taut bow at the neck, and left. He circled around the room, noting as he did so that the lady's head was bent to Reggie's as if they shared some confidence.

What had Mrs. Wentworth meant? Was it a ploy on behalf of Reggie? Or was she genuinely concerned? The lady seemed the last person on earth to behave altruistically. But then, what did he know of her?

In that moment, he scarcely cared. He slipped behind one of the heavy velvet draperies, and pushed open a door. The garden was shaped like a circle, in the center of which stood a massive marble urn that spouted rainwater into the rose beds. This was surrounded by a sort of circular bench that, in summer, would have provided a marvelous view.

Just now, all it provided was the opportunity for frostbite. He found Kate shivering there amidst the dying roses. "You're going to freeze to death out here," he said, stripping off his coat, "and utterly crush Reggie's dreams."

Kate gave a hysterical bark of laughter. "It is Reggie who drove me out here, blast him."

"My, what language," said Edward blandly. Gently, he furled the coat around her shoulders. "There. Warmer?"

"Thank you," she said on a snuffle.

"Now," he gently pressed, "what has Reggie done?"

She threw up her hands. "Oh, he begs me to dance, to stroll in the moonlight, to play piquet and talk about what used to be," she said. "In short, he wishes me to *still care*. And I will not—which he finds most disobliging. And that makes him testy. I wonder how much money he owes. It must be a quite desperate amount."

Edward was certain she was right, but he didn't say as much. Far be it from him to drive home the sad truth of Reggie's indebtedness.

On a sigh, Kate sank down onto a bench behind her knees. Left with no alternative—and no real wish to do otherwise—Edward joined her. Certain he'd regret it later, he circled an arm around her shoulders, and drew her to his side.

Kate tucked close, and her shivering eased. The chill was born, he feared, as much from fatigue as cold.

"These people," he said darkly, "are wearing you out."

"Oh, Edward. It is not that. I am not so faint of heart."

"Then Lord Reginald Hoke," he replied, "is wearing you out. I'd like to take my riding crop to that impudent dog."

"Oh, never mind Reggie," she said. "I'm just tired. I was having a difficult day even before he started in with his whinging."

Instinctively, he tightened his embrace. "What happened?"

She gave the curious laugh again. "I drove Peppie into the village for errands," she said, "to find the entire populace speculating whether I would finally marry Reggie."

"I fear the villagers do not know you as well as they think," Edward murmured, "if they imagine you a rug to be trod upon."

"Indeed not." She gave an exasperated sigh. "In any case, after that I came home to find we'd lost two lambs to pneumonia, and a letter on my desk from Uncle Upshaw. I had forgotten, Edward. I had forgotten I'd invited him. He is coming, but without Aunt Louisa."

"Damn it," he muttered. "Kate, I should go."

A long silence hung heavy over the rose garden. "Oh," she said softly. "Oh, Edward. I wish you would not."

"I have some knowledge of Lord Upshaw," Edward warned. "He is a staunch and stodgy conservative."

"—and a prosy moralizer," Kate added, "but I love him. And I respect him greatly."

"He'll be little pleased to find the likes of me at Belle-combe," Edward warned.

Beneath the weight of his large coat, her slender shoulders shrugged. "He likes none of Aurélie's friends," she said evenly. "Are you not here as *her* guest?"

He was, actually.

And it made him wonder yet again what Kate's mother was up to. For a woman who spent her mornings abed until noon, and her afternoons lazing about with her malodorous pug, she still seemed a woman of boundless scheming.

"Kate," he said quietly, "I'm sorry if I've seemed . . . *harsh* of late. But this should have ended. I care for you—deeply—and because of it—"

"Oh, please don't go," said Kate. "I know I oughtn't ask it. But I will feel so frightfully outnumbered if you leave."

"Dash it, Kate, does everyone expect you to marry that man?" asked Edward gruffly. "Will Upshaw?"

She shook her head. "Yes to everyone. And *no* to Uncle Upshaw. He never liked Reggie. He was pleased, I think, when I begged off the betrothal."

Edward dipped his head and set his lips to her forehead for a long moment. It was a kiss of comfort, and she didn't push him away. "Kate," he finally murmured, "I wish to God I had not come here."

"Well, you didn't, did you?" she said sharply. "I ran you down."

He had hurt her, he realized—and likely not for the last time.

"Stop flogging yourself over that," he said gently. "I was glad for the holiday from—" He couldn't find the words. A man could not escape himself; not for long.

"What?" she said. "What is that supposed to mean?"

"Nothing," he said, giving her hand a gentle squeeze.

"You look lovely tonight, Kate. That dress . . . well, there are no words, really."

Her head still tucked against his shoulder, Kate gave a muffled laugh. "I wore it with the notion of seducing you," she said in a voice of quiet confession. "But this does not seem like seduction."

And yet it was. It was the most dangerous sort of seduction. The kind that made a man ache with longing and regret, and wish for things he ought never have.

"Ah, Kate," he said, kissing her forehead again. "We are fools."

"Perhaps," she said.

And there seemed nothing left to do save kiss her. To run that awful risk of further hurting her. Besides, Kate had caught the resignation in his voice, and already lifted her head from his shoulder. So Edward tipped up her chin with his finger, and brushed his lips over hers.

"*Kate*," he whispered.

Kate's arm came up to curl around his neck, and the kiss fired to something hotter and sweeter. He felt her breath hitch. He stroked the seam of her lips, then pushed them open with his tongue, thrusting inside to entwine his tongue around hers.

She made a sweet sound of pleasure, her nails curling into the wool of his coat collar. She tasted tart, like wine, and smelled of soap and new-mown grass. Clean and pure.

Yes, seduction of the worse sort. The innocent sort, perfectly designed to entice a man who had known nothing but depravity. Any bought-and-paid-for female could seduce a man with her body and her wiles; some would do it just to prove they could. But this was a seduction of the heart. A longing so deep it drove like a spike into his soul.

He stroked his tongue sinuously along hers, one hand still set to the curve of her face, and felt her quicken to his touch. Her hand was pressed to his heart, warming his skin through the silk of his waistcoat. He tried to keep his mind on the door, to stay alert to any sound, but it was useless. She drowned him in desire.

But it was Kate who broke the kiss and pulled away, her breath a little fast.

"Kate?" he murmured, his eyes searching her face in the darkness.

"Come to my bed tonight," she said on a rush.

Already he could feel blood surging. His cock hardening. The will to say no vanishing.

Edward brushed his lips over hers. "Yes," he whispered. "Midnight?"

She nodded. "I had better go back inside," she said, scooting away and leaping to her feet. "You will come? I have seduced you?"

He felt himself smile in the darkness, and for once there was no bitterness in it. "You had me seduced, Kate, from the moment I opened my eyes at Bellecombe."

"Edward," she said quietly, "you don't have to say that. I know I'm not . . ."

"Beautiful?" he gently supplied. "Your beauty, Kate, is quiet. Elegant and graceful. And for however brief a time we are lovers, I would appreciate it if you didn't tell me what I think."

"Well. It seems you know your own mind, then." She started toward the door, but stopped to glance back at him in the gloom. "Edward, you're very kind," she whispered. "And I *do* know you. Forgive me for saying I did not."

"Kate, love, I am not that man," he said. "The man who opened his eyes and saw your face. The man who teased and flirted with you so blithely. That isn't me; it never will be. So I misled you. And I'm sorry for it."

Kate slowly shook her head. "Perhaps you have let your work—or your past—determine who you think you are," she said, her voice a little tremulous. "But there is another man inside of you. I know. I have seen him."

"You saw a man with a fractured skull."

She laughed weakly. "No, just a bump on the head," she countered. "I saw you, *Ned* Quartermaine. And you are a very decent sort of man."

But he was not. Nor was he even gentleman enough to correct her. Moreover, it would have done no good. Kate was half in love with him. Or in love with the notion of being in love, at least.

Still, Kate made Edward wish he'd lived his life a little differently. That he had not resigned his army commission in such a fury, angrily pursuing something he'd never been meant to have. Even the bastard son of the Duchess of Dunthorpe had had a chance to make something decent of himself.

But he had snuffed out that chance and—in a young man's fit of grief and rage—turned into something not so very different from what his father had been.

And now that man was going to Kate's bed. It was unconscionable, really. His intentions were not honorable. *He* was not honorable.

He rose and went into the lamplight, then extracted his pocket watch.

Midnight, it seemed, could not possibly come soon enough.

CHAPTER 11

A Romantic Assignation

"Kate, you should have a real maid," said Nancy, drawing the brush through her sister's hair. "A lady's maid, I mean. Like Mamma has Tillie."

"What, someone who's paid to listen to my tantrums? And to pick up the shoes I hurl across the room?" On a laugh, Kate lifted her gaze to the mirror. "No. I have you, Nancy. For now."

"For now," her sister agreed, drawing the brush again.

Nancy stood in her nightgown and wrapper just behind Kate, her luxuriant strawberry-blonde hair hanging down her back in riotous curls, shimmering in the firelight as she brushed out Kate's unusually elaborate arrangement.

They had always made do this way, she and Nancy; taking turns brushing out and lacing up and unhooking whatever required unhooking. Kate was the seamstress, expert at replacing buttons and darning up rips. Nancy had a way with ribbons and colors, often laughingly declaring that, were Kate left to her own devices, she'd simply dress in shades of brown so that nothing need match.

Given all that, a lady's maid had seemed an unnecessary extravagance. So, at the end of a late evening—if it ran past dear Peppie's bedtime—it was always just Kate and Nancy.

Nancy had found a stray pin at the nape of Kate's neck, and was working it free. "How did you find Aurélie tonight?" she asked evenly.

"Ooh, now there's a weighty question," said Kate, watching her in the mirror. "On the whole, she's been on quite shockingly good behavior. She isn't flirting *too* outrageously with any of the gentlemen, nor drinking too much champagne. And she's stopped pushing Reggie in my face."

"She still insists on seating you near one another at dinner," Nancy pointed out, tossing the hairpin onto Kate's dressing table.

"Yes." Kate sighed. "There is that."

"*Hmm*," said her sister, taking up her brush again.

Nancy wanted to talk about something, Kate could tell. A little anxiously—and selfishly—she glanced at the ormolu clock on her mantelpiece. Half past eleven.

She returned her gaze to the mirror before her. "So, how does Aurélie like Richard?"

"She adores him as much as I do," said Nancy. "Can you not tell?"

"And yet tonight," Kate murmured, "you danced with every gentleman present *except* Richard. Well, and Edward."

"Actually, Edward was the only gentleman I did ask," Nancy admitted, "but he turned me down. What is your point?"

"That Aurélie is flinging gentlemen at you," Kate grumbled. "Her new scheme, I daresay, is to torment poor Richard into doing something rash. Do be careful, Nancy, please."

Actually, it had been obvious for the last two days that Aurélie had surrendered to Richard's earnest charm and utter devotion to Nancy. But whether that would translate into support for Nancy's marriage—or something more devious—Kate could not have said. Perhaps she had been too fixated on her own desires to spare Nancy's a thought.

In any case, Aurélie's support, or lack thereof, scarcely mattered; in keeping with England's archaic laws, a woman was not thought competent to grant a daughter permission to marry. Only her father or her guardian could do so. And since Nancy's father was dead, that left only her guardian . . .

"Uncle Upshaw is coming," Kate warned. "By midweek, at the latest."

Nancy sighed, and tossed the brush onto the dressing table with a clatter. "Well, that will just ruin everything," she said. "Uncle will frighten Richard to death. And the fact that Aurélie thinks we should marry will just turn him further against Richard."

Kate widened her eyes. "*Does* she think you should marry?"

Nancy shifted her gaze and shrugged. "Oh, who can ever know, Kate, what Aurélie really thinks?" she said. "All she'll do is wink and smile and tell me to trust that all will come aright in the end."

"Yes, just like a fairy tale!" said Kate mordantly. She rose from the dressing bench, and gave her sister a hug. "I will speak strongly to Uncle Upshaw, Nan," she said, "*if* you're sure that no one else will do?"

Tears welled in Nancy's eyes—and, as with everything she did, Nancy was beautiful when she cried. "No one else *will ever do*," she said. "I wish to be Richard's wife. I wish to work at his side for the greater good of our parish. Why can no one see the honor in that?"

"I see it," said Kate, catching her sister's hands and giving them a squeeze. "I will talk to Uncle, and I will make him see it—or at the very least, Nancy, I will do my best. I promise."

"Your opinion will go twice as far as Mamma's, at least," said Nancy, blinking hard. "All she ever says is 'La-de-da, never mind Upshaw! He's just a stick-in-the-mud to be got round.' "

"Hmm. Well." Kate kissed her sister's cheek. "I'll do all I can. I promise. Night, Nan."

"Yes. Good night." Her sister was halfway to the door when she stopped and spun around again, her pretty brow furrowed. "But Kate . . ."

"Yes?" Kate was already climbing into bed by way of discouraging any lingering. "What is it?"

"What did Aurélie and Anstruther quarrel about tonight?"

"Tonight?" Mystified, Kate shook her head. "When? I didn't see any quarrel."

"A while after the dancing started," said Nancy. "Mamma tried to coax him onto the floor but he wouldn't go, so she grabbed . . . someone. De Macey? Afterward, she spoke a few words with Edward—with Mr. Quartermaine, I mean— then he stalked off somewhere, too. Outside, I think. And next I knew Aurélie and Anstruther were out in the passageway looking daggers at one another."

"Good heavens."

"Not shouting, mind," Nancy added. "Aurélie is too refined to hurl shoes or words or anything else outside her bedchamber. But I know her temper when I see it—and Anstruther's, too."

Kate winced. "I will talk to him," she assured Nancy. "Whatever Aurélie did—well, I shall undo it. Something to do with tomorrow's shooting, no doubt."

"Oh, yes. Probably." But Nancy didn't leave. "Oh, and Kate? I wanted to tell you—Mrs. Cockram cornered Reggie before dinner tonight."

"Oh, Lord." Squire Cockram's wife was the village's second-best gossip, nearly neck-and-neck with Mrs. Shearn. "What did she say?"

Fleetingly, Nancy hesitated. "She said the entire village was happy to see him home," she answered, "and that they trusted the two of you had 'grown up a bit.' That everyone was counting on him this time. I think the implication was clear."

"All too clear," said Kate sardonically. "Well. I think we

can assume that word of Heatherfields having been sold to Edward has not got round yet."

"No, not a whisper." Nancy wrung her hands a little. "Kate, ought I not have told you? I don't want to worry you. I *don't*."

Kate smiled. "It does not matter," she lied. "Good night, Nancy."

With a niggling sense of guilt for having rushed her sister away, Kate slipped from the bed and dashed back to her dressing room as soon as Nancy shut the door. She bathed and brushed her teeth all over again, and dabbed on a hint of rosewater.

Then, as she pulled on her best nightgown, Kate caught sight of herself in the mirror.

She felt suddenly such a fraud. She hardly looked like the sort of woman who made midnight assignations with a dangerous, dashing man.

She looked like Miss Katherine Wentworth, ordinary country mouse.

Kate sighed, and sagged down onto her dressing bench. Aurélie would have known how to go on—and probably would have given Kate advice if she'd had gall enough to ask for it. Even Nancy knew how to look tempting; it came to her innately.

Kate picked up the brush Nancy had tossed down and turned it over and over in her hands, wishing she could absorb a little of her sister's charm from it. Since their accidental tryst in the rose garden, it had dawned on Kate that everything between her and Edward had changed radically. How could she hope to please him now?

Before it had been so much simpler. Making love to a man with no history—no complications, no faults, and no memory—had been a fantasy. It had felt as though they clung to each other in some private and intimate world; an extraordinary place where the ordinary did not exist. Because, in a way, it had not.

But now her ordinary life was all around her and Edward was in the middle of it; no less desirable—but certainly no longer a fantasy. He was a real man with a well-remembered past and some very dangerous edges. She should have considered that more carefully before wriggling into her seductive green and gold dress.

Gowns like that were not meant for girls like her anyway. The dress didn't make her beautiful, it merely distracted from her ordinariness. And it complicated things. Because Kate's life was not going to return to normal when Edward left. She had foolishly let herself fall in love with him.

She was in love with wicked Ned Quartermaine, a man who was the very antithesis of what she needed. He was not *Mr. Edward*, handsome, pleasant, and slightly incapacitated houseguest. He was like an uncaged lion roaming loose in her house. He had a stubborn streak, a vile temper, and a scarred past.

Oh, there was great goodness in him, she was certain of it. But he was still the very last sort of man she should have fallen for—and the very last sort who should have fallen for her, because now he could doubtless remember every woman who had come before her. Every lover he had taken to his bed. And Kate didn't kid herself. There had been many, many women in Ned Quartermaine's bed.

She wanted to trust that, in Edward's eyes, she was desirable. But that was so very hard to do. Kate had once believed Reggie desired her—and only her. Oh, men routinely made such claims; she knew that now. But she had not known it then. She had trusted Reggie completely, both as a friend and as her fiancé. She had lost her good sense in his words of love and adoration, and utterly lost her sense of self in the plans they had made for their future.

And if she had perhaps not loved Reggie with a passion that made her heart soar, she had nonetheless loved him sincerely. She had been young, and he was just Reggie; she had known him—and his foibles—all her life. And she had just wanted to be happy. Not giddy. Not desperately, madly in love. She had never expected that.

Yes, in accepting him, Kate had been settling, and contentedly so.

But Reggie had not been settling. He had meant all along to keep Bess, the lovely but penniless widow he'd set up in Bloomsbury. For all Kate knew, he kept her there still—and two or three children in the bargain. She had learnt the hard way that one could not trust a word that came out of Reggie's beautiful mouth.

She slammed the brush down and willed her hands not to shake. This was stupid. Edward was not Reggie. Men—no matter what Aurélie often said in the midst of a shoe-slinging snit—were not all alike. And if Edward had wanted a beautiful, more experienced lover, she reassured herself, he could have chosen Lady Julia, who had certainly shown him her cards.

Caught between anticipation and anxiety, Kate glanced at the clock.

It was a little past midnight already. He was late. Perhaps he was still playing at billiards with de Macey. Or perhaps he had simply come to his senses. Or perhaps Lady Julia had shown him something besides her cards . . .

A little angry that she had just expended such worry over another man, Kate got up, put out her lamp with a flick of her wrist, then climbed back into bed. Only the fire in the hearth lit her room now. She watched it snap and lick at the coals, its shadows dancing up the wall adjacent, and wondered if this was all there would ever be for her.

A big, empty bed.

In what felt tonight like a big, empty castle.

IT WAS WELL past midnight by the time the Comte de Macey banked his last ball and put Edward out of his misery. The dandified Frenchman studied every shot as if it were an exercise in physics upon which the future of his nation hung.

He was, in short, a bloody good billiards player, and Edward's mind had been elsewhere.

In Kate's bed, specifically.

After racking his cue and paying de Macey his ten-pound wager—the largest he ever permitted himself—Edward glanced at his watch and wondered if Kate would have locked him out by now. Hastily, he retraced his steps from that distant corner of the castle back to the main staircase.

As he started toward the top of the stairs, however, he heard voices in the great hall. Looking through the balustrade, he saw Aurélie Wentworth and Richard Burnham standing on the threshold below. Edward hesitated on the landing, uncertain what to do.

The last of the guests were finally departing, for through the open door, he could see Jasper assisting Squire Cockram into the Burnhams' coach. The young rector looked anxious to follow. But Mrs. Wentworth clasped one of his hands between her own, her tone lightly teasing.

"And so you wish to marry my daughter, *n'est-ce pas*?" she said, her mouth curled into that odd half smile that seemed perpetually upon her lips. "She is very young, you know."

"Yes, I wish to marry her desperately." Burnham swallowed hard, poor devil. "More than anything, ma'am."

"That is all very well." She patted his hand a little condescendingly. "But to paraphrase our American friends, *mon cher*, to the victor goes the spoils of war."

He drew back a fraction. "One does not like to think of love as war."

Mrs. Wentworth laughed lightly and let his hand go. "Perhaps not, Mr. Burnham, but in my experience, it is very much so," she said, "and on every level. We fight a battle for love, sometimes every day."

"Indeed, ma'am?" Both hands free now, the rector was turning his elegant beaver hat around and around by its brim almost anxiously. "I never thought of it in such a light."

Mrs. Wentworth leaned very near. "Tell me, Richard—*may* I call you Richard?"

"Certainly, I wish you would."

Again, the almost wicked smile. "Then tell me, Richard," she said. "Are you that rarest of creatures every woman searches for?"

"Well, I hope so, ma'am. But what sort, precisely?"

"A fighter," said Mrs. Wentworth, "and a man who can be trusted in all things."

"I'm a rector, Mrs. Wentworth," said the young man a little stiffly. "I should hope I'm to be trusted in all things. As to fighting, where Nancy is concerned, I'll do what I must."

"Excellent, excellent!" said Mrs. Wentworth, giving his arm a parting pat. "Well, Richard, perhaps we should speak further on this subject one of these days?"

But Edward had already turned to make his way back up the steps. He had no wish to intrude—or to fall into the lady's clutches again—so he set off in search of an alternate route to Kate's wing of the house.

Still, unless he missed his guess, Aurélie Wentworth was up to something on more than one front. Had she given up on pushing Sir Francis upon Nancy? The gentleman's attention had clearly turned to Lady Julia, and to his friendship with Lord Reginald Hoke, for he spent most of his time in their company of late.

Edward thought of Kate, and considered warning her. But of what? What had he heard? On its surface, nothing but a faintly philosophical conversation between two people of reasonable intellect.

And yet there was nothing remotely philosophical about Mrs. Wentworth. There was a purpose, he would venture, in every breath the woman drew.

Still, Aurélie Wentworth was not his problem. Her elder daughter, however, was. In truth, Kate had become enough of a problem to keep him up at night with doubt and something vaguely akin to despair twisting at his gut.

He pushed Kate's mad, effervescent mother from his mind, and hastened down the servants' stairs.

THE CREAKING OF the door came to Kate as if in a dream.

She was locked in a long, barrel-vaulted room lined with elegant wainscoting, its fine furniture draped in holland cloth and cobwebs. There was a pervasive sense of abandonment in the air, and low beams of late afternoon light cut down its length, dancing with dust motes.

Where was she? A familiar place, and yet a place she'd never seen. It meant something, she was quite sure of it. She was struggling to surface from the haze so that she might puzzle out that meaning in her conscious mind. And then the hinges creaked again, and the door swung shut.

In the dream, Kate turned. But there were no doors that she could see, and she was still alone. Alone in a beautiful but barren place.

"*Kate.*"

"*Hmmm?*"

Kate came awake to a heavy warmth that tucked snug against her, its weight sagging into the mattress.

"*Kate?*"

She felt a large, warm hand cup her face, and the vestiges of the dream vanished.

"Kate, I'm sorry. De Macey plays slow as treacle, devil take him. I couldn't think of a good excuse to simply quit. Should I have?"

"Edward—?" She stirred, tried to roll toward him but he was on top of the covers, still dressed. "Did I go to sleep?"

He was kissing her throat now. "Yes, and put me properly in my place," he said on a laugh.

Kate set a hand to his chest. "I thought you'd forgotten me."

"Never," he murmured. He lifted himself away as if to study her face, and threaded a hand through her hair at her temple. "You're not that kind of woman, Kate. Not the kind a man forgets."

Kate reached up to twine her hands around his neck. In the firelight, with that golden curtain of hair falling forward to shadow his face, he looked harsh and handsome. He lowered his mouth to hers and kissed her slowly and intimately. She felt desire surge, then go twisting through her again, leaving her with a faint fear she might be incapable of refusing him.

After a time, he lifted his head away. "Your invitation—in the rose garden—it still stands?"

"After that kiss?" She gazed at him in the gloom. "What do you think?"

"Thank God," he said. "I'm no gentleman, Kate. I won't say no."

"Then say yes." Already Kate could feel his erection pressed against her hip, hard and insistent. "I'm saying yes, Edward. I want you to make love to me again."

He slipped a finger under her chin, his gaze holding hers. "I can never deserve you, my dear," he said. "And I should say, too, that—" He stopped, and looked away.

"What?" she whispered.

"That I'm sorry, Kate. Sorry things didn't turn out differently. That I didn't turn out to be something different. Can you understand?"

She shook her head.

"I regret that there can never be more than this fleeting *affaire de coeur* for us," he continued, dropping his hand. "But that's all it can be. We know that now, yes?"

She forced herself to nod. "Just make me feel that way again," she whispered. "The way you made me feel in your bed that night. I have tried, Edward, and I cannot stop thinking of it."

"I can do that," he said, gazing down at her, "and not even feel guilty for it."

"Why should you feel guilt?" she said. "I want this, Edward. It is not a mistake. It just is . . . us. It is our secret."

"A better man would, Kate."

"Nonsense." She lifted her head from the pillow, and kissed him again, her right hand shaping the hard length of his hipbone through his trousers. "And I have no expectations of you."

"But Kate, you should," he said. "Or rather, you should be with a man who warrants your expectations."

"Ah, and you've brought me a long list of these worthy fellows, have you?" she said dryly.

"I have not," he admitted, smiling at her in the gloom. "I don't know anyone who deserves you."

"Liar." She chuckled, pushing at him. "Sit up. I can't move."

He did so, and she realized he was already in his shirtsleeves. "I locked both the door to the parlor and the door to the corridor," he said, his hands going to the knot of his cravat.

"Good." Kate had scrambled from beneath the covers. Seated behind him, she took in the vision of his brocade waistcoat that stretched over impossibly wide shoulders, then winnowed down to his lean rib cage.

Leaning into him, she put her arms around his waist and set her cheek against his back as he expertly jerked free the knot and unwrapped the long strip of cambric. "There," he said, tossing it onto the bed.

"Here, let me." Kate shifted and let her hands start with the bottom button of his waistcoat.

He leaned back, and let his head rest against her left breast. "Well, this is companionable," he said as she worked her way up.

Kate smiled, then pulled his waistcoat off. "Perhaps I shall train to be a valet," she said, folding it neatly, "if this baroness business does not work out."

He chuckled, then began to slip down his braces, easing

them from each shoulder in turn. That done, Edward drew his shirt off over his head, shucking it inside out and tossing it in the direction of his cravat.

If his shoulders had looked impossibly wide before, they looked magnificent now. His was a warrior's body, thought Kate. Sleek, and beautifully made, with muscles that ran around his arms and extended down either side of his spine in thick, overlapping layers.

She set one hand to the white, puckered scar low on the turn of his rib cage. "Did this hurt?" she murmured.

He twisted around to look at it, as if he'd forgotten he had it. "Yes, like the devil," he said. "Took the business end of a bayonet in Ceylon. Ugly, isn't it?"

"I like it," said Kate honestly. "No one should be too perfect."

He laughed, and shifted around to face her. "Your mother made a similar remark about my forehead," he said, tucking a wayward strand of hair behind Kate's ear. "That my new scar would lend me character."

"Oh, Aurélie!" Kate rolled her eyes. "Pay her no mind. She babbles."

"Does she?" said Edward musingly. "I wonder."

Then he stood and turned to face her, his braces hanging around his hips, his lean, smooth chest warm in the firelight. Kate rose to her knees, and set her hands on his shoulders.

"You are magnificent to look upon, Edward," she said. "I'm sure you've been told. I don't even know the words."

"You don't need words, Kate." He reached up and pushed his fingers through her hair at the temples, and drew them slowly through it. "It's in your eyes. Your affection for me— your admiration—it's in your eyes."

"May I kiss you?"

He crooked one brow. "You needn't ask."

Kate set her lips to the turn of his shoulder and drew them across his collarbone; down along the beautifully shaped muscle that led to his breast. Fleetingly, she set her cheek to it, and felt his heart beating, slow and strong. His chest was smooth, with the merest dusting of hair that grew thicker and darker as it descended down the flat of his belly, only to vanish suggestively beneath the buttoned bearer.

She thought of Edward's mouth on her breast. On impulse, she flicked out her tongue, lightly brushing his nipple. He made a sound deep in his throat and his hands speared into her hair again, holding her to him.

"*Mmm*," he said.

"Is that a good sound?" she asked teasingly.

"Keep on, minx, and you'll find out how good a little too soon," he murmured, one hand easing down her spine.

She kept on, leaning fully into him to stroke, and eventually to suckle, until Edward's hands began to make slow, sensuous circles at the small of her back.

He gave a little growl. "Oh, enough of that, love," he murmured, setting her a little away.

His eyelids, she noticed, had grown heavy, and yet it was as if his gaze and his touch sent a newfound awareness coursing through her. He fumbled for the hem of her nightgown, and dragged one side up.

"I want this off," he rasped.

Kate felt inexplicably shy, but loosened the tie at her throat and drew it off. Edward's gaze heated at once. He returned her tender ministrations, his head bent so that his hair fired gold in the firelight as he captured her breast in his mouth. She made a soft sound and felt the need begin to go twisting sinuously through her.

Edward laved her breast, teasing the nipple with the tip of his tongue, then drawing it between his teeth to bite. Something that was pain—and yet nothing at all like it—shot through Kate. The wickedest, most tantalizing sensation that made the spot between her legs throb and pulse.

She must have cried out, for he released the pressure, then began to soothe and tease all over again. It was maddening.

Deliciously so. As if he pushed her toward something wonderful. Kate felt her nails dig into those broad shoulders, and let her head fall back.

"Edward," she whispered. "Oh, yes. I want to feel that again. That sweet sensation. Oh, I feel so greedy. As if I can think of nothing but myself and that delicious *feeling.*"

"What, and not of me?" On a choked laugh, he buried his head against her neck, his breath rough. "Ah, but never mind that. I can assure you, my dear, that when I look at you, I think about what I want enough for the both of us."

"*Umm,*" she said, pulling him closer. "And just how do you mean to satisfy that urge?"

"You know, witch," he rasped, but there was a new edge to his voice; something urgent, and yet despairing. "Oh, Kate, love. You are *exquisite.*"

And then Edward's mouth took hers, hard and possessive, his tongue thrusting deep. It was as if he claimed her. As if he meant never to let her go. Kate was utterly subsumed in the melting, liquid heat of the kiss, parrying his strokes with her own as her hands moved urgently over him.

His hand moved between her thighs, urging her legs wider. Kate was still on her knees, giving him every access; access he used to full advantage, echoing every sweet thrust of his tongue until desire drenched her and she gasped for breath. Her hands went of their own will to his trousers, pushing impotently at the waist. On an impatient sound, he jerked the first button loose.

Kate finished the job, her fingers moving swiftly but awkwardly, jerking and pushing until Edward stepped back, shoving down his trousers and drawers in a crush of fine wool and white linen, his erection rising up a little dauntingly.

She ignored the little frisson of unease, and watched him push off the rest of his clothing. Then he pushed her backward on the bed and crawled over her, the thick muscles of his arms bunching as he did so. His eyes were no longer somnolent but almost wild, his hair falling forward in a golden mane as he lowered his weight onto her body and bore her down into the softness of the bed.

Kate drew up one knee, her hand curling into the sheets. Oh, she wanted this! Wanted it so desperately, she would shut out all risk to her heart. She wanted the physical strength of him; wanted him thrusting his body into hers, joining them in that perfect, primal rhythm of loving.

Edward was so overwhelmingly male; she reveled in it as her hands stroked and touched, entranced by the hard sleekness of his body. She could feel the unmistakable weight of his manhood pressed into her belly. Impulsively, her fingers delved lower, capturing the hot, velvet hardness. It pulsed insistently against her palm.

"*Please*," she whispered. "Oh, Edward—this—please."

"*Shush, love.*" He was still kissing her. Her face, her throat. His tongue stroked the seam of her lips, lightly teasing. And then he was trailing a ribbon of heat between her breasts, moving lower and lower. He found her navel, circled, darted in. The pulsing, twisting sensation drove deep again, making her gasp.

He moved lower, his mouth hot and insistent.

"Wha . . . what are you doing?" she whispered.

"I'm going to enslave you, Kate," he murmured against her skin. "Or die trying."

His hands were set to either side of Kate's thighs as his tongue stroked down, all the way into the thatch of light curls at her joining, making her cry out, a thin, thready whimper.

"Edward?"

He looked up, his eyes almost feral in the firelight. "Let me take you this way, Kate," he said. "Let me give you something, love, to remember me by."

But Kate was already sure that this—and his memory— would be with her forever. When his tongue plunged into her heat, her whole body shuddered.

"*Umm*," he murmured, his tongue and his fingers lightly probing. The touch was so sweet, she still trembled with it.

"Oh, Edward, I don't think—"

"Yes, *don't* think," he murmured against her skin. "Just lie back, and let me prove wicked men do have their advantages."

She wanted to scold him; to tell him she loved him, and that there was nothing wicked about him. But the light, teasing touch of his tongue was beyond wicked. Beyond decadent. Yes, it was enslavement, or something perilously near it. For this, a woman might lose her moral compass entirely . . .

"Edward," she whispered. "Oh. Oh, God. That is . . ."

"Oh, Kate," he murmured teasingly. "Are you feeling enslaved?"

"*Yes.*"

She swallowed hard and tried to nod, both hands curled into the sheets now. The feeling had grown so intense she feared she might never return to herself. But the words choked in her throat, her head tipping back as she gasped and gasped again.

He stroked once more, a tiny, teasing lap of his tongue, and then she was lost to the pleasure, caught up in the throbbing intensity of it. As if he'd somehow severed her connection to the physical. Sent her shooting like a star in a streak of white light into a place where there was only him.

Only Edward. Only perfect bliss. The beauty of it washed over her. Drew her down into his warmth and cast her up again, sobbing. When she returned to herself, he held her in his arms, one heavy leg thrown over hers, surrounding her with his warmth and scent.

He smelled of soap and sweat and of her. His face was buried against her neck, his lips set lightly to her pulse point. "Kate, love," he murmured. "You are beautiful. Don't ever—*ever*—say you're not."

She relaxed into the mattress, content in that moment. It was as if nothing beyond this room existed, as if time had stopped. And she *was* beautiful. She felt it. She saw it through his hot, hooded gaze as clearly as she knew her love for him.

After a time, he levered up onto one elbow, heat kindling in his eyes—a heat that was for her and her alone, she was utterly certain.

Kate wrapped her arms around his neck, and rose up to kiss him. "Let me pleasure you," she whispered against his ear. "Show me how. I am, after all, your slave now."

He gave a low, wicked chuckle. "Ah, a baroness in servitude!" he said. Then he set both hands to her waist, and rolled onto his back, lifting her astride him. "On top with you, then."

Kate landed on a suppressed shriek, her hands splayed atop the wide wall of his chest. He urged her knees apart, into a position as wicked as it was decadent.

"There," he said, a roguish grin curving his mouth. "A man likes his sex slave to know her place—and you look especially fetching in that one."

Kate felt her face heat, but she pushed herself up uncertainly, and set one knee on the opposite side of his hip so that she fully straddled him. "Like this?"

"*Umm.*" Edward slipped his left hand between them, slicking one finger through the wetness between her legs, and the grin faded to something far more serious.

"Oh, Kate," he whispered. "Oh, my love, you madden me." Edward's right hand was weighing her breast in his palm as his thumb lightly stroked her nipple. "Yes, *perfect*," he whispered, "except for one small detail."

"Yes?"

"Rise up a little," he murmured.

"L-like this . . . ?"

"Yes, on your knees." He slipped the hard, velvety weight of his erection through her wetness. "Oh, God," he choked.

"*Just* like that. Just like that, Kate." He pushed himself a little inside her, and squeezed his eyes shut on a deep moan.

It was remarkable. And deeply erotic. His hands were at her waist, his thumbs dark against the pale flesh of her belly as he held her still to his slight motion. He moaned again, his grip slackening. Kate moved experimentally, and he pushed deeper, filling her and stretching her.

"*Ummm*," he said again, lower still.

"Oh, my. That is . . . remarkable." Empowered, Kate set her hands on his wide shoulders and rose up, then slid all the way down this time, impaling herself.

"Good God," he choked. "Kate—*oh*!"

She lifted again and met his first, powerful thrust. The time for talking was over; they were beyond it. He set a rhythm, lifting her at the waist though he hardly needed to; Kate thrilled to the power of each stroke.

She could feel his entire length drawing at her flesh, delicious and utterly carnal. Leaning forward, she bent her head to his and kissed him as he had kissed her, thrusting inside to plumb the depths of his mouth. The heat ratcheted up instantly, Edward's arms coming around her, clasping her to him as he drove himself up and into her.

Kate felt as if she had burst into an inferno of desire. She thrust her tongue as he thrust inside her, reveling in his hunger. Savoring the power until she sensed his release near. Lifting herself up again, she set her hands to his chest, her gaze locked to his. His breath was sawing in and out of his chest, a faint sheen of sweat across his forehead.

Then Edward's belly drew taut as a bow, and she felt that sweet, elusive sensation edge near yet again. It seemed impossible, yet she yearned for it. Over and over he drove inside her, edging her nearer that sweet cliff. And then she was lost to his strokes, as if the light and heat and bone-deep yearning had fused them into one physical presence.

"Come to me, love," she dimly heard him plead. Then she lost herself to the throbbing pleasure.

They came together in a glorious shattering of light, and Kate felt herself spin away again, utterly one with him as they plunged into that sweet, carnal bliss. So caught up in the ecstasy, she scarcely realized he had drawn from her at that last, perfect instant.

The light and pleasure faded slowly, and Kate savored it. When she returned to the real world, she was tucked against Edward's side, not entirely clear how she'd got there. He had snared his cravat from the bed, and only then did Kate grasp that he'd spent himself upon his thigh.

She was still grappling with her feelings about that when he hurled the cravat into the gloom, and pulled her harder against him. She cut her eyes toward his fine legs.

"You were being careful," she murmured, letting her lashes fall shut. "Thank you."

"I have to be careful." His breath was still roughened, his fingers of one hand tangled in her hair as he held her to him. "Because, Kate, I care for you. And nothing could alter the fact that what just happened was utterly . . ."

"Amazing?" she supplied hopefully.

He laughed, a deep, rasping sound. "Why is it words fail me with you?" he said. "It was not amazing, love. It was *disconcertingly* amazing."

"Edward," she murmured, sliding her lips down his damp throat. "Oh, sometimes I think . . ."

He kissed her atop the head. "Think what, sweet?"

"That I could fall in love with you," she blurted, "or that perhaps I already have."

Beside her, he went perfectly still, and Kate knew at once she had spoken too plainly. Worse, she'd said something he could never reciprocate. Her heart was already sinking a little when he made a soft sound of dismay.

"Ah, Kate," he said, rolling onto one elbow to look at her through his heavy-lidded green eyes. "It won't do. You know it won't."

"I know," she whispered.

His gaze softened tenderly in the firelight. "Yes, you love me in this moment," he said, placing his wide, comforting hand over her heart. "You love what I do to you. And I'm gratified. But tomorrow you'll realize it's not at all the same thing."

"You seem very certain," she said.

He dragged a hand around the dark stubble of yesterday's beard. Then he spoke very slowly, as if carefully considering his words.

"Sometimes, Kate, women think they must love a man to enjoy his body," he finally said. "Don't fall into that trap, I beg you. We are good together, you and I. Better than I would ever have dreamt possible. But don't let yourself love me, Kate. Just . . . don't. Take your fill of me, and move on with your life."

She gave a faint shrug, knowing there was no point arguing. Knowing, as surely as she breathed, that she had already fallen. And in the end, she would be no happier about it than he.

"You were once in love," she murmured. "Weren't you? You were betrothed."

"Kate, it's complicated," he said. "And ugly. May we leave it at that?"

"Of course," she whispered, turning to look at the dying fire.

He drew a deep breath and held it a moment. "The truth is, Kate," he said, "I don't know if I was in love. I was besotted, certainly, and hotheaded. But I was young—just eighteen, and still under my father's thumb. And Maria was younger, too young to know what she wanted. I see that now."

"But her family disapproved, you said."

His gaze shuttered. "Her parents were not pleased to discover our friendship, or who my father was," he said, "but it scarcely mattered; they had already arranged a marriage to a neighbor."

"Why?" Kate tucked closer. "What made him so worthy?"

"He had loaned Maria's father money," said Edward, "with their farm standing as collateral. He had no way to replay it, and Maria was his only child. So it was agreed this neighbor would marry Maria. In that way, the entire estate would pass to him upon her father's death."

"And Maria—had she agreed to this?"

Edward hesitated. "She said she had not."

"So she held fast against her father, I hope?"

"For a time, certainly."

"You do not know?"

He shook his head. "I left England," he said. "There was a fire in London—my father's gaming hell burnt. I didn't set it, but I damned sure walked out with what little cash I could save, along with his account books and enough incriminating evidence to hang him. Then I leveraged it, and forced Hedge into retirement, you might say. I put his cash into an annuity which I controlled, and purchased myself a lieutenancy in the Sixty-first Foot, then went out to Ceylon to make something of myself."

"And did you?"

"I did well enough, and advanced quickly," he said, "and I made some investments here and there. But I realize now it was a futile effort. I didn't quite grasp the size of Maria's father's debt to his neighbor. In my naiveté, I thought I merely needed to make myself respectable. But no mere army officer could ever hope to pay off a debt of that magnitude."

"Poor Maria," said Kate.

"She was confused, and desperately unhappy." Edward hesitated. "I think, Kate, that's what drew me into the whole, miserable mess. I look back now, older and wiser, and I think I just wanted to be someone's white knight. I was young enough then to believe such things existed."

"And now you don't?"

He laughed hollowly. "Oh, Kate, I have not believed in

white knights or fairy tales or the overarching goodness of mankind in going on two decades," he said. "I see human nature for what it truly is—plagued by the deadly sins, and venal in the bargain."

"Your world is dark, Edward," said Kate softly, "and hard."

"I would beg you to remember that," he answered, "when you're tempted to fancy yourself in love with me."

"Yes, I believe I shall shut that notion right out of my head," she said a little flatly.

"Kate," he chided. He leaned over to kiss the tip of her nose. "I'm sorry. You're neither dark nor hard."

"I wish I were harder," she said, and meant it. "Well, *c'est la vie*, as Aurélie would say."

"Your mother is not entirely wrong in her philosophy." He kissed her nose again. "Shall I go, Kate? Shall I leave you to rest?"

She sighed, feeling oddly fractious. "No, not yet," she said, glancing at the clock. "Tomorrow is Sunday; there will be no shooting. Have you any plans?"

"Anstruther and I mean to ride over to Heatherfields," he replied. "He's to give me a tour, and point out the worst of it."

"Heatherfields' decay frustrates him," she said, then hesitated. "He mentioned to me tonight that you mean the property as an investment. That you will never live in it?"

He shook his head almost imperceptibly. "No," he said vaguely. "I will never live there."

Kate had not realized until that moment how much his answer had meant to her. For a moment, she was a little ashamed.

Had she really toyed with the notion of continuing an illicit romance? And how had she meant to go about it? Simply send around for her gig and go trotting off to Heatherfields when lust struck?

Inwardly, Kate sighed at her own artlessness.

A long silence fell over the room, and for a time they

simply lay in each other's arms. The languor remained, and that delicious feeling of having been well loved and sated. But the intimacy had been pierced, and the ordinary world had again intruded.

It was as if he read her thoughts.

"Tomorrow, Kate," he murmured, "perhaps I should move upstairs. With the other gentlemen. That is, if I mean to stay on."

"*Umm*," she said against his chest.

"It . . . might be easier," he said, his lips brushing her temple. "Easier than knowing that, every night I remain here, you lie but a few steps away. Less tempting. Less complicated."

"Perhaps you're right," she said softly.

But Kate knew that nothing, after this, was going to be less complicated. Because she was doubly in love with Edward. And no woman could love such a man, and expect her life to be less complicated.

CHAPTER 12

In Which Aurélie Seizes the Reins

It was a novel experience to get up at one's usual hour of seven o'clock, only to find Aurélie Wentworth had risen betimes. But when Kate entered the breakfast room a quarter hour later, there sat the worthy lady in all her morning glory, the pug snoring riotously in her lap, and the Comte de Macey waiting on her hand and foot from the sideboard.

The room was otherwise empty save for Nancy, who rolled her eyes and tilted her head in her mother's direction.

"Good heavens," said Kate, hitching on the threshold. "I am like to fall dead from shock."

"Dead from lack of sleep, more like," murmured Aurélie without lifting her gaze from her newspaper. "Why, *mon chou*, do you speak as if I am some specter risen from the netherworld?"

"Really, Aurélie," Kate muttered, going straight to the teapot. "Have you even *been* to bed?"

"*Mais oui*," she said, giving the paper a straightening snap. "For today I wished to rise early. Great plans are afoot."

"That sounds ominous." Kate lifted the lid from the chafing dish to behold a steaming pile of eggs. "You always have plans afoot. But they never require that you rise before noon."

"*Oui*, this is true," said Aurélie agreeably. "But today is different. Today I mean to go to morning services. And tomorrow I mean to take Nancy shopping. All must be properly planned."

But the bit about shopping flew over Nancy's head. "To church?" She roused at the opposite end of the table. "Why? Mamma, what are you up to?"

"*Non, non.*" Her mother wagged a finger. "Not in front of *le comte.*"

"*Mon Dieu*, Aurélie," said de Macey, bending over to warm her coffee, "I have known you long enough—and well enough—to have noticed that you have children."

"Oh, have you indeed?" Aurélie smacked him playfully with her newspaper. "Well! Perhaps I go to church to confess my sins, de Macey? Indeed, you may have some knowledge of them."

"Not in some years, my pet," he replied absently, "not in some years. Much as it pains me."

"Oh, for God's sake," Kate muttered.

"Coffee?" asked de Macey, lifting the pot.

"No, thank you. I'm having tea." Kate sat adjacent to her mother. "What are you up to, Aurélie? I hope you do not mean to embarrass Richard."

For once Aurélie looked genuinely hurt. "*Moi, mon chou?*" she said, pressing her hand to her chest. "How can you think it?"

"You do like to tease," Kate chided. "And another thing, whilst the family is here alone—"

"Thank you, child." De Macey patted her shoulder and sat back down.

"Yes, I include you," said Kate tartly, "because I charge you, to some extent, with her supervision. Aurélie must quit flinging her pretty gentleman at Nancy. All she's doing is upsetting Richard. I saw his face last night every time she danced. And I cannot think Sir Francis has the least interest in her."

"No, no, not in the least," de Macey agreed. "Of that I'm quite certain."

Kate turned to look at him oddly, then gave a dismissive wave. "Yes, whatever," she said, "but Mamma—*Aurélie*—churns all this up deliberately. And now this business of going to church?"

Aurélie's pretty lips formed an exaggerated moue. "Perhaps, *mon chou*, I merely wish to be better acquainted with the man who desires to be my . . . er, my—"

"Your daughter's husband," said Nancy tightly. "Yes, Mamma, your son-in-law. You *are* going to have one."

"*Ma foi*, the mother of a priest!" said Aurélie, casting a gaze heavenward. "And then grandchildren! It is not to be thought of just yet. But tell me, *ma fille*, how badly do you wish this marriage, *hmm*?"

"Oh, Aurélie, more than anything!" said Nancy, leaning over her plate.

For once, Aurélie looked uncertain. "*Oui, ma chérie*, but consider carefully what *anything* is," she replied.

"Anything," Nancy repeated. "And Mamma, you really needn't send any more gentlemen to flirt with me. If Uncle Upshaw will not give me permission, Richard and I mean to wait until I'm twenty-one."

"Ah, *chérie*, you will have wrinkles by then," said her mother evenly. "He will not want you."

At that point, the conversation descended into utter foolishness, and a great deal of babbling and gesturing about a shopping trip to Exeter. Aurélie had somehow enlisted Anstruther to drive them. The latter meant to buy a new double-furrow plow that could only be had from a large ironmonger there; the former, a pair of red shoes, her old ones having had the temerity to pinch her toes last night.

Kate didn't care about her mother's shoes, though admittedly the plow was a matter of some significance. Nonetheless, she shut the racket out and ate her breakfast, saying nothing more. But matters were not much improved when, half an hour later, Lord Reginald strolled in, wearing a shimmering silk banyan over his waistcoat and looking like a true gentleman of leisure bent upon breakfast with his family.

"Mamma is going to church today," said Nancy a little triumphantly. "What do you make of that, Reggie?"

Reggie turned from the sideboard, and arched one satanic black eyebrow. "Heavens, Aurélie, are pigs flying?" he asked. "Or does Filou require absolution for all that curried crab he filched last night?"

Kate jerked to her feet. "I've a letter to write before services," she lied. "And the carriages to order. Just the five of us, is it?"

"Not I," demurred de Macey.

"And no one else means to get up, I daresay," said Nancy, covering a yawn. "So just us four."

Her mother lifted a faintly teasing gaze to Kate's. "Actually, *mon chou*," she said, "Mr. Quartermaine has already risen, dined, and gone down to Anstruther's office."

Reggie gave a sharp laugh. "Oh, that one won't darken a church door," he said. "Depend upon it."

Aurélie snapped over the page of her paper. "Actually, I believe he means to," she said. "Katherine, I trust you've no objection?"

"Why, nothing would please me more," she said, smiling at Reggie as she slid past.

As it happened, her mother was right. Edward strode up St. Michael's north aisle just behind Anstruther, not two minutes before the church doors were closed. To Kate's delight, he hesitated by the empty spot Nancy had vacated moments earlier in order to join Richard's mother, whose sister was visiting from Staplegrove. Having laid her prayer book there, Kate was rewarded by Edward's muted smile when she snatched it up again.

He sat down, his wide shoulders filling the space in a way Nancy's had not. And though he looked straight ahead without so much as brushing her arm with his, his warmth and his presence comforted Kate.

He was attired today in the tall black boots he'd worn the day of his accident, and looked almost dangerously handsome. Throughout the service, she had to resist the impulse to sneak surreptitious looks at his striking profile, and to wallow in her recollections of the previous night. Her mother was right; there had been very little sleep involved.

Her face flushing with sudden heat, she opened her prayer book to the wrong place, scarcely aware until Edward reached over and flipped back the page. Mortified, Kate snapped it shut again, and forced her gaze toward the altar.

Richard spoke as eloquently as ever, seeming little cowed by Aurélie's presence. After communion, everyone filed out into the churchyard, then scattered into random knots to pontificate upon that holy trinity of every little English village: the harvest, the weather, and the latest gossip.

Kate turned toward Edward, smiling genially. "Good morning, Mr. Quartermaine," she said, catching her toe on a clump of grass. "Heavens, this ground is uneven."

"Lady d'Allenay." Crooking one eyebrow, he offered his arm.

"Oh, thank you!" she said, taking it. "An inspiring sermon, wasn't it?" Then she dropped her voice to a whisper. "Just keep me away from Reggie," she begged. "I want to quell the village gossip."

He cut an odd glance down at her. "I rather doubt you'll quell any gossip by hanging upon *my* arm," he murmured, "but you're welcome to try."

Kate persuaded herself it was the lesser of two evils. Already Reggie was glowering at her, and she had no wish to encourage him. Having been espied by half her neighbors climbing out of Aurélie's barouche with him this morning was bad enough.

She looked about the churchyard to see that Nancy was, as usual, cozying up to Richard's mother. Along with Mrs. Burnham's sister, they had strolled across the street and now stood before the small rectory, their three heads bent in an intense conversation.

Aurélie had been surrounded by a trio of elderly village tabbies who, though they likely disapproved of her, wished nonetheless to exchange a few words so that they might speak of it later in scandalized whispers.

"Mamma and Nancy are going to be a while," Kate said. "Walk with me through the churchyard, won't you?"

"If you wish." But he didn't look as if he thought it a good idea.

After moving away from the crowd, they spoke little to each other. Whatever his misgivings, Edward seemed content to stroll sedately together through the grass, now gone brittle with the cold.

Soon they were deep in the shadows alongside the church, winding their way around gravestones. Snippets of conversation carried on the sharp air, though they were by no means out of sight of the congregation.

Kate pulled her cloak tight against the chill, and Edward helped her around the base of a stone that tilted precariously on a tree root. "Is all of your family buried here?" he asked.

"Yes, most," she said. "Some inside, and some out here."

"Ah, yes. Here is a Wentworth." He bent forward to scratch off a bit of lichen. "Harold, I believe it says."

"Yes, Grandpapa's ne'er-do-well younger brother."

He straightened up. "The barony has suffered more than a few of those, I take it?"

"Besides my father and my brother?" said Kate. "Yes, more than our share."

He laid his hand over hers on his coat sleeve for an instant, patted it, then moved on to a weathered marble obelisk some seven feet high.

"Infantry," he said admiringly. "Gad, the Fiftieth Foot!

This must be someone more worthy than the wastrel Harold."

"It is a memorial to Grandpapa's cousin James, for whom Papa was named," said Kate. "He fell at Vimerio, trying to hold the hill against the French. You were in Ceylon, did you say?"

"Yes, mostly." Edward circled the obelisk, reading its many inscriptions. "So, a lieutenant colonel, your cousin, and much decorated. The Fiftieth fought bravely at Vimerio. They killed two thousand of the French that day, you know."

"With only a handful of British lost," said Kate. "Cousin James was too brave for his own good, it was said."

"Do you Wentworths always go to one extreme or the other? Either saint or sinner?"

Kate smiled. "Yes, *Nothing by half measures* is practically our motto."

"Are you quite sure?" Edward winked at her as he circled the monument. "Because I've begun to suspect some of the outwardly angelic ones might harbor a secret streak of wickedness."

"*Hmm*," she said, lifting one eyebrow.

Then his face sobered, and he made an expansive gesture. "Do you know, Kate, I rather envy you all this."

"What?" she said. "A churchyard full of dead ancestors?"

He laid his bare, long-fingered hand along the top of the nearest gravestone and leaned into it, his gaze trailing pensively over row upon row of stones. "Yes, actually," he finally answered. "I envy you the history of it. The fact that you're rooted to this place with all its lore and legends. To know your people—to know with a certainty to whom you belong—it is a gift, Kate."

"It is, and that's why I'm working so hard to preserve Bellecombe." Kate cut a sidelong look at the winnowing crowd. "What of your family?" she said on impulse. "Do you know where they are buried?"

He hesitated. "The Earl of Oakley's line hails from the north," he said. "I've never been there, nor met any of them save Aunt Isabel. And my father died in Brighton last year."

"What was his name?"

"Hedge," he finally answered. "Alfred Hedge, a bully and a thug and an outright criminal who, so far as I know, sprung fully formed from Satan's breast. If the man had family, they disowned him."

"Good Lord," she murmured. "So I gather you had no siblings." *And nothing even vaguely akin*, she silently added, *to an ordinary family life.*

"Until I was ten I had my half brother Frederick, who is now Duke of Dunthorpe," he said. "He is two years my senior."

"Ah." Kate kicked herself for not thinking her question through. "Have you any contact with him?"

Edward shook his head. "Not since we were parted," he said. "He was twelve. It was . . . difficult. We had been inseparable."

Kate's face fell. "He must have been crushed."

"He cried," Edward quietly confessed, "whilst the servants packed my things. And Father—Dunthorpe—stropped him for it."

"He sounds like a bastard," muttered Kate.

"No," said Edward wryly "That would be me. That was, after all, the very point of Dunthorpe's exercise."

"Edward, don't," said Kate, her gloved hands fisting. "I dislike hearing you disparage yourself."

"I believe I'm merely stating facts," he said blandly.

Kate turned to face him, her hands set on her hips beneath her cloak. "Please don't take this the wrong way," she said quietly, "but you do not know the facts, Edward. You know only what your mother told Dunthorpe—and told him in anger, mind."

"You sound like Aunt Isabel," he said. "Always wishing to believe the best."

"I do not *wish* to believe anything," said Kate. "It matters not one whit to me if you're the butcher's boy. In fact, I might prefer it. Because one thing is certain: The three parents you did have all put their pride before their duty, and that is despicable."

"I know you mean well, but let it go, Kate." Edward's jaw had gone a little rigid. "As to disparagement, Lord Reginald over there looks willing to do the job for me. If that black gaze of his were a scythe, he'd have sliced off my head by now.

"Never mind Reggie," said Kate impatiently. "Tell me about Aunt Isabel."

"Isabel?" He looked surprised.

"Is she living? Do you like her? She clearly likes you."

His smile was muted. "She likes me well enough, yes."

"What balderdash," said Kate. "The lady gave you a watch worth a small fortune."

At last the smile deepened. "And I like her," he said, "very much. Though I rarely see her."

"Where does she live?"

"In Belgrave Square."

"Indeed?" said Kate. "Then why do you see her rarely?"

He hesitated. "It's complicated."

"It cannot be that complicated," said Kate tartly. "She is fond of you. You're fond of her. And she lives all of, what?—a mile from St. James?"

They had resumed their sedate stroll and had nearly reached the rear boundary of the churchyard. Even Kate, independent though she was, knew better than to disappear from sight of the crowd on the infamous Ned Quartermaine's arm.

She turned around and noticed Nancy and Richard by the tower door, speaking to each other intently. His expression was dark. Nancy's hands were both fisted at her sides, arms rigid.

Aurélie, thought Kate grimly, *what now?*

She wanted to sigh; her mother was nearly unmanageable. At least this visit had been relatively sedate and—until today, perhaps—without drama. Kate forced herself to smile. "You were going to tell me about your aunt?"

Edward shrugged. "I see her privately when I can, but it is awkward," he said. "The Quartermaine Club is hardly the sort of place one can invite someone like Isabel, Lady Keltonbrooke."

"Ah, so you live there." Kate considered it. "But you might buy a house."

"I might," he said.

"Or you might simply ask your aunt what she wishes."

He hesitated for an instant. "She wishes to see more of me," he admitted. "She is getting on, and she's childless. Frederick and I are all she has."

Kate paused to consider it. "Are you afraid of seeing your brother?"

Again, the faint pause before answering. "It would be awkward," he said. "Beyond that, I should prefer not to ruminate upon the past. Forgive me, Kate, but Anstruther has brought our horses round. I had better return you to your mother."

Anstruther was indeed looking impatient. "Yes, of course," she murmured. "I forgot. The two of you are off to Heatherfields."

By the time they reached the sunny front lawn, the last of the villagers were trailing through the lych-gate. She watched Edward stride down the path after them with his confident, long-legged gait and felt her heart oddly lurch. She really was quite hopelessly in love with him; it seemed not to matter who he was, or what he had done.

He was a good man, and whatever she might think of the way he earned his living, it was something that had been thrust upon him by circumstance—or so she told herself. In all other ways, Edward was everything that a gentleman should be.

In the street beyond, Fendershot was handing Mrs. Peppin

up into his dogcart for the drive back to Bellecombe. For a moment, Kate debated wedging herself onto the seat beside Mrs. Peppin so that she might avoid the drive with Reggie. But that was just foolish.

On a sigh, she turned to see that the churchyard was empty save for Aurélie, who stood just inside the porch, picturesquely framed in the ancient stone arch. She was waving good-bye to Anstruther, a waterfall of lace hanging from her sleeve, as Edward flung himself into the big black's saddle.

"Aurélie, your coachman is waiting," said Kate as the two men rode away.

Aurélie turned to look at her as if bestirred to the present. "Ah, yes," she said. "But a moment, if you please, *mon chou*. I must go back inside and speak to Mr. Burnham."

Kate arched a disapproving eyebrow. "Whatever for?"

Aurélie flashed her usual coy smile, and yet some inscrutable emotion lay just beneath it. "I was not jesting, *mon chou*, at breakfast," she murmured. "I mean to ask our good priest to hear my confession."

"How can you poke fun at Richard?" Kate chided. "Unlike you and de Macey, his duties are not a joke to him. He's very devout. Besides, you're not even Catholic."

Lightly, she shrugged. "*Oui*, but I am, perhaps, half a Catholic, on my mother's side? Besides, cannot a very sinful person confess to their rector and ask forgiveness?"

"No. Well, not as a matter of ecclesiastic obedience."

"But as a matter of personal absolution?"

Kate had never imagined debating church doctrine with her mother. "Well, it is permitted, yes. One can ask for absolution if one has sinned."

Aurélie smiled as if her point had been made. "And perhaps I may have sinned once or twice? And now I feel the need to tell the Reverend Mr. Burnham of it—and I wish to do so within the protection of the confessional."

"There is no actual confessional, Mamma. Honestly, sometimes I think you quite mad."

Aurélie gave a dismissive toss of her hand. "*Ma foi*, you are hardly the first to say so," she returned. "But if the wind will not serve, as they say, one must take to the oars. And if your sister is not at least halfway to the altar before I leave this dull, miserable wilderness, then I am a lesser mother than even rumor would have me."

"Oh, Aurélie." Kate just shook her head. "I hope you know what you're doing."

"I always know what I am doing." Aurélie looked at the tiny bejeweled watch that swung from a chain on her reticule. "So, you will meet me here in half an hour, *s'il te plaît*. And what has become of Nancy and Reggie? *Mon Dieu*, Katherine, go and find them."

She was already making a shooing motion with the back of her hand when the massive oaken door swung inward on shrieking hinges and Reggie strode out, his tall beaver hat clasped rigidly in his hands. Dark, hard eyes locked to Kate's as Aurélie brushed past him, almost unheeded, into the church.

"Mamma requires a moment with Mr. Burnham," Kate explained, turning to step back into the sun of the churchyard. "I trust you don't mind waiting?"

When he said nothing, Kate turned to fully face him.

"Actually, Kate," he said snidely, "I begin to mind waiting a great deal."

"I beg your pardon?"

"When it comes to you, all I do is *wait*," he snapped. "I have been *waiting* eight years now for you to accept my apology. I have been *waiting* for days here, in hope you might spare me so much as one heartfelt word. I have made my interests plain, and I have *waited*—holding my tongue, mind you—and in response you choose to insult me—"

"Heavens, Reggie, have you taken leave of—"

"—to *insult* me," he repeated, speaking over her, "by strolling about like some strumpet on that man's arm. And by God, Kate, I will not have it. It is beneath me to play second fiddle to the likes of Ned Quartermaine. And you'd do well, my dear, to remember it."

Kate widened her eyes. "Have a care, Reggie. Because you're on the verge of getting that heartfelt word you so long for."

But caution had left him. "I find it beyond the pale, Kate," he gritted, "that you'd dare be seen on his arm in front of the village. To invite him to Sunday services and parade him about when I have bowed down to you and groveled to you. When the whole bloody parish is holding its collective breath, expecting any day now to hear that—"

"What, to hear the truth about Heatherfields?" Kate coldly interjected. "For that's the only village gossip with any legitimacy to it, Reggie."

"How dare you throw a run of bad luck in my face," he said.

"With very little effort, to be honest," Kate answered, "for it isn't a run of bad luck, Reggie, that has ruined you. It is folly, plain and simple. And I trust that no one—yourself included—would ever be fool enough to suggest publicly that you and I might reconcile."

Reggie's clenched fists had gone white, his handsome face black with rage. "How dare you," he said again. "Why, if Stephen were alive, he would put you over his knee for this."

"Oh, he might try—*if* he were alive." Kate's emotions were rubbing raw. "Which he might be, Reggie, had the two of you not got yourselves rip-roaring drunk and climbed up that bell tower in the dead of night. And *if* you had not wagered him fifty pounds he could not balance on that bloody ledge."

Reggie thrust his face into hers. "I didn't push your damned brother, Kate."

"You didn't have to! Your presence—your constant challenging and teasing and taunting—it was always sufficient!" Suddenly, Kate burst into tears. "Reggie, you were older. Stephen looked up to you. How could you not be more careful?"

Reggie seemed unmoved by her crying. "Oh, yes, as usual, it's all my fault!" he snarled. "Damn it, Kate, I tried to make it right."

"To *make it right*?" she cried. "My brother *died*, Reggie. My whole life changed. This—Bellecombe—all of it—was meant for Stephen. Not for me. There is no making that right."

"Well, didn't I offer to marry you? To take those future burdens from your shoulders?"

But Kate's storm began to clear as swiftly as it had broken, and she blew her nose loudly on the handkerchief she'd shaken from her pocket.

"Listen to me, Reggie, for you'll hear these next two words but once," she said through the snuffles, shoving it back in again. "*I apologize.* Stephen's shortcomings were his own. No, you did not push him. Yes, you were devastated by his death. But you knew the barony would come to me, and your proposal was opportunistic."

"An outright lie!" cried Reggie.

"It is not," said Kate. "Grandpapa knew it—and he saw your disappointment when you learnt how cash-poor we were. Yes, I knew why you proposed, Reggie, and I was willing to accept it. But I will not accept a confirmed adulterer or a gazetted gamester for a husband. I have seen my mother live that life and *I will not*."

"Oh, Kate!" Reggie rolled his eyes. "Sauce for the goose, sauce for the gander! Aurélie was as unfaithful as your father."

"Not at first," Kate countered. "But that is neither here nor there, Reggie. What you must understand now is that *I will never marry you*."

"Kate, you don't know what you're—"

"Yes, I do," she cut in, "and further, you do not even *want* to marry me. Your nose is simply out of joint. I have been nothing but the ace up your sleeve for years now. You have always believed that, if it became financially necessary, you could charm good old Kate back into your arms."

"Yes, perhaps even back into my bed," said Reggie nastily. "Longing for another taste, Kate? I could be persuaded."

"Reggie, you cad!" Kate hissed. "You *seduced* me. You used Stephen's death as an excuse, and played upon my stupidity."

"Yes, that would be your version, my love." Reggie flashed a snide smile. "But as I recall it, you flung yourself into my arms, begging to assuage your grief, and I merely obliged you. After that, there was no one else you *could* marry. Shall I tell Ned Quartermaine all about it?"

"You would not dare," Kate warned.

"I do dare, and I shall," said Reggie, "if you do not announce our betrothal."

"*Betrothal?*" Kate's mouth fell open.

"Announce it," he commanded. "At dinner tonight. And do not trifle with me again, Kate, or you will learn I'm not to be trifled with at all."

At that, Kate drew herself up to her full height. "Well, Reggie," she said briskly, "you had better hurry along, then. Mr. Quartermaine is off to survey his new property, and if you try, you might just catch up with him. *At Heatherfields.*"

"Damn it, Kate—"

But Kate was striding away in the direction of the rectory. "I trust, Reggie," she said over one shoulder, "that you can make your own way back to Bellecombe. Because just now, I do not fancy sharing a carriage with you."

She did not turn around again, and instead marched up to the rectory and pounded on the door. Nancy came out at once, her head hung oddly low.

"Are we ready to go?" she asked, brushing past Kate.

Kate turned. "Yes, almost."

Nancy didn't look at her as they crossed the street. Something had happened, Kate realized. Had her sister overheard the quarrel with Reggie? Or had it been the thing she and Richard had been discussing outside the church? Was it, in fact, Aurélie?

Kate didn't have time to press Nancy, for as soon as they crossed the street, Aurélie flew out St. Michael's door, one hand clapped on her hat as if to hold it in place.

"*Dépêchez-vous!*" she ordered, motioning impatiently. "We haven't got all day. Julia and the others await us."

Neither Nancy nor her mother bothered to ask Kate what had become of Reggie. Both their minds were clearly elsewhere throughout the drive back to Bellecombe. Aurélie was looking oddly dreamy-eyed again, while Nancy just looked distraught.

When they arrived home, Aurélie went at once to her guests. Lady Julia and the gentlemen were lazing about with their coffee in the front parlor. Absent any shooting, and the hour being as yet too early for serious drinking, or even cards, the four of them were looking dead bored. Nancy brushed past without sparing them a glance.

"Come upstairs, Kate," she said quietly. "I think I had better speak with you."

Kate cut her mother a dark glance and followed Nancy up to her private parlor. Mrs. Peppin was there before them, replacing the bottle of cordial that Aurélie had been gradually draining.

"All right, Nancy, out with it," Kate demanded. "Is Mamma teasing Richard? Or . . . or *flirting* with him?"

Nancy's eyes flared wide. "Oh, no! Nothing like that."

"I should leave you," said Mrs. Peppin, turning from the sideboard.

Nancy threw up a hand. "No, Peppie, I need you. Come, sit, the both of you."

Kate was beginning to sense she might need a stout glass of the cordial. "Nancy, you're worrying me," she said, smoothing her skirts beneath her as she sat. "What in heaven's name is wrong?"

Nancy was hunched forward on the end of the chaise, her hands clasped. "It's Richard's aunt," she said.

"The lady visiting from Staplegrove today?" said Mrs. Peppin, her brow furrowing.

"Yes. Mrs. Lowell." Nancy lifted her gaze to Kate's.

"What about her?" asked Kate solicitously. "I hope she's not ill?"

"Oh, no." Nancy caught her lip between her teeth a moment. "It has to do with Mrs. Granger, who lives across the street from the Lowells' church."

"Mrs. Granger?" Kate was mystified. "Do we even know a Mrs. Granger?"

"A little," said Nancy. "Mrs. Lowell introduced us at the Midsummer Fair in Taunton."

Kate shook her head. She remembered the fair, for it had been a beautiful June day. She and Nancy had been invited to drive out with Richard and Mrs. Burnham, and to take tea afterward with the Lowells at the vicarage in Staplegrove.

"We met so many people that afternoon," she said vaguely. "What about this Mrs. Granger is so distressing?"

"You may recall Mrs. Lowell was actually gossiping about her that day," Nancy reminded Kate. "She whispered that Mrs. Granger had moved with little explanation to Staplegrove some years ago with a granddaughter in tow."

"Oh, yes," said Kate, a snippet of memory returning. "This Mrs. Granger had a child—her daughter's child—a pretty girl, but the name escapes me."

"Annabelle Granger," said Nancy. "Annie, she's called."

"That's right," said Kate. "The mother had been seduced by the girl's father, then died in childbed. It was a sad story."

"Yes, but a rich London gentleman owns the cottage Mrs. Granger lives in, and even the stables behind it." Nancy spoke swiftly, as if to force the words out. "It's been put about that he's the girl's godfather, or an uncle of some sort. Yet he rarely visits, and scarcely spares the child a word, according to Mrs. Lowell."

"Ah, the father," said Mrs. Peppin sagely. "'Tis ever the

way with rich gentlemen. They hide their troubles away in some little village."

"Yes, that's what Mrs. Lowell said," said Kate. "She was outraged. But we don't know the truth, Peppie. Perhaps the gentleman really is an uncle?"

Mrs. Peppin shot Kate a doubtful look. "With a story so vague as that?"

"I know, I know," said Kate, throwing up her hands. "You're likely right. Human nature is ever a disappointment. But Nancy, what has this tragedy to do with us?"

Nancy looked at her sorrowfully. "Oh, Kate," she whispered. "Mrs. Lowell says—well, she says that man is Edward."

"Edward?" Kate went suddenly still inside. "She says that Edward . . . keeps up this child?"

It was as if she could feel her own heart beating. As if time had caught, suspended on a silken string, as she struggled to make sense of Nancy's words.

"Not *Mr. Edward*—?" Peppie's fingers flew to her lips, as if she might take back her words.

"Mrs. Lowell recognized him at church," said Nancy sorrowfully, "and that great black horse of his, too."

The horse. Kate had forgotten it.

With Edward's identity discovered, she'd dropped all enquiries into its origin. But one rarely rode a horse all the way from London nowadays; the train was too fast.

"So you're saying that . . . that this Mrs. Lowell claims Edward is Annie Granger's father?" Kate managed to say. "That he owns the cottage they live in? That his money—his gaming hell money—keeps up the Granger family?"

Nancy nodded, biting her lip again. "Yes, and the Lowells deeply disapprove of him," she replied. "Mrs. Lowell says he comes round once or twice a year and strides about like he owns the place."

"Which he does, it sounds," interjected Mrs. Peppin.

"Yes," said Nancy. "That's where the horse came from. Edward pastures it there."

But the entire, ugly scenario was playing out in Kate's mind. Edward had recognized the church in Staplegrove the day they drove past it; he had not even pretended otherwise.

This, then, was the tragedy Edward had spoken of. The story of Maria, whose parents had refused his suit.

She died whilst I was in the army, Edward had said.

But how could that be? Could he have been so spiteful— or so distraught—as to go away and leave her carrying his child? Or had it all been one great misunderstanding?

It almost didn't matter; he had hidden away a child, and more or less ignored her. It was not abandonment, no—but it was close. And Kate had truly thought better of Edward than that.

"Miss Kate?" Peppie put an arm around her shoulders. "Oh, miss, sit up straight, lovey, do."

"But Edward . . . Edward has said nothing of this to me." Kate realized she had slumped forward on the sofa. Nancy and Peppie exchanged speaking glances.

"Oh, Kate!" Nancy slid to the very end of the chaise, and caught Kate's hands in her own. "Should I not have told you? Richard is so angry! Strange as it is, he'd taken quite a liking to Edward. And he said . . . he said I really *must* tell you. Perhaps I oughtn't have?"

"There, there, Miss Nan," said Peppie, but she was patting Kate's back. "Of course you did rightly. And as Miss Kate says, there's no knowing how this gurt scandal come about. Mayhap there's more to it than that newsy Mrs. Lowell knows."

Kate gathered her wits and stood. She needed to be alone. "Thank you, Nancy," she said. "You did just the right thing. I'm . . . disappointed, to say the least."

Left with little alternative, Nancy rose. "And are you going to confront him, Kate?" she asked. "Are you going to demand the truth? For my part, I should like to strike that handsome face of his a cracking good blow. I feel as if he has deceived us."

"But it's really none of our business." Kate forced a smile, though it cost her dear. "He's chosen to keep it a secret for reasons of his own. I shall not pry. After all, he isn't starving or beating Annie Granger, but merely depriving her of a father's love and companionship."

"But what a cruel, cruel cut for a child to bear!" cried Nancy. "How can you, of all people, excuse it?"

"I do not," she replied. "Children should live with their fathers regardless of how they came into being. They should not be hidden away as if they are something to be ashamed of."

But Nancy's outrage didn't relent. "Kate, you and I know too well what it's like to be dumped in the country and treated as an afterthought," she said harshly. "Aurélie, for all her faults, would have stayed if Papa had let her. You know, Kate, she would have."

"I'm not excusing Papa," said Kate. "But this is about Edward's failings, not his. And we must console ourselves that Edward is doing better than many rich men in his place would do. Yes, Nan, I'm crushed. The child is likely his. But what can it matter to us? He'll be gone soon."

"Not if Mrs. Wentworth has any say in it," Mrs. Peppin warned, "since she's taken it into her head to keep the fellow here."

"Then I shall tell Mamma the truth," Nancy hotly declared. "I . . . I shall insist she send him away."

"Nan, leave it be," Kate cautioned, rising as gracefully as she could. "He'll go soon enough. Certainly I shall not further detain him. Now, if the two of you will excuse me, I have some letters to write."

She watched them trail from the room, the withering smile still planted upon her face. But at the last instant, Mrs. Peppin cast a pitying look back over her shoulder. Then Nancy, too, turned around.

"Kate," she said, "shall I cancel my trip to Exeter tomorrow with Mamma? I should be pleased to stay at home with you and keep you company. I do not need to go shopping, truly."

"Heavens, no," said Kate. "Aurélie will have a fit."

But it was her sister's simple kindness that was Kate's undoing. As soon as the door shut, she flung herself across the divan, and began to sob.

She wasn't even sure why she sobbed—which made it all the worse. What had she imagined? That Edward would turn over a new leaf and fling himself at her feet? That there would be some sweet happy-ever-after amidst the wreckage of her life?

There would not be.

There would not be, and even Reggie, cad that he was, had sense enough to see what Kate's life was coming to. In fact, Reggie had likely given Kate the best offer she was apt ever to have—and that had been an offer of blackmail, more or less.

Certainly she'd get nothing better from wicked Ned Quartermaine, and on that score, Edward had not deceived her. He had made it plain that Kate could expect nothing of him beyond this; a strange bond born of a strange circumstance, and a passionate fling between the sheets.

And now she had to face the fact that Edward was not at all the sort of man she'd imagined—this, on top of the fact that she'd somehow convinced herself that owning a gaming hell might be forgivable. But to neglect one's daughter? That struck too near the heart for even Kate to contrive to excuse.

Oh, such men inevitably had a dozen pretty reasons. Certainly her father had; by the time Nancy had come along, with his marriage already strained, James Wentworth had ceased to spare his daughters a passing glance, and packed them off permanently to Somerset. And that abandonment, she fully realized, was precisely why Nancy was so angry with Edward.

But if challenged, Edward would doubtless say that his occupation made him unsuitable to rear a child. That men were temperamentally incapable of understanding daughters. Or, like Kate's father, that children needed fresh, country air.

But children—especially daughters—needed fathers. Someone to teach them how to ride a pony and wield a cricket bat. Someone to tell them that they were pretty, even if they were not.

Even if they were plain as a pikestaff, and gangly as a beanpole.

A child needed a father's love. And to deny it was selfish beyond reason.

On another wave of self-pity, Kate curled into a ball on the divan, and let her head sink into the pillow. Just then her door creaked open a crack, and then a little wider. Filou came waddling and snuffling across the carpet, his rheumy eyes solemn.

He simply stood at the edge of the divan, gazing up at her in what seemed to Kate like sincere sympathy.

"Oh, very well." Kate sighed, and patted a spot beside her.

Filou leapt up, his hind legs kicking and flailing for purchase. She reached out and hefted up his rump, and the pug flopped against her on a wheezy exhalation. She wrapped an arm about him, and snuggled him close.

He sighed again, gave a tremulous doggy shudder, and then began to snore.

Well, this is it, thought Kate. *This is as good as it gets for me.*

A flatulent, asthmatic dog. Or Lord Reginald Hoke, extortionist extraordinaire.

Kate chose the dog.

She put her arm around Filou, and drifted off into something like sleep.

CHAPTER 13

Miss Wentworth's Dilemma

Kate managed to avoid Edward for the remainder of the day, and with very little effort on her own behalf. In fact, she saw almost no one.

According to Mrs. Peppin, Nancy was closeted with Aurélie for two hours, planning their grand shopping excursion. Declaring the trip to Exeter too taxing to even contemplate, Lady Julia curled up in the library with a novel. Sir Francis and the Comte de Macey decided to take a long walk along the moor, while Reggie spent the whole of the afternoon in the billiards room with a bottle of Bellecombe's best brandy.

As to Edward, Kate heard no more of him, and supposed he spent the remainder of the day with Anstruther. So, after sending down her excuses at dinner—a headache, entirely real—Kate went straight to bed, only to be roused from a long, dream-fraught night somewhere near dawn by Mrs. Peppin, who was gently jostling her shoulder.

"My lady, wake up, do!" she was saying as Kate surfaced.

"*Umm?*" Kate levered up onto one elbow, dislodging poor

Filou, who had, for once, forsaken Aurélie. She pushed the hair from her face to see the housekeeper standing over her bed in a pool of yellow light, her lamp raised high.

"Peppie? What's wrong? Is it Mamma?"

"No, no, lovey," she said, putting the lamp down on Kate's night table. "Young Tom Shearn's in the bailey. He says Jenks has a heifer breeching down in the byre, and another calf behind it."

"Blast." Kate dragged a hand through her hair. "One of the Devons?"

"No, one of the new Herefords, lovey," she said, "and too expensive to let die, Jenks says."

"Jenks is right." Kate flung back the covers. "Blasted over-bred racehorses. What does Anstruther say? The Herefords were his notion. Did anyone send to Taunton for the veterinary surgeon?"

"Aye, but Jenks thinks there's no time," Mrs. Peppin reported. "And Anstruther's dressing to take Mrs. Wentworth to Exeter, says Tom, and dares not disappoint her. He said Tom was to come for you, and ask what might be done."

"*Exeter?*" Caught in the midst of filling her basin with cold water, Kate turned, incredulous, the pitcher held aloft. "And shopping takes precedence over a forty-guinea Hereford? My God, has Mamma run the whole world mad?"

"Just dress, miss," Mrs. Peppin encouraged. "He would not have sent for you a'thout he believed you needed."

"Very well, blast it," she said. "Put Filou back in Mamma's room, and have Athena saddled. Oh, and Peppie? Tell Fendershot to load my pistol, and put it in my bag."

Mrs. Peppin winced. But Kate was not about to let a cow suffer needlessly, be it forty guineas or four hundred, if there was truly nothing to be done. And some of the things that *could* be done to save the poor cow were horrid in and of themselves . . .

Well, just like the rest of her troubles at present, those alternatives didn't bear thinking of.

Still, some days, Kate wondered how her life had come to this. She had grown up expecting an ordinary life; happiness, marriage, and children. Even until yesterday, truth be told, she had not entirely given up on that dream.

And now she had suffered what was the most miserable night of her life since Stephen lay dying. Even the dog had apparently felt sorry for her. She was so angry. So deeply angry with herself, and yes, with Edward—and for what? For refusing to tell her about his daughter?

Did she really imagine herself such a significant part of Edward's life? Was she so naive that she believed being bedded by a man obligated him to share his life's story? His every sin and secret?—both of which were numerous, she did not doubt.

Oh, Edward enjoyed her companionship, she realized. But at the end of the day, perhaps she was no more important to him than poor little Annie Granger. No, she was just ordinary Katherine Wentworth, called to tend a laboring cow!

"As if I know bugger-all about that, either," she muttered to herself, and rather vulgarly, too.

It was just the sort of language one picked up around a farm. Language, really, that a lady had no business knowing, and should never have been exposed to. But she did know it; this was far from her first birthing. Sheep, cattle, and once even a draft horse; Anstruther and her grandfather had begun to drag her along to every crisis before Stephen's body had gone cold in the grave.

After all, what had been the alternative for Bellecombe?

For her to marry Reggie?

"Ha!" she said aloud. "As if *he'd* know what to do, the little nancy-pants. Better I should marry Tom Shearn."

With that sentiment in mind, Kate washed her face, dressed, and twisted up her hair into a ruthless knot. Having forgone her corset in favor of speed, she simply dragged on her boots, seized her crop from its hook, and went downstairs to find Tom.

AFTER OVERSLEEPING, A rare event indeed, Edward was required to rush down to breakfast. He'd spent the previous afternoon in the saddle, touring every corner of his new property. Now, as he dressed, he felt a faint sense of hope stirring—at least on one emotional front.

Yes, Heatherfields was so neglected it would take five or six thousand pounds, Anstruther had calculated, to set it to rights again. But oh, what a house it would be when finished! He had practically stolen the estate from Reggie, the damned, desperate fool.

Far from being a mere shooting box, Heatherfields was instead a tidy Elizabethan manor house of perfect proportions and once-elegant gardens, the whole of which was essentially unaltered by time.

Anstruther had been especially cast down by the nearly uninhabitable interiors, but Edward, strangely, had not. He had known Lord Reginald Hoke for the wastrel he was, and expected the worst. Far better the rooms were unaltered and unkempt, if it meant they had not been ruined by two centuries of bad taste and indiscriminate plastering.

Restored to its sixteenth-century glory, Heatherfields would be the ideal place for Annie to begin young adulthood. The sort of home to which prospective suitors might be brought; a house meant for landed English aristocracy, the very thing rich young merchants and sensible bankers' sons would aspire to become.

And they were just the sort of young men who could not afford to turn up their noses too thoroughly at Annie's uncertain parentage, and who, once wed, would not trouble themselves to quell the speculation that their new bride might—just *might*—be the granddaughter of a duke, however unlikely that scenario was.

But Edward was getting ahead of himself when the house might require years to be brought up to snuff—particularly if they uncovered the woodworm Anstruther predicted. By then, Annie would be ready for those rich young suitors.

And however awkward and infrequent Mrs. Granger might make his visits, Edward did want to help the child.

Engaged in tying his cravat, he caught his own reflection in the mirror and considered, not for the first time, his inadequacy for such a task. He wished suddenly he could ask Kate's counsel; not about just the renovations and the land, but about Annie. What did he know, after all, about a young girl's needs? Or how to launch her into society? Or—more daunting still—how to convince Mrs. Granger to even permit it?

The damned woman still resented him; resented both his help and his interference, even though circumstance compelled her to take both. She was still hell-bent on sheltering the girl, but could she not see that hiding Annie away merely made the gossip worse?

Oh, Edward had no quarrel with gossip if it could be turned to his purpose. The ambiguity about Annie's origin was likely better than the truth. But Annie was growing up. The world would have to be told . . . *something*.

He would have liked to tell Kate the truth—insofar as he knew it. But to what end? There was nothing for him at Bellecombe. There could never be. Kate wouldn't have him, and he wouldn't want her to. So why throw Annie on the pyre of his flamingly bad choices?

Suddenly, his cravat knotted to the wrong side. Edward's fingers clawed at the too-tight knot, then tore the damned thing off and flung it across his bed.

Was that what he wanted? To bare his soul to Kate? To promise his undying love, and swear to be a better man? Well, it would not work. His blood might be uncertain, but his past was all too clear.

Moreover, old Pettibone the headmaster had been right; there was a vicious streak in Edward that would not yield. Indeed, he had embraced it. It had enabled him to survive a harsh life, even as it marked him ever after. A double-edged sword always cut two ways.

No, better to simply savor Kate's companionship through the coming days, and forge something like an abiding friendship, if he could. He had no wish to involve Kate in some tawdry, ongoing *affaire*—and she wasn't fool enough, thank God, to permit it.

And yet, how was he to visit Heatherfields over the coming months and years without yielding to the temptation to see her? In his heart and in his memories, Kate and Bellecombe and even the staff were knotted as tightly together as this damned cravat he could not get untied.

He ripped the second off, hurled it aside, and buckled on a black stock instead. Whatever hard choice wanted making, it needn't be made today. Perhaps, if Kate's headache had waned, she might agree to ride over Heatherfields with him as he inspected the fences. What was the harm in asking? In fact, there was a great deal of wisdom in it, since she owned the adjoining property.

His spirits lifting at the notion of spending time with her, Edward shrugged into his coat and hastened downstairs to the breakfast parlor. Unfortunately, he found no one there save Aurélie and Nancy Wentworth. An overstuffed carpet-bag sat just inside the door, the pug curled on the rug beside it, snoring.

"*Bonjour*, Mr. Quartermaine," sang Mrs. Wentworth from beneath a lacy, broad-brimmed hat of pink silk. "Is it not a lovely morning to be off on an adventure?"

"Indeed, ma'am," he said, looking about the room in hopes of conjuring up Kate. "In fact, I think I shall ride round Heatherfields again. Has Lady d'Allenay come down?"

"Not a hair has been seen," said her mother with a toss of her bejeweled hand. "Katherine has gone out already, I daresay."

Nancy Wentworth didn't so much as look at him. Indeed, her hands lay fisted upon the table, white-knuckled. "There was a sick cow, Peppie said," she answered into the table-cloth. "She's gone to tend it."

"Oh," said Edward, disappointed. "How long does that sort of thing take?"

"All day, sometimes," said the girl.

"Ah. Too bad."

He went to the sideboard to pour a cup of coffee, musing upon whether to chase after Kate, or to simply await her return. He glanced again at the sleeping dog, and the carpetbag.

"Is someone leaving us today?" he asked.

"*Non, non*, merely shopping!" said Aurélie Wentworth a little loudly. "I have some gowns there which require lace and shoes and, oh, la!—all manner of trifles!—but the trifles must match, *n'est-ce pas*? So I take them. For matching."

"Of course." Edward took some kippers and eggs then returned to the table, but just then Anstruther appeared in the doorway.

"Well," said the estate agent a little gruffly. "I am come, Nan. If you're ready? Morning, Quartermaine."

Nancy Wentworth rose, but her face was bloodless. "Yes . . . yes, I'm ready."

Anstruther gave the girl his arm almost formally, and Mrs. Wentworth followed them out, waggling her fingers to Edward as a sort of afterthought.

"*Bonjour*, Mr. Quartermaine!" she said lightly. "We shall have all manner of things to talk about when we return!"

Edward could not imagine what, since he had no interest in female fashions, or their accouterment. He had never troubled himself to keep up the sort of mistress who required such attentions. He preferred Kate's manner of dress, now that he thought on it; simple, functional, and suited only to its purpose. Well, except for that green and gold confection . . .

As to Nancy, the poor girl looked a little sullen. And yet there had been a hopefulness in her eyes when she had looked at Anstruther. Clearly the girl was suffering mixed emotions over something, thought Edward. And why was

Anstruther escorting them anyway? Something to do with buying a plow?

Edward shook his head. Anstruther, for all his recalcitrance, looked to be as under the cat's paw as the rest of Bellecombe when it came to Aurélie Wentworth. But there was no helping the poor devil, so Edward sipped at his coffee, and returned to his musings about Kate in the green and gold gown.

KATE RETURNED HOME in the late afternoon with Tom Shearn riding alongside her. On one or two occasions, the poor man was nearly required to poke her upright, so physically exhausted did she find herself.

"A good day's work, m'lady," said the young man as they rode beneath the inner portcullis.

"Thank you for staying, Tom," she said as he leapt down. "It was more than poor Jenks and I could manage. Two calves, and most of the day. Who could imagine it?"

"Happy to serve, ma'am," he said, helping her dismount. "I'll just take Athena round to Motte, shall I?"

"Mercy 'pon us," declared Mrs. Peppin, meeting her at the door. "You look a fright, miss."

"Congratulate me, Peppie." Kate's smile was wan. "I'm a new mother twice over, and we're about . . . oh, twenty pounds richer?"

"So you may hope," said Peppie. "But Mrs. Wentworth will have spent that in ribbons today. Well, miss, let's get you a bath drawn. Stop staring, Jasper, you gurt gawka-mouth, and set to it. Happen you've not seen blood and muck afore?"

With a tug of his forelock, the young man darted off.

"Bless you, Peppie," said Kate. "What time is dinner?"

"No one's said, miss," reported Mrs. Peppin. "Half-seven, I daresay?"

Kate turned, already starting up the stairs. "What, has Mamma not returned?"

"Not a sight of her, miss, since eight o'clock when they set out for the village."

"The village? Why go through the village to reach Exeter?"

The housekeeper shrugged. "I couldn't say, Miss Kate, but turn toward it they did, for Hetty was up t' tower shaking out rugs and saw as much."

"Oh, well." Kate turned back to the stairs. "Half past it is, then. Aurélie and Nancy will have to eat something cold if they are late."

On the next landing, however, she bumped squarely into Edward, who was coming down from his newly situated room one floor above. Nerves already on edge, Kate felt her heartbeat ratchet up, and that familiar longing twist through her.

And then she remembered Annie Granger.

"Kate!" He jerked to a halt, eyes widening, and moved as if to catch her by the shoulder. "Kate, my God. Are you all right?"

She glanced down at her stained habit, but kept moving. "Quite all right," she said calmly. "The perils of being a lady farmer, I fear. Shall I see you tonight at dinner?"

He stood stock-still on the landing. "Yes, of course," he said after her. "But Kate, I wanted to tell you—"

"Can it wait until after dinner?" she said matter-of-factly, striding down the passageway. "I shall have more time then."

"Well. Certainly."

She didn't turn around again, but set a businesslike pace all the way to her room. Once inside, however, she slammed the door and bit her lip.

Then, on muttered imprecation, she went to the sideboard and extracted not the cordial, but a bottle of Anstruther's good Scotch whisky she kept hidden for just such a purpose. Pouring out two fingers' worth, she slung half of it back and let it burn, blinking her eyes rapidly—a response not entirely attributable to the whisky.

Good heavens, she hurt all over, and it wasn't just her heart. Her right arm felt as if it had been yanked from its

socket, and the left not much better. Moreover she was filthy.
No, she *smelled*. Of mud and blood and manure, and of the
sweat of the day, too.

She certainly didn't want to think of Edward or Annie on
top of all else.

She threw back the rest of the whisky, then hastened
through to her dressing room to strip herself bare. Soon she
could hear the clatter of the tub being carried in—the big,
copper contraption, too; the one ordinarily reserved only for
Aurélie's two-hour champagne-and-buttermilk soaks, the
preparation of which drove the poor dairymaid half mad.

Beyond the door, bless her, Peppie was exhorting the footman to carry up the cans faster, and in short order Kate was
floating in water up to her chin, the temperature so hot her
skin was turning red.

To her shock, Tillie, her mother's maid, came in—ordered
to do so, no doubt, by Peppie. The maid washed Kate's hair
in Aurélie's best *savon de Marseille* and rinsed it out in vin-
egar, then scrubbed Kate's arms, legs, and back in Mediter-
ranean sea salt. By the time she was finished, Kate felt clean
again—and regrettably spoiled.

Afterward, the maid combed her hair dry by the fire, then
curled and pinned it up in a fashion that was far too elaborate for Kate. But she was too tired to argue, and with her
muscles no longer aching, her thoughts once again fixated
on her heart.

She could not get Annie Granger out of her mind. And
yet, for the life of her, Kate could not remember what the
child looked like. Like Edward, perhaps?

And what would Edward's children look like? Golden-
haired and green-eyed? Handsome, almost certainly.

On a wave of sadness, Kate went to the wardrobe and
took out a shawl. She had to shake these blue devils off; she
had duties to attend. With Aurélie and Nancy away, it fell
to Kate to entertain Julia, de Macey, and Sir Francis. They
were likely trickling downstairs already.

But in her oddly peevish mood, Kate suddenly decided the color of her shawl was wrong, and flung it on the bed. The cashmere sailed onto her pillow like a cloud and landed with a soft rattle. She was halfway back to the dressing room when she realized that made no sense.

Curious, she turned around and marched back again. Lifting the shawl, she flicked back her covers. A fold of thick, cream-colored letter paper lay in the center of her pillow. With a strange sense of unease, Kate picked it up.

LADY JULIA HAD just stepped from her room and paused in the passageway to fondle her earbobs, as if wondering whether she'd made the best choice, when Kate burst from her room, the letter still in hand.

"Heavens, Katherine, you look frightful!" said Lady Julia.

"Julia," she rasped. "My God. Do you know anything about this?"

She shoved the letter into Julia's face. The lady took it, skimmed it, then burst into peals of laughter. "Oh, *Aurélie!*" she declared. "What next?"

"*What next?*" screeched Kate, snatching it back. "I shall tell you, Julia, what's next. Uncle Upshaw will have her head on a pike over Temple Bar, that's what's next!"

Julia had drawn back as if hysteria might be contagious. "To be sure, you're likely right," she said more soothingly. "Poor Kate. I'm so sorry for laughing. This is terrible. What can I do?"

Kate didn't even stop to think through her next words. "Go upstairs," she demanded, starting down the corridor, "and tell Mr. Quartermaine I need him. I'm going downstairs to find Peppie."

The latter was easily done; letter in hand, Kate flew down the stairs, almost plowing the poor housekeeper down.

"Lawks, miss, such hurry-scurry!" said the housekeeper. "Have ye seen a ghost?"

But reality was settling in, and Kate was beginning to feel

more sick than angry. "No, but I fear, Peppie, that I soon shall," she rasped, "and that ghost will be Mamma's. Uncle Upshaw is going to throttle her!"

Mrs. Peppin took the letter. "Well, burn my wigs and feathers!" she cried after a moment. "Getting *married*—?"

Just then Edward came dashing down the stairs. "Kate?" His boot heels rang hard on the marble as he strode through the hall. "Kate, what's happened?"

"Oh, Edward." Kate looked up at him with desperation in her eyes. "It is beyond comprehension! Aurélie has persuaded Richard and Nancy to elope!"

"Good God!" he said. "*Elope?* But . . . how?"

Mrs. Peppin thrust the letter at him. "And that, sir, is the very question," she said. "We know not how, but only who's behind it. Lawks, what's to be done, Miss Kate?"

Kate set a hand to her forehead.

Edward was reading the letter.

Think, think, she told herself.

"We must stop them somehow," she said determinedly. "Or—wait, perhaps Anstruther will stop them? He drove them. He has good sense."

"Someone had better stop them," warned Mrs. Peppin.

"It may be too late to stop anyone," said Edward, his handsome brow deeply furrowed.

"Oh, dear," said Kate. "Uncle Upshaw will be here tomorrow at latest. Truth be told, I expected him today."

Edward folded the letter, sliding it pensively through his fingers. "So Mrs. Wentworth means to get a special license from the Bishop of Exeter," he said, "so that Richard and Nancy can marry."

"Again, I can't think how!" declared Kate. "Without Upshaw's signature, she cannot do such a thing."

"It is quite true that a mother may not grant permission," said Edward. "Only a guardian—or a father."

"Well, Papa is long in his grave, and Upshaw is either in

London, or on his way here. And I can assure you he didn't give permission. Aurélie must have forged something."

"My dear Kate." Edward set a wide, warm hand at the small of her back. "Shall I go after them? You've only to say the word."

"I don't know!" Kate heaved a slow sigh, realizing she shouldn't have sent for Edward in her panic. Already she yearned to lean upon his shoulder—and his good judgment.

"Perhaps Peppie and I are overreacting?" she added. "Surely Anstruther will not let Aurélie hang herself. Or ruin Nancy. They will get to Exeter, he'll catch wind of her mad scheme, and turn the carriage home, won't he?"

"Kate," said Edward quietly, "I would not be too sure of that."

"What?" she said sharply. "Why not? Anstruther is a very sharp character."

Edward hesitated oddly. "How far is the drive to Exeter?" he said. "Forty miles?"

"A little less." Kate licked her lips nervously. "Why? What is your point?"

"Four people in Mrs. Wentworth's barouche?" he said. "It's too far, Kate. I'm sure they took the train, however much your mother may loathe it. They had to have done. Likely they were in Exeter before noon."

Kate quelled her anxiety and considered it. "Yes, of course you're right. But the Bishop of Exeter is as stiff as they come. He's not likely to be swayed by one of Aurélie's tearful tales, or her feminine wiles."

"Kate, my dear, it is possible they didn't go to Exeter at all." His hand made a slow, soothing circle at the curve of her spine, and she did not even glance about to ensure they were alone save for Peppie. "Your mother is very clever. They might possibly have gone north to Scotland."

"To *Scotland*?" Kate's breath seized. "To marry over the anvil? Richard would never agree to such a shameful thing."

"Then let's assume Exeter," said Edward. "But at all accounts, I think it best I go after them."

"Thank you," she said, feeling suddenly grateful. "But I ought not have involved you. I should go, too, at the very least."

"No." His eyes were tender, but his voice was firm. "Have the horses put to. There is a fast-looking gig in the carriage house. I saw it yesterday."

"With the curricle bar? It was Stephen's."

"Yes, it will be light and quick, and I shall move faster alone."

"Yes. Yes, of course." Kate was nodding. "There is some chance Mamma might actually listen to you."

"But you must stay here, Kate, in case your uncle turns up," he pressed. "You will have to tell him . . . *something*, but I know not what."

"I should tell him Aurélie has kidnapped Nancy," declared Kate. "For that's very nearly the case. Nancy was resigned to waiting Uncle out. Aurélie means well, I know, but she does not *think*."

But Edward was already starting back up the stairs. "I'll fetch my greatcoat," he said. "Where is the most likely train station? I'll go there first, and see if anyone answering their description has passed through today."

"I'll see to Motte and the gig," said Mrs. Peppin, turning toward the front door.

"Edward." Kate rushed to the staircase after him.

He stopped and turned on the step, looking down at her. "Yes?"

"I'm sorry," she said, clinging to the newel post. "About earlier. I was brusque."

"You were tired," he said. "Good God, you *are* tired."

Then, to her shock, he tipped up her chin on one finger, almost as if he might lean down and kiss her—and fool that she was, she would have let him.

"Don't worry, Kate," he said softly. "I will find your

mother. I *will*. But it's likely too late, and what's done is done."

"Oh, Edward!" she said. "I want Nancy to marry Richard. I do. But Mamma is just going to cause a big uproar, alienate Uncle Upshaw, and possibly taint Nancy's reputation in the bargain."

"My dear, your mother won't run the latter risk; she's not the fool you think her." Then he cupped Kate's cheek in his palm. "She's finagled a way to make this marriage, depend upon it. And Upshaw will be angry, certainly. And there may be a *little* uproar—but only if it starts here. In this house. Do you understand me?"

"I—yes, I think so."

"I will find your mother," he promised, "and you will stop the uproar. And in the end, all will come aright."

"I wish I had your certainty." She restored his hand with a pat and a little shove. "Go. Go before Uncle turns up on our front step."

"Right, then." Edward shot her a swift smile as he turned. "I'm off."

"And Edward," she called after him, "*thank* you."

CHAPTER 14

In Which the Parson Takes a Wife

It is always darkest before the storm, and by the time Edward returned to the castle with Aurélie Wentworth in tow, the night was black save for a waxing moon, and the storm had begun to rumble ominously in Bellecombe's great hall.

It had taken no great effort to find her; the lady had been standing on the platform at Wellington Station, attempting to hire someone to drive her to the castle. During their swift journey, he had not asked Mrs. Wentworth what had happened; it wasn't his business, and she offered up nothing save an explanation that she had quarreled with Anstruther, and left the others in Exeter.

The lady sat now beside him, uncharacteristically quiet as she held fast to the carriage; a wise precaution given his considerable speed. But he did not want Kate to worry any more than was necessary. At least Aurélie Wentworth had sense enough to be silent when a man was driving to an inch, and pushing his team to its limits.

When they turned onto the bridge across what had once

been Bellecombe's moat, however, she made a sound of dismay.

"*Mon Dieu!*" she said as he cut his team beneath the portcullis, "I am to be hung for a sheep this time."

He looked up, the tight stone passage having been successfully navigated, to see her staring straight ahead. In the inner bailey beyond, he could see servants hastening about, torches aloft, and a large traveling coach being unloaded.

His heart sank a little. "Lord Upshaw, I presume?"

"I expect so," said Aurélie in a resigned voice. "Ill timing indeed! But then, I knew I had to make haste. *Ma foi*, Mr. Quartermaine, this may not be pretty."

It would not. Already he could hear a booming, authoritative male voice demanding something of someone. Kate, he feared. Swiftly, he leapt down to hand Mrs. Wentworth from the carriage.

"Upshaw is about to slice someone to ribbons, it sounds," he said grimly. "It is not fair that it should be Kate."

"I know my duty, sir," she said, bowing her head almost regally. "I thank you for the swift journey."

He caught her arm as he turned to go. "Mrs. Wentworth, I think I have some notion what you're up to," he said, "and if you hope to pull it off, I suggest you hush Upshaw before the gossip gets out."

"Excellent advice, Mr. Quartermaine," she said, flashing one of her bemused smiles. "You have saved me much time, and Katherine much awkwardness."

After exchanging a quick word with Motte, Edward hastened after her. Aurélie Wentworth was walking stoically through the bailey, an overly large reticule swinging from one elbow, and her ostentatious hat hanging limply from her other hand, dwarfing her slight figure.

He caught up with her on the steps and entered on her heels. A tall, portly man was pacing the hall, still in his greatcoat, and clutching at his forehead with his hand.

Edward touched Mrs. Peppin on the arm. "Has word got round the servants?" he whispered.

The housekeeper shook her head. "No, and you may trust it will not."

Her expression resolute, Kate stood opposite the man. "Mamma!" she declared, relief sketching over her face. "Oh, Edward, thank you!"

"*Aurélie!*" said the portly man, whirling about with surprising speed. "Perhaps you can explain what in all blazes is going on here? Where have you been?"

"*Mon Dieu*, Archie, am I accountable to you now?" said Aurélie, rising onto her toes to kiss his cheek. "No one told me."

"Where Nancy is concerned, indeed you are!" he declared.

"Uncle, please!" said Kate. "Let us go into the library and sit down like rational people."

"Rational?" boomed Lord Upshaw. "A rash assumption, I fear!"

Kate turned and looked at Mrs. Peppin. "Peppie, may we have some tea brought in?"

"Certainly, my lady."

Kate gestured down the passageway. "Uncle Upshaw, I'm sure all your questions will be answered in due course."

"They will indeed, my girl!" he said grimly. Then he glanced back at Edward as if noticing him for the first time. "And just who, sir, are you?"

"This is my friend, Mr. Quartermaine." Aurélie Wentworth slipped her arm through his. "You will come with us, Edward," she commanded. "I fancy I may require an impartial witness."

What the devil he was supposed to attest to, Edward had no clue. He was far more concerned about Kate not bearing any blame for her mother's antics. He glanced at Kate, and crooked one eyebrow enquiringly.

Her face unsmiling, she jerked her head, indicating he should follow.

He knew, even then, that he should not. That he should step aside and go slinking off to his bedchamber with a bottle of brandy, and keep himself well out of the fray. But Mrs. Wentworth had an iron grip on his arm, and Kate looked as if she might need moral support. They trailed after Lord Upshaw, who looked rather like an oversized version of Mrs. Wentworth's pug.

Though he'd been careful not to ask any questions, Edward had a pretty good notion of what the lady had done, but the mechanics of it escaped him. Women like Aurélie Wentworth had secrets aplenty, and men wrapped around their little fingers.

When the library door was shut, Mrs. Wentworth didn't join them in sitting down around the table by the fire, but tossed aside her elaborate hat and began to move about the room with a restless energy.

"Well, madam?" demanded Upshaw.

Mrs. Wentworth swallowed hard. "*Alors*, Archie, you suspect the worst," she finally said, "and you're right. Nancy is not here. Indeed, she is wed. I have gone against your wishes and seen it done; you may rail at me as you will."

Her brother-in-law leapt from his chair. "How dare you!" he said, stabbing an accusing finger at her. "What is more, *how* can you hope to get away with it?"

"Oh, Mamma!" said Kate softly. "Please tell me this is a joke!"

"It's every inch a joke, for it simply is not legal," said Lord Upshaw, pacing the room. "So whatever Aurélie may think she's done, rest assured I shall have it *undone* by week's end!"

Aurélie shrugged her slight shoulders. "*Bien sûr*, Archie, you may try," she said. "But not, I hope, too soon? Nancy and Richard are enjoying a wedding night at Exeter's finest hotel. I should hate it to be interrupted."

Upshaw's eyes flared, black with temper. "By God, madam, this goes beyond the pale!" he said, slamming a fist down on a nearby table. "A wedding night! The chit is ruined!"

"*Zut alors!*" said Aurélie, eyes widening ingenuously. "Is she?" Then her pretty face fell. "*Oui*, you are likely right, now I think on it. Poor Nancy! No other man will want her now."

Edward was compelled to pinch himself to keep from laughing at the innocence on Mrs. Wentworth's face, but Upshaw was not amused.

"Yes, she's ruined!" Upshaw bore down upon her, Aurélie standing her ground. "Which is just as you intended, you scheming female! My God, Aurélie, have you any idea what you have done?"

"*Mais oui*, I think so," said Aurélie, suddenly serious. "I have made a mother's choice for my daughter which—if the law of the land were equitable—I would have every right *to* do. She has convinced me that she loves Richard Burnham, and that she is mature enough to make this choice. And so I have allowed her to make it."

"But you have no legal authority!" Upshaw repeated, in the tone of one speaking to a child. "You are a mere woman without—and I think both circumstance and law bear me out here—a brain in your pretty little head."

"*Oui, oui!*" Aurélie threw up both hands, as if in surrender. "It has ever been a failing of mine! No brains whatever! Alas, one muddles on."

"Oh, do not be impertinent with me, madam!" said Upshaw. "I will see this undone by every means that is legal. And she shan't have a penny of her inheritance so long as I can stop it."

Suddenly, Kate shoved back her chair. "Uncle Upshaw, I think that is quite enough," she said, rising.

The big man turned on her like a charging bull. Edward braced his hands to spring, but Kate threw up a hand, and Upshaw stopped cold.

"Sir, I fear you must accept Mamma's choice," said Kate firmly. "However it has come about, Nancy is married—and to a good and decent man of whom I earnestly approve—and she is spending the night with him. Even if we were foolish enough, we could not get to Exeter fast enough to undo this. So, as Mamma would say, *c'est fini*."

"So, Katherine, *you* were in on this little conspiracy?" roared Upshaw. "With your mother? The woman's amoral as an alley cat, and two-thirds mad in the bargain!"

At that, Edward did jerk to his feet. "I beg your pardon, Upshaw, but I would speak to you outside."

"Outside?" The man jerked, blinking as if trying to recall who Edward was. "I do not even know you, sir. And I certainly have no interest in discussing this business with you."

"Nonetheless, you will." Edward leveled a cold, hard look at Upshaw; one that had persuaded many a recalcitrant gentleman to full cooperation. "I account Lady d'Allenay and her mother as friends. No authority, legal or otherwise, gives you the right to speak to them in such a disrespectful tone. Temper it, sir. Or, as I say, we may go outside and finish this conversation."

"I have every right!" said Upshaw, but there was a whine in his tone now. "That child is my responsibility. I'm her guardian and her trustee."

"Then by all means, sir, explore your legal options to undo the marriage if you're willing to sacrifice Miss Wentworth's good name on the altar of your own pride," said Edward calmly, "but you will kindly keep a respectful voice in this house."

"Aren't you the fellow who didn't know his own name last week?" Upshaw grumbled. "You seem mighty sure of yourself now."

"Kindly sit down, sir," said Edward. "Lady d'Allenay had nothing to do with this."

Kate cut Edward a grateful glance. "I did not," she agreed, "but I do not scruple to tell you, Uncle, that I've come to believe you wrong about Nancy. She is old enough to know what she's doing."

"Old enough!" complained Upshaw, falling at last into a chair. "She knows nothing of life. She has scarcely been to London, or gone about in society."

"She has no interest in London or society; she's in love with Richard and wishes to help him do God's work," Kate countered, more bravely now. "Moreover, she's almost nineteen. Mamma was wed at barely seventeen, and bore two children by twenty. Louisa married you on her eighteenth birthday if memory serves. So if you wish to rail at Mamma, then yes, you may rail at me. I'm glad it is done. There, I have said it."

"It is not legal," Upshaw grumbled.

"On the contrary, Archie, I believe it is." Aurélie gave a Gallic shrug. "Or near enough as makes no difference."

"Madam, we shall see," declared Upshaw, a little more civilly. "I mean to call upon our family solicitors as soon as I can get back to London."

"I beg you, sir, not to call upon anyone," said Kate. "I think we must consider Nancy's best interests. Far better she should live a simple life than to have her good name tarnished by . . . by what? An annulment? Is that what you contemplate?"

"I do not yet know," said Upshaw, his lip curling in Aurélie's direction. "Perhaps, madam, you will be so obliging as to confess how you did it? Clearly, you persuaded someone to violate the law."

Aurélie shot an assessing, almost furtive, look at Kate.

"Oh, I'm not leaving," said Kate darkly.

"Perhaps I should," said Edward, planting a hand on his chair arm. "I will be just outside the door, Kate."

"*Non!*" said Aurélie sharply. "I think perhaps you, my dear Edward, already know?"

He hesitated. "I have some notion, ma'am," he admitted. "But it is none of my business."

Aurélie smiled and dropped her reticule on the table before him. "In the end, it might be," she said, sitting down opposite in him in a crush of silk, "and you are a man who is infamous for his ironclad discretion, I believe?"

Edward cut an uneasy glance at Upshaw. "I am."

Aurélie gave a swift shrug. "Keep your seat, then," she said, opening the reticule and extracting a thick pile of what looked like letters tied with a red ribbon.

"What is that?" asked Upshaw suspiciously.

"*Billets-doux*, Archie," said Aurélie in a low, sultry voice. "I've made, you see, rather a habit of collecting them—*many* of them—over the years. And alas, being, as I am, amoral as a cat—not all of them are from my husband."

"Your *affaires*, Aurélie, are of no interest to me," said Upshaw tightly, "nor were your husband's."

"*Oui*, but perhaps you might like to read one or two?" suggested Aurélie, smiling prettily as she pushed three across the table. "These are from a gentleman currently serving His Grace the Bishop of Exeter—serving, I might add, in a position with much power to act on behalf of His Grace."

"Then he has repented his sins, it is to be hoped!" said Upshaw.

"I am sure," said Aurélie, drawing them back again, "that he has. And I am sure we can all agree it would be best if his wife knew nothing of his brief moral failings, however well documented they might be?"

"You blackmailed a man with his own love letters!" exclaimed Upshaw. "I knew it! That is just the sort of thing, madam, you would do! Bed the poor fool, then bludgeon him with the evidence."

"Archie, you wound me!" declared Aurélie. "And in front of my daughter, no less. How am I to stop men from writing me letters pledging their eternal love—and their burning desire—and in such creative terms, too! *Vraiment*, I did not bed the poor fool; I did not need to. Men can be fools with no encouragement whatever."

"B-but you kept the letters!" sputtered Upshaw.

"*Oui*, a terrible vanity!" said Aurélie with a little half shrug. "But now, in the twilight of my life, as my looks fade and my figure falls, these letters, Archie, they comfort me. In fact, I think I shall be buried with them."

"No time soon, it is to be hoped," said Kate. "Mamma, really. Stop speaking of such things."

"*Eh bien*, the end, it comes to us all," said Aurélie evenly. "But it will not come to His Grace's dutiful assistant any-time soon—well, not at his wife's hand. Was it not kind of him to grant the Reverend Mr. Richard Burnham a special license to be married today?"

"Yes, and without her father's blessing, or her guardian's blessing!" countered Upshaw. "And thus it is patently illegal!"

"*Mon Dieu*, Archie!" Aurélie finally rolled her eyes. "The thing is legal—unless you're unwise enough to make an issue of it."

"And what if I do?" he complained.

But here, Aurélie shot Kate another glance, her face turning a little pink. "Actually, Archie, if you mean to persist, I *did* have Nancy's father's blessing," she said. "I took him with me to Exeter."

The room fell still as death.

"I will own, however," Aurélie went on, "that I'd as soon you didn't force me to make that public in the Court of Chancery, and thus embarrass my daughter."

"Oh, Mamma!" said Kate, clapping a hand over her mouth. "You didn't . . ."

"Oh, I did," said her mother. "You will recall, *mon chou*, that I asked your sister what she was willing to give up to have this marriage. I hope it shan't come to it, of course."

"But you . . . you *slept* with Anstruther?" said Kate.

Lord Upshaw gasped.

"That poor man! Oh, Mamma, how could you?"

Aurélie lifted both eyebrows a little haughtily. "Oh, it was not difficult, *mon chou*," she said lightly. "You should have

seen him in his youth! Even now, one must admit, John Anstruther is every inch a man."

Upshaw shook his head as if throwing off a bad dream.
"Aurélie, that does not make him Nancy's father," he said.
"Not in the eyes of the law. You cannot even prove that he
was her father."

Aurélie shoved the entire stack of letters across the table.
"*Non?*" she said lightly. "His Grace's dutiful assistant
thought I made a good case. I have Anstruther's love letters,
too. His angry demands that I let him acknowledge Nancy.
His insistence we go to France and get a divorce for me,
then marry. That we kidnap Kate and Stephen, and run off
to Scotland. On and on with his mad notions. It is a good
thing, Archie, *n'est-ce pas*, that one of us exercised good
judgment?"

"God help us," muttered Upshaw, whose bare forehead
was now sheened with sweat. "I think I'm having a heart
attack."

Aurélie plucked another from the pile. "Ah, and look
here! Here is James's sullen accusation that Nancy could
not possibly be his," she said, fanning herself with it. "Alas,
he was in Paris with his mistress the whole month of her
conception."

"And likely wished to throttle you when he got back,"
declared Upshaw, "a sentiment with which I find myself in
charity."

"Oh, James was not well pleased that his wife was in love
with his mother's godson," Aurélie acknowledged with another casual shrug, "but he had long ago lost interest in me,
and in the children he did have. He would never have paid
Nancy any mind. Indeed, he wanted rid of her."

"Oh, *Mamma*!" said Kate, covering her eyes.

"I am sorry, *mon chou*," said her mother. "But you know it
is true. Until Stephen was old enough to dice and whore, your
father spared even him not a glance. But Anstruther—oh,
ho!—he was very plainspoken. He wished his little girl

here, under his watchful eye. And here she was to stay, or there would be hell to pay."

"Well, what a fine mess this is!" said Upshaw. "Aurélie, *why* did you not tell me?"

Again, the Gallic shrug. "Because I was ashamed?" she suggested. "Because I had not the power to gainsay my husband, and go to my children and the man I loved?" She waved her hand dismissively. "So many reasons, Archie!— and none of them very interesting. Another person's tragedies never are."

"Good Lord," said Upshaw. He was mopping his head with a handkerchief now. "I am exhausted. I have to lie down."

Just then, the maid came in with the tea tray and the argument fell silent.

"Thank you, Hetty," said Kate. "What time is dinner?"

"Pushed to half past eight, my lady, Mrs. Peppin says," reported the girl. "Shall I have Jasper lay for nine?"

"Thank you, Hetty, but no," said Upshaw, slowly rising. "I have lost my appetite."

Kate came to her feet. "Hetty, make up the room across from me for Lord Upshaw," she said.

"Mr. Stephen's room?" said Hetty. " 'Tis done already, miss, and the bags took up."

"What happy news," grumbled Upshaw, starting from the room. "At least someone here is competent."

He followed Hetty out, and a moment later, only three of them sat around the tea table, staring at the untouched tray. A heavy silence lay over the room. Aurélie Wentworth's face had softened with that odd, wistful look Edward had glimpsed once or twice before, and he wondered, fleetingly, if anyone truly knew her.

John Anstruther, perhaps, did.

Edward had espied them once, caught in the throes of an argument. It had been the night he'd kissed Kate in the rose garden. Afterward, he'd slipped around to a distant door to discreetly return to the house, only to stumble upon Mrs. Wentworth and Anstruther alone in the passageway.

Their argument had looked deeply personal, with Anstruther's big hand locked around Aurélie's wrist, as if he restrained her from something. And yet, even then, Edward had had the impression that this was nothing new between them. There had been . . . yes, a physical familiarity between them. A passion, he now realized.

"How long, Mamma?" Her voice hollow, Kate had not lifted her gaze from the tea tray. "How long did you and Anstruther . . ."

"Have an *affaire d'amour*?" asked her mother. "Oh, la, child! When one is my age, one prefers not to count that many years."

"I believe, my dear, that what your mother is saying is that the *affaire* has perhaps not ended," Edward gently suggested.

"Oh, Mamma!" Kate whispered. "You? And Anstruther? *Still—?*"

"*Bah!*" Aurélie tossed her hand. "Much of the time the man is so stubborn as to be unbearable."

"But . . . but what about *le comte*?" said Kate, incredulous. "All those years with him—all those gentlemen forever surrounding you . . ."

Aurélie just smiled her vague smile. "Oh, *mon chou*, de Macey and I make better friends than lovers. As to Sir Francis, he, too, is de Macey's friend, and I had need of him. He does not admire me."

"Yes, you brought him because of Nancy."

"In part," said her mother, her lips making a little pout. "But Sir Francis would rather shoot with de Macey from daylight to dark. Besides, I have decided his eyes are too sly; I have surrendered him to Julia, much joy may he bring her. It is as well Nancy preferred Richard, and that you . . . ah, well, that is neither here nor there!"

It was very much here to Edward, though he refused to

hold Aurélie Wentworth's gaze. Even as she sat so quietly beside him, her hands folded in her lap, Kate drew the whole of his attention; drew from him the male instinct to protect and to defend.

He thought again of the pompous Lord Upshaw; of how close he'd come to dragging the man out in the passageway and bloodying his damned nose for the tone he'd taken with Kate.

Oh, he had looked controlled, perhaps, for it was a skill he'd honed relentlessly, but he'd been an inch from doing violence. One might dress a thug in Savile Row, but temper could not be shrouded.

No, as much as he yearned to care for her, he was still the last thing the well-born and well-mannered Baroness d'Allenay needed in her life.

"*Eh bien!*" Aurélie rose, then leaned over to kiss Kate's cheek. "I must go and change for dinner. If anyone asks, Nancy is wed and Upshaw has given his blessing—for he must, once his tantrum is over."

Edward stood, and Kate joined him, her arms crossed over her chest, her shoulders slumped. They watched her mother stroll from the room, the reticule stuffed with love letters still swinging from her elbow, her head still held high.

"Well." Kate turned to him with a wan smile. "I should go," she said, "and see if—if—"

Her words halted, her lower lip trembled tellingly.

"Oh, Kate," he said softly, opening his arms. "Oh, love. I know."

She fell into his embrace and he simply held her. "Oh, Edward! It has been the most frightful two days! Everything seems so . . . so *upside down*!"

"I would turn it all right side up if I could," he said, bending his head to kiss her forehead. "But Kate, you acquitted yourself well with your uncle. I'm always so proud of you. You were truly meant to be Baroness d'Allenay. And Lord Upshaw is formidable."

"He means well," said Kate. "I console myself with that thought." Then she lifted her head and set her hands to his chest, pushing away as if to study him. "Thank you for being my champion. You were daunting, Edward; so cold and so furious. I thought you might thrash the poor man."

He had no response to that; he merely held her solemn gray gaze. Then something inside her seemed to give way— some strange, mixed emotion went sketching over her face, and Kate rose onto her tiptoes, hesitated another instant, then shut her eyes and set her lips to his.

He returned the kiss, slanting his mouth hungrily over hers. And as he'd known it would, the embrace warmed and blossomed, unfurling in the heat to something far more sensual and hungry than a mere gesture of thanks.

He held her to him, inch to inch, his hand roaming down to stroke and shape her. The turn of a shoulder, the smooth, silken strength of her back, that sweet sway of her spine he loved so well; Edward's hands could have sculpted her in the darkness, so well did he know Kate.

Theirs was a rare passion; one that could not be contained, and Edward wondered yet again how he was to go on. How he was to look back on this time, and not think of her? How, even years from now, could he call on Annie, and not look across the fields and moors and wonder?

"Kate," he murmured against her lips. "You know how much I care, yes?"

She drew away with one last, lingering kiss. "I know you care," she said, her lashes sweeping down. "But you cannot stay, you've said."

"Not . . . stay, no," he rasped. "But perhaps I might be near?"

"Oh, *near*!" She sighed. "Sometimes I wish you'd never come to Bellecombe, Edward. That you'd never met Reggie, never bought his damned house. Or that I'd never learnt what it was like to want someone so much."

He threaded his fingers through the soft, loose hair at her temple and wondered what a man said to such words.

"Do you know, Kate, before I regained my memory," he murmured, "I feared that what I felt for you was just a sort of desperation; a lost soul clinging to the only rock he had. I told myself that when I was well again, I would not need you. That I'd be ever grateful—and ever fond of you—but that would be the end of it."

With a hint of reluctance in her eyes, she returned her gaze to his. "And now—?"

He inhaled deeply, and blew it out again. "It is not the end of it, Kate," he said grimly. Sometimes I wish for my own ignorance back. I still want to hold on to you, and it is just so unwise. There are a thousand men better suited for you than me. If I were any sort of gentleman, I'd encourage you to go find one."

"I am perfectly capable of it," she said, "should I wish to."

He forced a smile. "And if you do," he said, "you will always have my deepest regard. A part of me will always be with you."

"Oh, Edward." She did push away then. "Oh, that is just not fair!"

It was not fair. Certainly not to her.

He wanted to tell her the whole truth; that he'd long ago fallen in love with her—with her earnestness and her simplicity and that eternal, quiet beauty that enticed him like the loudest of sirens' songs. That his love for her fit perfectly into that small, black spot in his heart that had so long remained a void, and made him whole again.

He wanted to tell her he did not know how to return to the bleakness of his old life, certain he would find it all the more desolate for her absence. Kate had become his warmth and light and peace. And yet a part of him kept thinking there had to be a way to get beyond this.

But the only way he could see was to have her. To pull her down to his level, another Persephone dragged into the underworld, just to satisfy another's lust.

Was that how it had to be? Was there no other option?

Could he not *make* himself worthy?

But he had tried that once before, and seen it end in tragedy. And Kate was not waiting to find out, he gathered.

"Well," she said, letting her arms fall. "What a muddle this day has been."

Edward took the hint, and stepped back. "Don't think hard of your mother," he said, forcing a normal tone. "There are a great many people who've made a worse muddle of their lives."

"Yes, but Nancy!" said Kate. "Imagine how hard this must have been for her to hear."

Edward shrugged. "For what it's worth, Kate, your sister has learnt that her father is a good and honorable man," he said. "A man she has long adored. A father who wanted her near him above all things, even if he could not tell her the truth. A less honorable man would have ignored her existence."

At that, Kate's expression tightened oddly.

"And that would have been cruel indeed, wouldn't it?" she said coolly. "There are a great many men who think nothing of fathering a child and simply ignoring her."

Edward set his head to one side, suddenly wary of the edge in her voice. "Anstruther is not that kind of man, Kate," he said. "And Richard is man enough not to care about Nancy's parentage. Indeed, he may be much comforted by the knowledge, assuming he knows."

"Oh, he knows." Having turned to go, Kate looked back. "I realize what happened now. Mamma confessed to him on Sunday—though she took the precaution of asking absolution."

Edward's eyes widened. "And thus he'd be bound never to speak of it, even if it horrified him?" he murmured. "My, she *is* clever. Frighteningly so."

"Indeed," said Kate, setting her hand on the doorknob. "Well, I should go into the drawing room and see if everyone is assembling for dinner. Shall I see you there?"

He hesitated. "Will you excuse me tonight?" he said, after rashly considering it. "I'm still in my boots and breeches, and I have an important letter to write."

"Certainly." She flashed a tight smile. "I'll have a tray sent up."

"You are too good to me, Kate."

"Yes, perhaps." The smile faded.

Kate left the door open and started down the corridor, her spine as stiff and straight as a duchess's—just as her mother's had been. Edward watched her go, the rash idea in his head slowly turning into a remote, and somewhat imprudent, possibility.

KATE SET THE back of her hand to her lips where the warmth of Edward's kiss yet lingered. She felt a fool for leaning on him. But she would not deny she had been glad he had followed her into the library.

Well, glad at first. Now, after the kiss they had exchanged, she was just confused and angry. Dropping the hand, she set a brisk pace toward the drawing room, certain that the last two days really had been the worst of her life. Devil take it, why did the man have to look so handsome? And sound so profoundly rational?

If Annie Granger's secret had not broken her heart, Edward's words nearly had. And now her mother's secret lay exposed to half the family, and worse, to Nancy. Uncle Upshaw was still beside himself with rage. And Kate feared her next conversation with John Anstruther would be an awkward one indeed.

And yet the awkwardness had only begun, it seemed. Reggie was lingering in the great hall, his eyes fixed upon her as she approached.

"Reggie," she said tightly. It was as civil a greeting as she could muster.

"Kate, my dear girl." He stepped into her path with what

looked like genuine sorrow on his face. "The servants are whispering there was a great row in the library."

"There was a lively discussion," Kate admitted. "I've just learnt why Nancy and Richard went to Exeter. They eloped."

"Heavens!" His eyes flared wide. "I hope Upshaw didn't rake you over the coals for it?"

She shook her head. "Uncle? No. Why should he? But I will own that I'm surprised by the announcement."

Reggie caught her hands and squeezed them in what was apparently meant to be a reassuring gesture. "I was looking for you, Kate, to make an apology," he said, stepping respectfully back. "I behaved abysmally yesterday."

"Oh, for pity's sake, Reggie," she said, moving past him, "not that again."

"Of course not, another time," he said hastily. "But Kate, this business with Nancy, what may I do? Anything? Would Nancy listen to me? I can be on the first train to Exeter tomorrow."

Kate turned back to shake her head. "Thank you, there's nothing to be done," she said. "Mamma went with her, and Uncle gave his blessing with a little reluctance. Tomorrow would be too late in any case."

Reggie tried to look concerned. "So Upshaw will not try to undo it?"

Kate arched one eyebrow. "Certainly not," she said. "It is done, and they are alone together at an inn. Indeed, even if Uncle had disagreed with the match—which he did not— he'd likely hold a gun to Richard's head if he tried to get out of the marriage now."

Reggie merely stared at her for a long moment. "Would he?" he finally said. "Yes, doubtless you're right. Everyone will assume that Nancy has been ruin—"

"Reggie." Kate held up a hand. "I think we all know what people generally assume. But this is what Nancy wants, and it's done."

"Yes, yes, I'm sure." Then, his expression oddly distant, Reggie made her an almost courtly bow. "Well. We must wish them happy, then. I know I certainly do. I will see you, Kate, at dinner."

And then, as quickly as he'd turned up, Reggie was gone—or at least the person purporting to be Reggie. He had not spoken so kindly to Kate in an age.

Mystified, Kate shook her head, and went on to attend her guests. Sensing the mood, even Lady Julia looked cast down. After dinner, the hour being late, everyone retired for the evening.

Grateful for the peace of her bedchamber, Kate collapsed into bed, and spent the rest of the night in a fitful, feverish sleep. She dreamt of Edward; of the warm weight of his body pressing hers down into the softness of the bed. Of his heated touch, and passionate kisses.

But in her fantasy, there were no words. No explanations and no excuses. For logic had become the enemy, and Kate had grown weary of it.

CHAPTER 15

An Encounter in the Rose Garden

The course of true love never did run smooth, nor did the paperwork required to execute it. What followed was a bleak, misty day, much of which Kate spent closeted with Lord Upshaw, first attempting to make peace, and then trying to convince him that much could yet be done to protect Nancy's welfare.

To his undying discomfort, this required the presence of John Anstruther, who returned from Exeter on the first train up, and came into Kate's study bristling like a bear. He appeared to be sodden, weary, and spoiling for a fight.

However, a good night's rest had served to temper Lord Upshaw's outrage. He rose stiffly at Anstruther's entrance, hands clasped tight behind his back, holding his tongue as he'd reassured Kate he would do.

Anstruther, however, was blunt as he stood before Kate's desk. "I'll have nae whinging from you, Miss Kate, nor suffer any lectures from that one," he said, jerking his head toward Upshaw. "Say it plain. Am I to stay? Or go?"

She looked up at him incredulously. "I can't think how

you even ask," she said. "Have we not always been like a family here?"

"Aye, weel, things can change," said Anstruther, his great sideburns puffed out a little comically. "Myself, I wouldna' done it, Kate. Run off to the bishop, I mean. But your mither—once she takes a notion intae her head—"

Kate held up a hand to stay him. "Lord, don't even attempt to explain the workings of Mamma's mind!" she said. "Just sit down. Upshaw wishes us to reassure him that the glebe can support Nancy and her children in an appropriate style."

A little of the belligerence left Anstruther. "Oh," he said. "Oh, aye. Prime arable, no question."

The three of them sat down, and Anstruther took up the tools of his trade; his ledgers and his maps and his meticulously drawn tables setting out anticipated crop yields acre by acre. When they were finished, there being nothing, truly, to be displeased over, Upshaw pinched his nose pensively.

"Well, I need not remind you again, Kate, of your fiduciary duty to the Bellecombe estate," he said. "But you've hacked off a considerable bit of land and let it pass from Wentworth hands forever."

"Nancy will be a Wentworth forever, Uncle, to me," said Kate softly. "Besides, as Anstruther will tell you, that acreage was never entailed. It came to the estate through Grandmamma, and Anstruther was her godson. Why should it not go back to their side of the family? If, indeed, we must have a *that side* and a *this side*."

"And we still have the matter of marriage settlements," said Upshaw, unable to suppress a dark look at Anstruther. "Your daughter, sir, has married without any. That is the very purpose of a trustee, you know. To ensure such a thing does not happen."

"Aye, to protect her from fortune hunters, I know," said Anstruther uneasily. "But Nan has no great fortune, and Burnham's an honest lad."

"On her majority, Nancy will receive twenty thousand

pounds from my late father-in-law's estate, as per Aurélie's marriage settlements," said Upshaw pompously. "And as it currently sits, her new husband will have every legal right to take it to Epsom the next day and wager it on the first nag he sees."

Anstruther scratched his chin. "Aurélie did say something of it," he admitted, "though I dinna grasp the particulars. Burnham said we might draw up whatever we wished in that regard, and he'd sign it."

"Well!" Kate opened both hands in an expansive gesture. "There is no reason, Uncle, is there, that Richard cannot sign settlements postnuptial?"

"Why would he do so?" Upshaw demanded.

"Because he's a man of his word," said Kate firmly. "But there, Uncle! You do not know him. It's as good as done, trust me. Just have the papers drawn."

Upshaw, however, did not yield with perfect grace. "There is still the matter of the house," he said. "The current rectory is a mere hatbox, and the man has a widowed mother."

"The new rectory is of sufficient size, sir, to accommodate the three of them and ten children besides," said Kate. "Why do we not meet there tomorrow, the three of us?" She paused to consult her schedule. "How would eleven o'clock suit? If the house does not meet with your approval, Uncle, then we shall alter it in whatever way you wish."

"*Hmph*," said Upshaw. "You seem to have thought of everything!"

Kate laid her pencil down with a sharp *clack*. "Thank you, sir," she said. "I try."

An hour later, the trio parted, with Upshaw and Anstruther setting off in relative charity to Taunton, to engage a local solicitor to draft the settlement papers. It was further agreed that Upshaw would remain at Bellecombe an additional day to host a dinner party for the returning couple, in order to put the burnish of his approval on the marriage.

Kate followed them from the room, quelling the impulse

to search out Edward in order to share with him how the business had been settled. But the truth was, it really was none of his concern, and the crisis had been averted. Absent Upshaw's inclination to drag the matter into the protracted hell of Chancery, the marriage of a village rector to an unknown country miss was not going to draw any speculation.

Certainly de Macey seemed to have found the entire business soporific. Kate discovered him asleep in the library while, at a table nearby, Aurélie and Lady Julia played cribbage for sixpence a match.

In the back of the room, something deeper was at stake. Reggie and his new cohort Sir Francis were playing a card game that appeared far more intense than cribbage. She watched blandly as a great wad of banknotes changed hands—in Reggie's direction, for once—then she went to the window to peer out again at the weather.

It was not raining, but the skies hung gray and heavy. She considered riding into the village to personally tell Mrs. Burnham of the dinner party, but Jasper had likely left with the message by now.

Still, there was no denying Kate felt an odd and restless wish to flee the house. It was Edward, she realized; her need to see him—and for no reason save the pleasure of his company—was wrestling with her better angels.

A part of her longed for those early days when they had not known who he was. When he had been merely Edward, and not the notorious Ned Quartermaine with his pernicious gaming hell and his illegitimate daughter.

Her heart heavy, Kate went instead to the shelves to find a book to read. A comforting piece of fiction seeming most appropriate to her mood, she drew out a well-worn copy of *Emma*, and was halfway to her favorite chair when she recalled the sad subplot of poor Harriet Smith, the illegitimate and abandoned daughter of a gentleman.

That was too dreadful a subject to be borne just now, Kate decided. She turned around to slide the book into its slot just as Sir Francis swept past, his eyes a little blacker than usual, and his jaw set tight.

"Lady d'Allenay." He paused to give a taut but civil bow. "Good afternoon."

"Sir Francis, I'd advise you not to play with Reggie," said Kate lightly. "Tragedy inevitably follows—his, usually. But alas, occasionally someone else's."

"The tragedy was mine this afternoon," he said with a faint smile, "but I shall think of a way to win it back, I daresay, before the day is out."

Then he bowed again, and left her standing alone in the middle of the library. Watching him go, Kate felt a faint, unpleasant shudder. She adored the Comte de Macey, but she didn't care for his friend Sir Francis.

I have decided his eyes are too sly, Aurélie had said.

And Aurélie, as Edward was fond of reminding her, was not the fool she seemed.

THAT EVENING, EDWARD dressed for dinner in his most elegant black frock coat, worn over a jacquard silk waistcoat and a snowy white cravat, which he managed, through sheer happenstance, to tie flawlessly. Though the limited wardrobe he'd obtained in Taunton had served, he was more comfortable in the attire his valet had hastily sent from London.

He had seen almost nothing of Kate since they had parted so awkwardly the previous evening, and the fact that the awkwardness was entirely his fault did not escape Edward. He had spoken rashly, something utterly foreign to his nature. He had spoken, he feared, from his heart. How ironic, when most would have said he had no heart, perhaps himself included.

The awkwardness notwithstanding, he looked up in the mirror to inspect his attire, bristling with impatience to see Kate. A tall, lean man looked back, his stare unflinching. He was handsome enough, he supposed, though his jaw turned at a hard angle, and his eyes held no warmth.

He slid a hand around that jaw now, realizing he should have shaved again. In London his valet often shaved him twice a day. But he had not wanted the fellow here, for reasons he could not explain. Perhaps because, had his valet turned up, Edward would have felt compelled to be himself.

Here at Bellecombe, even with his memory fully restored to him, he was *not* himself. He was a more pensive, perhaps even kinder, man. He thought of the letter he'd penned last night, and wondered what Peters might make of it. Perhaps he'd turn up in Somersetshire to see if his employer had run mad.

Or perhaps not.

Hastily, Edward stabbed his neck cloth with a rare and flawless padparadscha sapphire that matched his ring, and then hastened down the stairs to find Kate to share his latest good news. Anstruther having kindly passed on to him the name of the rectory's construction superintendent, Edward had been able to persuade the fellow to take a look at Heatherfields.

With the first two stages of the rectory complete, Mr. Moreland had offered to take up Heatherfields as his next project. His crews of masons, carpenters, and plasterers, who were rotating seamlessly through the rectory project, could simply move on in turn to Heatherfields before returning to Bristol, saving Edward months.

But when Edward arrived in the drawing room, it was to find Kate engaged with Lord Upshaw. Oddly disappointed, he conversed pleasantly with de Macey until they were summoned for dinner. As usual, Kate sat at the head of the table, and Edward some distance away.

At least they were not long detained after the meal. Since Upshaw believed port akin to a vice, the rest of the gentlemen soon drained their glasses and rejoined the ladies for coffee. Kate was pouring, however, and chatting with Lady Julia.

Edward took his cup, his eyes catching hers, their hands

fleetingly brushing. Then he retreated to a corner where he might marvel at his own foolishness. He was like a besotted boy, he realized, and just about as impatient. Kate was not a toy to be trifled with; she was worthy of something far more significant.

Behold a virtuous woman, he thought, *for her price is truly above rubies.*

How ironic that she, of all women, should have been the one to catch his eye. There were few men who deserved virtue less; it was the antithesis of all that he had made of himself.

Tonight she wore a simple, more modest gown than the memorable gold and green affair, but the delicate shade of mauve set off her gray eyes to perfection, and hugged her curves in a way that still revealed a hint of lush cleavage.

"*Bonsoir*, Mr. Quartermaine," said a warm, sultry voice at his elbow. "A quiet beauty, is she not?"

He looked down to see that Aurélie Wentworth had slipped alongside him. She was without her pug, a rare occurrence, and her eyes were alight with what looked like mischief.

"Ma'am, your powers of perception are exceeded only by your audacity," he said, setting the cup down on its saucer with a soft *chink*.

"*Alors*, have I been complimented?" she said lightly. "Or insulted?"

Edward managed to smile down at her. "Complimented, Mrs. Wentworth," he said. "In my line of work, both perception and audacity are frequently rewarded."

"Ah, then I thank you," she said lightly. "Speaking of your line of work, I wonder if you might be persuaded to take a turn through the rose garden with me?"

He looked down at her in some surprise, but set his coffee away at once. "Certainly," he said after a quick glance to confirm Kate was still engaged. "If you do not mind the cold."

"I am never cold," said Mrs. Wentworth.

The drawing room opened onto the garden via three sets of French windows, heavily draped in green velvet. They slipped out, seemingly unnoticed.

Outside in the cool night air, Mrs. Wentworth circled her arm through his. "Do you know, Mr. Quartermaine," she said abruptly, "I would not have taken you for a fool."

"*Hmm*," he said. "And do you?"

She laughed lightly, steering him toward the massive marble urn in the center of the garden. "In French there is a saying, *Le coeur qui soupire n'a pas ce qu'il desire*," she said. "It was a great favorite of my grandmother's. Do you know it?"

Edward tried to puzzle it out. "Something about the heart's desire?"

"The heart that sighs has not what it desires," said Mrs. Wentworth.

"I see," he replied, more reservedly. "And you fear my heart is sighing, do you?"

She laughed again. "*Bien sûr*, dear Edward, your *eyes* are sighing," she said. "But the rest of your parts? Ah, you are a difficult one—even for me, the amoral-as-a-cat Aurélie, who always knows what men are thinking."

"I believe that, whatever it is, my heart shall have to survive it," he said, circling with her around the massive marble urn. "Now, you require my professional assistance in some matter? I hope, ma'am, that you have not acquired gaming debts."

"Certainly not." For the first time, Aurélie Wentworth sounded insulted. "But that is precisely what I wish to know about. Gaming debts. Specifically, Lord Reginald's."

"I am not sure how I can help you."

She pulled him down onto one of the benches that surrounded the urn. "You know people," she suggested in a sly tone. "You have ways of finding things out. Reggie is up to no good; I feel it. Lady Julia says he has had some bold talk of late, especially when he's in his cups too deep. I should like to know precisely how bad his debts are."

"He is insolvent, ma'am," said Edward tightly. "I do not need to make enquiries in that regard, for it's my business to know such things. The man has debts which cannot possibly be repaid, and he's being pressed aggressively by his creditors—some of whom are not especially benevolent."

"Yes, but you managed to get Heatherfields out of him," suggested Mrs. Wentworth.

"Because I am the least benevolent of all," said Edward. "I will not tolerate being cheated of what's owed me, and Reggie knows it."

But Mrs. Wentworth had stiffened, and was staring at the most distant set of French windows. Lord Reginald Hoke stood there, his back turned to the rose garden, and beside him stood the unmistakable form of Sir Francis. Their heads were leaned together in a vaguely conspiratorial manner, and from the intensity of both expressions and gestures, Edward guessed they were arguing.

"You have been guarding my wicket, Mr. Quartermaine," said Mrs. Wentworth musingly, "and diligently. I thank you."

Edward said nothing. Suddenly, Reggie appeared to thrust a hand inside his jacket, and present a wad of bills to Sir Francis. Sir Francis took them, then turned and set his hand to the doorknob.

"*Mon Dieu*, are they coming out?" murmured Mrs. Wentworth, leaping up.

"I doubt it," he reassured her. "Not when they see us."

"Ooh, I should like to know what that feckless creature is up to!" She flicked a glance at him. "*Dépêchez-vous!* Go in, go in!"

"And leave you?"

"*Oui, oui.*" She was already pushing him toward the door. "You are too large to hide."

"What are you going to do?" he asked.

"Eavesdrop!" said Mrs. Wentworth, hopping onto the bench in her high-heeled slippers. "I shall climb into the urn."

In an instant, she had seized the lip with both hands, and hauled herself over, tumbling in almost sideways in a *whoosh!* of crinoline and lace.

"Good God," he muttered.

But he could hear hinges squeaking in the gloom. Left with no alternative, he turned and set off toward the drawing room doors.

Sir Francis had already espied him. "Ah, someone is here before us!"

"No, it's too cold for me," said Edward. "Gentlemen. Do have that bench; it's the only spot out of the wind."

"Thank you," said Reggie stiffly.

"Good night, Sir Francis," he said, bowing a little as he passed. "Lord Reginald."

He went inside to see that Kate now sat with Lord Upshaw. Good Lord, was he not to have so much as a minute of her time? Impatiently, he refilled his coffee, considering as he did so that—for Kate's sake—he might better concern himself in extracting her mother from her latest predicament.

But Mrs. Wentworth, it seemed, needed him no more than did her daughter. Reggie and Sir Francis returned within ten minutes; Edward put down his cup, preparing to go around and into the rose garden to fetch her out. But he had no sooner stepped into the corridor than the lady herself breezed past.

"*Mon Dieu*, Mr. Quartermaine, do you leave us so early?" she said in a carrying tone. "I just went out to fetch a fresh pack of cards."

"Thank you, no cards for me," he said, discreetly brushing a bit of moss from her shoulder as he dropped his voice. "Madam, I salute your acrobatics."

"Well, then, we shall miss you," said the lady brightly. "Oh, there is Reggie! Reggie, where have you been, you wicked boy? I want you for whist."

He watched her sweep past him, realizing too late that she was dragging a dried rose twig along on the hem of her skirts.

With a muted smile, Edward turned and, after catching Kate's gaze with a parting nod, started on his way upstairs. The better part of a bottle of the efficient Mrs. Peppin's brandy, along with a good book by the fire, would doubtless prove less frustrating than staring over his coffee cup at what he ought not have.

CHAPTER 16

Lord Reginald's Conquest

For perhaps the first time in her life, Kate went up to bed with her arm hooked companionably in her mother's.

"With Nancy gone, Katherine needs me to brush out her hair," Aurélie had whispered as they passed Lady Julia. "I shall leave you to your flirtation with Sir Francis."

The offer to brush out her hair was a tender gesture, and one Kate had not expected of her mother. And so far as Julia was concerned, Kate was glad, for a moment, to focus on someone else's intrigues.

Tonight it was difficult to determine just who was seducing whom in that little liaison. Having coaxed Julia away from the card table, Sir Francis had urged the lady into a quiet corner of the drawing room, and plied her with poetry and madeira for the latter half of the evening. His flirtation had been so blatant, Uncle Upshaw had murmured his disapproval, and gone up to bed early.

As they turned down the passageway, however, Hetty approached from the opposite direction, carrying a mug and a glass of water on a tray.

"His Lordship's bilious again," the maid whispered when they met between Kate's door and Upshaw's. "I thought per'aps some warm milk and soda water?"

"*Mon Dieu*, a bottle of port after dinner would have better served," said Aurélie, pushing open Kate's door. "Virtue is rarely rewarded."

"Thank you, Hetty," said Kate reassuringly. "That's exactly the thing."

The girl nodded, and vanished into the room opposite Kate's suite. The room that, not so long ago, had been Edward's.

He had been wise, perhaps, to relocate, Kate thought. Tonight, having been unable to exchange so much as a word with him, she felt oddly cheated.

On a sigh, she went into her bedchamber to see her mother flinging off her things, and casting them onto Kate's bed in a vaguely proprietary fashion. First her reticule, shawl, and silk gloves, and then, of all things, she unhooked her crinolines at the waist, and with remarkable grace, simply pushed them down and stepped out.

"Ah!" said Aurélie. "Much better!"

Uncertain what to make of it, Kate decided to turn the subject. "Mamma, *is* Julia after Sir Francis?" she asked, settling herself onto the bench before the dressing table. "He seemed to have resisted her flirtations until tonight."

Aurélie shrugged, and kicked off her shoes. "*Eh bien*, Julia isn't as young as she used to be," she said evenly, "nor is she rich. But recollect, *ma fille*, that Julia first set her sights on Quartermaine, which likely put Sir Francis's nose out of joint."

"Yes, he was shooting with them for a while," Kate mused as her mother began to pull out her pins. "But he seems now to have turned his attention to Heatherfields."

"All of it, *mon chou*?" asked her mother.

Engaged in removing her earbobs, Kate flicked up a glance in the mirror. "All of what, Mamma?"

Her mother flashed a muted smile. "All of his attention?"

Blushing, Kate dropped the earbob in her jewelry box. "I'm sure I wouldn't know."

On a sigh, Aurélie tossed the first hairpin into its porcelain tray. "Ah, *ma fille*, can you not see how his eyes follow you?" she said. "And poor Reggie! His pique becomes comical."

"Nothing about Reggie entertains me," said Kate darkly. "And what is your point, anyway?"

"My point?" said Aurélie lightly. "It is merely this—if you are still clinging to your virtue, Katherine, I beg you will give it up and take advantage of that golden god fortune has put beneath your roof. He may be a little hard and a little wicked, but both those things will prove their advantages, trust me."

"Mamma," Kate chided. "How outrageous you are."

"*Oui*, sometimes even I despair of me," said Aurélie on a sigh. "But Katherine, one hates to see you squander your rare luck. As a baroness in your own right, you are accountable to no one for your wealth or your position. No man can take from you your home or your children, nor threaten you with poverty. And if you are quite, quite sure you shall not marry—"

"Quite, *quite* sure," Kate interjected.

"*Eh bien*, that is very sure indeed," said Aurélie with gentle sarcasm. "So, that being the case, why not enjoy life?"

"Oh, thank you very much, Mamma, for that sage advice," said Kate. "But unlike you, I have no interest in breaking men's hearts for sport. Nor have I even the ability."

At that, Aurélie looked truly wounded. "Breaking hearts for sport?" she echoed, dropping a hairpin on the dressing table with a sharp *plink!* "Katherine! Never have I done such a thing."

"But you have hurt Anstruther," said Kate a little accusingly. "Mamma, I know him. For all his gruff ways, he is not the sort of man who loves lightly."

"La, *ma petite*, Anstruther no longer cares who I am bedding," said Aurélie. "And I do not know if he ever loved me."

Something in her tone raised Kate's suspicions.

"Mamma," she said, turning around on the dressing bench, "have you been trying to bring Anstruther to some sort of point all these years? Is this what your very public *affaires* with de Macey and the banker and all the others have been about?"

"Katherine, do not be ridiculous!"

"I hope I *am* being ridiculous," said Kate. "You would have to be mad, Mamma, to think a man like Anstruther could be jealous of a fop like de Macey, however rich and dashing he may be."

Her mother's lips thrust into that perfect, pretty moue again. "*Oui*, apparently you are right."

"And de Macey—my God—he does not deserve to be hurt," said Kate. "I do like him—very much."

"*Tut, mon chou*, you quite waste your worry!" declared her mother. "I fear de Macey shall never have what he wants. But he does not want me—not now."

"Mamma, you make no sense," said Kate.

But with Kate's hair only half down, her mother had gone to the bed and flung herself dramatically onto it. "*Mon Dieu!*" she said into the ceiling. "Does no one ever believe what I say? Katherine, have I not always told you de Macey was a dear friend?"

"Well, yes. But I believed it a euphemism."

"Ah, Kate! You are so naive! For all my beauty, Macey has always enjoyed pursuing a vast array of lovers. And his choices can be . . . well, let us call it *exotic*."

Suddenly a picture of de Macey and Sir Francis walking together through the rose garden flashed into Kate's mind. She had come upon them unexpectedly, and suddenly there had been a glow of color across de Macey's cheeks . . .

"Oh," said Kate flatly. "Oh. Good heavens. Are you sug-

gesting that de Macey . . . or Sir Francis . . . that they might
be—"

"I'd begun to think it possible," said Aurélie. But I confess,
Sir Francis's flirtation with Julia tonight gives me pause."

"Good heavens," said Kate again.

But splayed across the bed, her mother merely yawned, as
if the entire business now bored her. "Do you know, Katherine, you have the most comfortable suite of rooms in the
house!"

"So you've often remarked," said Kate, pulling out the re-
maining pins as best she could.

"*Oui*, and had your father not died," said Aurélie wistfully, "they would have been mine."

Kate laid down her pins and turned around. "Mamma, did
you walk up with me just to wheedle my rooms away? I've
told you on countless occasions to simply *have them*."

Aurélie nodded, her elaborate coiffure scrubbing the
counterpane. "*Oui*, I think perhaps I should," she agreed.
"But what if I do not like them? What if, for example, the
morning light shines in too brightly? Or what if there are
roosters on this side of the castle?"

"These are easterly rooms, Mamma," she said on a sigh. "I
cannot alter the rays of the sun for you. But there are no roosters, I assure you. Shall I have Peppie switch us tomorrow?"

"*Mais non*, I shall simply try them first," she said, bounc-
ing a little on the bed as if to test it. "I shall sleep here tonight. You may sleep with Filou. But first, *mon chou*, have
you a nightgown? I find myself too fatigued to go and look
for one."

Kate heaved a silent sigh. "I am not sleeping with a dys-
peptic dog, Mamma," she said going to her wardrobe and
yanking a nightgown. "I can sleep across the parlor in the
valet's room."

"As you wish, *ma fille*." Aurélie yawned hugely, and
curled herself into a little ball.

Kate went into the dressing room to bathe and change into

her nightclothes. She was a little irritated at being put out of her own bed. But Aurélie was right; in a perfect world, the rooms would indeed have been her parents'.

The connected suite consisted of a large dressing room giving on to the master's bedchamber, then a connected parlor, followed by the valet's room, with all save for the last also opening onto the main corridor. Kate loved the privacy and comfort the suite afforded her. But she loved her vain and pampered mother more.

She crossed back through the bedchamber, pausing to kiss her mother's cheek, noting as she did so the feathery lines that were beginning to appear at Aurélie's eyes.

"There's warm water still," she said. "Don't go to sleep in your dress, Mamma, and mind the hem of my nightgown for it will be too long on you. Shall I fetch Filou?"

"*Non, merci,*" said her mother, who appeared to be already drifting. "Sleep well, *chérie.*"

After taking up one of her lamps, Kate crossed through the parlor and opened the connecting door to the valet's room. The space was rarely used nowadays, but the small bed was not uncomfortable. Kate crawled in and attempted to punch the feather bolster into a suitable shape, but Aurélie's words were tormenting her a little.

Aurélie had been quite right when she had said that Kate's situation was unique. While Kate was mindful of the dignity the title was due, one could not deny that a degree of latitude came with it. She would never suffer at the hands of a man as Aurélie had done—if, indeed, Aurélie had suffered.

Kate was beginning to believe that perhaps she had. That Aurélie's blithe and often shallow demeanor covered up something darker and sadder. Perhaps there was a lesson to be taken from it?

I still want to hold on to you, Edward had said, *and it is just so unwise.*

But was it *that* unwise?

Suddenly, she wanted to see him. To throw her ordinary

caution to the wind. To actually heed her mother's mad advice. She did *not* want to waste her good fortune, and live a life devoid of desire and pleasure.

Kate didn't approve of the life Edward had led or the choices he'd made, no. But if she waited until a paragon of virtue turned up on her doorstep, she might go gray. And a paragon of virtue, as Aurélie had hinted, was far less apt to tumble her into bed with any degree of skill.

Impulsively, she went into the parlor and picked up a recent edition of the *Journal of the Royal Agricultural Society*. After scribbling a quick note, Kate sealed it and tucked it inside, then pulled the bell.

In short order, Jasper appeared at the parlor door.

"Kindly take this up to Mr. Quartermaine and see if there is a light under his door," she said. "I promised him some reading on agricultural chemistry."

Jasper nodded cheerfully and trotted away again.

Kate flicked a glance at the clock. Not quite eleven. Edward being something of a night owl, it was unlikely he'd be in bed. Her mother, however, was. The faint stirring inside the room had quieted and the lamp had been put out. She hoped Aurélie was not ill.

She began to pace the floor a little anxiously, then went instead to the sideboard for a glass of wine. She had scarcely finished it, however, when a light knock sounded at the parlor door. Swiftly, she opened it.

His coats and his cravat already cast off, Edward stood on the threshold in his shirtsleeves, looking large, lean, and implacable.

Poking her head out, Kate found the corridor empty, and pulled him inside.

"Quick," she said, "in the valet's room."

She drew him into the circle of lamplight inside the little bedchamber.

The light flickered over one side of his face, casting up otherworldly shadows. Edward leaned back against the wide doorjamb, his arms crossed, his heavy, hooded gaze raking down her length.

He had been drinking, she realized.

"I take it you wished to discuss agricultural chemistry," he murmured, "in your nightclothes."

"Another time, perhaps," she said.

"Hmm," he said. "That nightdress is dishearteningly high-necked, Kate, for *any* sort of discussion. I count—what, eight buttons? And that robe can only be described as virtuous."

"Shall I take them off?" she suggested, cutting him an assessing glance.

"Kate." He bestirred himself lazily from the door. "It is late. What *do* you want?"

She felt suddenly uneasy. Perhaps this was a mistake? Or perhaps she should wait until he was fully sober? He suddenly seemed too large and a little intimidating.

"I'm not sure," she confessed.

"Then let me help," he said, stepping nearer. "Was it this?"

So saying, he tipped up her chin, let his lashes fall half shut, and kissed her almost ephemerally. It was the merest brush, yet it took her breath. Then, to her disappointment, he stopped.

His eyes drifted over her face, which had decidedly warmed. "Your move, my dear," he murmured.

She backed up an inch. "Have you been drinking?" she asked.

"More than usual," he admitted. "But come, Kate. You didn't send me that note so that you might chastise me for my bad habits."

She shook her head, and plunged forward. "No," she whispered. "No, I didn't. I wanted to ask you, Edward, what you meant by what you said in the library last night."

He did not pretend to misunderstand. "When I said I cared for you?" he replied.

She nodded. "Yes," she said. "And what I wish to know

is this: Is that all there will ever be for us? That you will always be fond of me?"

Something dark passed over his face then, and he backed her up another step. "What do you want there to be, Kate?" he asked. "Shall I swear my eternal devotion? Fall at your feet?"

"I just want the truth," she said.

He lifted his hand and cupped her cheek in that achingly familiar gesture. "The truth?" he said. "The truth, as you so succinctly put it last night, is that it would have been better for both of us if I'd never come here. Never bought Reggie's house. Never taken you to bed."

"And do you regret it?" she murmured, lifting her gaze to his.

He kissed her again, deeply and intimately, curling one arm about her waist as he thrust slowly inside her mouth, weakening her knees until she pressed herself to him for strength.

"There," he finally said, lifting his mouth but an inch. "Does that feel like regret? No, Kate. I regret only what it has come to."

"What has it come to?" she pressed. "What did you mean when you said you would be near?"

His heavy gaze shuttered completely, but his hand had begun to make those slow, sensuous circles at the small of her back. "I was thinking, I suppose, of Heatherfields, so close to you," he said, "and I hoped—damn me for a scoundrel—but I suppose I hoped we . . ."

"Here is what I think," she blurted. "I think we should be lovers. Not just now, but . . . but for a time. For as long as it suits us."

His eyes flashed darkly, his mouth opening to speak, but Kate forged ahead. "I know, Edward, that your home is in London, not here. I know the life you lead, and that eventually country life will bore you. But from time to time, mightn't you find it pleasant to visit? Mightn't we find a way to be together, for so long as neither of us finds the other tiresome?"

"Tiresome!" he said on a harsh laugh.

"Edward, don't laugh," she said. "I won't share you, by the way. I'm not . . . desperate. That's part of what I'm saying. If there can be nothing more, can't there at least be commitment and . . . and pleasure?"

He brushed her cheek with the back of his hand. "Is that all you want me to give you, Kate?" he asked. "Pleasure? You sell yourself short, love."

"I want you," she said. "Heaven help me, but I just want—"

He cut her off with another kiss, this one far less tender, the stubble of his beard raking her skin as he dragged his mouth hungrily over hers. His embrace was almost ruthless, his tongue plunging deep, his arm drifted lower until his hand cupped her buttock and lifted her carnally against him.

Through the wool of his trousers, Kate could feel the thick ridge of his manhood hardening against her pelvis. He thrust into her mouth again, tangling his tongue with hers, his thumb hooking her robe and tugging it off her shoulders.

"*Pleasure*, Kate," he murmured, his mouth skimming down until thwarted by the lace collar at her throat. "Oh, love. I can give you that."

His other hand, she realized feverishly, was working loose the long row of buttons down the front of her gown as his lips skated back up, lingering at the soft spot just beneath her ear, his tongue lightly teasing. Her heart raced, anticipating what was to come. What only he could give her.

The lace fell away from her throat, and the gown gaped. Edward dragged it open, a stitch ripping. He cupped one breast, lifting it high until the cool air touched her nipple. He bent his head, nuzzling and then suckling.

"Edward," she whispered. In response, he drew her breast into the warmth of his mouth, his teeth sharp and hard on her nipple.

"Oh!" she gasped, the sensation seizing her breath.

He bit again, then sucked hard, sending that dark hunger spiraling through her. All the way into her belly, down and down like some sensual ribbon twisting greedily at her core.

Her breath was already coming fast in the gloom. "Edward, I want—I want—"

"You already said," he murmured against her mouth. "Hush, and let me give it to you."

Suddenly, he lifted her off her feet and turned, setting her back against the door. Between them, his hand fumbled at his trousers. Fleetingly, Kate considered pointing out the bed in the shadows. The notion skittered away. Impatient, she hitched one leg instinctively over his hip, hiking up her nightgown as she wrapped her hands around his neck.

On a sound of pleasure, Edward forced his hand between them, dragging the fabric up over her belly.

He touched her intimately then, his fingers stroking between her folds until Kate trembled, and felt her flesh begin to slicken with need.

"Oh, Kate," he rasped, "So sweet, love. So silken."

He held her now with nothing save the strength of his arm beneath her bare hips and the weight of her back pressed to the door. "Please, Edward," she whispered.

"Please what?" he murmured, lifting her just an inch. With the other hand, he pushed his length through her slick folds, working her. Taunting her a little, perhaps, with the promise of what he could give her.

"Inside me," she whimpered. "*Please*."

"Is that what you want, Kate?" His voice was rough. "Say it, love."

"Yes. *Yes*." She tried to nod, swallowing hard, the world beyond forgotten as he teased her with his hard, velvety shaft. "I want it," she said. "You *know*—oh, Edward—*oh*."

His free hand found her leg, hooking her knee higher, opening her fully. Balancing her weight, he lifted her a few inches. On a rough, agonizing groan, Edward slipped his thick shaft into her silken wetness just an inch.

"*Umm*," she said, her passage tightening involuntarily. This was raw and carnal; not beautiful, no, but deeply erotic. And deeply addictive, she feared.

She worked her hips just an inch. "Edward, please," she softly whimpered. "I need—just—*oh!*"

He gave another agonizing sound, something torn from deep in his chest, then he thrust up hard, plunging his length deep. "Oh. God. *Kate.*" The words were little more than rasps.

A swift madness came upon them then. He pushed again, roughly and hungrily, stroking her in at the right angle. Kate cried out at the delicious sensation. Covering her lips with his, he thrust again.

"*Oh.*" She moaned the word into his mouth.

He set a furious rhythm, driving her higher, his hips powerful, his arm beneath her buttocks holding her to him. "Yes," she said again. "Like . . . oh, *oh.*" She could feel herself spiraling out of control. Into his control, dangerously tempting.

"Kate, Kate," he chanted. "Come to me, love. Oh, darling. *So* needy."

"Yes," she whimpered one last time. The need had welled up fast, like water against a dam, the heat pooling deep and heavy as he pumped in and out of her. Edward buried his face against her neck, sucking at her flesh and he thrust and thrust again.

Kate's skin felt alive, shivering everywhere he touched. Already she was coming apart, shattering to pieces, lost to reason and the world around her. Then Edward shifted his angle, pushed his hard flesh all the way into her, and she felt her whole body begin to shake.

Kate crested a wave of passion that was otherworldly, coming in a rush of sensation that flooded through her in great, shuddering spasms. She could feel Edward pumping furiously into her. And then he cried out, a deep, guttural sound. His head went back, the tendons of his neck cording hard, his golden hair falling like a mane behind him.

He jerked, and jerked again, his shaft throbbing inside

her. Then, on one last groan, he stilled, gasping. After a long moment, he let his forehead come to rest against hers.

"Oh, God," he groaned. "*Yes.*"

"Yes?" she whispered.

"*Yes*, Kate, to anything," he rasped. "Anything. You enslave me."

For a moment Kate toyed with a daring, dangerous question. Then good judgment came creeping back, and along with it the realization that in that moment, to ask it would have been deeply unfair.

And a terrible mistake.

On a sound of pure exhaustion, she let the leg over his hipbone slide back to the floor. Ever the gentleman, Edward let her slide down his length, then restored her nightgown to some semblance of order, his hair falling forward to shadow his beautiful face.

She threaded one hand lazily through his hair. "You need a haircut," she murmured.

He laughed. "My God, madam, you know how to keep a man in his place," he said.

"I'm sorry." Arms still twined behind his neck, Kate kissed him. "I'm no good at this—this knowing the right things to say. There seem no words, really."

His smile flashed in the gloom. "You're perfect, Kate."

She looked past him. "There is a bed in that corner," she suggested. "A very small one."

"Now she tells me," he muttered.

Then he picked her up, sliding an arm beneath her knees, and carried her to it.

"There is indeed, though not much of one," he said, settling her gently on it.

Kate scooted all the way against the wall, leaving just enough room for Edward to tuck alongside her. After prying off his shoes, he did so.

"Close quarters," he murmured, brushing his lips down her throat. "Ah, Kate."

"Yes?" she whispered.

His head lifted, his gaze softening to hers. "It has been a long time since I made love like a raw lad," he said. "Lord, up against a door with my clothes still on! I can only plead too much brandy, and too much . . ."

"Too much what?" she pressed.

"Desire." He looked away. "Merciful heaven, Kate, but I burn for you."

Impulsively, she kissed his forehead. "So will you consider my question, Edward?" she said.

"About . . . an arrangement?" he said.

"Yes," she said, toying with the button on his shirt. "About that."

He was quiet for a long, awful moment. Then, "Kate," he finally said, "we may have to have more than an arrangement. What we did just now . . . love, I was not careful. I know better. And yet—"

"We will not think of that," she interjected, kissing him again. "Just answer my question, Edward. Don't . . . leave me hanging. It hurts."

"Yes," he rasped. "Blast it, Kate, you're a damned fool to take up with me. But yes. Whatever you want, yes."

She settled herself against him, burying her face against his throat. He smelled enticing; of soap and sweat and of himself, that wonderful mingling of sandalwood and leather and his own musky essence. He smelled of strength and comfort—or what Kate had always imagined they would smell like.

Teasingly, she slipped another button free and stroked her tongue along his collarbone. "*Umm*," he murmured. "Keep on, minx, if you think this bed can hold us."

"I doubt it," she said on a choked laugh.

"Kate?" He kissed the top of her head. "Why are we in the valet's room?"

"Because he retired to Lyme Regis," said Kate, "when Grandpapa died. And Mamma took my bed tonight."

"Good Lord," he said. "Why on earth?"

Just then, however, there was a faint bump from outside the room.

Edward sat bolt upright, cursing under his breath.

"Wait," she murmured, grabbing his arm.

"Kate, the last thing you need is to be caught in bed with me—especially with Upshaw so near."

"It was just a servant," she said, "in the corridor."

But Edward got up and locked the door all the same.

The sound, however, came again—louder, and followed by a drunken giggle.

He sat down on the edge of the bed, one eyebrow crooked. "Servants?" he said doubtfully.

"That's Lady Julia." Frowning, Kate wriggled past and got up to retrieve her wrapper. "She was drinking downstairs with Sir Francis when Mamma and I came up."

This time there was a trill of laughter, but farther down the passageway.

"Well, she sounds sotted now," said Edward darkly.

"And apt to wake Uncle Upshaw," Kate muttered, throwing on her robe. "Wait here."

Unlocking the door, she went out and through the parlor to the main door. Cracking it, she peeked out to see Lady Julia entangled in a passionate embrace with Sir Francis, who had pressed her up against Kate's bedroom door while somehow managing to hold a lamp aloft.

"*No, no, Francis!*" tittered Julia, pointing drunkenly over his shoulder. "It's *not*. It's *two more doors*."

"Julia, my love, mind the lamp." Eyes hooded, Sir Francis kissed her. "I think I know which door is yours."

Kate had stepped out to scold them when, out of the blue, Sir Francis slipped a hand behind Julia, gave the knob a violent twist, and sent her tumbling backward into the room.

Suddenly, all hell broke loose. From Kate's bedroom came a bloodcurdling scream, almost theatrical in its pitch. Another, more hysterical scream followed, along with a string of blistering curses.

Kate rushed into the gloom of the passageway, slamming into Upshaw, who came barreling from across the way, his nightcap hanging over one eye. "What in the name of all blazes?" he bellowed.

"I'm sorry, sir," said Kate. "Lady Julia's a bit tipsy."

But Upshaw had marched across the hall, only to freeze upon Kate's threshold.

"*Aurélie Wentworth!*" he bellowed. "What in God's name?"

Kate pushed past him and into a scene of farcical mayhem. Lord Reginald Hoke was sitting up, bare-chested, in Kate's bed. Tucked beside him, Aurélie was propped almost comically on her elbows, a shock of curly black hair over one shoulder, her nightgown hanging loose off the other. Lady Julia was buckled over with giggles, while Sir Francis, still holding his lamp aloft, looked dark as a thunderhead.

"*Zut alors!*" Aurélie was scrambling upright. "Reggie, *mon amour*, we are caught out!"

"Damn you, Reggie!" Sir Francis shook his empty fist at the bed. "Is this your idea of a joke?"

"Sir, you will keep a civil tongue, and get out!" bellowed Upshaw. "And you, madam"—here he stabbed a censorious finger at Julia—"*you are drunk!*"

Julia managed to straighten up, and stab a finger back at him. "And you, sir, are a p-pompous pr-pr-prig!" she said, bursting again into giggles.

"*Eh bien*, Reggie," said Aurélie, patting his bare back. "It was bound to happen."

But Upshaw bore down on them like a frigate under sail. "Aurélie, for God's sake, have you no shame?" he boomed from the foot of the bed. "That man is half your age!"

"*Vraiment*, Archie, I am mortified!" said Aurélie. "Mortified, I tell you. But still, he is not *quite* half my age!

Reginald, *mon coeur*, must we surrender our dread secret once and for all?"

But Reggie had crawled from the bed, clad only in his drawers, and was backing away as if Aurélie were a snake, horror writ plain across his face. "*What* dread secret?" he uttered, snatching up clothes from the floor. "What the devil, Francis! What have you done to me, damn you?"

"I did what you paid me to do, you fatuous fool," Sir Francis gritted, seizing Julia's arm and dragging her out.

"Dear God!" Upshaw had clapped a hand over his eyes. "I do not believe this."

"*Ça alors*, Archie," said Aurélie, doing up her buttons. "You know I am incorrigible. But please, I beg you! I shall break with Reggie at once. Just do not force him to wed me. He's too young—and alas, *much* too poor."

"*Marry* you?" Reggie jerked upright, his arms filled with clothes. "Are you mad?"

"Now wait just one moment, you upstart!" Upshaw ordered, dropping his hand.

Out in the passageway, Lady Julia sounded near tears with laughter. Sir Francis was trying to quiet her.

Reggie stopped halfway to the door and turned back, a black, patently evil gaze trailing over Aurélie and Kate as he drew a tremulous breath. "By God, I know not how the two of you brought this about," he gritted, "but someone is going to pay, and dearly. Do you hear me?"

Kate finally gathered her wits enough to speak. "Reggie," she managed, "what were you doing in my bedchamber? Do you care to explain it?"

Rage shuddered through him. "Get out of my way, Upshaw."

Reggie's gaze was one of such unmitigated evil, Upshaw actually stepped aside.

But then, from beyond the corridor, there came a deep, languid voice. "Gads, Reggie!" said Edward. "Not really the done thing, cavorting about in one's drawers. Frightens the horses, you know. We could hear the din upstairs."

Kate peeked out to see Reggie jerk to a halt. "Go to hell, Quartermaine!" he gritted, shaking with rage. "I see your hand in this. Well, you shall *never* have her! *Never.* You may have taken my house, but by God, that's where it ends!"

Aurélie had hopped from the bed and was yanking on a wrapper. Shaken, Kate turned to Upshaw, and laid a hand on his arm. "Have a care, Uncle; this isn't what it looks," she quietly warned him. "Go back to bed and let me deal with it."

"Young lady, I will tell you—"

"Uncle, please," she said firmly. "This is my house. Go back to bed and we shall speak of it in the morning."

Upshaw's jowls quivered with indignation. "Then I hope, Katherine, that you know what you're doing!"

Kate hoped so, too. She also hoped her mother had not entirely lost her mind.

Her knees were shaking, she realized. She had dodged one scandal, only to find herself embroiled, potentially, in a worse one with her mother. Still, never had she dreamt Reggie could be so cruel.

And had his wicked trick succeeded . . . dear heaven! No one could *force* Kate to do anything, it was true. But even her title could not protect her from that sort of scandal, or the resulting censure.

A little sick at the stomach, she followed Upshaw out to see Edward loitering in the dimly lit passageway, his arms crossed. The Comte de Macey stood beside him, still in his evening clothes, his expression wary. Everyone else had vanished.

Without sparing either a word, Upshaw went back into his bedchamber and slammed the door shut.

"Well, that was interesting," said Edward.

"*Bonsoir*, Mr. Quartermaine!" said Aurélie, coming out behind Kate. "What extraordinary hearing you have!"

"Yes, it's often been remarked," said Edward calmly.

"Oh, *mon Dieu*, de Macey!" she said, seeing him in the shadows. "Did we wake you, too?"

Liz Carlyle

"No, I was coming up the stairs, my pet, when I heard you scream," he said a little drolly. "It was worthy of the Opéra-Comique. Are you cheating on me again?"

"Yes, *mon coeur*, with a much younger man," said Aurélie. "Edward, I trust we did not disturb your rest too thoroughly?"

"I shall survive it," he said.

"So shall I," said Aurélie, "if someone will fetch me a brandy."

"I suppose we are beyond any pretense or formality now," Kate grumbled, starting off down the passageway. "Besides, I could use a drink myself."

She went back into her parlor, and the three of them trailed in after her. Edward had apparently carried in her lamp and turned it up, softly lighting the room. Kate went straight to the sideboard and extracted Anstruther's Scotch whisky, deciding that French fortification was simply not up to the task.

De Macey followed her, and seeing Kate's hands shaking, took down the glasses with a soothing noise, and began to pour. Aurélie draped herself over the divan, and winked at Edward.

"How cozy this is!" she declared. "All of us here together in our dishabille, almost like a family."

"I am entirely dressed, my pet," said de Macey, pressing a whisky into her hand.

Aurélie took a sip, and wrinkled her nose in horror. "*Ma foi*, this is Anstruther's rot!"

"Just drink it, Aurélie," said Kate grimly, sitting down opposite her mother. "Now, kindly explain what just happened."

"*Mon Dieu*, I was caught in bed with my young lover!" said Aurélie, batting her inky lashes. "Is it not obvious?"

"The only thing that is obvious to me," said Kate, as Edward joined her on the sofa, "is that you manipulated me tonight. And that your name is in ruins. So out with it, Mamma. I must save you from Uncle Upshaw somehow."

"Oh, Archie!" Aurélie wrinkled her nose, and took another drink of the whisky. "He is bound to think the worst of me, regardless."

"Mrs. Wentworth," said Edward quietly, "I hope you won't make me tell your daughter what happened in the rose garden tonight."

Kate turned to glare at him. "Are you involved in this?"

"Unwittingly, I fear," he said. "I do know significant sums of money have passed back and forth between Reggie and Sir Francis recently—and no small amount of scheming, it would now appear."

"That I wouldn't doubt," muttered Kate.

"And tonight," he continued, "I collect your mother managed to overhear a bit of that scheming?"

Kate shot her mother a dark look. "Aurélie," she commanded, "out with it."

Aurélie just shrugged. "There was some vile talk between them," she finally said, "of attempting to compromise you. Reggie is in rather a snit that you've refused his proposal. He gave Sir Francis back the money he'd won at cards in exchange for a small service."

"Ah," said Edward. "So the point was, I gather, that Sir Francis would loudly burst in, pretending to be drunk, and discover, to his mock horror, that Reggie was in bed with Kate. And do so loudly enough to disturb everyone—particularly Lord Upshaw."

"Alas, Katherine sleeps like the dead," said Aurélie, shrugging. "He might have got away with it."

His expression darkening, de Macey had settled on the end of Aurélie's divan. "This is beyond the pale," he said grimly. "Reggie imagined Upshaw would pressure Kate into marrying if she were compromised—but to do it with certainty, Reggie knew he needed the perfect witness."

"And by that you mean Lady Julia, London's most relentless gossip," said Kate angrily. "It would have been dreadful, yes. But I would not have given in. Oh, Mamma! Why did you not simply *tell me* of Reggie's plan?"

Her mother looked weary. "Because, *mon chou*, Reggie would never have given up," she said. "Indeed, he still may not. But it is I who made the grave error of bringing him here, so it fell to me to fix it. No sane person could expect you to marry your mother's castoff lover."

"But what of you, Mamma?" Kate protested. "The scandal—the talk about Reggie—now *you* must face it. And face Anstruther, too."

Aurélie gave another of her languid shrugs. "*Eh bien*," she said. "He will never notice. And so I said to myself, Aurélie, you imbecile! You can easily bear one more scandal attached to your name! And so I did. I made a scandal. It is what I do well, *n'est-ce pas*?"

"Oh, Mamma!" Kate felt emotionally exhausted. "What will happen next?"

"Next?" Her mother lifted both eyebrows. "Next Julia will quiz me mercilessly. I shall maintain a stoic silence—after all, *mon chou*, half a story is always more intriguing than the whole. Thus thwarted, Julia will run back to London whispering her tale, and trying to find out from all our friends how long Reggie has been sharing my bed. And Reggie—well, he will give up, or so I pray."

"So we all pray," said de Macey doubtfully.

"Mamma, you ought never have done this," Kate warned. "I confess to grave unease. I fear Reggie will take revenge on you now."

"Bah! Reggie cannot trouble me!" said Aurélie with Gallic disdain. "What is he to say? The truth? That he tried to trap a dear friend into marriage? And by the most contemptible means imaginable? *Non, mon chou*, I think he will not admit to *that*."

"My pet, you're dangerously diabolical," said de Macey,

rising. "But I collect Katherine would like to scold you in private, so I will take myself off to bed. But on the morrow, I will be explaining to Reggie—and to Sir Francis—that our friendship is at an end."

Aurélie uncurled herself and rose, too. "Filou will be missing me," she said, covering a yawn. "Katherine, take back your bed now, and tomorrow you may scold me to your heart's content."

"Good night, Mrs. Wentworth. De Macey." Edward had risen to open the door. "I trust you will both sleep well."

"And you, too, Mr. Quartermaine," said Aurélie suggestively as she passed. "You must be weary, too, what with all the exciting events of this night."

EDWARD REALIZED THAT, under anything remotely akin to normal circumstances, no sensible person would have left Kate standing in her nightclothes with a gentleman who was half undressed himself—and a gentleman who had a less than stellar reputation in the bargain.

But nothing about this night had been normal—nor was de Macey or Aurélie, come to that. At present, however, he was more concerned about Kate. She had been suffering under no small amount of strain, he realized, what with her sister's elopement, and a houseful of guests cutting up her quiet life, topped off by Lord Upshaw's censure and now Reggie's betrayal.

And then there was her entanglement with him. Yes, perhaps he, too, shared some of the blame.

Kate was pacing back and forth across her parlor carpet now, the matronly wrapper whipping at her ankles each time she turned.

"This is dreadful," she said sharply. "I could throttle Reggie! And what *can* Mamma have been thinking? How am I to calm Uncle Upshaw now? This, on top of Nancy's elopement?"

Edward edged nearer. "Kate, I think this is just your mother's way of trying to help."

"Trying to *help*?" Kate jerked to a halt, and turned to him, incredulous. "In what way does this help any of us? If Anstruther had any love left for her, this will have ended it. And now I must try to convince Uncle Upshaw his sister-in-law is not insane. And Nancy—! Nancy just married the village rector! I have taken *such pains* to see that gossip did not taint her! Mamma simply didn't stop to consider how ugly this would look. And to have done it on *my* account? No. No, Edward. This is madness."

She resumed her pacing, and Edward followed her to the window. Her pensive posture put him in mind, strangely, of the way she had been looking through the drawing room window the first time he'd kissed her. He remembered that day now, in this poignant and dangerously charged moment— perhaps with good reason.

"Kate," he said, settling a hand lightly on her shoulder. "Your mother is cut to no ordinary pattern, it's true. But she's being a parent in the only way she knows how."

"Then why doesn't she learn better?" Kate cried, spinning around. "*Why*, Edward? Did Nancy and I not deserve it? How hard can it be?"

"Harder than you might think," murmured Edward.

But Kate stood rigidly by the window, shaking her head. "Then one finds a way," she gritted. "When you have children, you have obligations. *You raise them.* You watch over them, and teach them how to go on. But Nancy and I never had a normal family. We have never been . . . *parented*, if that is a word, in any ordinary fashion. We have always suffered Mamma's antics and Papa's neglect. And I am sick of it."

"Kate, you've just suffered a shock, that is all." He tried to set an arm around her shoulders but she threw him off. "You've had a brush with public ruin. You didn't realize the depths to which Reggie might stoop—nor did I, for that matter."

"I appreciate your effort to explain this away," she said a little stiffly. "But all I can think of is the fact that Nancy and Richard will be back tomorrow, and that we have a dozen of our neighbors coming to celebrate their marriage—and all people will be talking about is how the bride's mother got caught in bed with her sister's former fiancé."

"Richard's reputation will weather it, Kate," Edward said calmly. "And perhaps it won't even get out?"

She turned on him then. "Secrets always get out," she said a little bitterly. "Always. Scandals cannot be contained, no matter what subterfuge we engage. Do not kid yourself on that score, Edward."

A sudden coldness settled over him then, and he had the distinct impression they were talking about something a good deal more dire than her mother.

He went to the sideboard and pensively poured another whisky, though the last thing he needed was another drink. But he did need time. Time to think. To calculate.

Good old Ned, he thought. *Always figuring the odds.*

Kate was still standing at the window, staring out into the dark of night, practically vibrating like a tuning fork, radiating anger over something that had been, in his opinion, pretty damned clever, so far as complete and utter checkmates went.

"Edward," she said, her voice flat. "Earlier tonight you said . . . you said that we might have to have more than an arrangement. That you were not careful."

"I did, yes." He turned uneasily from the sideboard, certain now that her rage ran deeper than Aurélie's antics.

"What did you mean by it?" Kate was still staring at the glass, her arms crossed.

"I don't think it has anything to do with what just happened, Kate." He willed his voice to be calm as he felt his way through the minefield. "We're talking about your mother. Aren't we?"

"Nonetheless, I wish to know," she said. "God forbid, Edward, if I were to find myself with child, what would you do?"

"I would do the right thing." He watched her reflection warily in the glass. "And God help you, Kate. But what else could I do?"

"Yes, it would be frightfully awkward, wouldn't it?" she said, dropping her voice. "I am Baroness d'Allenay, not a nobody. You could not hide me away in the country on some small annuity, and see your child once a year, could you?"

"Well." He set his brandy down with a harsh *thunk!* "Well, Kate. It sounds as if we need to have a serious discussion."

She whipped around at that. "Do we, Edward?" she asked sharply. "Do we really?"

He held up one hand, but he felt his ire rising fast. "Kate, you invited me down here tonight," he reminded her. "I have tried, my dear, to keep my distance."

"Yes, you're quite right," she whispered. "You're a weakness for me, I won't deny it. From the very first, I have been unable to resist wanting you and craving the pleasure you give me. Even when I knew I ought not."

"And you *ought not*?" he said coldly. "Thank you, Kate, for announcing the obvious with such an air of discovery. Of course you *ought not*. I *ought not*. And yet *we did*. And we continue to. And yes, if the worst should happen, you would damn well marry me—and rue the day, I do not doubt. But that, my dear, is the risk we run. Did you not grasp that?"

"I did not," she said, "until it dawned on me that, in such a case, our child would be, at the very least, heir to the d'Allenay barony."

He closed the distance between them then. "Now, just wait a damned minute," he said, his hand seizing her wrist. "That sounded like an ugly accusation. Tell me *exactly* what this is about."

"This is about Annabelle Granger," she said, "and I think

you know it. Now, will you kindly relax your grip on my wrist?"

He let go as if she'd exploded into flames. "Well, if this is about Annabelle," he snapped, "then why didn't you just say so?"

Her lips thinning, Kate just shook her head. "It wasn't," she admitted. "Not at first. But now? Yes. Yes, I want to know what your relationship is with her."

"I am . . . her godfather, of sorts," he said gruffly.

"And are you her actual father?" There was a hint of a challenge in her question.

For a long moment, he weighed telling Kate to go to hell. But it was not an unreasonable question. Not for a woman who, as she pointed out, might be carrying his child.

"In confidence?" he finally said.

She hesitated. "Yes. In confidence."

"I am not," he said tightly.

Her gaze faltered. "And what if I do not believe you, Edward?"

He shook his head. "Then that is your choice, Kate," he said. "Like everyone else, you may choose what you think. You may choose to think me Annie's father or Annie's savior or Annie's rich Uncle Croesus. I generally do not trouble myself to clarify the issue. Because it matters just about this much"—here he gave a sharp snap of his fingers—"what other people think of me."

"But don't you think you should have shared her existence with me?" Kate demanded. "I mean, after all we have been—" Her words jerked to a halt, her face heating.

"Been to one another?" he finished, a bitter smile curling his mouth. "Kate, your desire for me might as well be mud on your shoe, as pleased as you are to have it."

"That is not what— Why, how can you—" She jerked to a halt, blinking. Then she shook her head. "I am sorry. You're quite right. This is none of my concern."

"I did not say that, Kate," he coldly countered. "I think we can make an argument that it is very much your concern. But don't put words in my mouth, and do not dare call me a liar."

She tore her gaze from his and turned. "I wish I didn't want you so desperately," she whispered.

"I can accommodate that," he said. "Say the word. I can be out from under your roof in ten minutes. But be very sure, Kate, that you understand who you're angry at, and why."

"I am angry at myself," she said. "Of that I am very, very sure."

There came a long moment of silence then, the night so still Edward could hear a clock ticking in the next room. He felt thwarted and angry and insulted—but most of all, he felt deeply wounded. Damn it, did he never learn his lesson on that score?

"I shall remove to Heatherfields tomorrow," he said tightly, turning toward the door. "I beg your pardon, Kate, for any offense I've given."

"Heatherfields is not habitable," she said, still looking out the window.

"Heatherfields will do," he retorted, jerking the door wide. "I spent too many years in the army to be put off by a dripping roof and a couple of rats. Good night, Kate. You will send word to me at Heatherfields or in London should the worst occur."

"Ah, yes. *The worst*." Her voice was distant; almost disembodied. "Thank you, Edward, for making that plain."

"You're welcome," he returned—just before he slammed the door.

CHAPTER 17

Lady d'Allenay's Advice to the Lovelorn

With her daily workbook carefully angled into a shaft of morning sunlight, Mrs. Peppin adjusted her reading glasses, then scribbled yet another line in the list headed *Dinner Menu*.

"Right, then, we've the sweets settled," she said with satisfaction. "Now, for cheeses Cook has put out the Stilton and the Camembert. We haven't aught else, miss, on such short notice."

"Yes, yes, I'm sure," Kate murmured, her elbows propped on Peppie's long table.

On a faint sigh, the housekeeper flicked a glance up to look across the table at her. "Miss Kate, do gather your wits," she gently chided. "You've not spared two words for this menu and you know His Lordship be partic'lar about his cheese."

"Sorry, Peppie." Kate tucked a loose strand of hair behind her ear, and sat more upright. "No, he likes Stilton well enough. But after last night . . ."

"Aye." Mrs. Peppin's nose wrinkled, cocking up one side

of her glasses. "We could serve up his Stilton on a solid gold platter, and he'd been no better pleased."

Having dashed straight downstairs after breakfasting alone in her room, Kate had given the housekeeper an abbreviated version of the previous night's fiasco. Peppie had replied sharply that it was her dearest wish Lord Reginald Hoke should burn in the hot fires of hell. But more importantly, she had reassured Kate that although the commotion had indeed been overheard, the servants had put it down to the usual antics of Mrs. Wentworth's friends.

"What a mess it all is, Peppie!" Kate propped her chin in her hand. "Has there been word from the rectory?"

"Mercy, yes! Jasper says Miss Nan come up on the first train," said the housekeeper, "just as Mrs. Wentworth said she would."

"I hope they will not mind coming to the dinner tonight." Kate jerked herself upright again. "Has everyone accepted?"

"What, with the rector wed so hurry-scurry?" Mrs. Peppin snorted. "Oh, aye, they'll all wish to eye Miss Nan's belly. At least I can cross Lord Reginald off the list." So saying, she leaned forward and drew a thick, black line over his name.

"De Macey has kindly ordered him to leave," Kate murmured, "to spare me the embarrassment. And honestly, Peppie, it cannot be too soon."

"Why, bless me, miss, but Lord Reginald left betimes," said Mrs. Peppin. "Dressed for riding, he were, and carrying naught but a postmantle and his coat. Left his man upstairs, Jasper said, to pack his trunks and come arter."

Kate exhaled with relief. "Well, thank God that's over," she said. "His valet may stay as long as he pleases. It's Reggie I wanted shut of."

Mrs. Peppin eyed her a little appraisingly across the table. "Well, seems we're soon to have the house half empty, then, what with Miss Nancy wed and Mr. Edward gone."

Something in Kate's heart sank low indeed. "*Has* he gone?"

"Heavens, miss, well afore breakfast!" she said a little accusingly. "Did you not know? Off on that gurt black horse o' his to stay at Heatherfields, he said, but how he's to live there I'm sure I cannot think, for the roof leaks like a sieve, old Cutler what keeps the place be deaf a post, and Mrs. Cutler as slammickin' a housekeeper as ever I knew."

"Mr. Quartermaine assures me he's not the least deterred by leaks or rats," said Kate, "so I doubt Mrs. Cutler's slatternly ways will much put him off."

"Oh, miss!" Mrs. Peppin eyed her darkly across the table. "How, pray, is he to have his eggs the way he likes them?"

Kate arched both her eyebrows. "Why, how *does* he like them, Peppie?"

"Dry, miss!" said the housekeeper, as if it were the Christian way, "and his bacon the same."

"—which would explain the overcooked breakfasts we've been eating round here," Kate added in an undertone. "I thought, Peppie, that you'd decided he was a rich scoundrel who'd left his illegitimate child hidden away in the countryside?"

Mrs. Peppin's gaze left Kate's. "Oh, well, it's not for me to judge, miss," she said a little guiltily. "It's hard not to like the gentleman, that's all I've to say in the matter. Ever so polite, and never a sharp word to staff."

Kate's head was beginning to ache—this, on top of eyes which had been so red and stained from crying, she had been compelled to hold a cold facecloth to them before coming downstairs this morning.

"Well," she said, pushing up from the table. "I'm off to the estate office to find Anstruther. After that, I'm meeting Uncle Upshaw at the new rectory to make sure he finds it good enough for Nancy. In between, if I've time, I'd better go round through the village and look in on the newlyweds, just to give them the cut of Uncle's jib."

"But what can Upshaw have to say about any of it now?" demanded Mrs. Peppin. "The house *or* the marriage, come to that?"

Kate shook her head. "There's nothing he can say, honestly, with Nancy having spent a night alone with Richard," she said. "Even an annulment, or whatever one calls it, would spell ruin for her. But Mamma has treated Uncle shabbily; as if his wishes were of no import whatever."

"I don't know, miss," said Peppin. "Seems to me His Lordship was being unreasonable and your mother cleverly got round him."

"Good heavens, you sound like Edward," Kate muttered. "Then end justifies the means! And perhaps it does. I do not know. But I'm going through the motions of trying to appease Uncle Upshaw because his feelings do matter, Peppie. He has been nothing but kind to Nancy and me."

"Oh, aye," said Mrs. Peppin, "in his own stiff-rumped and mighty way!"

"But he is family," said Kate, rising from her chair, "and one should not quarrel with one's family if it can be avoided."

"Well, blessed be the peacemakers." Mrs. Peppin had stood and was going through the pocket of her smock. "But about Mr. Edward—"

"What about him, Peppie?" asked Kate a little snappishly.

The housekeeper extracted a letter. "This came for him in the morning's post," she said. "From London, it is. Isn't he to be at dinner tonight?"

"Oh . . . heavens." Kate considered it. Edward was a new neighbor; one who had until today been a guest in her house. "I don't know. Give me the letter, Peppie, and I shall think what's best done."

Taking up her hat and her riding crop, Kate left the housekeeper's sitting room feeling more beleaguered than when she'd gone in—which had been quite a lot—and wondering if Peppie, too, meant to take Edward's side in this business.

Which was foolish, she told herself, when there was no *side*. She was not at war with Edward.

She was at war with herself.

And this morning she had awoken the most dreadful suspicion that she had somehow wronged him. He had said he was not Annabelle Granger's father. And Edward had never shown himself anything less than honest—almost blatantly so. From the very first, he had admitted things about himself he might easily have hidden, or glossed over.

But she could not think of that now, Kate reminded herself, going out into the sunlit bailey. Their relationship had been dangerous at best, and if it was truly over . . .

She found herself blinking back tears again, and hastened across the cobblestones into the shadows of the estate office, relieved to find it empty. After blowing her nose and dashing her cuffs beneath her eyes, Kate set about catching up the accounts that had been let go since her mother's arrival, while she lay in wait for Anstruther.

He came in half an hour later, his boots muddied and his attitude formal. He greeted her civilly, of course, and sat down at his great desk opposite to bring Kate up to date on the morning's events around the estate. She, in turn, went over the accounts. They were still looking for ways to come up with the cash to purchase the tin mine in Cornwall.

At the end of it, Anstruther sighed. "Nay, it's not to be, lass," he said, shaking his head. "Ask Upshaw, but to borrow money now, rates in the City being what they are . . ."

"No, no borrowing." Kate closed the account book with a heavy thud. "We're nicely above water, Anstruther, and we're staying there. I do not need to ask Uncle's advice in that regard."

Anstruther looked relieved, and set his hands on his broad, muscular thighs as if to be off.

"No, no, no," said Kate, throwing up a hand. "Anstruther, we are going to talk."

"Aye, we just did, didn't we?" But with a wary expression, he sat back down.

Kate drew a deep breath. "Something happened last night," she said. "A bit of awkwardness to do with Aurélie. I should hate you to catch wind of it, and think wrongly of her."

He set his head at a sharp, quizzical angle. "That's naught to do with me, my lady."

"Oh, don't *my lady* me, John Anstruther!" said Kate impatiently. "You're no more sensible than Aurélie, I begin to think. And by the way, just how long—and how often—have you been—er, *keeping company* with my mother?"

"*Hmph*," he said. "That would be our business."

"It was," Kate admitted, "until this week. Now out with it. Mamma will make me no sense; I needn't even ask her. We're a family, Anstruther. I wish to know everything."

"Then you'll have to wish on, miss," he said stiffly.

Kate scowled. Then, shoulders slumping, she shook her head. "Not *everything*," she said wearily. "Just . . . the *when*, and the *who knows*. What else can come back to bite us, Anstruther? I cannot guard your back unless I have some notion."

Anstruther was quiet a long moment, his huge index finger going *thump, thump, thump!* atop his desk. Then he stopped, and rubbed it alongside his nose. "A long while, then," he said, "if ye must know. Since you were a wee lass, and I came down to take up this post. And no one knows, as best I can tell ye."

"Were you . . . in love with Mamma?"

"Aye, long ago, I suppose," he said, "when I first met her. I'd just come down from university, and was visiting here. Aurélie was young still, Nan's age or thereabout, and your brother was just a babe."

"But nothing came of it?"

He shook his head. "Not until your father strayed some years later, and took to dice and drink," he said. "But I dinna wish to speak ill of him, miss, so I'd as soon leave it at that."

"You don't feel guilty, I take it." Kate managed to smile.

"I didna say that." Anstruther's expression was grim. "But in any case, aye, your mother and I have known one another long and well, Kate. Sometimes we've been friends; sometimes more."

Kate was beginning to think it was mostly *sometimes more*, for a great number of things seemed to be falling into place—this, despite the fact that she was so distraught over Edward she could barely think straight.

She drew a deep breath. "So—all those business trips to London all these years—for me and for Grandpapa," she ventured, "it was not just to save him the travel, or to save me the embarrassment of running into Reggie, was it?"

He gave a barely discernable shrug. "No."

Kate leaned back in her chair, and crossed her arms over her chest. "So, in summary," she said, "you and my mother met, fell for one another to some uncertain degree, and commenced an on-again off-again love affair both here and in London. And all the while, gossip has pegged her to the Comte de Macey, along with various other rakes, rogues, and scoundrels?"

"Aye, weel, from time to time, lass, your mother and I fell out," said Anstruther darkly, "when I didna do to suit her."

"Yes, but we're talking about a span of twenty years," Kate pointed out. "And Mamma's actual *affaire* with de Macey, I begin to think, was of very short duration."

Anstruther looked sheepish. "Aye, a few months," he admitted, "until I came to my senses."

"Ah, bucked up stubborn over something, did you?" she muttered. "Well, I need not know what. But Anstruther, Aurélie is a widow, and has been some years. De Macey can find someone else to use as wallpaper. Why don't you pursue her openly if you care for her?"

"What, *court* the woman?" Anstruther looked aghast. "Miss Kate, it wouldna do."

"I can't think why," said Kate. "Unless you're put off by the fact that she's mentally unhinged."

"I haven't the wherewithal to give her the life she should have," declared Anstruther. "I'm not of her ilk."

"Indeed not, you're a good deal more sensible," said Kate. "As to your wherewithal, I don't doubt for a minute you're rich as Midas. You've a lovely manor house at South Farm, and you're certainly as wellborn as Mamma. Her mother was the governess, you'll recall, and her grandfather little more than a jumped-up Parisian greengrocer."

"Nay, it wouldna do," he said again.

Kate shrugged. "You must suit yourself," she said amiably. "No doubt she's more than most men would wish to take on. But your post here could not be more secure, as you very well know, all your bad-tempered, self-sacrificing protestations aside. So if you wish to have her, but haven't the courage to pursue her seriously, then you must take the blame upon yourself, not me."

"*Hmph*" was all he said.

"Very well, then." Kate gave up, and snatched her hat and crop. "I'm riding into the village to drop in on Nancy and Richard. May I depend upon you to bring Uncle Upshaw out to the new rectory for our poke-about?"

"Aye, I'll bring the carnaptious, fykie fellow," grumbled Anstruther under his breath, "and will be wishin' my ears stopped wi' wax, I dinna doot."

"I have no idea what you just said," Kate replied evenly, "but I shall see the both of you at eleven o'clock sharp. Pray do not be late, for we've twenty-odd guests for dinner tonight."

"Aye, aye, I ken." He waved her away.

Then, her memory stirred, she turned from the door and extracted the letter. "Anstruther, could you drop this by Heatherfields, and tell Mr. Quartermaine we still hope to see him at dinner tonight? After all, he's our neighbor now."

Some inscrutable emotion passed over Anstruther's face. "Aye, lass, no trouble a'tall."

Then Kate snared her lip an instant. "And about that little dust-up last night—"

"No need," he said, waving her off. "Heard all aboot it already. And fair pleased with herself, she was, too."

"Oh," said Kate. "But Mamma is still abed and no one else has—"

Anstruther lifted his head from his ledger to smile thinly.

"Ah." Kate slapped her hat on. "Well. I see. I shall just be off, then."

Then, for a third time, she turned back. "Anstruther?"

"Aye?" He slapped his pencil down.

Kate hesitated, carefully considering her words. "Did you ever wonder if . . . well, if when a person wants what they cannot have, do they ever . . ."

He crooked one grizzled eyebrow. "Aye?"

Kate just shook her head, the explanation failing her. "Mamma, I mean," she managed. "Her capriciousness. Her willfulness. Could it be all of a piece?"

"All of a piece of what?" he said.

"Her *unhappiness*," said Kate.

His massive muttonchops twitched as if his jaw muscle was jerking.

Kate sighed. "There, Anstruther, I've said it," she went on. "I fear Mamma is unhappy—unhappy in her way, I mean. And though it certainly does not fall to you to *make* her happy, consider if perhaps what you want isn't so far removed from what she wants, and—"

"It is," he tightly interjected.

"Fine." Kate nodded, and seized the doorknob.

"That's to say, Kate, it must be." Then he hesitated a long moment. "But I shall think on it. Aye, lass. I shall think on it a time."

Stunned into near silence, Kate went around into the outer bailey and helped Motte saddle her horse. Athena was tossing her head in the cool, autumn air, but the stall beside her looked empty, and oddly forlorn.

Motte slicked a hand down Athena's withers. "Aye, the big fellow's gone orf ter 'is new home," he said soothingly. "More apples for you, me fine girl."

It was a cold comfort, those extra apples, thought Kate, thanking Motte for flinging her up into the saddle, and then setting off across the bridge.

All the way down the hill, in fact, and up the next, Kate's mind was in a tumult with thoughts of Edward. The certainty that she'd made a grievous error was growing within her, and a sense of desperation was building.

She kept telling herself—as she had for some time now—that even setting aside his treatment of poor Annabelle Granger, Edward was entirely wrong for her; that his past and his business dealings made him unfit even to know. That his being at Bellecombe, even as Aurélie's guest, had constituted a risk to her good name.

But it was almost as if she no longer cared. As if the weakness in her knees had sapped all power of logic.

Kate reminded herself of Nancy, and of the sweet promise that her marriage to Richard held. Of Aunt Louisa's three daughters yet to be married. Already they struggled with all the titters and gossip surrounding Aurélie's racy, headstrong behavior. They didn't need Kate to become the subject of wagging tongues. Aurélie, at least, was a widow, and permitted a measure of latitude.

But Kate, as always, was stuck somewhere in the middle—and a little tired, to be honest, of worrying about everyone else.

Her self-pity, however, was at once severed when she topped the last hill, and looked down toward the intersection at Edward's fateful milestone. There, by the more modern signpost that pointed toward the village, was a late lamb—one far too young to have been separated from its mother.

The poor thing was bleating so plaintively, Kate could hear it all the way down the hill, and even when she had nearly reached it, the lamb struggled, but didn't shy away as one might expect.

"Poor mite!" Kate murmured, curious. "I will set you back over the fence."

Dismounting, she draped Athena's reins in the hedge, and stepped onto the verge to examine it, and still the lamb did nothing but cry, its pink tongue trembling pitifully.

"Now, however did you get out, little lamb?" she asked, reaching down to scoop it up.

Only then did she realize the poor thing had got caught in a rope.

Kneeling, she realized it was not caught, but, horrifyingly, it had been *tied*. A thin rope had been wrapped around its pastern, and tied to the bottom of the signpost.

"Those bloody village lads!" she said to the creature, now yanking a little dangerously at the rope. "We shall have their heads, little lamb. Be still, and let me get this loose."

In a trice, Kate had the knot untied around its leg and turned quickly to scoop it up, drawing it to her chest. But Kate never made it back onto her feet. Suddenly, the lamb began to flail. And then there was a flash of white before her eyes, and Kate could not breathe.

She dropped the lamb, scrabbling backward with her bootheels, clawing at the hand clapped over her face, fighting to rip away the great wad of cloth that covered her mouth and nose. But Kate could see nothing; nothing but the distant hedgerow, and the little lamb skittering toward it.

And then Kate saw nothing at all.

CHAPTER 18

In Which Anstruther
Delivers a Swift Kick

The kitchen chimney at Heatherfields smoked. Ashy, acrid clouds roiled from its grimy maw, then drifted languidly to the bare, black-beamed ceiling—but not before scorching out Edward's nose hair and sending him reeling back with a cough that sounded of consumption and impending death.

Where was Vesta, he thought sourly, *when you needed her?*

There was no home here. Hell, there wasn't even a hearth. There was just a filthy, entirely antiquated kitchen with a massive black hole belching ash and ruin.

"Told 'ee it smoked," said the wizened old man behind him.

"You said, sir—and I quote—*it be ter'ble smeetchy*," Edward snapped, "though I begin at last to grasp your meaning." On a spate of sudden anger, he seized the poker and thrashed violently at the fire.

"Here now, mind 'ee the chimley-crook, sir, do!" cried the man. "The missus must hang the pot thereon."

"A pot of what?" Edward stood and turned, still grasping the poker.

Mr. Cutler threw up his arms as if to ward off a blow.

On a curse, Edward flung the poker aside. "A pot of what, sir?" he asked a little more gently.

"Supper," said the old man, "and d'ee wish a chimmer made up, sir?"

"A *chimmer*?" Good God, did these people not speak the Queen's English? "No, but I now need a hot bath. And what in blazes is a chimmer?"

Mr. Cutler looked wounded. "Upstairs, sir." He stabbed a finger at the filthy ceiling. "A *bed*-chimmer. Missus zaid I was vor ax o' 'ee d'ee mean to stay past supper? Or do 'ee go back to the gurt house?"

"Ah, a bedchamber," said Edward, his wrath collapsing in on him, only to become something like grief. "No, Cutler. I will not be going back to Bellecombe. I'm at Heatherfields to stay."

"Aye. Well a' fine then."

The old man nodded, but he might as well have been shaking his head, so doubtful of Edward's sanity did he seem.

And Cutler was right, Edward realized. He was a little mad.

Moreover, his arrival here had thrown the elderly caretaker into a muddle, and left his not-so-elderly "missus" less than pleased. She was out, so far as Edward could grasp from the Somerset accent, attempting to kill a chicken for his dinner.

Hands set stubbornly on his hips, Edward turned in a slow circle, taking in the miserable room with its scarred wooden worktable, and its massive Welsh dresser racked with dusty platters and plates, some of which still looked encrusted with only God knew what.

Then the stubbornness, too, fell into grief. Why was he forcing these poor, ill-prepared servants to bear the brunt of his self-loathing?

"I beg your pardon, Cutler," he said, pinching hard at the bridge of his nose. "This won't do, will it? Send to the White Lion and bespeak me a bed and some dinner, please."

The old man bobbed his head like an eager bird. "Aye, I can do it vor 'ee," he said more agreeably. "Will 'ee bide here?"

"Yes, for a time," said Edward, raking a hand through his now-sooty hair. "I'm going to begin hauling out some of this furniture so we can chop it into kindling."

The old man bobbed again, so amiable he likely would have nodded just the same if Edward had said he meant to set the house afire, strip naked, and dance in circles while it burnt. Which was, now he thought on it, a tempting notion.

Stooping beneath the low lintel, the old man hobbled out through the door that gave on to a series of weedy kitchen gardens that must once have been quite splendid. Edward watched him go, then dragged out the filthy kitchen table, its legs shuddering and scraping over the flagstone. After it went a battered churn and an ancient meat safe, its tin front rusting away, followed by a dozen rickety chairs, the bottoms all split out.

But when he reached the last chair, his rage half burnt away by his exertions, he instead fell into it, and considered his situation.

He should have told Kate about Annie, he realized, his heart sinking deeper still.

As soon as he'd remembered her existence, he should have told Kate. And told her everything, too. It wasn't as if he didn't trust her. But the story was so vile and his own guilt so heavy, he kept it inside. A part of him had also feared ruining the beauty of their burgeoning friendship, though it shocked him he might have—much less so deeply value—a friendship with a lady of such decency and character.

But it was not just a friendship, was it? It had become far more the moment he'd kissed her that afternoon by her parlor window. He hadn't even known who the hell he was, but the moment Kate had opened beneath him, sighing so sweetly into his mouth, he had known that he was lost.

He had claimed her in that moment—in his heart if not his head—and she had been his ever after. Except that he had never told her so. He had never told her that he loved her. Never confessed to her that something inside him had altered; had torn from its moorings and flown to her, and that she now held his heart, bitter and scarred as it was, in her slender but capable hands.

And now Kate was convinced that he was hiding something from her—which he was. He was hiding Annie as he had always hidden her; behind a curtain of anger and hurt and, yes, guilt. Guilt that he had not flown fast enough to her mother's side. Guilt that, truth be told, a part of him had rued his promise to Maria.

But he would have kept it, of that he had no doubt, had fate given him the chance. He would have married her, claimed the child as his own, and made up whatever vile pack of lies was required to ensure the story was believable.

Anything to save her suffering. Anything to save Annie from a fate that might have crushed her.

He propped his elbows on his knees and let his head fall into his hands, the scent of ash thick in his nostrils, his eyes stinging. He told himself it was the soot that made them burn, and even then he halfway believed it.

But he believed, too, that his life was in ruins, and there was nothing to be done.

Nothing but go back to Kate and beg her pardon and declare himself a changed man. Which he was, indeed.

Profiting upon the frailty of human nature held no satisfaction, but gave only a disgust. In small, destructive increments, Edward had allowed himself to become no better than that foul piece of humanity Alfred Hedge, and he knew it. He was merely better bred—by some small measure—and, if anything, far more ruthless.

How was he to impose that on Kate?

He could not. Not even if Peters turned up on his doorstep this instant with a portmanteau stuffed with cash in hand.

But what would Kate say of that? She was neither young nor foolish. She was an intelligent woman who managed a complicated life with skill and grace. Was he so caught up in regret and despair, he was unilaterally choosing a path without so much as considering her wishes? *Should* he tell her how he felt?

Perhaps she was so disgusted with him now it didn't matter. But for a man who had lived his entire life utterly confident in his ability to bludgeon his way through life's every challenge, Edward suddenly could not think straight.

But he could go to Kate and apologize for being a prideful ass.

And he would, by God, stop sitting here on the verge of tears. He would quit this pathetic mewling and remember what he did have, could he but set things right with Kate: a bond of quiet friendship that only a fool would fail to salvage.

It was a good thing he'd chosen that moment in which to decide this course of action, too, for he'd just got up from the wobbling chair and sent it flying toward the door with a swift, hard kick when a large shadow fell over the threshold.

"Quartermaine!" barked a harsh, familiar voice. "That you?"

"Come in, man!" Edward ordered, but Anstruther was already edging his way inside. "The place isn't trip-wired, for God's sake."

Anstruther's hard gaze swept the kitchen, his face falling. "Afternoon to ye," said the Scotsman, handing him a letter. "I was hoping to find Miss Kate aboot."

"To find Kate?" Incredulous, Edward flicked a glance at the letter, then shoved it away. "*Here?*"

"No' here, then?" Anstruther frowned. "And you'd be sure?"

"What?" Edward strode across the room. "Why should you think to find her here? Where the devil is she?"

Hesitance turned to something darker, and Anstruther shook his head. "No' at the castle," he said uneasily. "I've just come from there. This morning she bade me bring you that letter, then I was to head over to the new rectory to meet her. But she didna turn up."

Edward shook his head. "That isn't like Kate," he said quietly. "She's not with Nancy?"

"She was niver seen at the rectory, though it was there she was last going." Anstruther was twisting anxiously at the strap of his crop. "Something's amiss, Quartermaine. I feel it keenly."

"God *damn it*!" Edward kicked the chair back across the room. "It's Hoke, the scurvy bastard!"

"Aye, he was none too pleased to be thwarted last night, I hear," said the big Scot, narrowing one eye.

"Oh, he blustered a few vague threats." Edward dropped his tone, an ugly chill settling over him. "Or perhaps not so vague, after all?"

"I've sent Burnham all through the village, and Jasper across the home farm. Tom Shearn's calling on all the tenants—but quiet-like—and Upshaw's gone back to tear the house apart. But naught's been seen of her."

Edward was already shrugging into his coat. "That man is a rabid dog," he said, snatching his crop, "and needs to be put down. Where can he have taken her?"

"He had nae carriage," said Anstruther as they strode out of the house, both bending low beneath the door. "He would not dare take her by train. There's no inn or such place hereabouts as he might hide her; she's too well-known. No, I think she's here. On Heatherfields. It's what Reggie knows best."

"Good God, would he harm her?" Having already untied Aragon, Edward flung himself into the saddle and forced his temper down. If ever there had been a time for his cold, emotionless logic, the time was now.

Anstruther, however, didn't mount up. "I've been puzzling it out," he said scratching at one of his massive muttonchops. "I think he'd no' harm her. But Upshaw's dinner party is tonight."

"Dear God," said Edward. "Does he think to embarrass her before the whole village?"

"Aye, at the very least," said Anstruther, "for he's desperate—and desperate men, e'en the fickle and stupid ones, are dangerous."

"Yes, and what he's desperate for is to marry her," said Edward. "His debts are crushing him."

Anstruther gave a bark of sarcastic laughter. "Aye, weel, Kate canna help him there, even should she wish," he said. "Bellecombe's valuable but cash poor, and she's not such a fool as to risk borrowing money over him. Reggie just came back thinking she'd be easily charmed."

"Then he seriously underestimated Kate."

"Aye, he did. But you"—here Anstruther paused and gave his familiar, assessing squint—"now, you, I think, would not be such a fool, would ye? I think perhaps you grasp the lady's good sense, and her worth?"

Edward wasn't sure what Anstruther was asking, but he was sure of his answer. "I never met a woman more sensible or more worthy," he replied. "And she damned sure won't be wasted on the likes of Lord Reginald Hoke."

Anstruther gave a tight nod, as if granting Edward some sort of permission. "Gude, then how well d'ye remember the lay of the land?" he asked. "The empty cottages, the barns, the byres?"

Edward considered it but a moment. "I've pretty well memorized it," he said. "I'll search the northeasterly half, along Bellecombe's border."

"I'll go round the far side o' the village, then, to the old tithe barn," said Anstruther, "and work toward you. If we find naught, we'll meet up along the stream by the lower pasture."

Anstruther shoved a foot in his stirrup and hefted himself onto the great, gray beast. Then, as if it were an afterthought, he reached behind him for a worn saddlebag, and extracted a pistol.

"I shouldn't need that," said Edward, "to deal with the likes of Reggie."

"Expediency," said Anstruther. "I've got the mate. Should ye find that conniving fiend, fire it. I'll find you. Then we'll take the devil doon a hack."

KATE CAME AWAKE on a lurch of nausea. The air was damp, thick with earthy scents. Above her face, vaulting rafters swam, faded away, then straightened themselves entirely. They were black with age and rough-hewn.

A shed, she thought dimly. *Or a cottage?*

She lay upon something hard and cold. Gingerly rolling onto her right elbow, she clasped her hand to her mouth and tried not to retch. But the frightful, dank smell of the place struck full force then, and she staggered up.

Reeling across what had once been a flagstone floor, she made her way to the planked door. It wouldn't budge. Kate pounded on it with both hands, and there came a scraping, metallic sound. Flinging the door wide, she ran into the bracken beyond and heaved up her breakfast in the blinding light.

Behind her, someone cleared his throat. "Frightfully sorry, old thing. A wicked side effect, nausea."

Kate rose an inch, trying to think whose voice it was. Why it made her skin crawl.

Reggie.

Damn and blast, it was Reggie. What had he done? *Poisoned* her? Hands braced on her thighs, Kate tried to think. She had been on her way to the village. Someone had clapped something vile and sickening-sweet over her face.

Kate straightened and fumbled for her handkerchief to wipe her mouth. Drawing a deep breath, she felt the world coming back into focus. She stood in a landscape of bracken and heather. Far beyond it, the Exmoor rose up to meet the sky, the afternoon sun sending cloud-shaped shadows scuttling over it.

It was a familiar view. She had been drugged, she thought, and carted off somewhere—somewhere not far from home. Shoving the handkerchief away, she turned and marched back down the muddy, overgrown path, righteous indignation swelling in her breast.

Reggie stood propped against the door frame, a smug look of satisfaction upon his face.

Something about that satisfaction was her undoing. Kate hauled back and swung fast, backhanding him with all her might. Reggie's head snapped, cracking on the stonework. He staggered but a moment, then grabbed her and dragged her, clawing and biting, back into the cottage.

"You little—*bitch!*" He grunted out the words, wrestling her back onto what passed for a pallet. "Always—were—a hellcat."

Kate was fast, or would have been, but the drug had slowed her in both body and brain, and Reggie outweighed her considerably. She fought him hard, but to no avail, thrashing back with her elbows, scrabbling for a handful of shirt or hair or anything she could seize.

Eventually, however, Reggie got her facedown and threw all his weight atop her. Then the sickening smell pressed in upon Kate, and the darkness came again.

A SHORT BUT storied career in the British army, paired with nearly two decades spent raking out the pockets of some of the most duplicitous that humanity could offer, had honed Edward's instincts to a slicing edge. By the time he'd reached the edge of the moor, having moved relentlessly over hill and dale, through hedge, ditch, and every cowshed he beheld, three hours had passed and his blood was still like ice water in his veins.

He had learnt to smell deception before he saw it and to believe, like Machiavelli, that overcoming an enemy by fraud was as good as by force. Thus, when he saw the abandoned cottage with its attached shed half caved in, an uneasy certainty settled over him.

Returning to a copse on the far side of the hill, he secured Aragon and walked back to the cottage. Carefully selecting his angle of approach, he crept up to the windowless rear, a long wall spanning both house and shed. Within, nothing stirred—at least nothing that could be heard through the thick stone.

Nonetheless, he sensed a presence. Soundlessly he moved across the back in the direction of the shed. Halfway along he was rewarded by a faint snuffle, and the sound of shifting hooves. A quick glimpse around the corner, and he caught sight of a long, black tail swishing across a pair of red and black legs.

Kate's bay mare. Suddenly, he caught the rumble of a low voice from within the cottage.

Settling himself against the wall, he weighed what to do. He supposed Reggie to be armed; cowards usually were. He was not afraid of rushing the door, and expected he could tackle Reggie long before he got off a shot.

But that was a big gamble when Kate could get hurt. Spitfire that she was, Reggie had likely been compelled to bind her, rendering her incapable of movement or defense. No, better to flush Reggie out first.

Swiftly, he crept around to the side and stuck his head around front to examine the access points. One door with a low stoop and two windows, both shuttered. Glazing, if there had ever been any, had long ago been pried out. *Damn it.* There was no way to see what was happening inside.

Mentally calculating how far away Anstruther might be, Edward went around to the shed and released Kate's mare, along with a second horse, just as the voices took on an angry pitch. With the argument as cover, he led the horses away.

Upon his return to the shed, Edward began to quietly pile up straw and dry manure against the connecting wall, then topped it with dead bracken. Once the pile looked high enough, he double-checked the weapon Anstruther had given him. Then Edward pulled out his matches and sent up a prayer to Vesta.

WHEN NEXT KATE came awake, it was to find herself slumped in the corner, her hands bound before her by a length of filthy rope, and the handkerchief gagging her mouth. The rope went around her waist, painfully tight, hitching her from behind to something she couldn't see. An iron ring set in the wall, as best her numb fingers could make out.

Reggie sat on an old milking stool beneath a shuttered window. A blade of light leached in through the crack, casting an eerie, sharply angled luminance over his eyes.

"Hullo, Kate," he said softly. "Back amongst the living, are we?"

She lashed out with one leg, attempting to kick the stool from under him as she cursed him through the gag.

"What's that, my love?" Reggie leered. "Why, I would not dare take advantage of an insensate female! Besides, I had your virtue long ago, Kate, for what that was worth."

Stomping one boot heel impotently, Kate threatened to cut off his bollocks with a dull knife. The gag, unfortunately, spoiled the effect.

"Oh, just hush, Kate." Churlishly, he threw his arms across his chest. "You're still too drugged to run, and if you don't sit still, I mean to gas you again."

Snarling, Kate threw herself back against the stonework and considered her options. Her head was not clear, it was true, but she was beginning to make out where she was. Her eyes must have lit with recognition.

"Yes, the old cowman's cottage," said Reggie, showing his large, white teeth as he grinned. "We used to play here, Stephen and I. I thought you might recognize it."

When Kate said nothing, Reggie's smile actually warmed. "There's a good girl," he murmured, stretching out his legs. "Now, just sit quietly, my dear, and in the morning this will all be over."

In the morning?

What was the devil up to? Kate let her gaze dart about the one-room structure, considering her options—which were few, so far as her befuddled brain could make out. But what she could make out was the glint of a small pistol on the rickety gateleg table beside Reggie; not a proper sidearm, but something smaller, stubbier, and infinitely more lethal-looking.

"Oh, that's not for you, my love," said Reggie, seeing her eyes widen. "How could you think it? That's just for our protection today, in case someone manages to find you before you're thoroughly compromised."

"Compromised—?" Kate growled, though the gag absorbed the sound. "Are you mad?"

But of course he was mad; it went without saying. There was a feverish gleam in his eyes, and the strained, harsh look etched around his mouth had deepened.

"Kate," he said soothingly, "you really shan't have much choice. Half the village will be at Bellecombe tonight for the great celebration. I'm afraid our night-long absence will be much remarked."

On a groan, Kate shut her eyes. Uncle Upshaw's dinner party! And Reggie was right—everyone would be there.

And everyone would notice her absence.

"Yes, it *will* be gossip-worthy, won't it?" he crowed, seeing her dismay. "Tomorrow morning I'm sure you—and Lord Upshaw—will see the sense in an expedient wedding."

Kate kicked again, sending up a cloud of dust, but Reggie just laughed.

"Yes, Lady d'Allenay and her once-betrothed have slipped away to rekindle their passion," he said. "Or perhaps everyone will simply imagine your little sister besting you to the

altar put your nose out of joint? In any case, I shall delight in
Upshaw's outrage—not to mention Quartermaine's."

Pushing at the gag with her tongue, Kate stopped long
enough to grunt out another string of curses.

"Indeed, fit to be tied, I should imagine!" said Reggie
cheerfully. "And Upshaw will be only too glad to demand
I make an honest woman of you, Kate, since you will be
ruined—*just like your sister.*"

With a wrench of her jaw and a determined push of her
tongue, Kate dislodged the handkerchief. "You ruined me
years ago, you damned fool!" she cried. "Why didn't you
just tell him that?"

"What, and have you call me a liar?" Reggie's countenance darkened. "No, no, my dear, that won't answer. Besides, given that trick your Bedlamite of a mother pulled, it
will take a very public ruination to urge Upshaw's sympathy
to my side."

Kate just shook her head. "Reggie, your desperation's
driven you mad," she said. "I'm not Nancy; I'm of age and
I'm a baroness, for pity's sake! I'll never marry you. I'd
sooner cast my good name to the wind."

"You don't mean it!" he hotly interjected, leaping off the
stool and seizing his pistol. "You used to love me, Kate! You—
why, you *gave* yourself to me! You swore to marry me!"

"Before I came to my senses!" she cried. "I was just
grief-stricken, Reggie, by Stephen's death. Yes, I slept with
you and agreed to marry because I felt so alone. So over-
whelmed. Can't you understand that?"

"No, you . . . *you waited for me!*" he cried, waving the
weapon wildly. "I depended on you. And you were waiting,
Kate! It's not fair to now pretend you weren't!"

"Is that what you thought?" Kate cried. "Truly? That I
was . . . what, pining? Just biding my time until you returned
with some platitude about begging forgiveness?"

"Yes, for you'd no choice," he snapped. "No decent man

wants a soiled bride, and you're not even a beauty. Besides, I—I can make you do it! Do not try me, Kate! You don't know what I'm capable of!"

"You're capable of gross stupidity," she said on a snort. "That much is clear."

It was a terrible mistake to taunt him. "Don't laugh at me, you insolent bitch!" he shouted, leveling the gun at her head. "No one else shall have you, I swear to God!"

"Reggie," she said calmly, "move the gun away."

Instead, he shoved it nearer, the barrel trembling. "Oh, how it galls me, Kate, to come to Bellecombe only to find that scourge of humanity, Ned Quartermaine, cozied up in my place! That was a grave mistake, my girl. I will *not* have it. By God, *I will not.*"

Kate was suddenly frightened. Reggie no longer looked like himself; his face was twisted with rage, sweat beading on his forehead as his hand shook with the weight of the gun.

"Just let me go, Reggie," she said softly. "Let me go and we'll forget this happened. Don't be a fool."

"Oh, I'll tell you who the fool is," Reggie snapped. "It's you, Kate, if you think Ned Quartermaine will do a damned thing for you. The man is utterly without remorse or Christian charity. He'll toss up your skirts and go back to London laughing."

"And aren't you a fine one, Reggie, to speak of tossing up skirts and running off!"

"I didn't run, Kate, I just had a little f—" Reggie had cocked one ear toward a distant corner, his expression blanking.

Kate became gradually aware of a sound; a distant hum at first, rather like an angry beehive, and then more of a snapping sound. Suddenly, she caught a whiff of smoke.

Kate glanced up to see it gathering in the rafters. "Reggie!" she cried, "there's a fire!"

"Fire?" Reggie spun around, pistol in hand.

She could hear distinct crackling now. The adjoining cow-shed. "Reggie, untie me," she ordered, jerking against the iron ring. "Oh, God. My horse! Where's Athena?"

But Reggie was running from wall to wall, feeling them as if for heat. Suddenly the smoke was roiling down in great clouds between them. On the other side of the wall, the crackle was rising to a roar.

Genuine fear began to churn in her stomach. "Reggie, we have to get out!" she cried, twisting her hands behind her.

Neither the rope nor the iron ring would give. Reggie shouted something—a curse, she thought, and turned, still clutching his weapon. Through the haze she could just make out his eyes shying wildly. He tried the door, but it seemed stuck. He flung himself at the first set of shutters and began beating at them.

"Reggie!" The air was thickening with smoke. "Where's Athena? We have to get out!"

But Reggie had run back to the door. Finally he put his shoulder into it. A shower of sparks rained down from the rafters. Reggie panicked, and hit the door again. It flew wide and he bolted down the path. The door banged shut after him.

In that moment, Kate realized what true terror felt like. "Reggie!" she screamed. "You coward!"

Within seconds, a loud *ka-boom!* rattled the shutters. Kate screamed, and wrenched at the iron ring with all her strength. And then Edward was shouldering his way through the door, a look of grim determination on his face as he emerged through the smoke.

"Kate! Good God!" He shoved what looked like a pistol into the band of his trousers, and fell to one knee. "Did he hurt you?"

"No, but—oh, Edward!" She swallowed down her terror. "The fire! Athena!"

"Athena's well away, and the fire is just a ruse—for now," he said, his fingers swift on the knots. "Oh, Kate. Oh, love. I'm so sorry."

"Did you shoot Reggie?" she asked, relief flooding through her.

"Yes."

"Then you've nothing to be sorry for."

"I didn't kill him." He was tugging furiously at the knot behind her. "Should I have?"

"Oh. Well." She gave a thready laugh. "I'm so relieved to see you, I can forgive that small oversight."

The fire was above the wall and teasing at the far corner of the rafters now. Suddenly Kate felt the rope fall from around her waist, and Edward was up, hauling her to her feet.

Scooping one arm under her knees, he tossed her up and against his chest as if she were weightless, then shouldered his way back out the door and strode away from the burning building.

Reggie lay along the path—precisely where Kate had heaved up her breakfast—clutching one blood-soaked thigh. His pistol lay several yards away.

"You—you *shot me!*" Reggie screeched. "Damn you, Quartermaine! You *tried to kill me!*"

"I merely winged you," said Edward. "Pray don't make me regret it."

Kate looked down at the man writhing in pain, and suddenly, the hilarity of it struck her. "It warms my heart, Reggie," she said, "to see you rolling around in a patch of vomit."

"You little bitch!" Reggie seized as if with pain. "I may never walk again!"

"Another insult to the lady," said Edward coolly, "and you'll never breathe again."

Reggie shot him a vile look, then his face crumpled to near tears. Suddenly there came a hard pounding of hooves behind the cottage. Kate whipped her head around.

"Anstruther," said Edward, his somber gaze drifting over her face. "Sorry for the fright, but it seemed safest to flush Reggie out. Can you stand, my love?"

"Oh, yes, set me down," said Kate gratefully. "My arms were numb but they're just prickling now."

Gingerly he did so. When her feet hit the ground, Edward held her at a distance, his gaze sweeping down her, as if she were a fragile piece of porcelain. An instant later, Anstruther drew his massive horse around the cottage, throwing up mud and bracken.

"Kate, lass, are ye hurt?" he demanded, flying from the saddle.

"No, no," said Kate, dragging a hand through her hair. "Just filthy and a little nauseous. He clapped some sort of drug over my face."

"Weel, did he now?" Anstruther reached back his booted foot and swung it hard at Reggie's arse.

Reggie squealed at the blow, and tried to sit up.

"Aye, ye glaikit fool," Anstruther grunted. "I've wished to do that an age now."

"I can't believe you'd kick a man when he was down, Anstruther," said Edward dryly.

"Aye? Well, I can't believe you dinna aim a tad higher and save me the trooble." Anstruther was looking at the burning cottage. "Flushed him out and picked him off, eh? It wanted a new roof in any case."

Edward smiled at Kate and shrugged. "I've been in a mood to burn something down today," he remarked. "It was this or Heatherfields."

He had settled one arm around Kate's waist, and seemed deeply disinclined to let go.

On a sigh, Anstruther bent down and hauled Reggie up onto his good leg. "Weel, hop along ye game-legged eejit," he said. "You'll be wanting Fitch and his scalpel, I reckon."

"What's best done with him afterward?" Edward mused. "Truss him up like a Christmas goose and haul him before the justice?"

Reggie looked on the verge of tears now. Anstruther chewed on his lip a minute.

"I say we just get rid of him," said Kate flatly.

"Aye?" said Anstruther hopefully. "And bury him where?"

Kate gave a bark of laughter. "No, Anstruther, just make him go away," she said. "Haul him down to Southampton and put him on a ship bound for some hellish hot, midge-infested island."

"I can recommend Ceylon," said Edward dryly.

"*Hmph*," said Anstruther. He was rummaging through his saddlebag. "I'll have him shut up in the village jail for now," he said, extracting a length of rope and a large canteen.

"Thank you," said Edward. "Kate, my dear, I had better wait and let the worst of the fire go out. Will you—"

"I will be fine," she said firmly, taking the canteen from Anstruther. "I'm staying. Thank you both. Thank you ever so much for rescuing me."

Reggie having been well bound with the rope, the big Scotsman hefted him up with very little help from Edward, and tossed him sidelong across the saddle, his expression resolute. But the rope had hardly been needed; Reggie had fallen into what could only be described as a state of utter despondency, and all the fight had gone out of him.

Edward led Kate around the cottage and up the hill. From this vantage point one could see the ancient roof burning briskly, but there was no wind to carry the flames, and no place, really, for it to go, given the damp. But the surge of anger he'd felt upon seeing Kate bound and filthy had rushed through him and left him almost sagging with relief.

Kate found a thick patch of grass in the lee of the hill and sat down on a sigh. "Do you know, for an instant there I feared Reggie might really shoot me," she said, tucking her legs beneath her. "It came as rather a shock, really, for I'd imagined him too useless to seize initiative."

"Reggie has been seized by insanity," said Edward—who knew, he imagined, just what sort of madness Kate could inspire in a man's heart.

She looked up and smiled at him, then held up a hand. "Come, sit down," she said softly. "There's nothing to be done for a time."

Instead he went down on one knee and, having extracted a handkerchief from his coat pocket, soaked it with the canteen and began to gently wipe the dirt and soot from Kate's face. "You look a fright, Lady d'Allenay," he murmured, dabbing gently at a scratch on her temple. "I would still like to take a horsewhip to that dog."

"I'm tempted to let you." Kate lifted her chin for his ministrations, and when he was finished, she took a long drink from the canteen. Then, in a wonderfully unladylike gesture, she spit it some distance into the grass. "*Bleh!*" she said. "I think he gave me chloroform."

Edward held her gaze for a long moment, then laid his handkerchief aside. "Kate," he said quietly. "Oh, Kate, I ought never have let you from my sight."

Confusion sketched over her face. "Edward, I can't see how it's—"

But the sentence was cut short, for he had caught her in his arms. "Kate," he whispered into her hair. "Oh, Kate, my love. I could not bear it should anything ever happen to—"

"Nothing did," she interjected, pushing herself a little away so that she might look up at him. "Nothing happened, Edward. *You came.* And Anstruther came. And Reggie is an ass."

"I should never have left you." His eyes were locked to hers now, his hand cupped tenderly around her face as he pondered what he might have lost. "Not with that lunatic on the loose."

Kate broke the gaze, and turned away. "You didn't abandon me, Edward," she said. "I believe we made—perhaps foolishly—a mutual decision that you should go."

"Kate," he rasped. "Kate, love, look at me, please."

She did so, her eyes wide and honest in the sunlight.

"Kate," he said again. "*Was* it foolish?"

"Oh, Edward!" she said, her voice very small. "I lost my temper and I said things I ought not have said."

He set a finger to her lips. "And I was not honest with you, Kate," he said. "As soon as I remembered about Annie, I should have told—"

"No." She shook her head. "I was mad at Mamma—and perhaps even *that* was wrong—but I certainly had no right to demand—"

"I give you the right," he said swiftly. "I give you the right, Kate, to demand of me whatever you need, now and ever after. It's not as if I don't trust you. It *is not*. It never has been. It's just that Annie is a part of my life that I've always . . . well, reflexively clouded, is the best way to put it."

"It's not my business," she said, her lips thinning.

He took both her hands in his. "It *is*," he said, squeezing them. "But Kate, I did not lie to you. Annie is not mine; I was a world away in Ceylon when she was conceived."

"Oh, Edward!" Sadness sketched over her face. "And you loved Maria so much!"

"I suppose." Edward swallowed hard and felt the cold uncertainty inside him again. "It's so hard to know, when one is young. I was a hotheaded young fool, certainly, and she— well, like so many young girls, she loved the romance. The pursuit. The *drama*."

"The drama?"

He smiled faintly. "I expect you wouldn't understand," he said. "You were not melodramatic, I'd wager, when you were seventeen."

Kate laughed weakly. "No, I was painfully practical," she said. "But many girls do love to swoon over tragedy."

"And I was Maria's tragedy." He drew a deep, slow breath, then let it out again. "Kate, do you want to know? Shall I try to tell you what happened, as best I can?"

She gave a feeble shrug. "We do have time to kill."

"Aye, we do at that."

Edward stared down at the fire for a moment, contemplating how to explain what he barely understood. "I met Maria at Brighton one summer," he began. "I told you her father was horrified when I tried to court her. I was bold and impulsive then, and enraged that he found me unacceptable. And, as it would with any young man, that rage served only to make me more determined to have her."

"It is often thus, I believe, with young men." Kate smiled faintly. "What form did your determination take?"

"When Maria vowed she loved me, I insisted she refuse the marriage her father had arranged," he said. "I told her to wait for me; that I'd make myself worthy and somehow pay off her father's debt, then no one could deny us."

"And that's when you joined the army, you said," Kate murmured.

He nodded, still staring at the flames. "Yes, but a few months into it, Kate, real life settled in and I began to wonder if I was that much in love, or if I was just angry over being denied. I was always angry, Kate, in those days."

"I expect you were," said Kate almost defensively. "You had been through a great deal. You'd been torn from your family—from your mother and your brother—and left to make your way in a harsh world."

"It makes for a pretty excuse, I daresay," he replied. "In any case, Maria wrote constantly, waxing over her father's cruelty. How dreadful and overbearing her intended was. How stalwart and brave she was, crying herself to sleep every night. But there was something . . . something beneath all the words that began to trouble me."

"Enjoyed it rather too much, did she?" said Kate knowingly.

He winced a little. "I became uneasy," he admitted, "and I'm still not sure why. Perhaps I felt unworthy of such a noble sacrifice, or perhaps the drama wore me down, but I began to debate the wisdom of my obstinacy. It didn't help that, before I left England, her mother had accused me of coming

between Maria and their neighbor. She claimed Maria had
been happy about the match until I came along."

"Lies, I am sure," said Kate defensively.

He looked up at her from beneath his lashes, his mouth
twisting. "So I assumed . . ."

"But—?"

He sighed. "When I came home and found Maria dead,
her mother flung Maria's old love letters in my face," he
said. "Apparently, she had indeed written this man several.
So I had broken up . . . *something*. I had not meant to. *I had
not*."

Kate set her hand to his cheek. "Oh, Edward, how were
you to know?"

"She was young," he said again. "I . . . I should have
known. I should not have confused her. I should not have
ordered her to wait, then gone away and left her. I felt then
a little like I feel today—as if I had abandoned someone
I cared for—and should have protected—at the very point
danger edged near."

"Oh, Edward. That is just not so."

Kate was holding her hands in her lap now, clasped a
little too tightly. Down the hill, the roof was still burning—
well, smoking as much as anything—the dried and ancient
beams destined to eventually fall in, he thought. He could
feel Kate's gaze upon him, steady and expectant. And yet
he waited.

Waited for her to ask. As if that might absolve him.

"So who was Annie's father?" she finally said.

"The man her father had betrothed her to," he said. "He
had become impatient, according to Maria, of waiting for
what he'd been promised—what he felt he had *paid for*—
so he came one day when her parents were out to ask her
one last time. She refused him, she said, and he raped her.
Then he hurled her love letters in her face—according to
her mother—and told Maria that her duchess's bastard could

have the leavings, for hell would freeze over before he'd ask her again."

"Dear God!" Kate drew an unsteady breath. "And her father did nothing?"

"She did not tell him," said Edward, "or tell me, for that matter, until she found herself with child. By then the man had wed another. But what could her father have done? This neighbor practically owned him—his house, his farmland, Mr. Granger had mortgaged it all."

"But that is dreadful!" Kate swallowed hard, her knuckles gone white now. "That poor girl. What did you do?"

"I wrote her and told her to claim the child was mine; to refuse to be swayed from that story," he said. "It was madness, yes—but better, I thought, than the shame of having been raped. Wasn't it? After all, it was my fault for interfering."

"Oh, Edward! That simply is not so."

"But I told her to hold fast *no matter what*," he said, his voice hoarse. "Who was I, Kate, to tell her such a thing? I look back now, and realize that I barely knew her. I was just infatuated and angry. Petulant, really. It taught me well, Kate, that a man must be the master of his emotions, or they will bloody well master him. Worse, Maria had waited too long to tell me of the child. It took me weeks to get relieved of command and find a ship heading to England, and months to travel. And by the time I arrived . . ."

"By the time you arrived, she was gone," Kate whispered hollowly. "She was dead, and there was only the child. And she had told everyone the child was yours."

"Her parents knew it for a lie, of course," he said with a shrug. "But they didn't confirm or deny it. Instead, Granger maintained—and God help him, it's remotely possible he was truthful—that Maria had been playing us both false. That she'd *given* herself to the man, trying to dangle us both, and he'd ruined her—with no ravishment involved—then refused to do the right thing to spite her."

"Dear God!" said Kate. "But that is . . . that is . . . I have no words for what that is."

"Try *confusing*," Edward bitterly suggested. "Or the truth? Or a load of moonshine? Or was it just a weak and indebted man explaining away why he let his daughter be raped, and did nothing?"

"What did Mrs. Granger think?"

He shrugged. "She says she isn't sure," he admitted. "But she did have the love letters, so that much rings true. I challenged the man—tried to get at the truth—but he wouldn't say. I slapped a glove in his face, but by then his own wife was with child. So in the end, I just shot him in the arm and went the hell back to London. He lived. Granger didn't; he died, bitter and bankrupt, leaving Annie and his wife impoverished. That's when I took over Annie's care. Until then, I was not even permitted to see her."

"Dear heaven," asked Kate. "How does one take care of a child under such tragic circumstances?"

"I moved them to a village where no one would know about the scandal," he said, "and bought a large cottage. I hired servants and a governess—it seemed the least I could do—and I told Mrs. Granger to tell people what she damned well pleased about me, and I honestly have no clear notion what she has said. I believe I'm called Annie's godfather—a polite euphemism if ever there was one. I visit twice a year—though Mrs. Granger hates it, and truth be told, I hate it."

"Do you?" Kate's hand had snuck into his.

"The child knows nothing about me, and seems half afraid of me," he said. "And Mrs. Granger refuses to let me tell Annie about her mother and me, or even tell her who her father is. People whisper behind her back, and the poor child hardly knows why. But she's twelve, Kate. She's not stupid. Arrangements must be made. Something must be done."

"What a mess!" said Kate. "But . . . what sort of arrangements?"

"This." Edward opened his arms expansively. "That's what all this was for, Kate."

"What, Heatherfields?"

"Yes, for Annie," he said. "I had meant it to be a part of her dowry. A place that might help attract a decent husband when the time comes. Heatherfields, restored to its prime . . . just imagine it, Kate."

"Yes, a prospective husband might overlook a great deal for such a fine estate," Kate mused, "and if he were a kind and good man . . ."

"Just so." Edward fell silent a moment, then sighed again. "There. You know what I know, and good luck making any sense of it. As to Heatherfields . . ."

"Yes?" Kate encouraged.

He carefully considered his words. "I feel oddly reluctant now to part with it," he said quietly. "I find the neighborhood . . . endearing. There are likely fifty other houses Annie might have. But only one, I fear, where my heart might happily settle."

"Only one?" asked Kate softly.

Edward considered his next words a long, long while— though he had been considering them, he supposed, for an age now. He considered them so long, the cottage roof collapsed, falling in with a long, horrendous crack, followed by a shooting shower of sparks.

"Only one?" Kate said again. "I am content to sit here, mind you, until you find your answer."

"Oh, *Kate*," he said. "Oh, love."

"Do not *oh, Kate* me," she said tightly. "I'm the one who nearly died today. I'm the one who must now think of all the things she would have regretted never having done had that asinine Reggie managed to shoot me. Or poison me. Or bore me to death."

He twisted himself around then, and caught her, drawing her between his legs until she rested back against him.

Wrapping his arms around her, he set his chin on her head and together they watched the fire die out.

"You can do better, Kate," he said warningly.

"Better than what?" she asked lightly, feigning ignorance, he knew, to torment him.

There might be a great many years of such torment ahead of him, he realized—if he were very, very fortunate.

He sighed, and kissed the top of her head. "I'm a man of uncertain bloodlines and dubious character," he warned her. "My early years were spent bookmaking, calculating odds, and keeping the accounts in Hedge's hell—"

"Not by your choice," she interjected.

He laughed. "Keep polishing, but this one won't shine," he said. "I spent the last decade bankrupting England's aristocracy and lining my pockets with their folly. I have not always been honest, but neither have I been dishonest. I am that most disdained of creatures, Kate—a man with a certain moral flexibility. I have kept loose company and looser women. I'm rich as Croesus, and hardly a ha'penny of it was got honestly."

She sighed. "I know. But I have trouble reconciling all that with your marvelous green eyes and myriad other charms."

"If I take up residence at Heatherfields, you may avail yourself of my myriad charms at will," he suggested. "I will pledge them to you, my love, and you alone for all my days."

"And you think that would not get round, *hmm*?" she said sharply, crooking her head back to glower at him. "That servants do not gossip? That there is some secret passageway to my bedchamber? I assure you, Edward, that there is not. No. I will not do it. I may not be a ravishing beauty or a highly skilled seductress, but I'm holding out for more."

He gave a bark of laughter, and buried his face in her neck. "Kate, I love you so," he said. "Do you love me?"

"Desperately, damn you," she said impatiently. "I confessed as much some days ago."

"I love it when you curse," he said, the words muffled against her throat.

"I never did so before," she said. "I wonder why the tendency has so lately come upon me?"

He laughed again, and let his lips slide down the long, pale turn of her neck. "Kate, my beautiful seductress, I will give up all my wicked ways and quit London and gaming both if—"

"Good," she interjected. "You should. Wickedness is never rewarded, no matter what Aurélie says."

He let one hand stray higher, cupping her warm, plump breast. "*Never* rewarded?" he murmured, lightly thumbing her nipple.

"Well . . . almost never," she said a little breathlessly. "But there. I have interrupted you. I believe you were about to pledge your undying something-or-other."

"I was about to ask you to be Mrs. Niall Edward Dagenham Quartermaine," he said, "but then I realized you are Baroness d'Allenay, and will never be Mrs. *anybody*."

She turned in his embrace. "Does that trouble you?" she asked gently.

He shook his head, but his eyes, he knew, were sad. "Not in the least," he said honestly. "It only troubles me that you'll be saddled with all my bad baggage if we marry. Will you do it anyway, my girl? Will you have me for better if I jettison the worst? Society will talk, regardless. Upshaw will likely have an apoplectic fit. Your mother will lose all standing as the family's most outrageous female. So all in all, my love, I daresay you'd be better served by simply using me for my myriad charms."

She tightened her grip on his shoulders. "Edward," she said seriously, "do you *want* to marry me?"

"More than anything," he said fervently. "More than anything I have ever wanted in the whole of my life."

"Then I accept your proposal," she said, setting her lips to his.

And that, as they say, was that.

Drowning in his desire for Kate, Edward kissed her—deeply and possessively, for she was his. And he—heaven help her—was hers. Kate apparently agreed, for her arms left his shoulders and twined around his neck. Then her fingers plunged into his gold-brown hair, and somewhere in that process, Edward forgot he was supposed to be watching a building burn, while Kate forgot all sense of propriety.

And when at last they came apart, their breath coming a little fast and cravats and hairpins in a grave state of disorder, it was to the urgent realization that it might be best, after all, to seize Aurélie, and go straight down to Exeter at week's end.

"But that," Kate mused, shoving her last hairpin haphazardly into place, "will scarcely permit you time to shut up things in London."

"Ah, there is that." Edward's hands fell from their task of restoring her bodice to order and began patting over his coat pockets. "But perhaps I shan't have to."

He found the letter from Peters that Anstruther had given him some hours earlier, tore it open, his eyes skimming the first sentence.

"Well, congratulate me, my love," he said, lifting his gaze to hers. "The Quartermaine Club is no more, and we will shortly be several thousand pounds richer."

Kate's eyes rounded hugely. "How is this?"

His gaze softened to hers. "I sold it," he said, "to my second in command. I knew, my dear, that no matter what became of you and me, I had to get out of that business. I knew that, so far as you and I went . . . well, that not even a friendship between us would do if I kept on. I knew what had to be done."

"My friendship—just my *friendship*—is worth that to you?" she said, blinking her eyes a little rapidly.

He lifted her hand and pressed his lips to the back of it. "Your friendship is *everything* to me, Kate," he said. "And it is part and parcel to why we are going to have an utterly splendid, utterly happy marriage."

She preened a little at that, and drew back with eyes that had warmed to a brilliant, glowing silver. "Several *thousand* pounds of ill-got gains!" she said musingly. "That should buy me one incredibly magnificent wedding gift."

"Which is precisely"—here he paused to kiss the tip of her nose—"what I had in mind."

"I have always fancied rubies," she said, "and platinum."

"*Hmm*," he said as if considering it. "Might not a sapphire do as well? They are both corundum, you know."

"Why, I like sapphires very well indeed!" she declared.

"Excellent," he said. "One appreciates a little flexibility in one's wife. Now, up with you, Lady d'Allenay. After all, you have a dinner party to host—and perhaps, if you dare risk Upshaw's apoplexy—an important announcement to make?"

The Wentworth Weddings

In the end, due to an avalanche of logistical issues, real estate transactions, and family dramas—and despite a vast amount of impatience—Katherine, Baroness d'Allenay, and Mr. Niall Edward Dagenham Quartermaine announced their intent to be married; not immediately, but in late November.

It being widely assumed that wicked Ned Quartermaine had deliberately debauched the poor country mouse—the lady being, after all, a land-rich heiress, and the gentleman no sort of gentleman at all—their scandalous betrothal was immediately the talk of all London.

For all of a fortnight.

Then, most obligingly, the Earl of Brendle's heir fled to Gretna Green to marry his mother's allegedly pregnant lady's maid, only to get himself held up along the Great North Road by the maid's highwayman of a husband, whereupon the couple held the young lordling for ransom—thus trumping any scandal the Wentworth ladies might stir up.

Lord Upshaw breathed a sigh of relief, and sent the Earl of Brendle his condolences.

Even before the scandal, however, it had been decided the Bellecombe ceremony would be a small, intimate affair in the castle's private chapel. This seemed a good plan until Kate made the mistake of secretly inviting Isabel, Lady Keltonbrooke.

The starry-eyed bride then compounded this covert act—after pleading, not inaccurately, a general ignorance of her intended's kith and kin—with a vague and somewhat airy encouragement that Lady Keltonbrooke might bring with her whatever members of Edward's family as could be persuaded to attend.

Lady Keltonbrooke, having lived long enough in high society to know how to read between the lines, at once laid aside the letter and took up her own pen with a steely look in her eye. She had hardly dipped it in the inkpot, however, when her butler appeared bearing the calling card of Louisa, Lady Upshaw, on a silver tray.

If one doyenne of society is meddlesome, two constitute a coup d'état. And then, as the late and little-lamented Alfred Hedge might have said, they were off to the races.

By the time their guest list was finished, the train tickets arranged, the bedchambers aired and the joints laid on to roast, the wedding guests seemed destined to spill into the castle's inner bailey. Finally, the enterprising Shearns simply drove their hay wagon over to St. Michael's and began purloining pews, which Tom and Ike then shoved higgledy-piggledy around the chapel's edges.

The near-farcical logistics of cramming eighty-seven wedding guests cheek-by-jowl into a space meant for forty was exceeded only by the confusion that held forth at the altar. The primary cause of the November delay appeared at the back of the chapel attired in a bridal ensemble of ice-blue tulle and satin purpose-made by the illustrious modiste Madame Odette of rue Saint-Honore, Paris.

In her hair Aurélie Wentworth wore pearls twined with blue forget-me-nots, and on her face she wore the unmistakable, self-satisfied smile of a woman who had finally got her way around a recalcitrant man.

The bride was escorted up the aisle by her upright and saintly brother-in-law, Lord Upshaw, who had been assured by the firm-handed Anstruther that, would the poor man bear but one more scandal in Aurélie's name, her antics would be put permanently at an end.

After this show of feminine radiance and ruthless determination came something of an anticlimax. Lady d'Allenay, in plain, cream-colored silk, came up the aisle on the arm of her faithful steward. An awkward dance then followed as Anstruther passed Kate off to London's worst rascal, Ned Quartermaine, then wedged his rather imposing frame around the extra pews to squeeze himself in on his intended bride's right.

Lord Upshaw simply sat down to mop his bald brow with the fervent prayer that these two would, indeed, be the last of the Wentworth weddings he need ever concern himself with.

And at long last, the Reverend Mr. Richard Burnham—no stranger to scandal himself—was able to say, *"Dearly beloved, we are gathered here . . ."*

AN HOUR LATER, Kate found herself standing in the middle of Bellecombe's grand ballroom, one hand resting on her new husband's arm. "Good heavens, you could be twins!" she murmured, her gaze focused some distance away.

"There is a marked resemblance," Edward acknowledged, his eyes drifting over their increasingly exuberant crowd of guests.

Due to the presence of Aurélie's friends, the wedding breakfast was fast becoming a wedding supper, if not something worse. Kate's attention, however, was focused on the Duke of Dunthorpe.

A restrained, almost grim man, the duke was not quite

as tall as his younger brother, nor did he possess that lean, catlike grace which made Edward look so faintly dangerous. But in his hair and in his features and even in the intense green of his eyes, there was not a whit of difference between the two.

Just then, Jasper appeared with a tray of champagne. Edward snared two glasses, then turned with a muted smile to press one into his wife's hand. She took it, and looked up at him a little pleadingly.

"I do hope you aren't aggravated with me, Edward," she said, "for it is only—what?—one very *smallish* aunt, your estranged brother, and a few odd cousins who've turned up unexpectedly. Do say again that you're not angry."

His smile warmed. "No, my feelings for you, my love, turn in an altogether different direction," he said suggestively. "I am, however, a little put out at Aunt Isabel, for this was all her doing, she claims, and none of yours."

"Oh, I daresay," said his wife vaguely, "but I'm very glad your brother is here."

The duke chose that moment to leave his aunt's side and wade through the crowd. And then the awkward moment Edward had dreaded for twenty-odd years was upon him.

The duke bowed to Kate, and thanked her for her hospitality. Then he slowly extended a hand to Edward. "Ned, it is good t-to see you," he said.

"And you, Freddie," said Edward with excruciating politeness.

The handshake broke, then a heavy silence fell all around them.

After a moment, Kate cleared her throat. "Well," she said a little too brightly. "It is lovely to make your acquaintance, Your Grace. Do you make your home in London?"

"No," said the duke, "very rarely. We live in th-the country, my wife and I. Our children are small, and we pr-prefer a quiet life."

"Children, how lovely!" Kate murmured, her smile fixed in place. "How many have you, Your Grace, and what are their ages?"

The duke looked vaguely awkward. "We have th-three," he said, "and another expected any moment. Our Charles is n-nine, Margaret is seven, and our youngest—Edward—is four."

"Edward," Kate echoed.

"It is a family name," Edward interjected a little coolly, "and a common one."

"Er—yes, we traditionally have an Edward in each generation," agreed the duke.

He spoke stiffly and with little warmth, Kate noticed—but with the faintest stutter, which might be the cause, she thought, of his formality.

She decided to press her theory. "And what are they like, your children?" she said, determined to keep him talking. "Which is most like you? Which is the smartest, and which is the most mischievous?"

"Edward, I believe, is m-most like me," said the duke, warming a little. "He is a quiet child. Meg is very like her mother, and a pr-prettily-mannered girl. But Charles is Ned made over; smart *and* mischievous. Up to every rig, Charles is. You m-m-must . . ."

"Must what?" Kate prodded.

A brilliant hue was blooming across the duke's cheeks. "You m-must c-come and see them," he said, tripping awkwardly over the words, "if, th-that is, you w-wish, Ned—I beg your pardon—if you can bear it, I mean." Then he bowed stiffly. "I think Aunt Isabel wants me. I believe I had b-better go."

Kate's eyes followed him back through the crowd.

"Well, he's none too pleased to be here," said Edward tightly. "I wonder what Isabel threatened him with?"

"I think it is not displeasure," said Kate pensively. "He

stutters. And he seems sad; almost painfully shy, really. Was he so as a boy?"

Edward said nothing for a long moment. "Yes, Freddie was always quiet," he admitted. "Father used to strop him for stuttering, and tell him he was so hopelessly backward he wasn't worthy of being a duke."

"How very tragic," said Kate, still watching Dunthorpe blush and stammer his way through the crowd. "He did a good deal of damage, your father."

"Father!" Edward laughed, but without bitterness. "After all these years, I still call him that, and now I have you doing it, too."

At last Kate turned from the crowd. "I wouldn't be too sure he *wasn't* your father," she said a little grimly.

When Edward opened his mouth to protest, she threw up a hand.

"You don't know, Edward, nor do I," she said firmly. "Neither do we care. In fact, it's just as likely, I daresay, that Alfred Hedge sired the both of you—for if you and Dunthorpe don't share two parents, I'll be hanged. Blood runs too true for the pair of you to look so nearly identical."

"*Hmm*," said Edward. "I never thought of that." Then threw back the rest of his champagne. "Aunt Isabel always said the truth would never be known," he mused. "And do you know what, Kate? You're right. I do not care."

"Then you've made peace," she said, "or something near it."

He set the glass away with a gesture of finality, and circled an arm around Kate's waist. "Yes, I have," he said. "But now I think on it, Kate—now I look upon Freddie, and consider back over what his life must have been like—I wonder which of us had the worst of that terrible bargain?"

"He lost his brother," she said quietly, "and was left alone with a man who sounds like a monster."

Edward slowly nodded. "He was left under Father's thumb, I suppose," he mused, "whilst I was left to raise myself amidst the dregs of society. But neglect gave me a measure of freedom, at least, and I learnt early on that I needn't be obliged to anyone. That I could live—and prosper—by my wits."

"There are worse lessons, perhaps, and harder ways to learn them," said Kate. "Your father was not a kind man. And your brother still seems so painfully awkward, Edward. Perhaps you might go to him and say—well, I do not know. Perhaps you might say to him what you just said to me?"

Edward turned and smiled deep into her eyes. "Tomorrow, perhaps," he said, leaning very near and dropping his voice huskily. "Today I wish to think only of tonight, and of what you and I will be—"

"De Macey!" Kate's eyes lit with feigned brilliance. "Look, my love, who is standing just behind you."

Edward turned just as de Macey circled around him to seize Kate's hand. "My dear child!" he said with a sweeping, elegant bow. "So very sorry to not have made it back to Bellecombe yesterday. May I say that today, on this most blessed of days, you outshine even your dear mamma in your radiance."

"Oh, I do not doubt that," said Kate dryly. "Aurélie is not so much radiant today as she is victorious."

"Cat-in-the-cream-pot, I'd have said," murmured Edward. "And poor Anstruther! What a merry dance he shall be led."

The comte trilled with laughter. "Oh, he long ago learnt the steps to Aurélie's tune, *mon ami*, but she shall not be leading!" de Macey declared. "Do not grieve for Farmer John; he will have Madame Heartbreaker in traces before the week's out."

"Do you think?" asked Kate.

"I do," said de Macey, smiling wickedly. "It is what she craves, child. Her sort has no respect for a man they can get round with their wiles. Trust me, I should know. She and I—*mon Dieu!* Was ever a pair more ill-suited?"

"Well, you're a sporting fellow." Edward clapped a hand to de Macey's back. "Now tell me, have we settled that other little business?"

De Macey flashed an even more wicked smile, his elegant mustache lightly lifting. "Indeed, just as I promised," he said silkily. "Lord Reginald Hoke will be shortly arriving in the salubrious isle of Guadeloupe where he will be put to work on my sugar plantation."

"And he signed the papers without quibbling?" Edward pressed.

"But of course!" De Macey opened his hands expansively. "What choice did he have when I explained to him our offer?"

"What papers?" Kate interjected. "What offer?'

"Oh, my pet, a generous one," declared the comte. "Your husband offered *not* to have him hung for kidnapping."

"In exchange for . . . ?"

De Macey laid a hand dramatically over his heart. "In exchange for ten years of pondering his folly, my dear," he said. "Did I not tell you to trust me to deal with Reggie? He shall spend ten years serving an old friend faithfully. What more could a scorned man ask?"

"Oh, my God," said Kate quietly. "You *indentured* a nobleman's son?"

"*Oui*, to me!" said de Macey gleefully. "But as a . . . a . . . How would you say it? A clerk of the accounts? Yes, at long last, Reggie shall learn arithmetic. The dear boy needn't even sully those lovely hands of his in the field, child; he need only learn self-sufficiency. He has escaped his English creditors by fleeing to French soil, and now he will earn a wage."

"You're very kind," said Kate.

"Alas, I was once something of a fribble myself," confessed the comte. "But not, I grant you, one foolish enough to game his money away."

Just then, someone waved at de Macey from across the room. People were beginning to trickle out, Kate realized, though Aurélie was still swanning about the crowd, kissing cheeks and cooing at all her guests. Anstruther and Richard, however, were lingering near the door to either side of Nancy, who—despite a decided glow of happiness in her eyes—looked otherwise wan as they bent attentively toward her.

"Oh, dear," Kate murmured. "She is feeling not quite the thing again."

"Indeed, speculation runs rampant," whispered the comte behind his hand. "The wise and knowing Hetty advises that already the villagers count the months—but not, she adds, with any spite in their hearts."

"In either case, they count in vain, if they are counting on a scandal," said Kate.

No, if it was a minor scandal they hoped for, Kate very much feared they were counting over the wrong Wentworth. Indeed, Kate was beginning to regret having permitted Aurélie to put off their double wedding another fortnight while they awaited the favor of Madame Odette.

Just then, Nancy left her husband's side and came toward them, her color a little improved.

"Kate," she said, embracing her. "Congratulations. I am so happy for you."

Kate slid a surreptitious hand to her sister's belly. "And I for you, Nan, I hope?" she murmured into her ear.

They came apart, Nancy blushing furiously as she glanced back and forth between Edward and Kate. "Yes," she finally whispered. "It seems almost certain."

Kate caught her shoulders, and set her a little away. "Poor dear," she said. "Are you perfectly wretched?"

"Oh, yes!" said Nancy, her eyes welling a little. "Wonderfully, wonderfully wretched! Oh, Kate, I shall be twice blessed in less than a year. Thank you. Thank you for *everything*. I only wish for you my same happiness."

Nancy kissed Edward before leaving.

"She *is* happy, my dear," he murmured, taking Kate's hand and squeezing it. "And just look how Richard's gaze follows her. He'll make an excellent father."

"I have never doubted it," said Kate.

De Macey had slipped away. Aurélie was still babbling effusively, this time to Mrs. Granger, who had been persuaded to attend by Richard's aunt. Kate and Edward had welcomed Mrs. Granger warmly, and said no more. But Kate hoped that her attendance was, perhaps, the beginning of a tentative friendship.

Already Aurélie appeared to be making inroads with her irrepressible charm, though Anstruther had risen from his chair. Kate could see that his patience was at an end.

Kate shrugged, and turned to her husband. "I believe, my dear, that I should like to rest before dinner," she declared.

"And by rest," he murmured, "I hope you mean *not* rest."

"Just so," she said, curling a hand around his arm in a more proprietary fashion.

They strolled in the general direction of the door, pausing to accept the well-wishes of those few people to whom they had not yet spoken, reaching it just as Anstruther hitched his arm through Aurélie's and hauled her from the room. Kate and Edward followed them down the passageway, the four of them alone, it seemed, for the first time in a week.

In the great hall, they chattered aimlessly while Aurélie's coat and muff and warming blanket and hot bricks were fetched. When the bricks were found not to be ready, Anstruther simply dragged her out.

"Oh, haud yer wheesht, Aurélie," he grumbled. "Dinna ye think I can keep you warm from here to there?"

"Why, John Anstruther, I'm sure I do not know!" she declared, jerking to a halt on the cobbles. "Sometimes you have a cold, cold heart."

At that, he simply swept her up and carried her across the bailey. Edward helped Jasper carry out the two bags Aurélie had left waiting, while Hetty followed with Filou, who was curled up in a large wicker basket.

"Do you really think you can manage that woman?" Edward muttered once Anstruther had loaded her up into his carriage.

Anstruther grunted. "In the long run, laddie? I dinna know. But in the short of it? I'll be sorely tempted to lay the business end of my crop to her arse."

"I hope you won't," said Edward darkly.

Anstruther grinned, motioning for the dog to be handed up. "Nay, I'll not do it," he confessed, "but I'll have to threaten it often enough, I dinna doubt."

Edward opened his mouth to advise against it, then remembered de Macey's wise words. Anstruther had been warming the woman's bed for nearly twenty years, he decided. They both had to know what they were getting into.

"Well," said Edward uncertainly, "good luck with that strategy."

"Thank ye," said Anstruther, leaping up into his carriage.

Edward contented himself to strolling back into the great hall where his bride awaited with some impatience.

"That *rest* before dinner?" Kate reminded him, tapping her tiny, silk-shod toe.

"Indeed, my love," he said.

Then, following Anstruther's good example, he swept up his bride and carried her—giggling and shrieking—all the way up the stairs and all the way down the corridor to her suite.

Once inside, he kicked the bedchamber door open and dropped her, still laughing, in the middle of the bed. Then, going back into the parlor, he extracted a long, thin box he'd hidden behind the divan.

Carrying it back into the room, he presented it to his bride with a de Macey–like flourish. "Lady d'Allenay," he said, "your wedding gift."

She squirmed back upright, the ivory silk bunching most

delightfully around her derriere. "It is an oddly shaped box," she teased. "I thought I was getting platinum and sapphires?"

"Not exactly," he said tucking himself beside her. "Something infinitely better."

Eyes dancing, Kate opened the box.

"Oh . . . my," she said a little blandly.

Inside lay what could only be described as a ring of utterly hideous proportions; a great, jagged stone that looked like nothing so much as a lump of blue-black coal, and mounted in a thick setting made from a metal so lacking in luster it could not possibly have held any value. Scrolled inside the ring, however, was a document.

Slipping the ring off the scroll, Edward took Kate's hand and slid it onto her finger, kissing her cheek as he did so. "As I said earlier today, my love, with all my worldly goods I thee endow."

"How touching." Kate waggled her fingers a little, then held the lump to the light. "Well, it is certainly original in its design. I rather doubt any other bride has ever seen the like."

"I'm sure they have not," he said, "for I shall have you know, Baroness d'Allenay, that that is the famous Wentworth sapphire."

"Is it?" Kate looked at him and giggled. "I never heard of the famous Wentworth sapphire. And it is still rather ugly, my love, but I shall treasure it all the same."

Edward kissed her, then removed the ring from her hand, smiling. "It is ugly, my love, because it is uncut," he said, holding it to the sunlight "And it will be called the Wentworth sapphire, for it shall be your choice how it is cut, and yours to hand down to your Wentworth daughters."

"My Quartermaine daughters," she corrected.

"As you wish," he said. "But the ring is deservedly yours, nonetheless, because it is one of the finest purple-blue sapphires ever to come out of Ceylon. I know, you see, for I mined it myself."

"Yourself?"

"Well, not literally," he said. "But I told you I went to Ceylon to make something of myself, you will recall. One cannot do that entirely on an officer's pay. So one of the things I did there was to purchase—using more of Hedge's ill-got gaming revenue—an interest in a mine which, at the time, didn't look like much."

"And now?" she asked a little breathlessly.

"And now it looks like a rather great deal," he admitted. "Little by little, I've channeled the club's profits into the place, and gradually bought out the other investors. I must say the old place is becoming quite a profit engine, and it's how I learnt what I know about mining."

"I see," she said, her eyes widening with amazement. "I wondered about it at the time."

"And this," he said, tapping on the stone, "will likely be a pure, perfect sapphire to exceed one hundred and twenty carats when cut, my love—larger than even the famous Stuart sapphire in the Queen's Imperial State Crown. It is, in short, nearly priceless."

"Good Lord," she murmured. "And the unique setting?"

"Is pure tin," he said.

"Tin?"

He extracted the paper from the box. "From your new tin mine," he said, "in Cornwall. The one you and Anstruther have been lusting after this age."

At that, her eyes turned to saucers. "You . . . you *bought me a tin mine*?" she said. "As a wedding gift?"

"I did," he confessed. "Was that utterly unromantic of me? It seemed the only thing you truly wanted."

"Besides you?" she said on a laugh. "No, Edward, it is actually the most romantic gift ever given, for it is the gift of a husband who truly knows his wife, and does not mind if she is plain and pragmatic."

"My girl, you are nothing close to plain," he chided. "As to pragmatic, if you wish, I shall manage the mine for you," he said, "but only if you wish. Indeed, I can look after all your industrial concerns, *if* you wish. After all, you will have your hands full with the estate, and Anstruther . . . well, Anstruther will have his hands full with Aurélie."

"She may *not* interfere with his work!" declared Kate, who had put the ring back on, and was turning it this way and that to admire it. "It is out of the question."

"Well, good luck with that strategy," said Edward—the same words he'd spoken to Anstruther himself mere moments earlier. He didn't expect either of them to fare well with the task.

"Oh, I have a plan," said Kate, "to keep Aurélie busy. Trust me. But first, let me kiss you, my darling. I'm sure these are the most famous wedding gifts a bride ever received."

She did kiss him, and very thoroughly, too. And Edward kissed her back. Eventually the box tumbled to the floor, the deed to the tin mine soon following. And when, sometime later, all the kissing and tumbling was done, Kate still wore the ring, if nothing else.

Edward pulled her back against him beneath the bedcovers, spooning her so that he could set his chin atop her head. "So tell me this grand plan to keep your mother in line," he said. "I have little confidence, honestly, that you shall pull it off."

"Well," said Kate, "I think I shall prove you wrong. If you've no objection, Edward, I mean to ask Anstruther to take over the west wing of the castle that extends beyond the walls. It is a complete house with its own entrance and bedchambers—quite ample, really, save for the kitchens being a tad minimal. And in that way, I will be able to keep an eye on Mamma."

"This sounds to me as if Aurélie will simply have more of an audience," Edward warned. "And what will you do with South Farm? Anstruther is keeping up the manor house."

"Well, I thought perhaps we might put Annabelle and Mrs. Granger there," she suggested, "until Heatherfields has been properly done up. It is larger and finer than any cottage, and it will give Mrs. Granger status. It will move them into our sphere, and into Richard's parish. She already knows him a little, and knows his aunt well. And now he is your brother-in-law."

"Kate, that is . . . brilliant," he murmured. "As in, *Aurélie*-brilliant."

"Yes, manipulatively brilliant, I think you mean," said Kate a little smugly. "Mrs. Granger will get used to us, Edward. And in time, it will seem the most natural thing that Annabelle should drop in here, or that I might go there in passing. We will wear Mrs. Granger down with kindness, I feel sure of it. We will become normal to her. Ordinary, even."

Edward kissed his bride's cheek. "You are the very best of wives, Kate," he said, "and we have been married only— what, four hours? But I still think Aurélie will be underfoot."

"No, I think not." With that, Kate pulled his hand down to her belly. "No, given the pallor of Nancy's face today, and the unsettling event I have recently suffered, I think Aurélie will be spread thin."

"*Ohh*," said Edward, making a slow circle with his hand. "Oh, Kate. Oh, my God."

"She'll complain bitterly, of course, that she's far too young to be a grandmother," said Kate, wiggling back against him. "After all, she has not yet come to grips with being a mother. But mothering is hard work, whereas *grand*-mothering consists primarily of doting and entertaining and pampering."

"Ah!" said Edward, understanding dawning. "I begin to see the logic in this."

"Indeed," said Kate. "Was ever anyone more knowledgeable about what is required to pamper and dote? Did ever anyone appear more entertaining to you?"

"Indeed not, my love," said her husband. "Aurélie will be Grand Empress of Grandmothers, I do not doubt."

"Yes," said Kate on a snicker, "and when she takes them

out in their prams, she can tell the cooing passersby that she's their elder sister."

"Kate, my love, your plan is brilliant," he said. "My hat is off to you."

"Oh, not just your hat," said his wife. "Under these bed-sheets you're as naked as God made you—which was very fine indeed, by the way."

He pressed his lips to her hair again, and made another slow circle on her belly. "Kate," he said quietly.

"Yes?"

"Are you perfectly sure you're carrying my child?"

"Well, I'm perfectly sure I'm not carrying anyone else's," she said a little tartly. "But am I absolutely, totally sure? No, not . . . *quite*."

"Good, then, we should make *absolutely totally sure*," he murmured, sliding his lips slowly down her neck. "Because, old Reggie once pointed out, I'm not the sort of man who likes to sit on a mere profit when a little effort might turn it into a windfall . . ."

At Avon Books, we know your passion for romance—once you finish one of our novels, you find yourself wanting more.

May we tempt you with . . .

- **Excerpts** from our upcoming releases.

- Entertaining **extras**, including authors' personal photo albums and book lists.

- Behind-the-scenes **scoop** on your favorite characters and series.

- **Sweepstakes** for the chance to win free books, romantic getaways, and other fun prizes.

- Writing **tips** from our authors and editors.

- **Blog** with our authors and find out why they love to write romance.

- **Exclusive content** that's not contained within the pages of our novels.

Join us at
www.avonbooks.com